Praise for Denise Williamson's novel
The Dark Sun Rises
— 1999 Christy Award Finalist —

"*The Dark Sun Rises* is an incredible book that belongs on the shelf next to the likes of *Uncle Tom's Cabin.* The book is powerful testimony of the abuses of slavery, the corruption of worldly slave owners, and the quandry of godly slave owners. Joseph, however, turns his anger into forgiveness and strength and gives witness to the incredible redeeming power of God."

Christian Library Journal

"I believe this novel is one of the most important literary contributions to racial unity we've seen in years. The writing is beautiful, the history is astutely accurate, and the story is absolutely essential for anyone looking for answers to our country's racial tensions."

Jo Kadlecek, author of
I Call You Friend: Four Women's Stories of Race, Faith, and Friendship

"Character portrayal is vivid, and the flavor of the pre-Civil War South is richly captured. Compassion, faith, fear, brutality, and ignorance of both slaves and Southern whites are woven throughout a compelling story that keeps readers on edge until the final page."

Church Libraries

"The author appears to be a messenger from God to this nation, calling us to look back and consider our failures and to respond to God about them. The book also shows the triumph of God's grace and love for those who are lost, oppressed, and helpless."

Joseph Zintseme,
YWAM

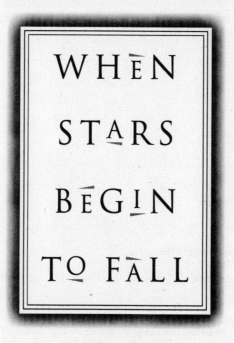

WHEN STARS BEGIN TO FALL

DENISE WILLIAMSON

BETHANY HOUSE PUBLISHERS
MINNEAPOLIS, MINNESOTA 55438

Published by Bethany House Publishers
A Ministry of Bethany Fellowship International
11400 Hampshire Avenue South
Bloomington, Minnesota 55438
www.bethanyhouse.com

Printed in the United States of America by
Bethany Press International, Bloomington, Minnesota 55438

Library of Congress Cataloging-in-Publication Data

Williamson, Denise J., 1954-
    When stars begin to fall / by Denise Williamson.
        p.   cm. — (Roots of faith ; 2)
    ISBN 1-55661-883-2
    1. Antislavery movements—Fiction.   2. Underground railroad—Fiction.
3. Philadelphia (Pa.)—Fiction.   4. Afro-Americans—Fiction.   5. Quakers—
Fiction.   I. Title.
PS3573.I456255 W48   2001
813'.54—dc21   99-050404

To honor those who have paid
the price of prejudice.
Many of their names have been forgotten,
yet through history's lamentation,
echoes of their voices still are heard.

DENISE WILLIAMSON is a full-time writer with seven published books and numerous magazine articles. She has also worked as an environmental education specialist for the Pennsylvania Bureau of State Parks. She and her family live in Pennsylvania.

ROOTS OF FAITH

The Dark Sun Rises
When Stars Begin to Fall

My Lord! What a morning!

My Lord! What a morning!

My Lord! What a morning!

When the stars begin to fall!

—A HYMN OF THE NEGRO CHURCH

FOREWORD

PASSION. NOT THE HEAVY BREATHING KIND but that which speaks of commitment, zeal, and purpose. The kind of passion that compels Denise Williamson to take pen to paper and bring forth book two in the ROOTS OF FAITH series. This saga continues to grip our emotions, teach us our history—the good as well as the painful—and challenge us to grow beyond our comfort zones. Her research is sharp and unflinching, her characters bold and courageous, holding to a faith that will not yield and to a God who will not fail.

Okay, I admit that I love these books! I love the fact that this installment shows Joseph as a man desperately seeking a "normal" life as a free person of color in a community trying to do the same. Their constant fear of the past serves as a reminder of a fragile present and a tenuous future. I love the way Williamson goes against all that school history books have taught. Here, black folks fight and fight with dignity, grace, "mother-wit," and cunning. There are no losers here, no one passively surrendering to injustice and inhumanity.

I love the fact that historical facts and figures, laws and statutes take on human form and fullness, ever pushing us toward understanding the past in order to correct the future for ourselves, our children, and our children's children.

I love the fact that after reading it one searches for a friend, a comrade, a fellow "Roots" devotee with whom to talk, discuss, analyze, and exchange thoughts and perceptions.

And finally, I love the fact that I leave *When Stars Begin to Fall* richer as a person of faith but challenged to live as David said:

"The salvation of the righteous comes from the Lord; he is their stronghold

in time of trouble. The Lord helps them and delivers them; he delivers them from the wicked and saves them, because they take refuge in him." (Psalm 37:39–40, NIV)

Oh, for the faith walk of David—and of Joseph Whitsun.

B. M. Cook
Writer

AUTHOR'S NOTE

HISTORY HAS HAD AS MANY VOICES as it has had people. Most are silent now. To focus only on the most popular or the most easily obtained records in this nation during the era of slavery is like sequestering oneself in a practice room with those who boast they have the best voices, while later missing the full performance.

My prayer through the research and writing of *When Stars Begin to Fall* has been that the Spirit will train our ears, our minds, and our hearts to hear from many different voices in the years of 1851 and 1852. Using letters, journals, newspaper reports, and commentaries, I listened as intently as I could not only to those who were our nineteenth-century brothers and sisters in Christ but also to their opponents and foes.

This is only one story. Many more need to be told out of the records and memories that remain.

PART ONE
The Child of Mystery

When I consider thy heavens,

the work of thy fingers,

the moon and the stars,

which thou hast ordained;

What is man, that thou

art mindful of him?

PSALMS 8:3–4a

PENNSYLVANIA, NOVEMBER 1851

CHAPTER 1

GRAY-HAIRED BARNABAS CROGHAN did not hear any knocking at the door, yet he suspected it because the floor boards of the log house vibrated under his feet, a sure sign that someone had come up to their porch.

Sitting across from him at the oaken kitchen table, Joseph Whitsun did hear sounds, and the younger man looked to the right into the dark main room, which was their parlor. Joseph stood a moment before Barnabas saw faces at the window that until then had looked out onto a still November night. They were Negro faces, familiar ones, which was a comfort to Barnabas, for as hard as he tried not to think on trouble, he sensed it coming because of all that had happened in Lancaster County since September, when a white master from Maryland had been shot trying to claim his runaway slaves. The site of the violence was a farmhouse just thirteen miles south of this cabin where he and Joseph had lived for the past six years.

Stiffly Barnabas rose when Joseph opened the door. Cyrus, a good-natured lad about sixteen years old, rushed in. He was the only son of Tort Woodman, a woodchopper who lived on Welshman's Mountain, which formed the rough northern boundary of their town, Oak Glen. Another boy followed Cyrus in. Barnabas knew him too. He was Renny, the fugitive slave who boarded with the Woodmans, their farm being an inconspicuous patch of cleared ground on the mountain's far side.

Cyrus was the one in pain, his right hand wrapped in a sack his father used for collecting herbs that he bartered as part of his forest livelihood. Renny had his friend by the shoulder, as though to give him strength. Drafts of icy air circled Barnabas's feet, for the door stayed opened. Oak Glen's sturdy, serious-minded pastor, Cummington Brown, came in next, followed by his twenty-year-old daughter, Angelene.

Words were exchanged, which were useless to Barnabas because of his deafness. Joseph and Angelene headed through the parlor, guiding Cyrus and Renny toward the medical room that Joseph maintained at the end of the hallway to the rear of their small old house. This left Barnabas with Pastor Brown, who did not know how to speak by manual signing, the language he relied on. The grave-looking reverend took down the slate and chalk that were always in the rack by the door. Moving into the dim light that came from the lantern hanging above the kitchen table, the steady man printed a few quick words. *Ba, watch the windows and door. I think the boys will be followed.*

CHAPTER 2

"CYRUS, DID THIS HAPPEN while you worked?" Joseph asked, seating the injured youth in the chair beside the table in his small one-room clinic. As he questioned Cyrus, Angelene lit both lamps mounted in wall brackets. Cyrus would not speak, nor Renny, leaving Joseph to assume that both boys had come from the kitchen of Meade McCreary's tavern near the Brinkerville railroad station, where they were employed nightly to shuck oysters and steam crabs.

As gently as he could, Joseph extended the injured, wrapped hand. Cyrus bent in agony. His mouth gaped wide. "Renny shot me!"

Joseph uncovered the ugly wound. Even though he had been a doctor for years, he cringed. There was a musket ball lodged in the palm, but somehow even more misery had been added, for Cyrus's skin was blistered from wrist to fingertips. "What happened here!"

Tears dripped into Cyrus's lap. Renny still refused to speak. "Did you two think it would help a gunshot wound to scald the flesh?"

Cyrus screamed. "He wa' lookin' for some way to cover up what he done. He didn't care that it put me into hell fires—no!"

"Renny, when did this happen? How did this happen?"

Suddenly the other youth defended himself. "We wa' shootin' at lighted candles, an' *he* put up his hand—"

"Afta *you* missed! While *you* wa' only s'pose to be loadin'!"

"We didn't have the time what Cyrus wanted to take. I needed to learn to use that gun straight off!"

"Why?" Joseph asked, mourning over both young men.

The youths exchanged their first glance to each other. "We both want to be part of the secret Black Guard," Renny admitted with some reluctance but also with pride. "An' me bein' city-born, well, I never did fire no gun 'fore t'night."

"What did your daddy say about you having his firearm out after dark?" Joseph pressed Cyrus, though the boy was already suffering. "And how does this explain your terrible scalding?"

Cyrus put his head down. "It weren't my daddy's gun, sah. It wa' Mr. McCreary's old musket what Renny found. I told him to leave it be, but he took it just as the sun was goin' down."

"That man don't even know he has that gun!" Renny said. "It's been up in his shed attic that long!"

"You took McCreary's gun and fired it without his permission?" Joseph said with alarm.

Cyrus cried like a child. "Renny did! I just put up the lights! Then when he shot me, we both got scaired. That's when Renny got the idea to burn my hand so McCreary wouldn't ask no questions 'bout why I couldn't work. We went to the kitchen, an' that's when he spilt the b'ilin' water all over me!"

"I saved you from havin' to answer to that buckra!" Renny was as remorseless as any old-time slave Joseph had ever seen during his own time of bondage so many years before.

Cyrus looked through his tears. "We both went on home then, by horse, but when my daddy saw my hand, he said we best get over here, an' on foot so that nobody would see us come. He said he'd have to go down 'long Arnold Creek where we wa' to make sure we didn't cause no trouble for any of the real Black Guard what wa' s'posed to be meetin' there." He stopped to suck his lips because of his pain. "Am I gwine lose my fingers?"

"I don't think so."

"He can't!" Renny fumed. "Then McCreary'll know it's more than just a burn."

"That's all he cares about! That *he* don't get caught!" This time Cyrus complained to Pastor Brown, who had been quietly listening to every word.

"Pastor, he don't know nothin' 'bout slavery!" Renny pushed himself back against the white plastered wall while Cummington stayed right inside the closed door. "He don't know what happens when somebody drags you back down over the Mason and Dixon Line. I'm not lettin' McCreary or anybody do that to me! I don't want nobody to know that I'm not Cyrus's cousin, for true."

Memories from Joseph's own past came to him like demons as he watched Renny wincing.

"Dr. Joseph! It do hurt!" Cyrus laid his head upon his arm.

Angelene had already set out the surgical tools, for since Joseph's time in Oak Glen, she had become his skilled assistant. He looked first at her kind, pained face, then at Cyrus again. "I know it does, but now I must remove that ball."

"I don't know if I can stand you to do it, sah!"

Renny groaned. "You free, Cyrus! You all don't know 'bout pain! Let somebody hang you by you' thumbs. Let somebody beat you till *all* you' flesh done look like that." He pointed to the hand.

Quite unwillingly Joseph's eyes shifted to him. "Renny! Did your former master do that to you?"

"He did that to my daddy!" the boy said without a blink or a frown. "He did that 'cause my daddy wa' his coachman, an' just *onc't* he left his massa's new carriage uncovered in a rainstorm."

Renny's hardened posture reminded Joseph of a callous grown over once tender skin. It set Joseph's teeth on edge and made him put his hands against the table so that they would not shake.

"That's why I ran!" the boy went on. "An' that's why I swear I'll *kill* my marse just the way William Parker of Christiana done if my buckra marse ever comes up here lookin' for me!"

"You were wrong to take McCreary's musket," Joseph said. He found his hands would stop trembling only as he focused solely on picking up the smallest of the surgical knives. "Renny, you brought this on yourself and on your friend."

"I put everythin' back! McCreary won't know what we done."

"Even so," Joseph whispered, waiting for the courage to trust his steadiness, which was returning, "Cyrus paid a high price for your actions, don't you think, young man?"

Renny's tone did change. " 'Bout that, I am sorry."

Joseph saw Pastor Brown reach out to the older boy in his misery. At that same moment the clinic door was pushed open. Cummington squeezed in closer to the rest of them, while all held their breath. But it was only Barnabas who looked in on them, his face full of worry. With great rapidity his hands moved, making signs and symbols that Joseph understood as easily as if he had been hearing the other man speak.

Yet Renny nearly interrupted his concentration by his rough words. "What's you' ol' *white* houseboy want with us all in here?"

Joseph found himself grasping his knife like a weapon. "Don't you ever call Mr. Croghan that!" His passion to defend Barnabas felt awkward, even terrifying, yet he knew that all his nerves were already set on edge because of what his deaf friend had just said. He spoke to Cummington, aware that they all were in danger. "Ba can see several white men out on horses in the street. He thinks McCreary might be one of them."

"What now?" Cyrus cried.

Joseph laid down his tool, using hand signs for Barnabas while he also spoke aloud. *"Ba, bar the front door. I need time to get this surgery done!"* Joseph knew his old friend was wise and that he could be trusted. But could he trust his own shaking hands? Cummington came and laid his hands on top of Joseph's while Barnabas left them and closed the clinic door.

"Take these towels," Joseph said to Renny and to Cummington as he nodded to the linens stacked at the table's edge. "Press them all around that door so that no light can leak out. Even if they enter my house then, it's possible that they won't look in here."

He glanced at the room's window, but that was already sealed by the thick shutter Ba had made so that no one could see in, either from the houses of Brinkerville or from the main pike running between Philadelphia and Lancaster City, a distance of more than sixty miles.

"What can I do to help you?" Angelene asked him as the crowded room turned deathly quiet. She was as small as a girl, yet she knotted her shawl with confidence to make it stay in place while she prepared for the work. So often Joseph had had reason to admire her maturity, which far surpassed her years.

"Keep your hands free to help me," he said. "Pastor, will you please come hold Cyrus and keep him still?" With these two helpers in place,

Joseph put his mind to his work, silently praying to God for the ability to do what needed to be done now, for time could not be wasted. "Not a sound!" he warned everyone, "in case someone does come into this house."

He started probing the raw flesh. Cyrus grimaced in agony but with a bravery that kept him silent. Still against the wall, Renny crouched like an ill child, his face to his knees. He moaned.

Angelene stood ready to receive the bloodied piece of lead that Joseph soon grasped with forceps. She wrapped it in a scrap of dark cloth the moment after he had it out. Before Joseph could speak to ask for it, she had a cloth dressing folded for him, then a long rolled bandage. They worked in silence.

Cummington dared to whisper. "I think the sooner I leave with Renny the better. I think he needs to be put on the Underground Railroad tonight."

Everyone there knew the meaning of the words he spoke. He was talking about the secret route of connections that could get a runaway slave safely through all of Pennsylvania and into Ohio or New York, and from there, the whole way on to Canada.

There was a new kind of pain in Cyrus's face. "You want to take him away? How can you? Dr. Joseph said that Mr. Croghan already saw men out there lining the street."

"I was thinking of the schoolroom door," the pastor said. "It opens to the rear yard." This classroom that Cummington spoke about had been added to the cabin soon after Joseph's and Ba's arrival to Oak Glen. It was accessible from the same hallway that connected the clinic room to the house, and there was a door leading out from it, which the students used to carry in water from the well and wood for the stove.

Cummington spoke mostly to Joseph. "Those men out there could start asking questions that would lead them to know that Renny is a fugitive."

Joseph had to agree. He feared what might be happening outside even now. His best hope was that even angry white men would not force themselves across the threshold of his house since Barnabas Croghan lived here too, and he was white.

Cyrus, who had endured the surgery so nobly, now quietly sobbed. "If you take Renny, I know I will never see him again."

"You know of Constable Long, don't you?" Cummington said to both youths. "Well, he's already given this town warning that he can ask for a show of clear identification from us all, and that he will do so at the slightest intimation of violence."

"This weren't violence, but an accident!" Renny protested.

The pastor frowned. "This time, son, you're the one who doesn't understand. Since the uprising in Christiana, many a *free* black man in this county has been harrassed unjustly. Some have suffered physical harm, and some have been arrested."

Joseph wiped his hands and turned his attention to Cummington. Keeping the cloth around his fingers, he tried to hide temors that had started anew.

"Renny has no freedom papers," the pastor went on. "There is no safer plan now, than helping him get away before any danger comes."

The boys were silent.

"Do you think I can get out through the schoolroom door?" Cummington asked Joseph. "Do you think it's safer to try that than to stay here and risk having men force their way in to find us?"

"I think that Renny must be taken from Oak Glen," Joseph said drily. "Even if he will not have to face McCreary and the others tonight, he will have to do so soon. The tavernmaster could ask for his identification papers then."

Joseph's heart pounded, and not only because of the danger now. They all knew the possible fate of runaways who were caught and sent back to their masters. Remanding, it was called, and by the current law it could be done legally all through the North *and* with the aid of federal marshals and private agents who made a profit from such work. What nobody but Northern Negroes and a few passionate white abolitionists seemed willing to talk about was that remanded men and women were often horribly punished once they were back in slavery's hold. Some were maimed, some even killed as examples to other slaves that they better not think on freedom.

Joseph saw Angelene sadly nod in agreement. Her hair, braided in neat rows, was almost completely covered tonight by the white cap she wore. Bowing to the hem of the shawl hanging from her shoulders, she wiped tears from her eyes. "I'm so sorry, Cyrus," she said to the younger boy. "I know you two have grown to be like brothers."

Though the parting was painful, Cummington did not delay. "Renny, come!" He pulled away the cloths from around the door and cautiously opened it.

Oh!" Cyrus mourned, looking askance at his friend. "I don't hold nothin' 'gainst you, Renny, an' I do want you safe, not back in slavery no more!"

Renny's eyes glazed with fear. "Don't let them have me, Pastor! Don't let them get me, please! I'm worse off than a dead man if that happens!"

"Yes, we know."

Hearing nothing unusual out in the hall, Cummington led the way while Angelene rolled up all the soiled and bloodied cloths around the musket ball that she already had concealed. "I'll go out with you, Daddy. I'll burn this all in Joseph's stove so that there will be no telling signs of any gunshot wound."

"No, Angel." Her father turned back. "To get to the kitchen you have to go through the front room, and anyone outside can look in and see you."

"Still, I think I should take my chances," she said firmly. "Who will care if a woman goes to work in the kitchen? See, I can hide this all in my shawl and go out to the woodbox. I can make it look like I'm only adding more wood to the stove. Then I'll even start to make some coffee. If they want to know what we have been doing in here for so long, let them come in and look at that bandaged hand. The scalding on Cyrus's fingers can be seen, for only the palm is completely covered."

Her words directed their thoughts back to the way the boys had planned it, that McCreary would think they had run to Joseph, Oak Glen's medical practitioner, only because of the scalding. There was wisdom in cleaning the clinic, and both men knew it. "All right," her father relented with a worried sigh, and a spike of nervous pain hit Joseph in his stomach.

Joseph stayed by the table with Cyrus while the others left the room. He asked that the door be left ajar so that he could listen. For long moments after he and his patient were alone, he heard nothing. Finally Joseph walked out into the hall himself. Barnabas was just coming down the short dark corridor to find him. The older man's hands moved like lightning. *"They are still outside, and more than before! I played the fool and shrugged my shoulders when they knocked. But now they see Angelene, and they know she can hear."*

"Yes." Anxiety made Joseph's own voice sound faraway. By then, Cyrus was right behind him, the bright bandage obvious in contrast with the dim surroundings. Joseph paid close attention to the commotion he now heard coming from the street.

Angelene joined them to stand where no one could see them from the windows. "What should we do? They seem determined not to go away."

"I'll speak with them now," Joseph decided. It might help Renny and Cummington get away safely if he drew the men's attention. The moment he stepped forth, Barnabas followed directly behind him. Angelene stayed in the hallway holding on to Cyrus, perhaps to steady the boy, or to be steadied by him. Barnabas had barred the door. Joseph removed the beam.

The instant he had the way unlocked, Meade McCreary pushed open the door, not seeking permission. The tavernmaster's eyes glowed angrily above cheeks that bristled with gray whiskers. He was followed in by a younger man, Mr. Long, the recently installed constable of Brinker Township, and then by Rotham Harley, who was their nearest white neighbor and the farmer who had sold Cummington Brown the parcel of land on which the Negro town of Oak Glen now stood.

It surprised Joseph to see Harley, for though the man was not now active in the Religious Society of Friends, he had been raised as a Quaker, and he still held to some of their modest ways, as his suit of plain gray proved. Before this moment Joseph had never seen him in association with either lawmen or tavern owners. Whatever Harley might say to explain himself was put off by McCreary's boisterous confrontation.

"I know Renny and Cyrus are here. Those boys had my gun today, and while I was figuring what to do about that, I saw how they spilt oyster water all over themselves and ran off. I first went to seek advice from our constable, and that's when I learnt that other citizens were there with their complaints too. Those men waiting out there heard shots fired down by Arnold Creek." He was pointing to the window. "Everyone knows it's Negroes arming themselves for riot against the law!"

Constable Long was slightly conciliatory. "Mr. McCreary didn't actually see the boys with his gun, but he found powder spilt in his storeroom, and when he checked on his old musket, it was not wrapped as it had been before."

"Those boys were so shook up about their first misdeed that they couldn't even come in to do a night's worth of work!" McCreary's voice rumbled as before. "They were so nervous that I'd find out about my gun, they spilt hot water all over themselves and then fled the kitchen. I've come to give them a piece of my mind in the constable's presence. Otherwise, I might give in to my instincts and whip them both to show them just how good they've had it working for me."

To Joseph's amazement, Cyrus stepped out alone from the hallway. "I'm sorry, sah. I know we shouldn't have touched you' property—"

Oaths spilled forth from the tavernmaster's mouth. "Where's the other boy?"

Cyrus seemed faint as he glanced toward Joseph. "He was so scaired, sah, he ran off!"

"You imbeciles! I tried to do something to help your kind, and look what payment I get for doing it. I'm warning you, boy, you had better never set foot back on my property even after your burns do heal. And you tell that to your cousin, too, when next you see him!"

McCreary turned to Long, then to Harley. "I am a law-abiding citizen. Constable, I'm asking you to speak to these Negroes. Make it plain to them that the only rights they have in this county are the rights we choose to lend to them. Remind them that they are *not* citizens, nor will they ever be. Finally, speak to that one!" He pointed again to Joseph. "*Who* does he think he is, putting himself up so high as to pretend to be a doctor? And *what* does he think is, trying to protect a house for himself by having a demented white man live under his roof, when that poor deaf-mute can't do better to help himself."

Joseph saw Constable Long swallow hard. "Joe Whitsun only aids those of his own color," Long said weakly, perhaps as much to defend himself in letting this happen as to defend any good reputation he might have thought Joseph had. "I've never heard any complaints from the county's real doctors about what he's doing, and I think that goes back all the way to the time when he came here saying he was qualified to treat the colored sick who had scarlet fever. In that epidemic and other times since then, I believe the real doctors are grateful that they do not have to do so much to help the local colored population."

"Negroes cannot be doctors according to the law in this Commonwealth!" McCreary's words were true. Inwardly Joseph trembled.

"He's only treating his own," Constable Long said again, "and he calls himself their practitioner, not their physician." Joseph felt Harley's eyes hard upon him, but the farmer said nothing.

"If there weren't so many fugitives on this mountainside, Joe Whitsun never would have come to stay!" McCreary surmised harshly. "Now that the revised Fugitive Slave Act has been passed, you lawmen have more power to rout any vagrant intruders who are hiding out from their masters here—even those who have been living here for years."

McCreary looked straight to Harley. "And to think you sold your wife's family property to a black preacher so that he could start a Negro town! Surely you could have thought of some better way to profit from worn-out, overgrowed land."

"It was a gesture of peace and goodwill," Harley said, though his first words of the evening did not hold much conviction.

McCreary laughed at him. "Just how much peace and goodwill do you feel now that we have Negroes arming themselves at night around Brinkerville, just like they did in Christiana weeks before all hell broke loose there?"

Harley looked at the floor.

McCreary turned to Joseph. "You'd better understand that nobody here is going to let Brinkerville be put on the map the way Christiana was as a Pennsylvania town bloodied by Negro rioting! All you colored people here better know that you will keep to your place, or we can ship you to Africa—or to the gallows on convictions of sedition and treason. Can't we do that by law, Mr. Long?"

The local officer shifted uncomfortably. "Treason is what the men from Christiana, black and white, will be put on trial for," he admitted. "Treason for encouraging anarchy to prevail instead of supporting governmental law." Then he turned silent too.

McCreary himself went on talking like a man campaigning for public office. "Compromises are in place now through the Congress to keep the North and South from going to war against each other. The least you Negroes can do is have respect for the laws that are meant for the nation's continued union and prosperity." McCreary then opened the door for himself and went out. Constable Long followed him.

Mr. Harley seemed reluctant to be counted either with them or separate from them. "This is not as I had wanted it to be," he said, delaying, while the small eyes in his sallow face looked directly on Joseph. "In good faith, I accommodated Preacher Brown's desire to have a town for you colored people built around the old Brinker meetinghouse, which I first lent to him to be his African church. You must know, I never dreamed that church-going Negroes would take up guns and sickles against a federal officer and citizens, as they did in Christiana. We don't want that to happen here."

Barnabas had his hands moving, for he had been able to understand some of what the man was saying by watching Harley's lips. Yet Joseph, as a black man, felt hesitant to translate every one of dear Ba's angry words. He did say aloud, "Mr. Croghan and I never thought *we'd* see the day when white men from the North would drive suffering Negroes back down to slavery."

"No one in Pennsylvania should tolerate bloodshed, as God is our witness!" Whether Rotham Harley proclaimed this as a threat or a promise or even a prayer, Joseph could not tell. Without looking back or speaking a word of farewell, Harley went out to join the others, now milling with the other five or six men who had been in the street all this time.

Joseph closed the door, still shivering in fear. Angelene came from the shadows, and he found the strength to take her hand because she, too, seemed numbed by fright.

"Do you think they will find Renny and my father?" she asked.

"God forbid it." Those were the only words of comfort he could truly say.

CHAPTER 3

THE RUDE VISITORS had been gone less than one quarter hour when Cummington came back to the house by way of the unlocked schoolroom door. Cyrus's father, Tort Woodman, was with him, and both men looked grave. By then, Joseph, Cyrus, Barnabas, and Angelene were gathered around the kitchen table. As she had promised in the clinic room, Angelene had the kettle boiling on the stove for coffee, though no one there seemed eager for it.

"Renny's safe," Cummington announced as he and Tort sat down in the last two vacant chairs.

Joseph felt amazed that it had taken such a short time for the pastor to move Renny into a secure place. "God be praised!"

All of them around this table knew that their pastor was a "station-master," the name given to one who maintained a hiding place along one of the invisible and unpublished Underground Railroad routes. Yet none of them, Joseph included, knew where this closest safe house was, for

that was part of Cummington's cautious plan. Even so, it was known that
Tort did have his own part to play in connecting fugitives with Pastor
Brown. All of them in company this night knew that the woodchopper
was an Underground Railroad conductor, one who knew the landscape so
well as to be able to lead runaways from one stationmaster to another
without a light on even the darkest nights.

According to what Tort was saying now as the coffee brewed, he had
instructed the boys to come to Joseph, but by way of Cummington
Brown's back door, for there was danger associated with Joseph's practicing medicine illegally just as there was danger in hiding fugitives. Yet all
of them here believed that both were forms of Christian benevolence that
could not and should not be discontinued regardless of the risks.

Barnabas moved out of his seat to help Angelene set the cups around.
Because she was the teacher in the school, as well as Joseph's assistant in
surgery, Angelene was as comfortable in this kitchen as in her mother's
across the street. "What if others had come to Oak Glen this evening
looking for help while you were away?" she said, posing the question to
her father while she placed a cup in front of him. "How would we know
where to hide them or what to do until your return? Mother or I might
hear the knock at our back door, but then what would we do?"

These were questions that Joseph had considered too.

Cummington looked at them all. "I say there is no cause for worry, at
least not at present. Anyone who comes to my house will find a safe
haven."

Only Angelene dared to press him more. "I don't understand how you
can say that, Daddy, when you are the only one who knows where Oak
Glen's safe house is."

He looked at her. "Then be satisfied just to know that I *can* say it, for
now, with full confidence." The puzzlement caused by his words hung in
the air, but no one said anything more about it.

Sitting beside Cummington, Tort obviously enjoyed having warm coffee poured into the cup held between his gnarled hands. "The new fugitive law sure makes it harder on folks who are runnin'," he observed after
taking a loud, long sip, "but it also makes it harder on those of us who are
tryin' to help." Though his voice sounded rough, he had a quiet way
about him.

He glanced to Angelene, who was again beside the stove. "It's not no
game, young sister. Black folk has died tryin' to get away from bondage.
An' now black folk have kilt so that others can go free. You' daddy's right

to be so cautious, 'cause it counts for you' safety an' the safety of every other person in this town, as well as for the runaways."

"But what if you bring them to us and my father's not there?"

Tort looked to Cummington. "The man of God says it will be all right, an' so it will be. That's enough for me."

Cummington nodded as though pleased that Tort was also putting the matter to rest. "Let us give thanks to God that Renny is safe. And also give thanks to the Almighty Father for protecting Cyrus, that no more harm came to him than just the injury of his hand. Renny could have killed him by the same kind of accident."

"The hand will heal in time, I feel sure," Joseph put in, wanting his words to encourage Tort as well as Cyrus.

"Then I can take him on home?" Tort pushed aside his cup.

"Yes. Of course you can bring him back any time if you think it's not healing properly."

"I'd say nettle an' witch hazel should be applied from this night till the scabbin' comes," the father said with sagelike wisdom earned from living on the mountain more than twenty years.

Joseph nodded, for he had learned much from Dr. Ellis, the Quaker, who had secretly trained him, but also from this man. "I agree, Brother Tort. In the event that you observe swelling or fever, however, you bring him back here."

The Woodmans started for the door, the son following the father. Barnabas went with them, obviously watchful about having them enter the night. When the door closed behind them, Cummington said to Angelene, "I want you to go home too, Angel, for your mother's sake. She knows something of what's happened tonight, and I don't want her to be across the street alone and worrying."

Again Angelene's stature seemed small for all the responsibility she carried so well. She was the Browns' only daughter, born after three sons. Her mother, Azal, had been Joseph's first patient in Oak Glen after Pastor Brown had traveled to Philadelphia looking to Dr. Ellis for help in the scarlet fever outbreak of 1845.

Though Azal had lived, Joseph could not prevent the permanent damage done to her heart by the fever. It had caused her to suffer weakness and lethargy to the present day. It was Sister Azal's plight that had prompted Joseph to leave Philadelphia in order to establish a new work here, for he saw that Oak Glen needed not only a doctor but a school as

well. For the first years he did both, until Angelene took over his responsibilities as the teacher.

Barnabas had been with him then. Before the older man unleashed
his skills to refurnish this cabin, they had lived with the Browns. Angelene had been a girl of fourteen when they came, and all of her brothers
were still at home, so the house was crowded. Now those young men
were away in different parts of Ohio pursuing occupations while also following their father's footsteps to serve as Underground Railroad station-
masters in that state.

Because Cummington still had coffee before him, Joseph volunteered
to escort Angelene home. Though she usually passed freely from one
house to the other, Joseph felt protective of her because of the night's
events.

To his surprise Cummington said, "Let's all walk together. I've been
meaning to talk with you, Joseph, and tonight has shown me that I must
not delay in that any longer. If you would come across with us to my
study now."

Clearly Angelene was waiting for her father to say more. Joseph felt
the same way, for he could not guess what was on his pastor's mind. Then
Barnabas, seeing them all head to toward the door, voiced concerns of his
own. *"What is the matter?"*

Angelene translated Barnabas's signing for her father, since her skill in
manual language was nearly equal to Joseph's. It caused Cummington to
go and shake the older man's hand in an act of compassion. "Tell him,
Angel, that I'll not keep Joseph long."

Barnabas did not need a translation, for he understood much by actions and inferences. *"Dr. Joseph hasn't even had time for supper!"* Barnabas
protested as though he were Joseph's father.

Joseph translated this, and Cummington smiled kindly. "Tell Ba he
should keep that pot of stew I saw on the stove warm, Joseph. I'll send
you back to him soon."

Walking between Cummington and Angelene, Joseph faced the chilly
night. The Browns' house was a two-story structure with four windows
facing front on both the first and second floors. It had been the second
house to be built on the old Brinker property, which had come to Harley
and his wife through an inheritance. The first house had been the cabin
that Joseph and Ba now occupied.

When the Browns purchased the property in 1842, Cummington repaired this house for himself. As long as Joseph had been in Oak Glen,

the second-story window that was farthest to the right had always been lighted at night by a lamp. In that window a small neat sign read *Quilts for Sale.*

Despite her physical limitations, Sister Azal continued to be an artist who used cloth to make incredibly beautiful quilts. Since her bout with fever, quilt-making had become her main occupation. She sewed beside that window several hours each day. As usual, tonight she had two finished quilts on display, their colors and details quite distinct in the lamp-light.

This window was the brightest on Oak Glen's rural street, for most residents went to bed at dusk to save oil and tallow. Joseph had heard some say that Cummington Brown was imprudent for letting that lamp burn, yet others speculated that the pastor allowed it so that the clergy-man's house could be identified by night. Because Joseph knew that their pastor was also secretly a stationmaster, the lamp in the window never proved to be puzzling to him. He assumed, without asking, that conductors like Tort relied on its glow for direction as they brought slaves in and led them away with so much stealth that few in Oak Glen knew they lived near a stop on the Underground Railroad.

The pastor's study was the first small room off to the right after they came into the wide entrance hall. Since Angelene had come across to Joseph's cabin wearing only her shawl for warmth over her dark dress, she went directly to the stairs while her father paused to hang his coat and hat. It gave her a moment to look at Joseph only. She eyed him with much unspoken concern. "I guess I'll say good-night, Papa," she said, yet lingering, certainly hoping to be included in their conversation.

"Good night, Angel," her father returned, either unaware of or disinterested in her hinting. "Joseph, go on into the study. I'll bring a candle from the hall."

Because the unlighted room was familiar, Joseph could have entered. Instead he paused because of Angelene. "Good night," he said, feeling that he was much like an older brother coming to visit home. "Thank you for all you did for Cyrus and for Renny."

Her smile was warm. "Good night, Joseph."

By then her father had the candle and Joseph followed him into the study. Cummington pointed to one straight-backed chair. "Sit down." He turned another one around, which had faced his desk that held his opened Bible. Joseph tried not to be uneasy.

"May God lead and direct our words," the pastor said. Though the side window was too dark to give any view, Cummington still looked that way, perhaps to watch the candle's blurred reflection. By day, their church could be seen through those panes, a square, yellow sandstone structure that had been abandoned for several decades before Cummington took it over as the house of worship for Mt. Hope African Church, the congregation he had founded.

"Sometimes you are as strong as iron, Brother Whitsun, but sometimes I see you tremble, as I did tonight."

Only after saying this did Cummington look Joseph in the eyes. Even in the privacy of this room with a pastor he trusted, Joseph found it hard to hear those words. He bowed, shamed because of this weakness that was beyond his control.

"Your hands are steady when you work. Tonight I took note of that too."

"Yes!" Joseph tried to focus on his confidence, yet when he dared to look at the pastor, he knew that a great source of disgrace for him had been revealed, and he felt helpless.

"When it happens, it seems that you are always with those who have been or still are slaves."

"That is true, sir. I know it," Joseph managed.

"Then do you know the reason for this trembling?"

Joseph thought he did know. "Please don't ask."

Cummington's face filled with concern. "Brother Whitsun, I've known hundreds of former slaves. Secretly I've helped that many to escape. I feel that sometimes now I can see beneath the surface to their souls. I feel that way about you. I should have spoken sooner. Honestly, I had hoped that you might speak to me."

Joseph held his breath.

"What I've seen in others makes me believe that someone you know, someone you care about, did suffer in slavery. Or perhaps still suffers now."

There was no way to avoid the other man's eyes.

"We must speak about this, Joseph. I hope you understand. I must know which of us will be in danger if Constable Long does call for any investigation here. With increased regularity, agents and masters are searching through Pennsylvania for former slaves. They are emboldened by the law." The pastor leaned back against his chair.

Joseph shivered.

"This will be spoken about in confidence. Do not fear. That is why I wanted to make sure that even Brother Barnabas would not find reason to ask you anything about this conversation. What you say will not go beyond these walls." He motioned with hands that were stained from the weekday work he did in the apple orchard he maintained to support himself and his family.

His face looked square and brave as he sat with his eyes closed for a time, certainly in prayer. "Brother, you know my past and Sister Azal's. Our parents were slaves in New York until gradual emancipation in that state freed them. I think you've heard how my mother continued working for her former master, while my father started his own business selling ice and coal. Because of their hard work and their frugality, I had a monetary inheritance as well as a spiritual one at their passing. This is what I used to buy the land for Oak Glen."

"Yes, sir, I do know these things."

"You know, too, how I felt God's hand on me to look for land where we might start a church and a respectable God-fearing town. My sons Earl, Wesley, and Jack were adolescent boys, and Angelene only a girl of eleven when we came here to this house."

"Yes, sir. Three years later Ba and I arrived."

"I'm refreshing your memory so that you can know without a doubt that God did ordain me to comfort and guide those who escape out of slavery's hell."

"I don't doubt it, Pastor Brown."

"Well, now, you see again how much you do know about us. But it's occurred to me many times that we know almost nothing about you, except that you were secretly trained in Philadelphia by the Quaker doctor, Leon Ellis, whom I know also from the Pennsylvania Abolitionist Society. You were his first colored student, working with him for years before you found Barnabas and went off to New England to see if you could learn a language for the deaf."

"Yes, sir. Ba and I were with the Christian man, Thomas Gallaudet." It felt easy to face his past as it related to Ba's friendship. "I think you know that Barnabas lost his hearing in a fire when he was in his forties. He was trying to save his cattle when hay stored in the barn caused great explosions that destroyed his ears. His wife and grown children hired an attorney to declare him unfit to keep his farm. He had been a county commissioner, but all that was ignored once his deafness came. They were terrified of the changed sound of Ba's voice when he could no longer hear himself speak, as though something terrible had gone wrong with his mind. It made him vow to never speak again. A son wagoned him to Philadelphia and left him to live on the streets."

Cummington raised a hand. "I wish to keep the discussion centered on you, Joseph. I've heard nothing about your family. Your father. Your mother. This has weighed on my mind."

Joseph pulled in a slow breath. "My mother was a slave."

Cummington nodded, as though he either expected it or knew what kind of courage and agony it took to make that short admission. The pastor spoke gently, but his question was probing. "How is that possible when you are from Philadelphia, and free?"

Joseph eyed him as his hands began to quiver. This time he felt it futile, maybe even dishonest, to try to hide them. The muscles in his face tightened too. "I think you already know."

Cummington never looked away. "My dear son. How long did you yourself endure slavery?"

Joseph forced himself to say it. "Twenty-one years."

CHAPTER 4

PASTOR BROWN GOT OUT OF HIS CHAIR. He came and put his hands on Joseph's shoulders like a mantle of consolation. "What agony, brother! What pain you have endured."

Joseph had the terrible feeling of sinking down, as though the seat and the floor were both falling away. He felt like dropping to his knees. The terrible burden of the secret was off his back, but still it consumed his energy and his breath. He could hardly avoid tears, so he covered his face.

The older man stooped slightly to look him straight in the eye as soon as Joseph would allow it. "Ah, Brother Whitsun. Take heart! Our Jesus says, 'Blessed are they that mourn: for they shall be comforted.' The comfort comes *with* the mourning, son. Not always before it!"

Joseph looked down. His past was known. Suddenly he wanted the meeting to end. He fought to compose himself. "You don't have to guess anymore about the reason for these tremors." He lifted his hands, exposing them as they shook violently.

There was much silence before Pastor Brown replied. "Don't be hard on yourself. There is a *truthfulness* in mourning. Do not despise the gift of grief. There is a great *vulnerability* in admitting our fears and our pain. There's a *reckoning* with the truth that can come only when we do so." He paused as though to let his words pierce Joseph's heart. As though he saw what a struggle it was for Joseph to sit there and listen.

"We cannot always be strong. Indeed, God does not require it, though I think you do require it of yourself."

Joseph felt more tearful and more confused. "I must! Otherwise I would just lie down and die from the agony! It is not just *my* suffering or the suffering of those I see. It is everywhere! Seen and unseen. You yourself said that you have known hundreds of slaves! How much can any man take of injustice, unless he steels his mind and heart to try to save himself from the agony?"

Cummington stepped back. "You can find rest in the Lord. I feel I need to say it again: You can rest in God. He is just and sovereign and all powerful. Suffering will end, and each of us will be present for the day of reckoning."

Joseph wished that he had the nerve to stand and flee.

"Picture yourself at the mercy seat of God. Share your pain with Him there."

"God is divine! What have I to say to Him?" Joseph knew his words sounded irreverent, but he did not stop them.

"God does see, but what you *choose* to tell Him is not the same as what He knows. You have anger toward Him. I understand, but *you* must bring that before God, or someday you may find yourself denying that He is your rightful, divine head."

Joseph looked away. Usually he was concerned about politeness, but now he did not care. "What does it matter! God knows, either way! The past is past! It cannot change!"

"You are right. The past does not change. But it is the foundation on which we build our present and our future. That is why I am asking you to speak about it now. It is important for your own safety in the future, and perhaps for the safety of Oak Glen as well."

"I am no runaway slave! I have a manumission paper. I came into Philadelphia with it tied by a cloth around my arm."

Cummington sighed. "I am glad! Please go on. Tell me how and why you were freed. Manumission is rare in this day." He sat down.

Truly Joseph wanted to seal off all memory. "I am sorry, Pastor, but I choose to forget! I have my valid paper. I don't see how Mr. Long or even a federal officer could take my freedom from me, so what danger is there?"

"The terrible danger that you are not truly set free—not yet, brother, not while all this agony is still the master of your heart, mind, and soul."

"It is my past, and you agree that the past cannot be changed!"

"Yes. Now can you agree that God is wise enough and powerful enough to use even your past for His divine purposes?"

Joseph could hardly see for his tears, which he did not want to shed. He turned his head, refusing to let Cummington know the extent of the weakness flooding over him. "As a Christian I know I should say yes, but right now I cannot and still be honest!"

"Be truthful! Why, Joseph, is it that you are known in this town as a man who would willingly give up his life for others? Why is it that Dr. Ellis and all our colored brethren in Philadelphia say the same about you? Is it not because your trials have already wrought a courage and a compassion in you far deeper than most have?"

Joseph shook his head. "I made a vow to God that I would not give up being His servant in freedom." He allowed himself to think back, but only to his journey from Charleston to Philadelphia sixteen years ago.

"God is your Master. That is evident! Now I challenge you. Let Him be your divine *Father* too. The One who loves you without conditions. The One who loved you even before you made your vow to serve Him. The One who loved you in your deepest and most hurtful times of pain."

Joseph moved his tongue to the roof of his mouth to feel the scars of wounds inflicted on him while he had been a slave on Delora Plantation. Even to let himself think on that name brought him more torment. It was like removing a barrier so that again he was vulnerable to all sorts of mental enemies that had been walled out for years. Real physical hurt coursed through his limbs. He doubled over.

Cummington did not allow him to writhe in silence alone. "Oh, your past does eat you like a cancer. You war against it, and you cover it very well. But tonight I realize how wrong I've been to let this go on without confronting you. I was just as wrong as you would be as a surgeon to ignore physical disease."

"Some diseases are fatal! And probing then is only cruel!"

"But God can lift this burden you carry. God can deal with the human sin that brought you to this place of suffering."

"I have friends in slavery," Joseph admitted haltingly. "I left them there! Even my mother! Will God overlook that sin in me on His Judgment Day?"

"You cannot be their savior. I'm sure they never expected you to be."

"Still, I deserted them! They are in chains and in torment to this day."

"Where are your friends? Where is your mother?"

His teeth were clenched. "South Carolina. On a rice plantation. That is, unless they had been sold or worked to the grave."

The pastor sighed his wonder. "And yet you were freed?"

"It is a long story that I want to forget!" Yet while he said this, Joseph's conscience was pricked. "I would be slighting God if I did not tell you one thing. My master did free me because of his conviction under Christ. But what of the others? Why was I the only one? How can God be served or satisfied by one drop of recompense in a sea of injustice?"

"How did you gain so much education in so little time?"

It was another act of God, Joseph knew, yet he was hardly willing to speak about it. Every good thing had been countered by so much sorrow. "As a boy I taught myself to read. When my master found out, he did not punish me but secretly sent me on to a colored school. His purpose was to settle in his own mind if Negroes could have intellects equal to whites." He stopped. "You know the man who was my teacher. It was Daniel Alexander Payne, then only in his twenties."

"Reverend Payne! The recently appointed historiographer of our churches!"

"Yes, the same!" Unexpectedly a chill ran through Joseph's spine. "He was forced out of Charleston in 1835, the same year I gained my freedom when Master Callcott died."

"Then you followed him north!"

"No, sir, I had no idea where he was. But a few years after I started studying with Dr. Ellis, I heard he was going to be at one of the city's Negro conventions where issues concerning our race were to be addressed. I was able to go and meet with him briefly. I learned there how he had traveled first to New York, then to a seminary in Gettysburg, Pennsylvania, where he was able to further his own education while continuing to teach."

"After that Payne moved to Philadelphia and opened a school," Pastor Brown added from his own knowledge of the man.

"Yes, but Ba was very sickly then, and I was responsible for his care, so I did not see him often."

"Reverend Payne recently published a book of poems, which I've purchased as a Christmas gift for Angelene."

"I would like to see it, sir!"

"You will. I have it upstairs. Oh, God *has* been at work on your behalf."

Another chill passed along Joseph's spine. "But why, sir? Why have I been preserved and liberated but not others?" For the first time in years, Joseph allowed himself to think about his sweet, wonderful wife, Rosa. Now dead.

"God is God. We must trust Him even when we cannot understand Him. I urge you to stop blaming yourself for things you cannot change. And stop blaming God for things He did not choose to change. Trust Him that He does love all those whom you love. And accept this more difficult truth as well: He also loves those whom we think cannot deserve His love. Even those whom we would rather hate."

Slowly, like the coming of a dawn, Joseph realized there was another reason why he had not wanted to face his past so unreservedly. There was another emotion inextricably bound to his grief. It was anger. Even now, unadulterated rage wrangled to be exposed from his heart and from his mouth. He clenched his fist. His hands shook again.

"Joseph."

Burning hate coursed like hot blood through his consciousness. The pastor's voice became faint by comparison.

"To have God's peace you must be willing to see all things as God sees them: Time. Life's purpose. Even your enemies."

"I was cut. Whipped. Penned." These details Joseph could spew aloud, but there were other tortures, especially against Rosa, that were too terrible to ever speak about again.

"It is the same evil, the same root of sin that tortured Christ. They pulled out His beard. They flayed His back. They spit on His face and cursed Him, and He was their God."

"They did it to us only because of our color!"

"Joseph. Listen! Your suffering qualifies you to be an ambassador for Christ. What hope do we have except in a Savior? The whole world is bound by sin. We are too, if we let it have its hold over us. Because you have suffered, you are qualified to speak on the evils of sin and on the impossibility of finding freedom through any other way but the way of Christ."

"I cannot forgive them all, if that's what you want of me!"

"But Christ within you can. His death and life are all about forgiveness, and His mercy is open to all. I say, begin to pray for mercy, that even our enemies will not have to face God's wrath. That's what Christ endured the cross for—that not one human being would be lost from God's love."

Joseph slumped in the chair and Cummington began to pray out loud. Joseph had the sense of feeling the man's resonant voice more than hearing it, and the feeling was like oil running down, seeping into his spiritual wounds.

He remembered then that even in some of the worst of his tortures, he had felt this same presence—divine and infinitely greater than the sum of his emotions, senses, and understanding. After praying for a long while, Pastor Brown grew silent. Joseph opened his eyes, then his hands. They were not shaking. The room seemed filled with an unnatural calm, like a night after a storm.

Pastor Brown spoke again. "I need to tell you some practical things. I think it best that you not show your manumission paper to anybody unless it becomes absolutely necessary as an action to preserve your freedom. So odd a document could cause a stir. Some might question its validity, and we have no power in the courts now to speak on our own behalf."

It was something Joseph had considered but dismissed, for he was legally free, and the law should respect that. "Barnabas has seen it, and Dr. Ellis, when I first came to his house."

"That's not a problem. I trust those two men. In a time of crisis, it might even benefit us to have Dr. Ellis as a witness and an advocate."

Joseph found the pastor staring at him.

Seeming slightly self-conscious, Cummington explained. "You've done so much and accomplished so much since slavery. Your testimony could be a great encouragement to others, for you know as well as I do that many who come out of bondage have no will or hope or spirit left in them. They have no desire to be either moral or productive. They do not care to seek after God. I think your words could help them."

"As God is my witness, I will not speak about this again!"

"It would not have to be told under your own name. It could be published in a booklet as Frederick Douglass and so many others have done.

Of course, you may not be able to face doing it right now, but the idea causes me to think on the book of Revelation, where it says, " 'They overcame him'—that is, the accuser of the brethren—'by the blood of the Lamb, and by the word of their testimony; and they loved not their lives unto the death.' "

"It feels like death to speak about it! And there is plenty of death in slavery, believe me. Mind, body, and spirit."

"Yet it might be so important for our churches in America to hear about it. Even how you could have faith in those times. The Negro wants freedom! Indeed, the white man needs it too! The message of your life, as I see it, is that humankind will never have freedom until hatred is conquered, and cruelty and greed. This can come only by submitting to God. You said you were manumitted when the Spirit of God convicted your master of right and wrong. Perhaps if your story is published, other *white* men would be convicted to do the same. At the same time, black men will be encouraged to press on as you are pressing on."

Joseph looked at him, overwhelmed. "It would be too painful."

"Someone else will benefit from knowing the truth about your past, and that is Angelene," the pastor said after some hesitation.

"Sir!"

"She does worry about you, Joseph. You must know that. She is inclined to interpret the struggle she senses within you as your indifference toward her."

"I don't mean it that way. She is like a sister to me."

"She was a child when you came, and she loved you as a child loves. But she is not a child anymore. I am not betraying her confidence by saying that she believes she does love you. I know she has told you this herself. I know because then she comes home and cries before her mother and me."

Joseph looked away. "Sir, now you know why she must not put her hopes toward me. I will stay resolved to press on to the end of my days doing what is right, but there is no love of life left in me. I hope you can understand why. To exist and not cave in to despair, I think on duty and obedience and responsibility. She is looking for love and joy, and she deserves it."

"I will not betray your confidence, Joseph, but I think she should be told."

Joseph stared at the blind dark window. "Even if I were not caught as I am by my past, I would be too old for her. I am thirty-six years old, sixteen years her senior! If you could speak with her about that—"

"You need to tell her. Tell her why you cannot, or will not, reciprocate the kind of love she wants to give to you."

Joseph glanced at him. "From the first time she spoke about her feelings, I was sure she was taken more by *what* I am than by *who* I am. Now you know my ugly interior. I am one of the few educated men she does know. Yet outside Oak Glen she could know many. Believe me, many will be taken by *her*, once they meet her. I pray God will lead her to an honorable young man."

The pastor chuckled. "She talks with you about many things, doesn't she? I suppose she tells you how much she wants to be part of the abolition movement and how she wants to travel with me when I go to the various conventions?"

"Yes, she mentions it," Joseph admitted, feeling somewhat lightened in spirit. "She seldom hides her feelings or her ideas." In that way and in many ways, she was so different from him. Suddenly another image of Rosa, dead, arrested him. It was almost as if he could reach out and touch her cold face. He was forced to stop speaking. His hands quavered anew.

Cummington studied him, but this time he asked no questions. "Healing does take time. I need not say that to you, a doctor."

Joseph agreed outwardly by his nodding, yet inwardly he decided that his crippling from the past would never end.

"I must consider Azal's health as well as Angelene's great zeal to fight the evils of slavery," Cummington said, going on about his family while looking quite sober. "There's no part of abolition these days that's free of danger. I must think on how such risks will affect my dear wife as well as Angelene. I have contemplated taking Angelene with me to the next set of meetings in Ohio. Then she could see her brothers. If Azal had the strength to travel, I would surely take her too."

He paused, then smiled, though solemnity still consumed him. "Perhaps Angelene could use her talents and her eagerness to help the cause in this way. Perhaps she could write your biography in time for us to carry it out of state. That would ensure the concealment of your true identity."

"I'm not sure, sir," Joseph said. "I'd have to think about it." In truth, he felt sure that he would not do it. He felt sure that if his pastor knew what his story was, he would keep his only daughter far from the truth of it.

Joseph could not imagine telling any young woman, and especially Angelene, the details of his time in slavery. She was too innocent. Far too young and pure in spirit. To tell her truth like that would crush and pollute her. He would not let himself be the one to mar such beauty. Yet the pastor seemed more to favor it as the moments passed.

"In the process of doing that together, Joseph, she would come to know you better. It might be the right way to let her hear about your past. Then you and she can decide what foundation it does lend to the present and the future for you both."

Joseph stared at him. "Would you want your daughter to marry me?" It was a question he had never raised with Cummington Brown before.

"Joseph, I already love you like a son." There were tears in the pastor's eyes. "All that I've learned tonight only makes me care about you and respect you all the more."

Joseph left the house certain that he would not speak about slavery ever again, not for the cause of the abolition, not to explain himself, and surely not as a project in authorship for Angelene, though she had the talent for words.

Of all the burdens he did feel while crossing the dark street to go home, at least one had been lifted. He felt confident that Angelene would soon have the opportunity to travel. In doing so, she would soon meet other learned Christian men—younger, more handsome, and more hopeful than he. Her pretty head would be turned by one of them, and finally he would be freed from the guilt of continually making her unhappy by his own unhappiness.

CHAPTER 5

THE MOMENT HE SAW JOSEPH LEAVE the pastor's house, Barnabas got up from the rocking chair he had placed by the front window. He had been watching continuously, his squirrel gun resting on his knees, since his friends had crossed the dirt street. After Long, Harley, and McCreary had intruded on their property, he had been unsettled. If any more men came here bearing threats against anyone in Oak Glen, he would be ready to defend them and himself.

When Joseph came to their porch, Barnabas opened the door. He never saw Joseph look more haggard or worn down by worry than he was now. *"What happened over there?"* he signed.

Joseph's eyes met his, then he opened his hands wide, as though he chose to answer with just one careless action. *"Nothing!"*

Barnabas did not believe him, yet he kept his peace. He pointed to the clock hanging on the kitchen wall that they could see from the door. It was now half past nine. *"You need to eat supper,"* he said after pointing.

Joseph did follow him to the table. He sat down as Barnabas lifted the iron pot filled with cooked cabbage and potatoes back onto the fire. While they waited for the meal to heat, Barnabas went to the kitchen shelf and took down the chess board and the box of chessmen that he had carved and painted himself. There had been years in his past when he never would have believed that he would be eager to play such a game, or with a Negro.

He brought the board to the table just when Joseph reached for the book he had started reading before Cyrus and Renny had come. It was one of the many thin, handwritten cardboard-bound journals that Joseph had put together for himself. All together the books were a history of his medical cases since the start of his practice with Dr. Ellis at the Infirmary for Colored Patients in Philadelphia.

Barnabas did not hesitate now to show his disappointment that Joseph would choose to do more work after his long and trying day. It was Barnabas's opinion that men in their prime, as Joseph was, should draw some pleasure from the fruits of their labor. But the serious-minded bachelor who shared this house with him always seemed burdened by so many responsibilities. Barnabas knew it was in part because of the times in which they lived. It also had to do with how great Joseph's vision was to make life better for American-born Africans.

Yet the only crown of glory Barnabas could see Joseph receiving for all his diligence was the halo of gray coming prematurely to his coal-black hair, which Barnabas cut short whenever they did each other's barbering.

It rankled him that a man as talented as Joseph could work so hard and gain so little. It had not been so for him when he was Joseph's age. Back then he had been a prosperous farmer along the Delaware River. That was until the day he lost his hearing.

"Supper. Then chess," Barnabas declared with all the force he could muster, for he was tired also and his aging fingers felt nearly too stiff for words. He had spent his day mostly in the barn and at the woodpile splitting firewood. Then in the late afternoon he had cut a cabbage from the garden and taken potatoes from the cellar to cook the meal.

"Forgive me, Ba." Joseph called him by name, putting the symbol for the letter B close to his heart. "I must study because of an ill child in Orphans' Cottage. I saw her this morning."

Orphans' Cottage was the house for homeless white children managed by Brinker Township. Joseph had just started making weekly visits there a month ago at the request of their neighbor, Rotham Harley of

Brinkerville, who lived directly across the Pike from Oak Glen. The lane to his farm was an extension of the one street that ran through Oak Glen, until it disappeared the other way as the road winding up into Welshman's Mountain.

Harley served on the orphanage's board. Late in September he had reported to Joseph that they would have no more funds until Christmastime to pay for a regular physician to ride across the mountain to see to the children's needs. Since Joseph lived much closer than any white doctor, Harley promised to pay him for any medicines he would need if Joseph would do the weekly visiting without a fee. Harley also gave his word that no one but he and the orphanage's house mistress would have to know that a Negro was tending to the children.

Barnabas was against this plan from the first, but Joseph agreed to it because he believed that no one should be made to suffer because of poverty. All this time Barnabas had worried because of the state's unwritten code against black men doing any kind of medical work. Joseph's manner at the table now seemed to reflect his own kind of deep concern. *"What is the trouble?"* Barnabas said, pushing the chess board aside as well as his hopes for playing as he sat down beside his closest friend.

Barnabas should not have been surprised, though he was momentarily, when Joseph began to speak about the orphan rather than about himself or his reflections on the uncivil visit by the white men that night. *"She loses weight. Always tired."* Joseph moved his journal so that Barnabas could easily read the page. In Joseph's clear handwriting and with many drawings along each margin, Barnabas saw paragraphs about cancers in the abdomen. *"I fear a t-u-m-o-r."* Joseph pointed to the printed word and also spelled it with their manual alphabet, using his supple, slender fingers.

Initially every word presented a challenge, for it had to be learned either from Gallaudet's collection of symbols or else made up by their own agreement and remembered. Barnabas tried not to let himself be shaken. *"For you, I fear s-t-a-r-v-a-t-i-o-n,"* he said, trying to lighten the terrible mood that seemed to have trapped them both. He spelled his last word too, for they had no ready sign for that one either. *"You have not eaten all day."*

To emphasize his concern, Barnabas called Joseph by name, making the letters *J* and *O* over the pulse of his upturned left wrist, which was the place for signing doctor. *"Please, feed your stomach now, not your mind only."*

Joseph smiled wryly. *"No one is helped by my stomach."*

Barnabas found himself unable to stop speaking his concern. *"Harley might blame you if that child stays ill."* He weighed an even more sobering thought, then said it too. *"Or if she dies."*

He saw Joseph's shoulders fall. *"I know. I need your wisdom, Ba, not your worry."*

"Those men today, did they speak about the orphanage?"

Joseph shook his head, but Barnabas knew him so well that he could see that not all the truth was being exposed. *"They said something about your doctoring. I saw such words on the constable's lips."*

Joseph grimaced, then agreed. *"He told everyone there that I was a doctor to colored people only."*

"What did H-a-r-l-e-y say?"

"Nothing." His hands opened again to make the sign.

Barnabas sighed. *"You must not return to the orphanage!"*

"She needs a s-u-r-g-e-o-n."

"You must not be seen touching a white child. Especially after today!"

"I have touched her. It was needed to find the cause of her great pain."

"You must not do the s-u-r-g-e-r-y!"

"I will not. But I must go back to see that she is taken care of. When I came home this morning, I went to the schoolroom and asked Angelene to go with me next week. Angelene will do the e-x-a-m-i-n-a-t-i-o-n. If the tumor is bigger, then she will show the schoolmistress why the girl must be taken to another doctor right away."

Barnabas turned the page in Joseph's book. He found notes written on a sheet of paper. *"This girl is thirteen years old!"* It panicked him even more.

Joseph nodded.

"Do you know what this can mean?"

"Yes." This time Joseph frowned.

Barnabas could not contain his worry. He rose and paced the floor. Had he known that Joseph would be called upon to look after more than infants or toddlers, he would have spoken his negative counsel from the start, no matter how desperate these orphans were. These days there was much anti-Negro talk published even in Northern newspapers that centered on the fear of *miscegenation,* or the mixing of the races. It was believed nearly everywhere that black males had vile natures that could drive them to take advantage of innocent white females.

There was no guarantee that Harley or the housemistress of the orphanage did not believe this too. Joseph eyed him, and that hurt Barnabas deeply. He came back to the table. *"I trust you!"* Barnabas hoped he did not have to say that. *"It's Harley and others I don't trust. It's what they might say of you!"*

Then Joseph stood, but only to rescue the pot that had been boiling wildly, which Barnabas could not hear. *"We should eat,"* Joseph said, turning the concern around so that now he was the one looking after Barnabas.

Both of them sat down with the food between them. In contrast with the slim man of African descent, Barnabas felt himself a doughy grandfather, keenly aware of his own sixty-seven years. Instead of having Joseph's frosting of white, he had only a few brown strands of hair remaining. Time had even blanched his wiry brows. Now he pressed his fingers to his brow, wondering if he could eat at all with so much worry churning within him.

Joseph tried to cheer him. *"Let only one bad thought remain,"* he challenged. *"Know that after we eat, you will lose at chess."* For the word "chess" Joseph showed the sign they had invented—two horses coming face-to-face as he put crooked fingers to his right temple then against his left one.

He waited until Barnabas could no longer keep from smiling. Joseph nodded then with satisfaction. *"Now, let us pray."* Joseph indicated that he would say the blessing. He did so, his lips and hands moving. Both men held their eyes open, their minds and hearts also, to reverence God.

Afterward, the atmosphere in the warm room seemed relaxed. Yet Barnabas began to think that any catastrophe to befall Joseph would likely destroy him as well, for Angelene Brown was the only other person in Oak Glen to understand Gallaudet's manual language, which Joseph and he had taken years to learn together.

Joseph was the one who had rescued him, the one who had showed him hope and kindness when no one else in the world seemed to care. Joseph had found him sleeping under a Schuylkill River bridge on the western skirts of Philadelphia. By then Barnabas had become a frost-bitten soul, barely breathing within his sack of bones. For years he had been begging drams of liquor day and night to drown his pain. Then a Negro bowed down to reach him.

This young man had medical training, given to him in secret by a Quaker doctor who believed in the equality of the races. What humbled Barnabas even now was that after Joseph found him, he rented a room on one of the most dangerous streets so that they could have a place to stay together in a town were black men and white men did not live as equals. Instead of continuing to work for his teacher Dr. Ellis, Joseph began taking menial jobs, from shining shoes to waiting tables, so he could have money and the time to nurse Barnabas back to health, all the while trying to convince him that his silence could be broken.

Their earliest bond had been literacy, since both could read. In the months when they studied under Gallaudet, Joseph worked as hard as any deaf student to learn the language in order to help him.

Suddenly Barnabas felt Joseph's touch on his shoulder. Barnabas bowed to hide the dampness that had come into his eyes. He felt selfish, thinking on what might happen to him if anything happened to Joseph. By all Joseph had done, the younger man had literally saved Barnabas's life and restored a purpose to him. Now Barnabas felt that he must be ready to do everything he could to save Joseph, though he did not have a young man's vigor.

Joseph seemed determined not to let him ponder such things. *"Don't you worry, Ba! When I win at chess tonight, I will not expect flattery, so don't you look so sad."*

CHAPTER 6

BORDERING THE SOUTH SIDE OF PHILADELPHIA, the streets of Southwark were woven into tight, dull squares like the warp and woof of soot-filled fabric. Ludlow Row was one of Southwark's many crowded, short dirt lanes in this settlement known for its lack of streetlamps and water pipes and its wealth of epidemics and vice. Harriet Mason had lived in the tenements of Ludlow Row for twenty of her forty-two years, seven of them with a husband, John. John had been raised for bricklaying by a Virginia marse, but now he lived free, earning a cooking room and a sleeping room for them both by collecting the rents from their colored neighbors.

Mr. Ludlow, the white man who owned the property, had it organized this way so he would not have to set his own foot down anywhere on the parcel that gave him the doubtful honor of bearing his name. And John willingly accepted the duty, with its benefits, just so nobody there would have to worry about any white man coming by.

John could have paid straight out for the first-story rooms they had and more had he wanted to, since he had a good salvage business going just around the corner in Dresden Alley. For his storehouse there he bought damaged cargo from the captains on the wharves just a few blocks to the east. This he sorted and sold, by pushcart and wagon, to customers both colored and white.

All who lived in the row understood that John took the dishonorable work of being Mr. Ludlow's collector in order to keep that white man from meddling in their lives. Like so many other city landowners, Mr. Ludlow had long ago put up these two tall, ramshackle buildings in the rear yard of his first house so that he could rent his sturdy brick dwelling to Irishmen and Germans while making more money from poor colored folk who would pay by the week for drafty, wood-framed rooms.

Harriet felt the cold air seeping through ill-fitting floorboards when she got out of bed to dress. It was dark, and John still snored under the comfortable layers of blankets and quilts. She went first to the kitchen right across the hall to feed the fire in the stove so the rooms would get warmer.

John had too much manly pride to step inside any kitchen except to eat from its table. That gave Harriet freedom to have this room almost to herself. From behind the woodbox she took out the large basket she hid there week after week. It was nearly as wide around as a shipping keg for wine and she had it covered up with sailcloth, lent to her by one of the sailors who rented a room upstairs.

Most of the tenants were free seamen who needed rooms only in winter when the Delaware River port might ice over. But in the tenement across from hers, there were at least two families of runaway slaves—the Cocherons and the Jamisons. They had named themselves after the Maryland towns on the eastern shore from which they had escaped. Harriet and John themselves weren't fugitives anymore, for four years ago, using her literacy and his money, they had bargained with their former marses by letter to buy themselves free, paying over six hundred dollars each for their own flesh, bones, and blood.

Harriet had learned to read and write from her white friend, Mayleda Ruskin, who was coming this morning to visit after having not been in Ludlow Row for close to seven years. That's what had Harriet up and moving about so early.

Not being so strong as she had been in her prime when she had toted water and such to Marse Arne's kitchen, Harriet now carried her big basket with both her hands and headed to the door. It was filled to the brim with the finished sewing she had worked on all through the week without John knowing it. Today Mayleda would bring her another, filled with new work to do.

Already having her black shawl around her shoulders, Harriet lugged the evidence of her labor into the twilight outside. To her surprise two small children stood waiting for her on the narrow walkway that ran straight between the two tenements, which felt like a path drawn through a cave or a tunnel because of the stifling closeness of the buildings on each side. With her arms free, she could easily touch both houses at once without even stretching out her fingers.

"This the mornin' when you' white friend Missus Ruskin's comin'?" Suzannah Cocheron asked as both little girls, just five years old each, blinked up at her. Their faces shone even in the dimness like those of heavenly cherubs bundled up against earthly cold in brown coats, red scarves, and multicolored mittens made from scraps of yarn.

"Yes, it is," Harriet answered, not forgetting that she had invited the children and their mothers for this happy reunion, because she wanted them to know her friend. "Will you' mamas come?"

Margrace Jamison pouted and shook her head. "I don't think so. They don't think that you an' a white lady will have tea t'gether as friends, like you says."

"Then why'd they agree on sendin' you two?"

"Our daddies!" Suzannah declared. "Our daddies remember *Mista* Ruskin, and they says they liked that man!"

"Well, they had better say that, for my brother Collin an' Mr. Ruskin were best friends, just like Sister Ruskin an' me. I wouldn't have my outdoor kitchen, an' you' families wouldn't have so nice an oyster-selling business if it weren't for that friendship 'tween my brother Collin an' Mrs. Ruskin's husband, Brother Sprague."

The girls grew serious and silent, maybe out of respect, for they knew they were talking about those who had died and gone on to gain their heavenly rewards. "Girls, I'm gwine down to the kitchenhouse to put the kettle on for some sweet sassafras tea." She waited, knowing that the reference to warm drink would entice them to come and keep her company.

"Can we help you any?" little Margrace said.

"Yes, you can!" Never having had any children of her own, Harriet was happy for their reply. The girls followed her like goslings behind the goose as she went down between their houses toward Dresden Alley. To her left, the tenement that the girls lived in was throbbing with sound as men and women talked and babies cried. On the right, her house was mostly quiet.

Directly across from the outdoor kitchen Harriet used for most of her cooking and baking, the girls' fathers were already busy hitching their mules to their fancy green wagon, trimmed in yellow and red. The older sons of both families were filling the wagon with barrels of oysters shipped up from the Chesapeake Bay. Only ten years ago these men, their wives, and oldest children had been in bondage. Now they were part of the city's growing fugitive population, and they were some of the prosperous ones.

Currently Cocheron and Jamison had business accounts with the same free colored watermen in Maryland who still supplied their marses' tables. But now they were profiting from ordering shellfish to be shipped by boat or by rail to the city so that they could sell it in the street. The daddies both took time to wave a greeting to their daughters, and the girls boasted out loud, "We's invited to Sister Mason's party with her white lady friend! An' we gwine help her now."

Harriet's kitchen had been built for her by her kind brother Collin just years before his passing. It was a copy of the one she had worked in as a tidewater slave, which made John worry why she loved the place so. Collin had dressed the logs and split the cedar shingles with tools he bought through a loan offered to him at no interest back in 1840 by Sprague Ruskin, Sister Mayleda's husband. That's how she and Sister May had first met, through the two men's agreement.

And that's what kept them close friends still, though now they saw each other only briefly one day a week, when Harriet would take her finished sewing to Dr. Ellis's Infirmary for Colored Patients, where Mayleda Ruskin volunteered her work as a nurse. Today, instead of walking over an hour to deliver the new supply of hemmed sheets and bandages to the hospital, Harriet was glad to be taking the heavy basket only as far as her own kitchen. Carrying it in, she set it down on the wide rough table that filled up more than half of the kitchen's space. Having seen Harriet at the infirmary one week ago, Mayleda suggested that they might meet in her kitchen once more, as they had done nearly every day during that peculiar and bittersweet winter when they together had shared a room right here in Ludlow Row in the building the little girls lived in now.

Mayleda's daughter, Judith, was away with her Ruskin grandparents on a trip through Europe. That meant Mayleda would be alone for the next several weeks, and that made this visit seem possible. Surely both women wanted it. Harriet had said that Thursday must be the day, for on Wednesday nights John kept his storehouse open so that colored men in Southwark would have a safe place for dicing and gambling, which, of course, she disapproved of mightily.

Every Thursday, then, John slept almost to noon, and since Harriet feared he would not welcome Mayleda's coming back, they agreed on Thursday as the right time—in fact, the only time—to come together. Theirs was a friendship that few in this town would understand or even tolerate, yet a reunion in Harriet's kitchen seemed worth the risks in order that they might savor once more the happiness they both had known when Collin and Sprague lived and they all had been the best of friends together.

Every day but Sunday Harriet was busy in this kitchen making something to sell on the street. With John to provide so well for her, Harriet did the work, in part, to help the families of girls who worked for her as hawkers and vendors, the ones who would sell her pepper-pot stew on the corner of Front and Fitzwater Streets, and the ones who balanced baskets of her fresh-baked breads or cakes on their heads to take into Philadelphia proper.

This morning, the hearth was still warm from yesterday's fire. Harriet crouched down and blew on the coals so that some of them brightened like cats' eyes shining in nighttime lantern light. Because the kitchen was still chilly and dark, the little girls did not come in but only lingered at the door. Harriet snapped tinder, then broke kindling to encourage new flames.

It was Mayleda's husband, Brother Ruskin, who had made this building possible, and Harriet was looking forward to showing it off to his dear widow, how it hadn't changed or aged one bit after all their years of separation. Brother Sprague Ruskin had been the younger son of a wealthy Philadelphia banker, Tyrone Ruskin. Sprague's loan to Collin to build this kitchen in 1840 was the first loan of its kind made to a Negro by that gentleman. When Brother Ruskin's daddy learnt of it, he told his son either to mend his ways or leave the family.

Daring young Sprague, full of zeal to see colored men able to prove themselves, did the latter. Cut off from work, family, and even inheritance, Sprague Ruskin soon set up a business of his own, finding white investors—mostly Quakers—who would lend money to Negro artisans for them to start businesses in the city. Just as Harriet's husband had been a mason for his marse, so Collin had been a carpenter. When Collin and Harriet escaped from Maryland, they faced a penniless existence in this town where work was more often given to strange-talking white folk than to native-born black men.

Harriet could do laundry and cleaning, but Collin could find no job worthy of his skills. That is, until one summer night after they had taken up residence here in Ludlow Row. Harriet's brother saw Sprague Ruskin for the first time at an outdoor meeting on Fitzwater Street, where a colored preacher was telling folk to get right with the Lord and get right down on their knees to do so. That young, wealthy white man in portrait-perfect clothes surprised them all and scared more than a few by doing just that. Afterward, only Collin was daring enough to speak to this new white convert.

That's when Brother Ruskin told Collin he had great hopes of helping Negroes start in business, and that's when Collin risked stating that he had ideas about being a carpenter for hire. What Collin needed was tools, he told this Mr. Ruskin, and money to buy his first round of lumber. So that's how Harriet's kitchen came to be, and how Sprague Ruskin, and soon his wife, Mayleda, and their baby, Judith, all became the only white folk to be welcomed in Ludlow Row. At least by some, though not by John.

Harriet sighed over the fire's snapping. She was commencing to feel both happy and sad about this day. The girls must have heard her, for they came in. "You done said we could be here, ma'am," Suzannah reminded her with uncertainty. "Is it still all right with you?"

"Of course it is!" Inwardly Harriet vowed to keep her melancholy spirit shut away. Yet still she kept thinking of the past while she took down the jar filled with willowy, spicy-smelling roots of sassafras.

Within months of building this place, Collin had paid back Sprague Ruskin's money in full, having soon found other work for himself. Harriet had been unmarried then, though she knew John because he collected the rent. More than once Collin tried to persuade John to borrow from Ruskin so that he could work as a mason, but John didn't want anything to do with anybody from the marses' race. Even so, John did build the kitchen's chimney and the hearth for her and Collin, but with tools that Collin borrowed. To this present hour it remained the only brickwork John ever did in the North, though he had quite the skill for it.

"Sister Mason? You gwine have walnut cake with you' tea this morning?" Margrace asked, looking cautious about interrupting the silence. The girls were politely standing by the table, but with their gazes fixed upward to the square tin on the shelf high overhead.

"Nope! That was all sold yesterday." Harriet let her words fall hard on purpose, then at once she tended to their little broken hearts. "But I do have big, soft, round ginger cakes set aside for today."

"Ohhhh!"

"My daddy says that the Widow Ruskin used to live right here in our row." Margrace dared to speak what was on her mind.

"That's right. After her husband passed, an' Brother Collin too, we lived in a room t'gether with her little daughter."

Margrace took a step back. "Is her little daughter comin'?"

"No, darling, an' she's not so little anymore. I think by now she would be ten or eleven years old."

They nodded soberly, for to them that sounded like a great many years.

"When little Judith did live here, she was younger than you are now." They nodded again, this time to show their maturity.

"Well, get you'selves up to the table. You can share that bench there. In a moment, I'll have you put out the cups and saucers." They moved obediently and sat quietly for a time while Harriet broke off a small piece from her precious loaf of white sugar, which she usually saved for making icing. Today she would celebrate Mayleda's coming and put it in the tea.

"How come you' kitchen don't have no door?" Suzannah questioned, appearing already bored with the waiting.

" 'Cause my brother put up a piece of high picket fencing instead. He set it out there a few feet away from the doorway so I could have privacy but some ventilation too, it being very hot to cook in here in summer. Plus, then I have a place to grow my rambling yellow roses."

"They all dead now," Suzannah observed.

"They won't be come summer," Harriet assured her.

"How did you' brother die? An' Mista Ruskin?" Margrace asked while both girls looked at her directly, making Harriet believe that it was a question they both had been wanting to ask for some time.

"Well, this is where the story 'bout our two friendships gets sad," Harriet confessed to them both. "My brother an' Sister Ruskin's husband, they both died the same day. Maybe the same hour, side by side."

The girls sat blinking until Harriet found the courage to go on. "You see, they were both on a stage comin' home from York City. It was in

February at night, an' the roads were icy. Mr. Ruskin wa' riding on the outside with Brother Collin 'cause the stage driver wouldn't let no colored men be inside on his coach's seats."

"So the white man Mista Ruskin stayed on the outside too?" Even at her young age, Margrace determined what a surprising fact that was.

"Yes, he did, darlin'. If he hadn't, Mr. Sprague Ruskin would probably still be alive today." She paused. "As it was, they died together just as they had worked together. You see, my brother was a business partner with Mr. Ruskin. That's a very unusual thing for a man of color to be a partner with a man who is white. It was Brother Collin's job to help Negroes trust Mr. Ruskin, an' it was Mr. Ruskin's job to help white men trust colored men."

The explanation about the business did not seem to interest them much. "So when did Sister Ruskin come to live here?" Suzannah asked.

"Well, after her husband died, she went to stay with friends in a faraway place called Boston. But there was hardly a month went by when she an' I didn't write letters back an' forth to each other, for in all the years we'd known each other, she'd been teachin' me to read an' write."

"Ain't that illegal?" Margrace wondered.

"No, darlin', not here in the North. That's one reason I want you an' Suzannah to get to know Sister Ruskin. I want you two to be settin' good goals for you'selves. I want you both to soon start readin' an' writin' an' thinkin' about school."

Suzannah took her arms off the table and commanded her little friend to sit more properly too. Harriet smiled. It was a start.

"So when she comin'?" Suzannah asked, still as poised as a lady but swinging her feet that did not reach the earth.

"I need to get this tea made first."

"An' then them cakes down!" Margrace added helpfully.

"Yes, that too." Outside, they heard the familiar cluck and whistle of the men driving the mules out. Ladylike posture was cast aside in favor of jumping down and going outside to wave good-bye. Since there was little for Harriet to do till the water boiled, she followed the girls.

"Mornin' to you all!" Caleb Cocheron said when he saw them come from behind the piece of picket fencing. "That fire of yours sure do smell warm an' invitin', Sister Mason." The man was as talkative as his child.

"Come for tea," Harriet offered while the children stood on either side of her skirts looking hopeful.

"I'd like that, but we got an awful lot of street to cover. November an'

December's our best months for sellin'." He tipped his hat as he stayed seated on the wagon bench, then he winked at his girl. "I do hope I can count on *somebody* savin' me a piece of tea-party sweets. This is the day when Missus Ruskin comes, eh?"

Suzannah would only grin impishly, so Harriet said, "Yes, it is. I'll tell you what. I'll put back six good ginger cakes if you do me the favor of keepin' back a few nice stewin' oysters for John's supper."

Margrace's daddy, Foster Jamison, was on the wagon bench too. "Sure can do!" he pledged. "That is, if I can get a similar portion." Caleb snapped the reins. Foster waved. "Have a nice time!"

Harriet smiled and said she would, in part because these men did not think it fearsome for Mayleda Ruskin to be coming back among them. One of the last things Collin and Sprague did before death came so suddenly was to secure a loan for these men to buy their mules from a Quaker in Byberry.

Harriet knew that the debt had long ago been paid and that the men were much more properous now for being able to sell out of a pretty wagon rather than out of pushcarts as they had done before.

In a way that John would not let himself understand, these men accepted that both the good times and the tragic times were what drew Harriet and Mayleda close, even across the line of color. Though the women had not been able to keep alive their precious men's dreams for business, they could at least preserve a friendship that had been dear to them all.

The mules' hooves soon made hollow sounds as they moved from the row into the cobblestone alley. The girls stood with her, even after their daddies and brothers had disappeared, having rounded the corner to go east toward the wharves.

After the noise of the wagon faded, Harriet heard another sound—a terrible wailing. It caused her to rush forth to the row's end, and there she saw Mayleda coming at a run from the west.

Her friend's face was pink under streams of tears. Mayleda's plain bonnet was pushed off her head, exposing her thick black hair pinned back severely. "You can't believe what happened!" May cried. "A girl jumped to her death, just in front of me! Now!"

Harriet took hold of her. Mayleda sank in her embrace. At the same moment the girls pulled at Harriet's shawl. Then May saw them. She sealed her lips.

"Come into the row!" Harriet told the panicked younger woman.

She led Mayleda in, but then left her to stand alone near the oyster-men's stable while she took Suzannah and Margrace by the hands back to her kitchen. They waited beside the bare, thorny rosebrush while Har-riet went in and got down the cake tin. Coming back to them, she spoke as though she had not another care in the world. "Are you two big 'nough to carry this back an' share it with you' families t'night?"

"Yessum!" Suzannah said, with eyes nearly weeping.

"Then you do that, an' don't you think on Sister Ruskin's words no more. You understand!"

They left her, cautiously looking outward toward Mayleda with small squinting faces even while they walked toward home. Mayleda came in farther, fumbling to tie her bonnet in place. By the time Harriet got to her, her thin but stout-hearted friend had dried her tears with her gloved hands. Her face looked gray now, as gray as her clothes. Slightly shorter than Harriet and much more slender, Mayleda worried aloud. "Oh, that I said such terrible things in their presence! I should have stopped my tongue."

Harriet steadied her, for she was like a stalk of wheat in the wind. "Come into the kitchen! Get you'self warm!"

"No! That girl's body is still in the alley. When she jumped she pulled a little boy from the window with her. I saw him, alive! I went to help him, but he limped away into one of those houses that were condemned last year for typhoid fever and later set afire."

"I know where you mean."

"I think he might try to hide in there. There were two men looking out the window that the children jumped from. One had whiskers. The other was bald. That's all I could see." Mayleda's hands went before her face. "Oh! That children would be so sorrowful as to try to kill them-selves."

"This girl and boy were colored." Harriet felt no need to make it into a question.

"Very fair, but Negro, yes! I know it's dangerous, Hattie, but would you go back with me? I don't think that little boy will trust me because of *my* color, and I fear he's injured."

"Didn't nobody else see this 'xcept those two men an' you? An' where do you think those two men are now?"

"I don't know. The alley seemed deserted when I started down it. And after the girl jumped, it got just as quiet as before. Thinking on it now, I believe anyone who was close by was probably staying well out of view.

There was a one-horse wagon filled with hay near the house the children came from. I imagine it belongs to those men. I'm thinking they were getting ready to take those children somewhere, and that's when the girl decided to try to end their lives. Oh, that she would do so right here in the City of Brotherly Love! The slave laws now make Philadelphia nearly as sinful as Charleston!"

"Or Maryland." Harriet pensively added her own indignation.

Mayleda brushed down across her skirt. "I'm sorry. I am thinking more clearly now. I should go back to Dr. Ellis. There is too much danger to have *you* come with me, for those men might be there looking for the boy. And if they are slave catchers . . ." Her voice faded. "I was thinking only of the living child."

"An' we gwine think of him still!" Harriet declared, knowing the risk but choosing to ignore it. "Go on! Lead the way to where you think he is!"

CHAPTER 7

MAYLEDA WAS HARDLY BACK INTO THE ALLEY before she turned around to face her friend again. "I just remembered! I was bringing you more sewing in another basket from the infirmary. I must have put it down next to the girl, for I don't have it now!"

Harriet's dark face was hard and lined like marble. Injustice and cruelty were not strangers to her. "We'll look for that too! Now hurry!"

Mayleda drew resolve from Harriet's courage. At the same time she knew the danger she was leading Harriet into, for the fugitive slave law restricted everyone from interfering with efforts to return runaway slaves to their southern owners, no matter how young the victims were. Even so, she led Harriet almost at a run for more than a block, until they were well past the intersection of Dresden Alley and Second Street.

"It happened just up there!" Mayleda stopped and pointed. "Harriet, I don't think you should go any farther. I don't think any harm will come to me if those men see me coming back. But for you, it might bring trouble."

"I am a free woman!" Harriet fixed her eyes straight ahead. "You already told me you didn't think the colored child would come to you, so let's go an' find him."

Mayleda could see no activity up ahead. "The wagon's gone!" Harriet pushed her to move. A few more paces and Mayleda saw a pile of hay where she thought the girl's body should have been. "I think it's hay from the wagon."

Harriet proved herself brave by going on ahead. A moment later the older woman toed the dried grass. She even reached down while Mayleda still kept her distance. "Lord have mercy, May. There's a dead cat here layin' in a pool of blood. It's neck an' bowels slit wide." She dared to touch it. "Still warm! Still nimble!"

Mayleda walked in a daze and took hold of Harriet's arm while silently chiding herself. She was a nurse, after all. How could she lose her courage like this? She had faced horrible times before, none worse than the hour when she had been called upon by the coroner to identify both Sprague's and Collin's remains. She shuddered as this memory flooded her vision now. Her knees bent. Harriet caught her around her waist. "May, let's look for the boy."

"Yes!" she managed, her voice an echo of Harriet's concerns. "The wagon's gone! My basket too. Perhaps the men have taken him!"

"Or maybe they chose to leave him in their haste to get rid of the girl's corpse," Harriet reasoned. "Which one of those houses did you see him go near?"

"That one." Mayleda nodded to the first roofless structure on their right, a blackened shell without any glass in the window frames.

"Come on!" Harriet pulled her to the ruined threshold. Mayleda raised her skirts and went in after her friend. Inside, she reached for Harriet's hand, but the debris was too thick to give them space to walk together. Burnt timbers crisscrossed above them and around them like a giant spider's web. They crept like flies, sensing and fearing their own mortality.

Pulling up the hem of their dresses, they crossed a pile of plaster. Every inch of the old, creaking floor was covered in ash, spread deep like flour on a dough board. Every place they stepped they left shoe prints, something that Harriet noticed at once. Not speaking out loud, she silently mouthed her thinking to Mayleda, while pointing to their ashen pathways. Then Harriet made it clear that she was looking for another smaller set of prints.

Soon they were found. The impressions of tiny bare feet led straight to a fireplace, its wooden panels gone. A dove flew out through the wreckage on whistling wings, causing Mayleda to cry aloud. Harriet was already at the hearth, stooping down so that she could peer up inside the wide, old-fashioned chimney.

Immediately dust started pouring down from the opening like dirty snow. Mayleda saw Harriet shut her eyes before she spoke. "Honey, you don't need to climb no higher. We come to help you."

There was more shuffling and another sifting of soot. "You don't have to flee, child! We come to take you someplace safe."

Mayleda wondered where that would be, for they were more than twenty blocks from Dr. Ellis's little hospital. She looked behind her, fearing that the men could come. If she and Harriet were caught now, they would be as trapped as the child, and the boy would easily be taken from them. But there was only silence, both in the house and outside.

Harriet still looked up as Mayleda cautiously bent down beside her. She searched Harriet's face, knowing that the other woman, too, could hear the breathing in the chimney that sounded wild and fast as a bird's. Then a drop of blood, like a drop of rain, stained the ashes. Harriet's lips pressed together. "You' hurt, child. You' cold an' scaired, I know. Come down. It's Aunty Harriet here to help you."

Mayleda looked up into the chimney for herself. It was dark. Her friend put her hands to the small of her back, for Harriet was less limber than Mayleda and already tired from their awkward position. When Harriet spoke the next time it seemed to be only to Mayleda. "If that boy has the strength, he can get hisself all the way to the roof an' make off without us to help him. But he won't have no hot supper that way. An' no bed for the night."

There was another scraping sound. They shared smiles. Perhaps the boy would choose to trust them after all. A second more and bare feet showed. Then stick-thin legs. A rumpled, too-small, blood-soaked shirt appeared over a marked little body. Finally they saw his face, gray with ash and streaked with tears. Harriet reached in over the hearth and caught him. The boy fell into her arms, unconscious, like a stillborn child.

"Oh, Hattie!" Mayleda mourned the grim scene.

Her friend didn't wait a moment but sat back in the dirt with the child drawn to her lap, mindless of her clothes. The boy was icy cold when Mayleda touched him. He hardly had any more muscle on his bones than a stack of twigs should have had. "Oh, honey! Oh, darlin'!" Harriet cooed over the little stranger. She gathered his hands into hers and blew upon them. He revived, panting and droopy-eyed. "Sister, go get Dr. Ellis!"

"If they find you, they can hurt you too! You go. I'll stay!"

"You know I cain't hail no hansom to take me 'cross town!"

The boy's eyes opened fully as though tracking their words. The color of those eyes was close to being gold, and they glowed with distrust. His hair, full of soot, was curly and the same shade as oakwood stripes shaved with an adz. In her sympathy Mayleda touched him again. This time he pulled back, garnering strength from somewhere to nearly escape Harriet's grasp. Harriet hugged him tighter. "Sister May, go!"

Mayleda ran east to Third Street. Then she turned and raced one block north. Desperately she started looking for any public conveyance heading away from the wharves. On Cedar Street, she called out to every passing vehicle, but in the early morning no driver seemed to care that a woman was crying out for help.

Her anxiety actually gave her strength. On foot she made her way several blocks closer to Dr. Ellis's infirmary. Yet by the time she came to Fifth Street, her lungs were on fire. Still she ran one block more before she felt herself staggering.

This was an ugly, dangerous part of town. She always avoided it, yet now it was her quickest way to help. Foul-smelling doorways hung open, revealing dark rooms and musty cellars. She rushed on, hoping that her fear would move her as her anxiousness had, but she was truly out of strength. Mourning her weakness, she slowed to a walk, panting loudly. *If only Sprague still lived. He would be the rescuer, not she and Hattie.* This thought, as raw as the wind, hit her fully.

Mayleda was so tired that no amount of worry or cold could spur her to go faster. While she stumbled on, a white hand reached out at her from a doorway. She smelled rancid breath before she saw the rough, unshaven face. "Oh no!" She pulled away as the stranger grappled for her cloak. "No!" She screamed, tearing away from the hideous grasp. This new terror caused her to race straight into the street, directly between two teams of horses moving in opposite directions. "Watch out! Get out of the street!" Angry drivers called.

Mayleda reeled from one danger to another. A flash of blue inside the window of a stylish coach caught her eye. Then the woman dressed in the blue looked through that same window. The door to the expensive vehicle opened while the coach continued to move. "Mrs. Ruskin?" the woman cried as their view of each other was broken momentarily by the passing of other conveyances.

"Yes! Yes, it is!" Mayleda cried as she recklessly ran toward this person who knew her. The driver of the carriage pulled the coach to the curb. At the same time a pretentiously dressed gentleman showed himself beside the lady as he climbed out to met Mayleda on the street. It was Dr. Dickens, the Ruskin family's dentist. Both the man and his wife were only mild social acquaintances for Mayleda. Though she was hardly ever seen with her in-laws, she had attended a lecture series on temperance with them last spring. Mrs. Dickens must have recognized her from there.

Now the woman was again gazing at her, while Dr. Dickens said, "Ma'am, what are you doing here?"

"I must get to Dr. Ellis's right away! There's a child injured down in Southwark!"

The woman in the coach glanced with worry to her spouse. Dr. Dickens made the decision. "We'll take you where you need to go."

Traffic moved around them as Mayleda tried to catch her breath. She gazed out the window from the coach's plush interior. "I must get to Eleventh and Pine. That's the location of Dr. Ellis's infirmary."

Dr. Dickens shouted the destination out to his driver. Mrs. Dickens started to ramble on about how they never would have come to this part of town, except to find a Negro to sharpen their children's skates. She said how pitiful it was that Africans chose to live like beasts here, even though Philadelphia was without a doubt the most civilized of northern cities. While she spoke so vilely, Mayleda could only try to still her breathing as she took account of her ash-marked garments. She folded some of the stains beneath the edges of her cloak, but surely not before the couple had seen them.

Though they acted well-meaning, Mayleda felt cautious, for they were true friends of her father-in-law, Tyrone, and of her unmarried brother-in-law, Anthony, who was ten years older than she. Mayleda had no hope that they supported the cause to abolish slavery, judging from the woman's ignorant words. The federal compromises of last year had rendered abolition quite unpopular among the gentry. Now the talk in high society was on keeping slavery in order to save the Union from civil war.

"So you do still come down among these indigents, even without your husband," Dr. Dickens observed. "I thought the Ruskins said you were doing only charity work at a hospital now."

"That's true," Mayleda gasped, not going any further to try to explain why she chose to have a reunion with Harriet Mason while her in-laws and daughter were far away. She knew how possible it was that the Dickens would tell her brother-in-law, Anthony Ruskin, where they had found her, which might cause her conflict with Sprague's family to be opened wide again. Right now they had true legal power to keep her from ever permanently leaving the rooms she had now in the family's mansion on Chestnut Street.

Back in 1844, patrons from the Ruskins' bank had recognized her as she walked through Washington Square with Judith, who was then just four years old. It was early spring, after the winter she had spent with Harriet in Ludlow Row. The Ruskins' friends followed her home, and then within hours, Tyrone and Anthony were both at the tenement door, ready to forcibly remove her.

Though she went with them peaceably, they still took the matter to court, winning an injunction to prohibit her from ever endangering Judith again by taking her out among the Negro population. The cost of breaking this legal prohibition was also stated: Mayleda could lose custody of her child and be deemed mentally unfit for parenting if she insisted on maintaining her relationships with those of color.

Perhaps it was this very ruling that Dr. Dickens considered when he spoke. "Mrs. Ruskin, I am surprised, nearly appalled, to find you as we did. I thought you had dismissed your low associations in favor of better ones."

"I do hope you are not involved with a *Negro* child," Mrs. Dickens added. "I do hope you have not gone against the Ruskins' wishes just because they are in Europe with your precious girl. The last time I spoke with your mother-in-law, she assured me that you were not anywhere unsafe but only working as a nurse now at a small hospital." She looked at Mayleda's plain ruined dress. "She did say that it was a Friends' hospital, and that you still choose to affiliate youself with those Quakers."

Mayleda refused to feel ashamed. "It's true."

"Where do you go for your meetings? That is what you call them, isn't it?"

"To the infirmary where we are heading now," Mayleda said quietly. Perhaps it would help to justify why she was involved in the hospital. Perhaps they would not ask, or notice, that Dr. Ellis had founded the work to benefit colored patients. Folding her hands, breathing a prayer, she kept looking out the window.

She had wanted to have a happy morning with Harriet in order to help her remember those years when Sprague had been alive and they all had been working together to make their dreams of equality seem real.

The longer she lived as a widow, dependent on rooms and provisions from her in-laws, the more she feared losing that tremendous sense of brotherly love and freedom she had known as Sprague's wife. With all that was happening in the nation and with Judith growing up in the luxury of her grandparents' home, the good things about her past life seemed hard to hold on to, even difficult to believe in, as her world was so much different now.

Dr. Ellis's meetings and his infirmary were two things besides Judith that Mayleda could still love and cherish. For the most part the Ruskins did not prevent her from attending Quaker meetings or working as a nurse there. They seemed satisfied to tell others, such as the Dickens, that she was still a Quaker, still involved in acts of extreme charity as part of her chosen religion.

She also suspected that they were content to have a reason for her not to be part of their own church, so they would not have to appear with her as she wore plain, unattractive clothes or held to her unpopular ideas about the Kingdom of God being a classless society of the Spirit, encompassing all nations, races, and levels of economy.

The Dickens' carriage was only two blocks away from Dr. Ellis's now. Mayleda leaned to the door. The wife kept trying to engage her in more conversation, but all of Mayleda's somber reflections kept her feelings inward. "When do you expect your daughter's return?"

"Before Christmas," Mayleda said, distracted because they were so close to her destination. "Oh, here! Now! On the left!"

"Our driver knows!" Mrs. Dickens sounded offended.

Mayleda pulled the door's latch as if she were an impatient child. The door opened and she leaped out even as the coach was still rolling to a stop. She turned only to slam the door, forgetting nearly every politeness. "Oh, thank you!" Her words were distressed, for she feared there had been too much delay already. The child could be dying. Hattie could be in trouble.

Rushing up the front walk, Mayleda pulled on the heavy walnut door. The infirmary's interior was warm, heated by coal. Aware that she must not distress the patients, she did not call out. Rather, she glanced up the banistered stairs to her left, which went to rooms where medicines were mixed and where some of those who were being trained by Dr. Ellis had their sleeping quarters. Listening, she heard no sound on the second floor, so she ran to the ward that stretched east to west in the rear of the voluminous old building that once had been a bindery for religious books.

Six beds for women and six for men lined the walls, the room quiet and bright. Between each simple bed was a long narrow window, remnants of the days when workers glued and stitched books in the natural light now tempered by muslin curtains. "Sister Claire!" she called softly, seeing only one nurse. "Where is Dr. Ellis?"

"Working with the pharmaceuticals, I think, Sister Ruskin."

Mayleda hurried back to the hall, then up the stairs, taking the steps where she had only paused to listen before. Now she cried out, for the ward was below her. "Dr. Ellis!"

A short man nearing his seventieth year came to the supply room door at once. He was spry for his age, but gray of hair. "What is wrong, Sister Ruskin?"

"There's a child injured in Southwark! He's a fugitive, we think. We fear abductors. Another child was killed! Sister Mason is with him. She's in danger too! Oh, please come!"

"Of course!" He took her gloved hand as though pleading for her to be calm. "I see the urgency! We will not delay!"

Then Oliver Catos, the young brown man whom Dr. Ellis was training to be a physician like himself, came to the supply room door. "Hitch up the carriage, Brother Catos. I think thee heard the reasons for Sister Ruskin's distress."

"I did!" The practitioner who had been with Ellis for several years straightened the silver-rimmed glasses he wore, which looked just like the doctor's own. While the young man who was in his twenties ran off by way of the back stairs, Dr. Ellis shuffled quickly across to his office to claim the leather bag he always had filled with supplies.

Then he and Mayleda went down the back steps too, coming out at the kitchen near the huge stove. A robust woman whom Mayleda knew by name was volunteering as cook that day. Her kerchief-wrapped head was bowed over the cutting board, where she prepared onions to be steamed. The doctor called to her as they hurried on toward the door. "Sister Parks, please go tell Sister Ellis that I am going to Southwark to see about a child."

In all of Philadelphia, in fact in all of the North, this was the only place Mayleda knew where God's design for unity showed itself among so many persons of different colors. It was Dr. Ellis's policy to use only surnames for his entire staff. Mayleda was the only white worker besides the Ellises to be there. Sister Parks, sharing their concern at once, hurried off. They went out the same back door following her. Brother Catos was just bringing the small one-horse rig to the door.

As soon as Mayleda and the older doctor joined him, Catos drove down the brick driveway and out through the infirmary's opened iron gates, which had been put in place to guard the former business. "He's in Dresden Alley between Second and Third," Mayleda told him with only slight relief now that they were on their way.

Oliver careened the carriage right, then left. "The child feared my touch but not Sister Harriet's," she reported as they sped along.

"Then Brother Catos will be the one to attend him," Dr. Ellis concluded at once. "Unless, of course, we find ourselves among unwelcome company." He then spoke to Oliver directly. "In that case, thee should maintain thy appearance as driver only. If there must be consequences to this rescue, thee and Sister Ruskin must allow me to face them and accept them for us all."

Mayleda exchanged glances with the young man who still was driving madly. "Sister Mason's there now!" she said, speaking her dread. "If agents do come, what will happen to her?"

Her companions did not answer.

CHAPTER 8

THE MOMENT BROTHER CATOS had the horse stopped, Mayleda moved to get out, but Dr. Ellis held her back with words. "I want thee to stay here."

"But Harriet's in there! I must go!"

Perhaps he did not think it was worth delaying, for he let her slip from the vehicle then, though his face was tense and his eyes full of concern. He went through the charred door first. Oliver followed him. Then Mayleda. The burnt building was quiet and now a thousand times more ominous as Mayleda had new fears of what they would find. In an instant, however, she saw Harriet alone with the boy. She was still on the floor, but now she had her shawl off and wrapped around the child so that he was barely visible in her lap.

"You must be freezing!" Mayleda worried about her friend while the men took a first look at the child in her arms.

"His life blood's drainin' from the wound in his side." The little boy's eyes flashed at Harriet's words. His vision fixed itself on Mayleda first, then on the old Friend, then on Brother Catos, who reached for him cautiously. As before, the child clawed and tried to scramble away, though he had looked nearly lifeless when they walked in. Harriet spoke soft words to him. Then Oliver Catos was able to take his wrist as he searched for a pulse.

Mayleda wanted to take her cloak off and share it with Harriet, but she dared not move for fear of spooking their young patient.

Tenderly, with much empathy, Brother Catos uncovered the boy's body and examined him wholly as Harriet continued to hold him. "There are broken ribs, Brother Ellis. Internal injuries. Perhaps a punctured lung."

Even Mayleda could have guessed this because of the stain of blood in the foam around the child's flaccid lips.

"Yes." Dr. Ellis gravely agreed to everything said. "He must be moved at once."

"So no one came to find you?" Mayleda sighed her gratefulness as Harriet stiffly yielded the boy to Practitioner Catos. He slipped his arms under the boy's shoulders and knees, and the child did not protest. After Catos had him, Mayleda helped her friend stand.

"Nobody came!" Harriet said, looking weary but glad. "My guess is that those agents knew the boy was hurt, an' hurt bad, so they decided it would be less *un*-profitable to let him go than to have to give account of him dyin' to whatever marse paid them to track him down."

Mayleda knew that slave agents could be held responsible for the condition of fugitives in their care, yet she countered some of Harriet's words. "He's not going to die, Harriet. God will see to that!"

"That boy's been branded on the hand an' shoulder," Harriet said. "He's nearly naked an' starved. It will be mercy if God takes him. Just promise me one thing, that you'll stay with him an' not let him pass alone."

"He won't be alone! Not for one moment!" Mayleda pledged. Oliver already had him at the door. Dr. Ellis was right behind him. "Let's catch up, then we can take you home."

"No, you won't," Harriet protested, taking her first stiff steps alone. "You take that boy to the infirmary straightway!" Showing herself mindful of the blood on her hands, Harriet laced her fingers. "I can find my own way. You take care of that little lamb."

"I don't want to leave you!"

"Sister, you see what can be done for that child."

Mayleda hugged Harriet around the shoulders, kissed her on the cheek, then parted to be with the doctors and the boy.

As a girl on Marse Arne's Chaucer Plantation, Harriet had seen hawks tumble out of the sky to snatch unsuspecting sparrows. Those little brown birds had had no mind on death till it came right down upon them. Hurrying through the cold now, her shawl and clothes stained with the young slave's blood, Harriet felt like one of those tiny birds, unable to see danger but perhaps having it near, nonetheless.

Against her own wisdom she started running, lifting her skirt to let her stiff, aching feet go as fast as they could. She knew she might be drawing attention to herself, but she felt fearful in the alley.

When she finally turned into Ludlow Row, she found John right in her path, between her rose fence and the neighbors' stable. Though she could not recall when the man had last belittled himself to go into her outside kitchen, he must have done so, for he had her teakettle in his hand, holding it by its handle. Cautiously she drew near him. He waved the spout like a spear.

In his roughest voice he demanded, "Where have you been? One of the stevedores had to come in an' rouse me, for you' chimbley was a'smokin' to high heaven, an' the smell of burnt somethin' or other was fillin' up the whole row."

"Ah, I put in sassafras root an' let it burn dry. I'm sorry, John. I heard about this hurt child in the alley, an' I plum forgot 'bout the tea." She knew her hands and clothes proved her words.

He looked at her appearance. "A bleedin' child!"

"Yes. A little boy."

He knew her too well. "Free or slave, Harriet? You tell me!"

"What does it matter? We were runaways once—"

"How was he injured? Why were you the one called to help?"

They were questions she didn't want to answer.

"The same man what got me up says he saw you go out with a *white* Quaker woman." He shook the dry pot again, then threw it down. "You'd better not say it wa' Missus Mayleda Ruskin still comin' 'round afta I warned you not to see her anymore."

"You judge her by her color."

"You right I do! For her dead husband's daddy is old Mr. Ludlow's banker. An' her brother-in-law is Mista Anthony Ruskin, the lawyer an' politician what wants to write up legislation that will drive *every* Negro out of this state."

"Those men aren't her blood relations!" she reminded him. "If she could live someplace else, she would, but the Ruskins have her child, an' she has no money 'cause of the business Brother Sprague an' Brother Collin had t'gether."

"Shush! Don't you call any white man *brother*!" he said with indignation. "That white man Sprague used *you'* brother to make his business work for him, just like his wife still does use you."

"May an' I lived as sisters for months in this row. We shared a room an' hardships an' work, an' all the time, color was blind to us! She taught me to read an' to write. All the mean things you say an' think 'bout her, they are not the truth!"

"What about this almost bottomless basket of sewin' I found? You sewin' for her, ain't you, while you' hidin' it from me! Now the brothers in this house tell me how you go to see a white Quaker doctor to bring this work to him an' take another basket home. You still workin' like a slave."

"I'm not. I sew for *colored* patients in the infirmary that's run by the Quaker who trains *colored* nurses an' even *colored* doctors, called practitioners, to care for our own."

"*Colored patients, colored doctors!* Pshaw! Harriet! You sew for *her*! The rice planter's daughter, reared in the South."

"How did you know about her family?" Harriet gasped, aware of Mayleda's past but thinking it was secret.

"Woman, there's plenty I do know. Collin told me."

"Why? I didn't even know my brother knew. He shouldn't have said nothin', God rest his soul."

"He learnt it from Sprague an' then he told me, thinkin' that would convince me that some whites can change. Well, it don't! It means to me that she seeks you out to be her *help*, just like her mammy an' her papa put the yoke on other colored folk."

"It's not true!"

"Soon as you get one white comin' near, then you have ten or a dozen more. They like hornets, protectin' the nest t'gether."

"Mayleda is alone. She has few friends among those of her own race 'xcept for those white Quakers what support Dr. Ellis's work. Sprague Ruskin was out to make a difference in this world. An' my brother Collin too. Now it's Sister May an' me carryin' that on! They *were* doin' something to help each other an' to make this city better. Now' me an' Sister May, we want to do that too, even if it's only by our friendship!"

"Don't you care? It was that kind of work that got Collin kilt!"

"Don't you remember? Sprague Ruskin died too! Sister May an' I have sorrows an' heartaches that we can still share t'gether."

"Gal, when you gwine stop livin' like you' grief was just yesterday? You don't owe that Missus Ruskin nothin' in that her husband died! It wa' her race, not ours, that broke they bodies by makin' colored men ride in a place unfit an' unsafe. Now you tell me. Was that her what lured you to the alley to look afta a child?"

His eyes suddenly flashed someplace farther behind her. She turned and saw what he was looking at. Two white men stared in as they stood at the bottom of the row. "You know who they are?" he whispered, his eyes never moving. He stared at the threatening view of well-dressed gentlemen in dark suits with knee-length cloaks and low slouched hats who looked toward them.

"I don't!" she gasped.

He pulled her around to face him. Walking to her piece of fence he twisted off a dead rose, which still held to some of its faded petals. Taking the sharp flat knife he carried in a leather holder on a belt for his salvage work, he cleanly cut the stem. In low tones he commanded her to work with him. Awkwardly, silently, they pruned the bush, one stalk at a time.

"So how many hornets in the hive?" His voice was rough but quiet. He would not let her look around to see the men again.

"May Ruskin's no hornet! She's got nothin' to do with those men comin' now."

"So you do know who they are!"

"I don't, but I am guessin' they slave agents lookin' for the boy. The child jumped from a window to get away from somebody. A girl too, an' she died. It's got to move you' heart!"

His voice got lower. "You in no position to save runaways!"

"For the child's sake. For the pride of our race, I wouldn't say no, not to May an' not to a child. Though she be white, Mayleda Ruskin do care, just like as I do. An' just like you should! You wa' a slave boy. You know what it feels like to be scaired an' whupped an' all."

"I'm gwine warn you one more time. The friend you onc't knew here now lives with the Ruskin family in one of the biggest an' probably most orneriest white hornets' nest in all of Philadelphia! Mista Tyrone Ruskin, the daddy, holds funds an' invests funds for those what trade southern rum from here. An' sugar. An' cotton. Rich people in this city all depend on slaves just as much as if they had they own Negroes in quarters on a street."

Giving into her fear, she glanced over her shoulder, regardless of her husband's warning. "John, they gone! It's not Sister May's fault that they came here."

His face was drawn like a man twice his age. "Right now *white* Pennsylvania citizens are sittin' in prison over in Moyamensin' awaitin' trial just 'cause *they* would not help a federal deputy in Christiana get back slaves for a marse. Now, if the courts of this nation's gwine do that to *white* folk, what might they do to the likes of you?"

"I know there's reason to fear the laws of Congress, but we must also fear the laws of God. We are to help each other."

"You want to help? Then you help those what are already here an' doin' good. The Jamisons an' the Cocherons, they wives an' they children. If you lure white men to start lookin' 'round, they gwine soon find out that those folks are fugitive."

"I didn't mean no harm. That little boy has brand marks. He's been sorely mistreated, yet he's nearly *light* enough to pass for *white*. An' still he suffers so!"

"An' you surprised! You know it wa' probably his marse what sired him. All white men want is the sweetness of the mama, not no bright yeller child born from their seed."

Harriet looked away in disgust, knowing that his words were likely true.

"It was probably his white daddy what branded him an' whupped him. It's probably that white daddy what's payin' Dawes an' Pudget to bring the boy back. Yep! A slaveowner can afford to *hate* his half-breed son. He can *afford* to abuse him, but he cain't afford to lose him, for every slave, born of his own will or another's, is *money* in his purse."

"Then *you* know the names of those white men who were just in the alley! Pudget? An' Dawes?"

"The one with gray whiskers is Davidson Dawes. The plump pig of a man, that's Hubert Pudget. They slave agents, all right, known all over the North an' the South, both sides of the Line. I tell you, if those two can get a cat to walk on its hind legs, then they can find some way to remand it to a marse as his long-lost nigger. That's what kind of miserable folk they are."

Harriet shuddered, thinking on the cat in the alleyway. Under her breath she spoke her grief. "I hope the boy dies an' finds God's mercy before he can be taken by men like that!"

John turned away. It showed that he was milder in manner now than in the days and years that came right after their marriage, for back then he would have had sharp words for her about her hope in God.

Now it seemed like mercy that he only called her to come into the house so that nobody else could see her. When they were inside, he led her to the sleeping room and told her to sit down. "You gwine stay here 'cause I got to go to the storeroom, an' I want you safe. Don't you show you' face at any window or door."

She felt vulnerable as she sat before him on the bed. For a moment she had an odd but wonderful sense that he might kiss her, though he was not known for his tenderness. Perhaps he was uncomfortable with the kindness coming forth from him, for he started to explain everything in a most businesslike manner. "I almost done worked the skin off my bones to buy you' freedom an' mine. I'm not gwine lose what it took me so long to get."

She put her face down. In her mourning heart she knew he was right. There was cause for worry. They could be in danger, and their neighbors too. "I understand."

Surprising her, he raised her chin with his thick hands. He looked young and ready for romance, but it all lasted only the space of a breath. "I don't want my wife actin' like nobody's slave, do you hear me? No more sewin' for Missus Ruskin! An' no more gwine out under the slave catchers' view." Then he straightened and went out through the door.

For the first time in a long while, Harriet felt a sense of loss at his leaving.

CHAPTER 9

CHARLES POWELL LIVED ALONE in rooms above his store. When he heard knocking at his door late Thursday night it worried him, since for most of his thirty-eight years he had had no kind relatives and only one close friend, already gone to the grave.

Rolling out of bed he reached for his trousers hung on the bedpost. Pulling them on under his nightshirt, he padded across the uneven floor, hurrying from the bedroom to the front room, then to the window, beside the table where he always left a lamp burning in case some customer called late. But this knocking was not at his store door, rather at the narrow, seldom-used Spruce Street door that opened directly to the front stairs of his second-story quarters.

Shading the lamp with his hand, he looked out the window, unable to see any person, horse, or conveyance below. Taking the light he hurried to the stairs, his six-foot frame fitting closely in the passageway, his shoulders nearly touching the walls as he went down. Undoing the latch, he found the elderly Dr. Leon Ellis standing outside. The man had his cloak up over his head so that much of his distinctive low-crowned hat was hidden.

"Come in, sir!" It had been years since this Quaker had come to his house for a visit, though often the man was his customer. "What brings you here, and so late?" Charles stepped back so there would be room for another on the stairs. The lamplight bobbled. Immediately Dr. Ellis requested that Charles lock the door.

Urgency spurred the aging Friend to climb the steps. He paused, out of breath, only when he was at the top. "I suppose thee can guess that I come with a purpose that contradicts human law." His words were intense.

Though Charles had been a friend of Friends since his youth, he had never come to own the Quaker faith. He was not part of the small meeting that gathered weekly in the man's infirmary, nor did he keep abreast of news about Dr. Ellis's activities to protest slavery's continuation in the South. "Sit down. Let me put wood in the stove. It's cold in here, for I conserve fuel at night."

"It's fine, Brother Powell." The smaller, older man always showed him the courtesy of addressing him as one who shared his religious convictions. His small gray eyes were still warm despite the chilly room and his anxiety. "I thank thee for this welcome."

"Have you a horse? Your carriage?"

"I walked, that I might be less conspicuous."

"Sit down. Please." Charles said it again, concerned for the aging man because he still was standing. He motioned to the closer of the two chairs at the table but also to the old black, spindle-backed Windsor positioned by the stove. There was a time when the doctor had been a regular guest to this room, back when Elim Peabody lived. Brother Peabody had been the store's first proprietor, and as a boy, Charles had been his apprentice.

Dr. Ellis availed himself of the closest table chair while gently making comment. "Thee does keep everything in order. Brother Peabody would be pleased."

"I can make you tea or chocolate."

Dr. Ellis shook his head, smiling slightly. "Again, just like Friend Peabody." Dr. Ellis dropped his cloak off his shoulders but kept his hat on, as Friends were apt to do. "Sit down with me, Brother Powell." The mild smile came again, contrasting strangely and strongly with the worry

Charles saw in his face. "Thy generous manner confirms why thy name keeps coming to my mind in prayer."

Charles did sit down to face him, which felt strange, for when he was a boy and Brother Peabody lived, it was always Elim and Dr. Ellis who had sat in these chairs. Instantly Charles felt melancholy, thinking back all those years to when the kind yet demanding Brother Peabody had been his guardian.

The doctor seemed to notice. "Are you well, Brother Powell?"

"Oh yes, I am."

"It has been a long time since I have been in this room."

"I was thinking the same, sir."

The doctor pulled at his gloves but did not remove them. "I will get to the point. I have an injured boy who must be removed from the city."

"If you need my team and wagon, you can have it."

"Do not be quick to promise. The child is a fugitive slave."

Charles felt ashamed for closing his mouth, but certainly the doctor expected it. Though he had continued on with Friend Peabody's mission to sell "free products" that were not grown, harvested, or manufactured with chattel labor, he had not let himself be counted with those who opposed slavery publicly.

"You want to move him tonight?" Charles asked, quite uncomfortable with the silence. Maybe by coincidence both he and the doctor looked at the clock hanging between the doors that opened into the two small bedrooms, the one on the right being that which Charles had occupied since Elim's death.

The Friend kept his eye on the clock face. The time was almost midnight. "The child is not strong enough now. Indeed, he may not survive to make the trip at all."

Feeling the sadness, Charles leaned forward. "I want you to know, I do think slavery is cruel." He struggled to put his beliefs into words, for since Elim's passing he had not had many reasons to speak about anything but slave-free products. "Otherwise, I would not keep Brother Peabody's store. It is not just because this is my inheritance. I never expected the property to come to me." Inadvertently Charles looked at the floor where he had found the merchant sprawled in death one morning. Charles had then been only nineteen.

Friend Ellis's soft gaze was still somehow piercing. "Thee does not support the *rescue* of a fellow human being? Only that commerce will not abuse him?" The silence grew again. "This boy is only seven or eight years old. I can tell that by the number of molars he has. Because of poor nutrition and treatment, thee might judge him to be no more than five."

Whether the doctor knew it or not, he could not have told Charles anything that would have pulled at his conscience more, for he had been a street urchin before Brother Peabody decided to take him in. Charles confessed his thinking. "You know I was an orphan discarded by my dead mother's family after my father died. They thought of me as Irish and therefore worthless, even as they had my father when he lived."

Dr. Ellis kept staring at him. "The child has suffered greatly, even before this present injury."

Charles felt every word. Even so, his highest reasoning could not support his deepest empathy. He tried to explain. "I am not wise. My only education was right here at this table when Brother Peabody took his hours at night to instruct me. I can only act on what I understand. Brother Peabody taught me that I must do what is right, but sometimes I do not understand what is right to do."

His choice of words caused him to throw up his hands, for he felt awkward to be so large a man but so small a thinker. "There! Doesn't that one foolish sentence itself prove how simpleminded I am?"

"No. Thee speaks from the heart. That is not so much simpleness as purity. A pure heart is needed by anyone who does want to know truth."

"There's no reason to compliment me, sir! Abolition and any draining of slave power away from the South are said to be detriments to our nation and an offense against our God."

"Thee must consider who speaks thus."

"But I do! Those who say this are learned, high-born men elected to our Congress. And some are great preachers trained in the universities. And then there are the city's merchants, who never are troubled when they work in partnership with the strongest ruler I think this nation's ever had: *King Cotton*."

"Thee truly cannot be convinced that slavery is wrong? That is why thee avoids fellowship with known abolitionists?"

Charles spread his wide hands. "I have this store because of Friend Peabody's generous trust in me, and thereby I can make slave-free products available in this city. By doing so, I give others and myself the choice *not* to have material goods at the expense of enslaved Africans. I can live with less and with less quality, and I urge others to do the same. But I cannot deceive myself to think that this benefits slaves. No, it benefits our consciences only! The world we call *civilized* is bound to slavery. A shop such as mine might change a mind or a heart, but never a whole nation."

Dr. Ellis smiled wryly. "Thee is an eloquent speaker."

"No! I only express the restless feelings I mull night and day. I suppose that most, perhaps even you, might view me as a hypocrite, selling to abolitionists while not adopting the cause myself. Constantly I pray that I am not."

"So thee does not think it is God's will to free men, women, and children from other men who will claim ownership over them?"

"Dr. Ellis, in my heart of hearts I wish I did! That is what I am trying to say. I do not know how to be morally convinced that it is right to take a slave from his owner when *Congress* has voted to keep slavery legal. Are we to be anarchists, doing whatever we will against the state? And worse than that"—he pointed to Brother Peabody's Bible lying open on the table—"the Word of God does not condemn slavery. Not from Jesus to Paul. Not from the first word to the last."

"Thee honestly seeks to know the truth. Yet alone."

"Where can I go? Fancy churches love slavery more than I. Humble meetinghouses love it less! I fit nowhere."

"Dear Brother Powell, we have only a worm's brain compared with the Almighty Father's. Does thee think about that? This is wisdom: To know that we cannot understand the mind of God. Therefore, we must accept our inability to *intellectually* assume God's ways. Yet we can be transformed in our hearts as the Spirit moves in us. Our work is to fear God, not to understand Him, for it is the *fear* of God that makes us to act wisely."

"How does one know if he is fearing God?"

"Do not despair if such wisdom does not first come through thy understanding. It will come through thy obedience to the Spirit. What does God want of thee now?"

Charles' frame felt too large for the chair. He stood. "Right now I can see no farther than His great commandment, 'Thou shalt not steal.' According to the laws of this nation, what you propose to do *is* stealing. Taking a man's chattel. I would not take a man's horse or claim his property just because I disapproved of his ways—"

"A Negro is not a creature or property! In the eye of *mortal* justice, let me be a thief so that *Immortal God* will not count me among those who sin against their brethren! I believe the Spirit has shown me that the most despicable kind of thievery is when one man steals another man's right to his own humanity. There is but one God who desires that all men have the freedom to choose so that each man might choose God's good care for him."

"What you say seems true, but so many disagree. Congressmen. Preachers. See! It leads me to think that I am too ignorant to even *know* what is good judgment. Most learned men say that Africans are fit only for menial tasks. Perhaps they are. They say it is God's mercy, not a curse, that savages find their way here, even in chains. That it is better for them to live as slaves with Christian owners than to die wholly ignorant of Christ in their own savage lands."

"Ah! That is the most simple of all thy questions to answer. Ask Africans to speak for themselves. Listen to what they say. There are colored believers in our meeting. Come. Start by asking these same questions of them."

Charles ran his hand through his straight dark hair. He had never talked to a Negro on any subject but produce, for sometimes he bought goods from colored farmers who were sparsely spread west of the city, and often he sold produce to Negroes who came to his store by way of the Easton Alley door. Silently he pondered even Dr. Ellis's ability to judge rightly. At one time this man had been the head of surgery at Pennsylvania Hospital, but he had given that up to start his Infirmary for Colored Patients. Charles' consternation brought forth an idea. "Sir, I know the Bible teaches that we are to obey our elders. With Brother Peabody gone, you are as close to being my elder as anyone. Perhaps here is God's answer: I am to obey *you*."

"There can be fines and imprisonment if thee does help."

"I know the law. But if something is God's will, then it must be done. That is what you have just said to me, and I do agree. So I think this *is* my answer: If you need me, I will go."

The doctor suddenly showed caution. "Thee is known for *not* being part of any antislavery group, while others, myself included, are probably being watched by slave agents, maybe even by marshals. I suppose thee knows about the hamlet of Christiana and how a Maryland man was shot dead and his son wounded when they went with a deputy to try to claim their runaway slaves."

"The people in the store speak of it continually, especially now that the trial will soon commence in this town."

"Any known abolitionist who leaves the city by wagon or carriage can be suspected of illegally removing fugitives. Anyone caught doing so can be imprisoned. Castner Hanway and the others from Christiana are facing charges of treason, I think, because they put their conscience before obedience to a deputy's orders."

"You came to me because others might not be so suspicious of my travels out of town, I understand." Charles' resolve was made certain now by Dr. Ellis's obvious sorrow. "Whatever you ask of me, I will do." He felt grieved when the doctor frowned.

"I thank thee, but no. The risks are too high for that. Thee must be convinced that this is *God's* will. All must be done under the Spirit's compulsion, for thee does believe in Christ."

"But where will you find another driver if I say no?"

"God knows."

"I feel for the boy. I do!"

"Thee must not do it for the child's sake either. Human affections will fail. Thee must do it out of love for God."

"Instead of encouraging me, you make it harder!"

"I did not come expecting an answer tonight."

"But how will we communicate again if secrecy is so vital?"

"I can come freely to thy store. I can come with a list of supplies for thee to bring to the hospital."

"What? I am to say aye or nay to you in public?"

"Say, 'I can come today' or 'I cannot come today.' Then I will know thy answer."

"You are saying that you will give the order on the very day when we need to go?"

"I might have to. I am still trying to consider the best plan. When I order supplies, they must be the products by which to build a hiding place on the wagon bed for the child and his nurse."

"A nurse?"

Dr. Ellis ignored his questioning. "Does thee still hire help from the street when thee travels?"

"At times."

"Thee would hire a colored worker?"

"I have, for they are the ones that fill the alleys now."

Dr. Ellis looked at him fully. "If thee is willing to deliver the supplies I request, hire no stranger to help on that day. I will ask my Negro assistant Brother Catos to pose as thy hired man. In truth, his business will be to stay near the child, for he has enough training now to be a doctor."

Charles had trouble believing that. It made him doubt the rightness of the aging Friend's judgment just a little more. "You mentioned a nurse. Is she colored too?"

"No, the nurse will be Widow Ruskin. She is the one who saw the child pulled from a Dresden Alley window by an older girl who died instantly when she fell three stories down to the street. There were slave catchers watching."

Charles cringed at the description, in part because he knew the woman who had witnessed this horrible event. "I thought Mrs. Ruskin lived with her in-laws now. What was she doing back in Southwark?"

"Visiting Sister Harriet Mason. I suppose you know her."

"She comes to the store. I know her because of Mayleda Ruskin. There was a time when they both came together." He paused, for that was years ago. He had not seen the widow since she left the dreadful place called Ludlow Row, a few blocks from here, where she once had shared a room with that Negress for one full winter.

"Sister Ruskin started attending our meeting of worship while she lived in Southwark. Though it displeases the Ruskin family, she continues to do so. They know she volunteers at a hospital for the poor. She has not confided in them that it is the hospital I started for Negro patients."

"I can't believe they would let her do such a thing. There's no forgetting the stir that was caused by the newspaper reports that she was seen roaming the streets with her child after Sprague Ruskin's passing and after she had secretly moved herself back into this city from Boston." Charles himself had not been able to understand the woman's actions, how she could ever think it wise to live with colored tenants when her husband's wealthy family was right in the same city. "I thought by now she would have been adopted into the society of her in-laws."

Dr. Ellis chuckled slightly. "Then thee hardly knows Sister Ruskin at all! Her in-laws do not counter her wishes to serve at the infirmary because she insists so strongly that serving the poorest of the poor is part of her religion. The family allows her to pursue this mission daily during those hours when her daughter, Judith, is being tutored.

"She dares to declare to the Ruskins that they may face harsher judgment in eternity if they keep her from giving to those who need help. They have her leaving and coming by way of their servants' door, through the kitchen, but other than that they do not try to control her religious activities. Indeed, Sister Ruskin lives almost like a recluse. Many in the city are not even aware that she still has rooms in their house."

It grieved him to learn of how Mayleda was being treated, and Charles said so.

"Her goodness and obedience are known to God." The Quaker smiled. "In the same way that her husband helped colored men, Sister Ruskin has found a way to help women. She distributes sewing that our hospital needs to have done. She selects the women, and we pay them for their labor. Sister Harriet Mason sews for the infirmary but only as way to give of her talents, since her husband will not spare any amount to support God's work."

"Mrs. Ruskin is taking a great risk in doing all this!"

Dr. Ellis looked at him. "She believes it is God's will."

Charles diverted his eyes, for there were feelings deep within him that he did not want to have revealed. But Dr. Ellis seemed to read his emotions as easily as he could have listened to his words.

"You knew her in her time of mourning, Brother Powell. She has made peace with God concerning the tragedy that she and Sister Mason share. Sister Ruskin was on her way to Ludlow Row to take sewing to Sister Mason and to have a small reunion with her in her outside kitchen when she saw the children fall."

The first few times Charles had seen Mayleda Ruskin in his store following Sprague Ruskin's death, he had not recognized her. Nor did he even know that she was white, for she always came in with Harriet and by way of the rear door used by colored clients. The day he finally caught sight of her face under her hood, he knew she was Sprague's widow, for the man had often brought his wife and child to the store.

The doctor put his gloved hands together, pulling Charles from his reflections. "Sister Ruskin has told Sister Ellis and me all about how thee helped her during the winter of 1843. How thee lowered prices for her and increased the measure. How thee brought her firewood at night and stacked it at her door."

"I've never told anyone. I didn't know she knew."

"She's said it was thee who kept them alive that winter."

"It was a long time ago, sir," he said modestly. "I have not seen her since she was forced by the Ruskin family to remove herself from Ludlow Row."

The doctor surprised him. "I have seen her looking out the window at thee when thee comes to bring supplies."

The casual statement stirred sad, uncomfortable feelings within him. In his mind's eye, he still had a clear view of Mayleda eight years ago:

petite, dark-eyed, dark-haired, with a vulnerable innocence that lighted her countenance with beauty. He felt his own face coloring, though by anyone's standards he was a confirmed, austere, even brutish bachelor. "It is too dangerous to let her go with this fugitive, Dr. Ellis."

"She believes God is directing her to stay with the child until he can be settled. The first practitioner I trained lives in southern Lancaster County. I want the boy taken there, for I think he can be safe there, and I know he will have the best of care."

"But her presence could endanger this mission more, don't you think? The Ruskins favor slavery. I read the papers, how her brother-in-law, Anthony, is starting his campaign to be state senator. What would happen if his sister-in-law were discovered to be part of a slave rescue?"

"Sister Ruskin feels that Mr. Anthony Ruskin will do anything to protect the family's name. Because he has the support of so many federal officers, she believes that any rescue in which she has a part would never even be brought to the commissioner's attention if discovered. She hopes that this could help us all. She feels certain that the Ruskins, father and son, would work together to get any case dismissed before their name and the word *abolition* could be mentioned side by side in public."

"You don't agree, do you, sir?"

"The issue is obedience to God. Not consequences. Her daughter is in Europe with her grandparents, so she feels freed to go. Since we brought the boy in this morning, she has not left his side, and while he did seem to fear her at first, he clings to her now, as she has had unflagging zeal to show him faith and love."

"Still, I don't think it's a good idea. Even if she cannot be harassed publicly, I fear they could make it worse for her at home. Indeed, what would keep them from putting her out?"

"The law. After it was discovered that she had chosen to live in Ludlow Row with colored friends, the Ruskins took her to court. The judge ruled that she must come under their financial protection and supervision until Judith is twenty-one, or until either of them is married to a gentleman approved of by the family."

"That news never reached the papers."

"Sister Ruskin told us. If she fails to comply with the agreement, the family can exercise its right to apply for sole custody of her daughter based on the charges that were brought against her in 1843."

"What charges?"

"That she was incompetent to raise her own child because of where and how she chose to live. That she endangered their granddaughter physically and morally in Ludlow Row."

Charles drew a breath. Already, today, Mayleda Ruskin had taken inordinate risks that he did not approve of for a woman alone. "What about slave catchers, Dr. Ellis? Surely they will have no mercy if they find her? Shouldn't you be concerned, for didn't you see that there were such men in the alley today?"

The man's soft eyes did mirror his own worry. "We are praying that the two men who had the boy will not pursue him now because of his weak condition. He may die, and then they might be liable for any part they played in making the children attempt suicide."

"Do you know which agents they were?"

"Yes, probably they were Davidson Dawes and Hubert Pudget, for they often hold captured slaves in that part of town. Sister Ruskin did see their faces."

"Then they must have seen her!"

"They must have."

"Then that should settle it. She should not go!"

"That is thy opinion, but is it God's? We plan to conceal her with the child." The doctor looked at the clock and stood. "I should not have stayed so long." He extended his hand, and Charles shook it with mild frustration that he would leave so abruptly. Charles followed the slow-moving brother down the stairs.

After Charles released him into the night, he felt unnerved that Dr. Ellis had not pressed him in the end to make his decision. And it felt unholy that he had not just readily volunteered. Locking the door, Charles leaned against it. Thoughts of Mayleda Ruskin, lovely and alone, overwhelmed all others. *Could he, should he, let her risk such a mission with any driver but himself?*

He was forced then to admit something about himself. He was drawn to make his choice based on his feelings about her, not on the child's need or even on the rightness or wrongness of this work before God.

Upstairs, the clock chimed one.

CHAPTER 10

WHEN DAWN CAME Charles was groggy, as though awakened from an all-night dream. Out in his main room, the table chairs were askew, sound evidence that Dr. Ellis's visit had been real. Indecision still swirled inside his brain.

Untrue to his nature, Charles shaved haphazardly and skipped break-fast, going straight to the old Windsor to sit down. Having brought the Bible from the table with him, he opened it to the Psalms, anxious to read and pray in earnest. He stayed one hour, but nothing spiritual seemed to be accomplished by his urgent sincerity. In fact, he felt cha-grined toward himself for presuming that God would speak to match his schedule.

Standing, he put the book back on the table and took his keys from the peg, his waistcoat also, pulling the latter over the clean, wheat-col-ored shirt he wore with heavy trousers. Close to the stove was the top of the winding back stairs that went down to his store. Years ago Brother

Elim had hung dark curtains at the head and bottom of the narrow passageway to cut off the draft, and those curtains were there still. Pushing aside the first one he went down to the second, then out to his counter, for the stairway ended directly behind it. The counter itself was a worn oaken piece of furniture, blackened on top by the touch of countless hands.

Under it he kept his cashbox and a shelf with ledgers, but all this he left in place as it was his first duty in the morning to see to his horses. He went through his front storeroom, crowded with stocked shelves and crates, then descended the few wide steps that separated this room from one slightly below it, on the level with Easton Alley, which spanned the shop's back wall. This second room was much like the first except that it had no bright windows like those facing Spruce Street. The natural light for this room was produced only by the twelve small glass panes put together in the door.

Brother Elim had always used this room for waiting on colored customers. Charles continued the tradition. He kept his old coat on a hook by the alley door, and he put it on now and went outside to face a brisk morning, though not as cold as last night. Over him the sky was shell gray with a whirl of pastel colors. Already a cluster of young colored males, often called bucks, were on the cobblestones between his mercantile business and his barn. Without a word or a look toward these boys, Charles went in to his mares.

The barn felt warm because of the two huge black Conestoga mares he kept side by side in separate stalls. These equine giants were his real partners. He depended on their health and their strength to take him to and from the farms and iron works spread throughout the Susquehanna and Schuylkill river valleys where he obtained much of the produce, wood, wool, and cast iron he sold.

Conestogas had been bred for the heavy work of pulling wagons by the same name over the eastern mountains as settlers moved west. Brother Elim had had a pair before him, but these Charles had trained and worked with on his own. They were prime specimens in a city where the breed was rapidly dying out, as lighter horses were being favored now that railroad cars moved many long-distance loads. The animals' withers were nearly level with his chin when he went in to them. Marcy and Maude gave him their own kind of greetings, nickering and nudging him while he worked to break the ice from their water buckets, fork hay into the mangers, and scrap out the muck from their stalls.

He spoke to them as though they were his children, and they fluttered their hot hides beneath his touch while he curried and brushed them. He checked their legs, their hooves, their shoes, even though he planned to spend his day at the counter. Before he was ready to leave, a bold young Negro dared to enter the barn, brazenly opening the door when Charles had it closed. Charles considered his property and privacy intruded upon. He glowered at the dark face and bright smile he saw in the subtle light.

"Sure has the makins' of a bery fine day, boss!" the Negro said. Maybe he was as old as twenty, but his bellowing voice and slim waving hands reminded Charles of a gangly child about to get himself into trouble. "Thought you might have somethin' for Tom here to do. Mebbe you need somebody to ride out with you. Then I'm you' boy!"

"No! There is nothing for you to do." Charles looked at him, but not for long. "Tell that to the others too. Tell them it would be better if you just moved on." He disliked having the indigent colored males so near.

"You sure 'bout that, sah?" The boy almost hopped beside him as Charles went toward the door.

"I am!"

The Negro took his dirty cap in his hands and brought it to his chest. "Mebbe t'morrow!" He scampered off to join the others, who were all as black as he.

No matter what scientists and theologians were saying, Charles thought it sad how Negroes had been brought to this cold climate from their deserts and jungles. The whole gang here jostled and joked as though they might be too dull to understand the ravages of the cold upon their ill-clad bodies. Like most street Negroes, these wore bedraggled clothing. In some of the popular magazines and newspapers, cartoonists were regularly capturing this image of Northern Negroes well—pants above the ankles and coats with the sleeves worn-out.

In this group there was one with a blanket pulled over his shoulders and one with a cloth tied over his head in place of a hat. As before when Charles crossed the alley, he tried his best to ignore them. Yet once he was inside and hanging up his coat, he looked out through the small windows in the door to watch them from a distance, thinking again on what Dr. Ellis had said in the deep of the night. It seemed strange that Negroes clustered as they did, always bantering with their odd-sounding words.

He reflected on his own unhappy years in the street, for he had stolen and scavenged and endured the cold just as these bucks did, but almost always while alone. Friend Peabody had found him eating the outer leaves of cabbages in the same storehouse beside the barn where he now kept many of his supplies. In contrast with his former distress, the Negro vagabonds never appeared as lonely or as unhappy as he had been.

A knock at the front door turned him fully around. Taking out his old gold pocket watch, which also had been Elim's, Charles saw it was far past opening time. He hurried upstairs.

Four gentlemen dressed in all shades of dour gray could be seen through the wide front windows. They peered in and Charles wondered about them, for he did not think he knew a one of them. Turning the key, he let them in.

"Why, man, we thought perhaps you were not open on Fridays." The youngest of them, who was also the one speaking, seemed good-natured as he strode in leading the others. The little brass bell above the entryway rang until they all had come in and the door closed behind them.

The young man removed his high, finely brushed beaver-skin hat. The others did the same. That is when Charles saw that he had been wrong. He did know the last gentleman in the group. He was Mr. Anthony Ruskin. Charles recognized him from infrequent encounters he had had with him at the bank and near the street entrance to his prestigious law office. His likeness was now on expensive illustrated literature being spread around town for the start of his senatorial campaign. At once Charles retreated to his counter. The lean Ruskin, having fine dark hair and a receding hairline, followed him. "You are Mr. Powell, aren't you?"

"Yes, sir?" Charles was greatly surprised that Ruskin knew his name. Immediately he feared this visit had something to do with Dr. Ellis's visit only hours earlier.

Anthony Ruskin seemed to feel no need to identify himself, but he did introduce the others. "This is Mr. Hudson of Crystal Hall Tobacco out of Richmond. Mr. Neice, who grows cotton in Georgia. Mr. Saunderson, who resides in the city at present, as their factor."

"Good morning, sirs," Charles responded quite uneasily, for Mr. Ruskin had never crossed his threshold before. "Is there something I can do for you gentlemen?"

Ruskin grinned. "None of us has ever seen the insides of a free-products store. We had some time before I open my office, so we all decided to come here."

Except for Ruskin, the men were already scattering. He continued to speak while the others looked around. "We are taken by the name for your kind of establishment." He pointed to the words painted on the windows: *Peabody's Free Products*. When I tried to explain the intent to these gentlemen, they were amazed that anyone would try to supply what the public needs apart from Negro labor."

"*Slave* labor, sir," Charles said feebly, while woodenly fearing that at any moment the attorney would begin to speak about his sister-in-law or the events that had happened only yesterday.

"Oh, right! *Slave* labor!" Charles' daring to make the distinction seemed to humor the lawyer. A twinkle came to Ruskin's eye. "Some of what you have here is grown by Negroes, isn't it? I remember my father saying that, for I know he's stopped in once or twice since the business has been handed down to you."

"Yes, sir." Brother Peabody had had his meager account in Tyrone Ruskin's bank, so Charles did the same now.

The one called Mr. Hudson rubbed the tobacco leaves that were hanging ready to be cut into plugs. "Where did you get these?"

Charles felt himself truly a man of few words in their presence. "Lancaster County, sir."

"Where's that?"

"West of here, sir."

The southern planter sniffed loudly. "Pennsylvania tobacco?"

"Yes, sir."

"This grown by some of your northern niggers?"

"No, sir, that's from white farmers."

He seemed to feel justified then. "I tell you what, even my darkies wouldn't be happy to have this to roll between their thumb and fingers." The others chuckled lightly, Ruskin included.

Charles watched with anxious eyes. He put himself to sorting apples near the counter so that he would not appear idle.

Mr. Neice wove his way back through the coffee and buckwheat to come to him. "Are you a Quaker, then?"

"No, sir." Even this Charles said with caution.

"I didn't think so. You don't wear odd clothes. I hear them called Friends. I do like that. A church full of *friends*. I thought this kind of place was always run by Quakers."

Mr. Saunderson and Mr. Hudson came close, as though to involve themselves in the discussion. "Elim Peabody was a Friend," Ruskin said from the middle of the room. "Charles Powell was once his apprentice, then his heir."

The young Mr. Hudson, who had come in first, was forthright. "How come you are not a Quaker if the man who trained you was one? Must be you born to it?"

"No, sir. For one thing, a Friend must be convinced that war is sin. I am not convinced, sir," Charles said.

"Nor I am, man!" Hudson smiled widely. He went on gamely. "Let me hear what you are willing to fight to the death for!"

Charles was taken aback. "Sir, I've made the choice mostly to honor the past—what I know of my family. I believe I had a grandfather who fought for the independence of this nation."

"So that's why you have your star-spangled banner hanging up there!" Neice pointed to the flag Charles had behind the counter. It was one of the few changes he had made when the store became his own.

"Yes, in honor of him," Charles said quietly.

"My father served under Washington at Brandywine," Mr. Saunderson boasted.

Hudson laughed. "If Powell's granddaddy had half the girth of chest that he himself has, that poor fellow would have been an easy target for the old lobsterbacks."

Charles added the emotion the others lacked. "He did die, sir." It was one of the few things Charles knew about his mother's family, that her father had never returned to Philadelphia after the war. His sacrifice was a commendable exception to the rest of his sad heritage.

Anthony Ruskin drew all the others together. "Powell, explain why you have a second storeroom down there."

Charles was suspicious of the man's motives. It sounded like a trap, and suddenly it felt like one. "The Negroes come in there," he said, awkward about a truth that had never bothered him before.

All the men showed interest. "Then you are *anti*-slavery, but not *pro*-Negro?" Hudson asked with a grin. "Isn't that interesting!"

Charles stammered the truth. "I guess I am."

Saunderson drilled him even more. "Well, then, tell us what you think should be done with the Negroes that come up across the boundary line. Surely you see them swarming like bees here."

"I am not the man to ask," Charles faltered as his eyes inadvertently met Ruskin's.

"How can you oppose slavery when you see the piteous condition of niggers on their own?" Neice observed.

Charles didn't answer. The question did trouble him.

Saunderson opened his mouth. "Three-fourths of the world's cotton is produced by slaves now. Did you know that? There's a beautiful harmony to it all when it's managed rightly."

"I do know the figures," Charles admitted, feeling small despite his physical size.

Looking around, Saunderson spoke again. "You have no rice here. No pecans, and only inferior qualities of textiles, tobacco, and sugar. What are you trying to prove by maintaining this business? Doesn't it strike you that your enterprise is about as foolish as trying to empty the sea with a thimble?"

"I do it for those of us who would rather have slave-free products," Charles dared, though he did not feel noble about it. "I admit I do not understand the Negro, but I do not think it is humane to have whips and auction blocks and chains for live beings that seem so much like us."

"My goodness, man, neither do we," Mr. Neice said. "But you have to understand the African's small mind. He comes from a dark land, where savage tribal chiefs will sell each other."

Saunderson agreed. "My granddaddy remembered those days before our Atlantic Ocean slave routes closed. He knew men who visited African ports. They'd tell of niggers bringing other niggers to put them inside the huge rock pens they had there. They had them bound by sinew to sticks. All very primitive."

Neice was shaking his head in agreement. "Yes, so when dealing with the darkies now, it is sometimes the unhappy truth that you must resort to what they do understand and know."

Hudson gave his opinion also. "Well, let the truth be told! Slavery could be one hundred percent humane if you folks up here would just do a little more to help us. It's the messages that your *Friends* here speak that encourage our Negroes to steal away."

"I don't understand," Charles said, feeling all their hot gazes upon him.

Hudson tipped his head to Ruskin. "Well, here's a honest Yankee for once, who admits his need for insight." The tobacco farmer began to speak at length. "Mr. Saunderson was right when he said there is a harmony in slavery. Have you been to the South, Mr. Powell?"

"No."

"Then allow me to tell you what you will not hear from any Pennsylvania Quaker. A well-ordered plantation is prettier than a clipper ship under full sail. Smoother than any machinery you can name. If you'd come South I'd show you my own property, and you'd see it for yourself."

He paused. "I take it you are a religious man."

Charles was quiet about himself.

"Well, I am, so I appeal to you by reason of God's design—how He formed a race inferior to ours intellectually but so well made for outdoor labor. If you visit me, you will find that I take good care of my chattels, for I believe that is a part of my role under God. You would see my darkies so content, I believe, that you might soon be selling tobacco from Crystal Hall." He smiled.

Charles had never heard slavery so eloquently defended.

"And that is where what I said before has great relevance," Hudson went on. "If you want slavery to be humane, then you must do *your* part up here to make sure the slaves know the North can be no paradise for them. You see, they take anything they hear and conjure up what they want to believe. That makes them restless. It forces the use of those primitive controls, which we spoke about before. If they had no myths about liberty and prosperity for them here, then they would stay satisfied."

"Anyone who has seen Negroes in the North should pity them." Mr. Neice pointed toward the windows of the Easton Alley door. He and Mr. Saunderson both walked to the top of the wide stairs.

"Are any of those out there runaways?" Saunderson asked.

Charles remembered the face of the youth who had come into his barn. "I don't know, sir. I don't make that my business."

This caused Mr. Ruskin to pull something from his coat. "In light of what Mr. Hudson just said, I believe it must become everyone's business here in the Commonwealth." He handed Charles a four-page pamphlet titled *Unity and Peace: Our National Heritage*. "You do know that I hope to contend for a senate seat in the next election?"

"Yes, sir."

"Well, here, I believe, is one of the most important issues for our time. This short text explains the benefits of compulsory colonization for all Negroes from Pennsylvania. It's a plan to see every colored individual removed from this state, either to be sent back to Africa or to the West Indies."

"Mr. Ruskin's plan engages well with what we all have said," Mr. Hudson added happily. "If you all had no darkies up here, then no slave in his right mind would ever attempt to cross the line between slave states and this one. To find any that did would be as simple as plucking flies from pink ointment." His comparison won approving nods from the others.

"Read over that for yourself," Ruskin told Charles. "That's why I took the time and expense to put it into print, because I do believe in its importance. Perhaps before you go to the poll box, we can speak again."

He said this all cordially. Still Charles feared the visit had something to do with the politician's knowing about Friend Ellis's hopes to help a colored child.

All four of them soon gathered at the front door. They were not yet outside when the bell over the alley doorway jangled, the signal that someone had come in by the back way. The gentlemen turned as Charles looked down to see several colored boys from the street striding in. With the exception of one, they went straight toward the coal brazier, which Charles usually had burning by now on cold days. This morning, however, he had neglected the fire because of these visitors. Even so, it was apparent to these men why the boys had been drawn in.

"I see you give *free* heat to them," Mr. Hudson chortled. Though he had been the first to come in, he was in a position to go out last.

The Africans must have heard him, for they looked up briefly. Regular customers usually had nothing to say about the presence of Negroes in the back room. Charles recognized the one who had called himself Tom because his coat had holes worn in the sleeves large enough to expose his lean gray elbows. Though that boy had been eager and vocal while alone with Charles, he was as furtive as the others now.

"There's a waste of good flesh down there!" Saunderson dared to say aloud. "It's a pity to see them miserable when they all could have practical work."

"You'd better watch them, Mr. Powell," Mr. Neice advised, his words hardly any quieter than Saunderson's. "They all are the kind that can *free* your free products as they probably *freed* themselves. By thievery!"

Charles was only too eager to bid the men good-day. When they finally did go out, he put himself to work with the apples again, this time quite conscious of the boys still moving about on the lower level.

Then one of those Negroes started to climb the inner stairs. The eyes of all the others were on him. For the first time in his years of owning the store, Charles felt fear at being alone with colored customers. Of course he could overcome this one slim black youth, who might be coming to take offense at what the white men had said, but he would not be able to win against them all.

He breathed a prayer while considering how many times violence had already erupted in this city because of the races. He saw the irony of having been asked only last night to aid a Negro, while now another was approaching to do him harm. When the African was right at the counter, Charles made his arm muscles hard. "You boys *do* pilfer from me, yet never once have I called in the law to hold you accountable!" He pulled himself up to his full size and made his voice even stronger. "But now you listen! That does not mean I will tolerate violence!" He dared to point to the Negro only inches from him. "Boy, now you go back down those stairs."

The Negro who wore spectacles did not move.

"You heard me! Now!"

"Yes, Mr. Powell, I heard you." Then the colored youth, black as iron and with a head of woolly hair, laid a piece of paper down on top of Ruskin's pamphlet, which Charles had placed upon the counter. "I am Brother Oliver Catos, Dr. Ellis's medical practitioner. Will you or won't you come today?"

CHAPTER 11

MAYLEDA WAS STANDING by the infirmary's upstairs window alertly watching for a wagon to come through the back gate. For more than an hour she had been moving nervously between the child's bed and the window, where the chill of the bright day leaked in from outside. A noise in the hall pulled her back once more toward the little boy who lay panting and unconscious.

It was Dr. Ellis's wife, Sister Eleanor. She opened the partially closed door and came in. "It is too early to expect Brother Catos to return," she said, knowing Mayleda's hopes as she went again to the window.

Mayleda knew this was true, but already she had changed into the warm, plain country-styled dress Sister Ellis had given her to wear. She had on layers of woolen skirts, thick socks, and borrowed boots, all so quickly obtained by the female members of the Ellises' small antislavery force. The older woman, clad in white and gray, sat down in the chair that Mayleda had been too agitated to use.

As always, Sister Ellis's hands were busy. She had a needle, fabric, and thread. "There, in a few more minutes thee shall have an extra pair of warm, loose-fitting trousers to take for the boy, remade from a pair of the doctor's old ones." The sister held up her work. She had already made the boy one set of trousers overnight. The same women who had donated clothes to Mayleda had collected socks and undergarments and a pair of shoes for the child, though at present he lay too ill to be dressed in anything but flannel.

"Thank you," Mayleda said, her arms wrapped around herself and under the heavy wool shawl on her shoulders.

"Thee is scared," Sister Ellis observed with sympathy.

"I am. For him." Mayleda nodded toward the child, limp and gray, whose breaths sounded as though they were painfully catching on his small fractured ribs. She viewed him through tears. "It seems impossible that he can live even now. How will he survive on the road in the cold?"

"We have prayerfully decided that he must be moved. If he can live, then he will do so in Oak Glen. That is our hope. Thee cannot stay with him forever. Practitioner Whitsun is the man to do the surgery, then perhaps the boy can convalesce in peace, undiscovered and undisturbed."

Mayleda shielded her eyes so that Sister Ellis would not comment on her tears. The older woman seemed to try to give her even more assurance. "Brother Whitsun had severe lung ailments when he was carried to us. He was in bed almost a year before God saw fit to heal him fully. He is a tender, caring man, Sister Ruskin. Thee needn't fear about giving up the child to him."

"I don't, ma'am. I just fear the journey. How likely it will be that he will die in my arms." She looked away from the other woman. She had had too much death already in losing Sprague. "If my husband still lived, we would keep this child ourselves, I know. We would have found some way to hide him right here, so that he would have been saved from this awful ordeal of traveling over fifty miles to another doctor."

"Thee tortures thyself with things that cannot be."

As though it were an echo in the stairwell far down the hall, Mayleda heard the tall clock striking twelve. She folded her hands to her chin to keep herself from touching the child in his tenuous slumber. "Oh, Sister Ellis! I think about the woman who brought him into this world. How could you go on not knowing your own child's fate, even if you conceived him unwillingly?"

"Thousands of our colored sisters do endure it." The older woman said this, not looking up from her work.

"I think about the father too! How can any man conceive a child and then perceive it as a slave? It was one of the many evils I could not reconcile while living in the South."

Oddly, the other woman smiled. "Perhaps the child will find a real home among the people of Oak Glen. Since this Mr. Pudget and Mr. Dawes have not come here to try to get him back, I believe they have given up trying to make their profit from him. It would be good if they would think him dead, then they would not pursue him, and the boy could grow up free."

"If he can survive!" This time Mayleda did not resist laying her hand gently against the child's burning cheek. "He has pneumonia, I'm sure. His fever is rising."

The woman got out the chair and motioned for Mayleda to sit down. "Thee should rest. Once thy journey starts, there will be no time for sleep." The child groaned and coughed like a very old man, but still Sister Ellis pointed to the seat.

"That does break my heart to hear him!" Mayleda cried while she reluctantly went and sat down, for she was weary but also too distressed to consider her own needs. The boy coughed again. This time his eyes came open. He swayed his head violently on the bed.

Sister Ellis, being closer, took his hand. "Little Lamb! Thee is safe!" They all had been using Harriet Mason's gentle name for him.

Still the child looked around wildly until Mayleda stood and put herself into his vision. Quickly she went to him. Even with so much weakness he raised his arms. "I cannot think why he wants me to hold him. It must hurt his little chest so. And it must be suffocating now that his fever rages." As Mayleda spoke, however, she lifted the child and drew him close while sitting down on the bed. There were cramping pains in her back and shoulders once more, for most of last night had been passed this way with the child in her lap.

She kissed him on his sweaty forehead and felt his bony frame relax. Sister Ellis brought a fresh wet cloth to lay upon his brow. The activity caused the child to look to Mayleda with dulling eyes. Though he had not spoken a word, Mayleda felt compelled once more to speak to him. "Soon a wagon will come, and you must not be afraid. We are going to take you away from this city called Philadelphia. We are going to a safer place where no one can find you. Practitioner Catos, the colored doctor you know, will travel with us. We will go to Dr. Whitsun's. He is a Negro too."

She did not know if he understood her distinctions concerning race, yet she thought them important in keeping the child's trust. With a light touch, she brushed her hand across his unruly hair. He sighed and closed his eyes.

Mayleda had started attending the Ellises' meetings and working at the infirmary only after Brother Whitsun had moved on, so she did not know the man. Still, she tried to take courage from Dr. Ellis's belief that his first medical student was as skilled at surgery now as he himself. She took comfort, too, in how many times Sister Ellis spoke of Brother Whitsun as a man with great compassion. *Now if only Little Lamb will live to meet him.*

"I think someone is coming," Sister Ellis said, going to the window. "It is Mr. Powell with his wagon!"

"Mr. Powell?" The name made Mayleda's heart race. "I thought it would be someone from our antislavery society."

Sister Ellis looked pensive. Mayleda could not exactly read her mood. "Brother Ellis did confide in me this morning that he had sought out the merchant late last night, for the very reason that he is not known to be part of our abolition group."

Mayleda still was holding Little Lamb, but she had enough strength to stand with the child to get a glimpse of the driveway in the rear yard between the Ellises' house and the infirmary. "He has a full load of bricks and a Negro helper," she observed, as she stretched her vision to look down. "Perhaps it's just coincidence that he comes now."

"No, dear! That is Brother Catos with him, in pauper's garb."

"It is!" Mayleda was amazed, for Oliver Catos was the son of a prosperous plasterer, whose father and grandfather had also been established as artisans in this city. Oliver regularly took great care in how he dressed, and usually he spent the allowance given him by his father on the fanciest clothing he could find. The Ellises worried about his expensive choices, and they admonished him, for they feared that his good heart and wise head might be obstructed by vanity. Mayleda thought he showed courage now to dress as a poor man just to help their cause.

"Those bricks are to provide a hiding place for thee," Sister Ellis said. Mayleda laid the boy down, but she stayed right beside him. "Brother Ellis told me this too. It is part of the plan."

Mayleda hardly heard her words as she looked out the window yet another time. She saw Charles Powell, strong and sturdy. He set the huge wagon's brake and climbed down. It was not the first time she had watched him from this window, but now it would be followed by the chance to speak with him again, face-to-face, after all these years of change since her days in Ludlow Row.

Brother Catos was out of the wagon too, closing the gate so that they would have more privacy. Though the sun was high and bright, the rear yard still looked cold, as it was in shadows. Mayleda watched Charles a moment more as he went ahead to check his horses. Behind her, the child starting whimpering softly. It was a new sound. She turned. The boy's response gave her hope, for it seemed his first attempt at communication. He extended his hand toward the window. "Yes, the wagon is here!"

She tried to sound happy and brave. He raised his arms to her once more. Even this slight amount of activity increased his gasping. Continually now his mouth opened like a fish's without water.

Sister Ellis came to help her and she spoke to the boy too. "Here are the new pants I have just finished for thee. Now Sister Ruskin and I will help thee dress for thy journey."

Oliver Catos had been reared by parents who were careful never to give the world cause to degrade or demean their family. They worked hard, dressed well, and kept a neat house, yard, and carriage. They practiced religion and temperance and made themselves as polite as their children. Still, they were despised as often as they were accepted by white neighbors and white businessmen.

Now, for the well-being of a colored child, Oliver had let himself be seen walking and riding through the streets in a slouched hat with a broken brim, an oversized coat that had no buttons, and knee-patched trousers. It was the first, and maybe the only, time Oliver ever volunteered to adopt the inferior image that seemed so wholly bound to his race. It made him nearly sick in his stomach to keep himself moving in the light of day, looking as he did.

Already he had suffered greatly for his decision, and right in Mr. Powell's store. The merchant had judged him as a tramp in an instant and treated him like a vagabond, when he should have known who he was, for often they had met either in the store or here at the infirmary's back door. The morning had forced Oliver to conclude that Charles Powell was like so many others who chose to remember him only by race, not by face, having no recollection of him as a person when he met him unexpectedly. All this whirling through Oliver's mind felt as intolerable as his threadbare, unbecoming clothes.

The moment he could, he left Powell to find Brother Ellis inside. The old doctor met him on the back stairs as he was coming down. At once, his astute teacher sensed his agitation. "What! Has thee been confronted by agents? Or followed?"

Oliver swallowed hard. "No. Everything went just as you had hoped. Powell is here. I will go up for the child."

He started to do it, but Dr. Ellis took his arm. "Wait. Something is wrong. Tell me the truth, Brother Catos."

"It is nothing that will risk the child's safety."

"But it will! Are thee and Brother Powell at odds?"

"What? Were you expecting it? Or are you blaming me?"

"I care not to blame anyone, but thee knows that a house divided cannot stand. Unity is essential as we face this risk."

"There is nothing I can do about how Mr. Charles Powell chooses to perceive me!"

"Brother, speak to him. He can learn from thee if thee will make it possible."

"I need be with him no more than three days. One cannot change a man's perception in that amount of time. Sir, do not expect it of me!"

"What happened between thee and Brother Powell?"

"I would rather not say. Let it be as it is. I will not endanger the child over it. Nor will I be the cause of delay."

"It would be better to have no doctor than one who compounds strife."

"It was he who insulted me! Yet for the sake of the boy I will be demeaned, if need be! Know that I will! I have a grand heritage of silence practiced by all the men named Catos in my family who have come before me. Not one of them did ever open his mouth to speak contrary to a white man. Trust me! For three days, and the sake of this child's life, I can do the same!"

The doctor still held him, but it was like a sign of his support and empathy now. If Brother Ellis heard the bitterness within him, he chose not to confront it. Looking at him for only a few moments more, Dr. Ellis released him to finish taking the stairs. Hard as Oliver tried, he could not remember how or when he had become so bold in speaking his mind to the doctor who had chosen him out of a class full of colored students at Friends School to receive this secret training in medicine.

He could not even decide why he felt able to say things to Dr. Ellis, things that black men would usually say only to one another. It was almost as though one could forget about one's color within these walls. Yet at the same time, there was no other place like this place, where he felt more affirmed as a *Negro* man.

It was Dr. Ellis's example, Oliver knew, that had given him the mettle and grace to dress as a poor slave in this attempt to save a child and free him. He entered the boy's room and found Sister Ellis and Sister Ruskin waiting.

"What took you so long?" Sister Ruskin fretted. "I feared that you had met up either with the slave catchers or a marshal."

Even though her tone was harried, Oliver felt no insult from her as he did from Powell when that man spoke. Oliver knew the widow well. He trusted her thoughts. There was no doubting the goodness in her heart or her love of fairness for all. Though he had not known her husband, there were colored men everywhere who testified that Sprague Ruskin had had the same rare, pure qualities as she.

One look at the child told him that his concerns must not be for himself any longer. "Has Dr. Ellis seen his condition?" Instinctively he put his fingers to the boy's wrist and found the pulse shallow but racing.

"Yes, he was just here and did the same," his wife said.

"Yet he still wants us to take him?"

The worry in Sister Ruskin's face was almost like pain. "He says there is a need for surgery. That there may be splintered ribs pressing into the lung. He believes it would be better to try the surgery in Oak Glen rather than here, for the child will not be able to be moved at all afterward."

For the first time since the boy had come to them, Oliver was fully convinced that the child would die. He understood the reasons why the child should not be kept here, but when he picked him up now, weak and bundled in his travel clothes, he felt certain he was carrying the boy to his death. He hid his thoughts from the two kind, vigilant women. "You gather your own things, Sister Ruskin. I will take him."

While Charles had been alone, he had turned his team around so that they were headed for the gate. There was a broad circular brick path remaining in the backyard from the days when wagoners had brought in supplies or carried books away from the bindery. Though this place was familiar, the anxiety he had now certainly was not. It seemed like an endless time of waiting until Oliver Catos, the Ellises, and Mayleda Ruskin came out through the rear door.

His horses, Marcy and Maude, impatient in harness, tossed their heads, making the bells strung between their collars seem to ring as loudly as church bells. It seemed foolish now for him to have left them on the harnesses, but he always traveled with bells so that others on the road might hear his team coming. To travel in silence might in itself risk drawing attention to his journey, yet now as he saw his passengers coming, he wished he had decided to leave the bells at home.

Dr. Ellis approached him. He said nothing about the wagon or its supplies. "While thee hastens to lift Sister Ruskin up into the wagon bed, Brother Catos will climb on and be ready to take the boy into hiding." The doctor glanced at the gate that had been closed and to the street, which was still partly visible behind it. "I counsel thee to hurry."

In his barn before the team had been hitched, he and Oliver Catos had used the bricks and boards to construct a small hiding space directly behind the wagon seat. They had used the plans and sketches that the young African had carried with him in the doctor's own handwriting. Charles now felt hesitant about committing Mayleda Ruskin to such a small, dark, and cold place, and for a ten-hour ride.

The woman he had not seen in years came to him dressed like a poor farmer's wife. She looked small and uncertain as she met his gaze. Her lips were tight, her eyes moist and sad, giving him clues that she was as worried as he. His hands chilled with his thoughts that he must touch her now, even before he could think of one worthy thing to say.

There was no resistance on her part, no hesitation. She loosened the cloak she had pulled around her so that he could put his hands upon her waist. He had never touched a woman before, and now he was touching her, someone who had been on his mind often in his loneliness. He did not know whether to repent or to give praise for the extraordinary moment, which passed so quickly. When she was up on the wagon and he had released her, she looked down. "Thank you, Mr. Powell."

"Hurry, sister, and get into the hiding place!" Mrs. Ellis said, standing by her husband. "No one must see thee. No one must suspect what is happening here."

Oliver Catos was standing on the wagon's edge. He waited while Mayleda crawled into the narrow space. Then Catos took the child as Dr. Ellis held him up, bundled so that Charles did not have even one look at the little fugitive whom they might be risking life and liberty for. He regretted that Catos kept his eyes averted from him. Charles knew he was the cause of the tension between them.

Catos disappeared into the hiding place too, but he was back out in the light before a minute passed. Then he started stacking bricks to seal the place at once. Charles got up on the wagon, and in silence he helped him to complete the task. The plan, of course, was to make it look like a solid order of bricks being taken from the town to the countryside.

Charles' experience of being so close to Mayleda still affected him as the chill that had started in his hands now seemed to go through his spine. He trembled unexpectedly after he jumped down and right before Dr. Ellis laid a hand upon his shoulder. Catos climbed down too, then went to the wagon seat.

"Godspeed!" the Quaker doctor said. "I will open the gate for thee."

There was darkness in daytime. They were enclosed in a little space with the boards less than an inch from Mayleda's head. When they started moving, the rocking of the wagon rained down sand from the countless bricks above her, threatening the child's breathing and irritating her own useless eyes, which were nevertheless wide open in the blackness because of her worry and discomfort.

All this worked together to form a new kind of terror in Mayleda. While the child had braved pain without sound before, he now writhed and tried to scream. She was forced to press her hand against his mouth, even when she believed it could suffocate him. "Oh, Little Lamb!" she pleaded quickly and in whispers. "Be still. Please! It's Sister Ruskin. Sister May! You know me! We must be quiet now. We must be patient and brave."

She took her hand away, so fearful that she might have stopped his weak breath or bruised his frail trust in her. Unable to see, she tried to kiss his face, for in the infirmary he had responded to this demonstration of affection, often lifting his hands to her while she lightly planted her lips upon his forehead. This time her mouth bumped hard on either his cheekbone or his nose. Still, she felt the tension easing in his scrawny limbs.

Overjoyed that he was still able to accept this all as part of her care for him, she said, "Listen to the merry bells on Mr. Powell's horses. Listen! You cannot cry out and listen too!"

When he stayed silent she praised him. "There! That's right! Good for you! You do hear the bells. They are playing for you! *Free-dom! Free-dom! Free-dom!*"

Leaning even closer in the small space, she kissed him again. This time she tasted his salty, secret tears, though he had never cried while they could still see his face. His skin was rough with the sand still sifting down. "I know you are in pain. God knows it too! We must think on freedom and pray for it."

"Sis-ter May?" His voice was as clear and as soft as hers.

"Little Lamb! You can speak!"

"Where's my sis-ter?" His words sounded weaker.

"Oh! That was your sister on the street?"

He did not answer, but she heard and felt one quiet sob.

Mayleda believed she did understand the small child's thinking. As long as he was in the city, perhaps he hoped to see the girl again. It tore her heart to think how dazed the little boy had been when he removed himself from the corpse. "Oh, my dear little friend! Your sister has gone on to a different place. A better one than even we are going to. When we are safely to Brother Whitsun's house, I will tell you more. For now, try not to be so sad, for you will see her again."

The boy did stay quiet. Too quiet.

"Are you all right, Little Lamb?" Within the bulky blankets and because of the noise and motion all around them, she could not sense him breathing, nor could she find his pulse.

Perhaps they had been on their way only five or ten minutes. She could not imagine now having enough faith or discipline or strength to keep on going for *hours* more. The child in her arms might have breathed his last already.

Then she, too, made herself listen to the harness bells, in an effort to hold to her sanity. "*Oh, Je-sus! Je-sus! Je-sus!*" she prayed out loud and in desperation, according to the rhythm she heard outside.

CHAPTER 12

THE PIKE TOWARD LANCASTER CITY was familiar to Charles, for since the days when he had been Friend Peabody's apprentice he had come this way to trade manufactured goods for produce in season, local cast iron, and firewood.

For the safety of himself and all those who were with him now, he prayed that this trip bore every resemblance to his others so no one would suspect that he was transporting a fugitive.

It was Friday, cold but clear. Many other wagons, carriages, and drays were making use of the good weather and the good road, most of them going east toward Philadelphia. When he and Oliver Catos weren't under the eyes of other drivers, there were businesses, tavernhouses, and residences strung along the way that prevented Charles from stopping anywhere to check on Mayleda and the child.

By his watch it was more than four hours before they came to the first truly secluded place, where the pike ran through a wooded rise.

Without consulting the Negro beside him, who had been wordless all day, Charles drove his mares to the edge of the road and stopped them under big, leafless hickories that cast down their long shadows. With hardly a glance at Catos, Charles turned his head. "Mrs. Ruskin!" he called over his shoulder. "Finally we are at a safe place. Are you all right?"

There was no answer, which panicked him. "Mrs. Ruskin!"

Catos spoke. "I heard her crying some time ago."

Charles was instantly angry. "Why didn't you say!"

"We cannot open the hiding place!"

Charles discarded his words. He got out of the wagon, with Catos following after him.

"What are you doing?" the Negro demanded.

"I'm getting her out!"

The young black man dared to grab him. "This is not safe! We must find a hidden place!"

"This is good enough. Time is of the essence!"

"No! *Caution* is!"

He ignored Catos. "Mrs. Ruskin! I'm coming to get you out!" The woman did not call out, but he heard her sobbing once he was up and standing in the wagon bed.

"You won't do it!" Catos ran back to the driver's bench. Hopping up, he took the reins and pushed the brake, rolling them forward as they were at the crest of the hill.

"Don't you touch my wagon! The woman is in trouble."

"We all are in trouble if you lose your head, sir! Or your courage!" Though the reins were threaded wrongly in his hands, Catos actually drove the horses forward.

"Stop!"

"Not till you do, sir!"

Then Charles saw a rider coming from the west. He was on a fast horse and soon was upon them. Whatever the cause of his haste, the stranger still stopped at once.

"Hallo!" the rider called with a friendliness common among the local country people. "Do you have some problem here?"

Catos yanked the horses. They jolted to a standstill. Charles, still on the wagon, nearly lost his balance. Catos once more took the silent demeanor of hired help.

"No problem!" Charles assured him awkwardly, while the speaker looked them both over with some obvious doubt. "I was just checking the load."

The man tipped his hat and rode on, kicking his horse to pick up speed again. Charles jumped down. He went up and climbed into the wagon seat on the side where Catos had been riding for the whole length of their journey. The black youth said nothing. Charles was well aware of his own fuming, yet Oliver Catos had been right in his judgment. "I'm sorry," he admitted truthfully. "And not just about now. About how I've been treating you from the start. You surprised me in my store. I though you were one of those that usually loiter outside." He stopped, for Catos would not look at him, and nothing he had said seemed to make the atmosphere better between them.

Catos did speak, however, but he changed the subject. "Aren't we near the village of Pleasant Points?"

"We are." Charles was surprised that Catos would know.

"Then there is an Underground Railroad safe house near here. I thought I recognized this section of rocky hillside. Please, drive on! I will show you the way."

The young dark man looked straight ahead, as though wanting no degree of friendship. Charles hesitated, barely conscious that he was doing so even after Catos had given back the reins.

"I thought you wanted to help her! Drive on! I know a safe place."

Charles spoke to his mares so that they did pull. He was reluctant to trust Catos, and he felt obliged to explain. "I don't know any Quakers in this area."

"I didn't say they were Quakers!" Now Catos looked at him. "See where the fence ends, then the rocky lane? Turn left there."

Oliver sighed out some of his frustation when they were deep into the woodlot on the ragged, private track winding through the bare young forest. Mr. Powell was on the course he had requested, but when the white storekeeper saw the pens for goats and fowl on both sides of the narrow lane, he pulled his horses to another stop.

"You must be mistaken," the merchant told him. "This can't be the entrance to any reputable Underground Railroad station. This is just not the kind of place that houses a stationmaster."

"But it is!" The hours of silence and cold had Oliver feeling wholly irascible. This was a place to which he had been twice before, not with Dr. Ellis, but with colored men, members of the city's Vigilance Committee, which was the largest and best organized effort among Philadelphia Negroes to aid runaways. When he had been here with leaders from his own race, Oliver had been able to admit that being on the property of a poor black farmer was foreign to him. But now with Powell, he acted only with certainty, as though he knew the proprietor well.

With obvious skepticism Powell urged his mares to move forward, and they continued down the rutted path. Dogs tied to short, thick lengths of rope barked as they approached the rambling house, built half of log and half of milled boards. It stood under ancient trees. Without saying anything, Oliver jumped down and ran ahead. A gray canopy of smoke from the chimney hung in the otherwise empty boughs. He went up onto the porch and knocked on the door. The whole place smelled delicious, of cooked onions and ham.

In a moment someone came up behind him instead of from the house. It was the same small, tough-looking brown man in worn clothes whom he had met before. Today the farmer had a live fat hen hanging upside down from each hand. "Brother Simeon Bart?" Oliver said, turning around, the first name easy for him to remember but the surname coming hard.

"That's me," Bart replied, looking more toward Powell's wagon and Powell himself.

"I'm a friend of Brother Still and Brother Purvis. We have some *cargo*, sir. We were trying to get to Oak Glen from Philadelphia, but with the distance and the cold—"

"You bein' followed?" Bart cut him off with his words, then with eyes that flashed far out on his lane.

"No, sir. It's that we're carrying a sick child and a woman hidden inside those bricks."

Bart opened one of the many crates scattered around the worn yard and threw the hens to confinement. "You tell the driver to bring his wagon 'round 'tween the house an' the barn." The urgency in Bart's voice comforted Oliver greatly.

"He welcomes us!" Oliver said, running back to Powell and not concealing his satisfaction. *Let him know that not every Underground Railroad conductor is a white man.* "Mr. Bart says to drive your wagon over there."

Soon their wiry, hatless host was nodding to have Powell lock the brake. And Powell was back at the wagon's gate a second later and up into the bed, dismantling the rear brick wall with a vengeance.

Oliver climbed up too, not to remove bricks, but to be ready to take the boy. Standing there, waiting, he collected his thoughts. *The child's welfare depends on me. I am the only doctor here.*

Powell reached in with one hand, his shoulders being too large for the space. He got the child out right away because Sister Ruskin had sidled her way forth with the boy on her lap. The blankets were away from his face. Oliver could see a drawn, lifeless form. Powell lifted the boy and handed him over without a word. Oliver felt no breath. Still he delayed, because there was reason to be worried about Sister Ruskin too.

She came out with her face wet from crying and squinting because of her trials in the dark. Yet her attention was on the child. "Oh, Oliver, is he dead?" she cried, using his first name, which was never Dr. Ellis's practice, or hers, at the infirmary.

Mr. Powell steadied her while she tried to stand. She stared only at the boy.

Simeon Bart spoke. "You all come into the house."

Sister Ruskin's legs were so numb that Mr. Powell had to carry her while Oliver transported the child. Inside the plain kitchen, they encountered Bart's large family at the table. The children ranged in age from toddlers to a group of strong adolescent boys and girls, some of whom were helping to bring bowls of soup to the others.

Simeon's wife rubbed her hands on her apron and joined the man in his worries. "They just brought a young sick fugitive," Bart said. While he spoke, Powell put Sister Ruskin down lightly to stand on her own.

The woman looked at them all, then opened a door behind the table. "Bring the child in here."

There was a homemade bed with a thick down mattress. Oliver laid his charge upon it. Removing his broken hat, he said, "I work as a medical practitioner. I have a sack of supplies to bring in from the hiding place." Yet he found no need to go for it, for Mr. Powell readily said he would get it.

Sister Ruskin rubbed her arms. "Is he still this side of heaven?"

Oliver pulled away all the wrappings from the skeleton-like body. The wound had reopened. Blood stained the inner covers.

"Yes, he's still alive." As soon as Powell was back, Sister Ruskin searched for more bandages in the sack. While Oliver decided what he must do because of the bleeding, Sister Ruskin focused on the boy's congested lungs. "I don't see how we can take him farther. All those hours in the wagon, I thought he was dead."

Oliver concluded that he could only wrap the child's abdomen again.

Splinters of rib bones had migrated toward the skin since he had last checked the injury, but he left them as they were. No surgery could be attempted until the child was in a place where he could be kept still afterwards, for days of convalescence. "We were trying to get to the house of a Mr. Joseph Whitsun," Oliver dared to say to Simeon.

"For sure!" the farmer agreed with no hesitation. "There is a safe house there too."

Oliver was surprised that he would say this in the presence of white folks.

"Mr. Bart, you know Dr. Whitsun, then?" Sister Ruskin asked.

"Last winter he saved my wife's life. She had dead twin babies trapped inside her, an' he rode here through the snow to take them out through her belly, right out there upon our table."

"Oh, Brother Catos, maybe Dr. Whitsun can be called to come here again," Sister Ruskin said at once. "Then the child would not have to travel."

The boy was gasping and groaning between breaths. His eyes were closed. His lips were dark and his fingers also. It seemed that death must soon come. Oliver considered the danger to this family. There was only a slim chance that surgery would help the child, but a long recovery would be needed if the boy did survive. "How much farther to Oak Glen?" he asked, conscious that Mr. Powell had not said a word since they had been in this house.

"By the pike, twenty miles, but over Mine Ridge and down the other side, less than half of that."

"Is there a road wide enough for my team?" Powell did ask.

"I have a cart," Simeon replied. "I can take the boy in that. It won't draw no attention as you' wagon on the mountain would."

"I want to go too!" Sister Ruskin said. "I promised the child I would stay with him all the way to Brother Whitsun's."

"Mayleda!"

Oliver was surprised to hear Powell call her by her first name. The woman looked at the white man. "You have done what you can," Powell reasoned. "Now I think you should leave him with his own."

Oliver saw her eyes narrow. "I promised the boy I would be with him until we arrived in Oak Glen."

"He's not going to know," Powell said with some tenderness as he motioned toward the bed.

"I will know!" She moved to take the boy's limp hand. Oliver was amazed when the child opened his eyes. "All the way here I talked to him about freedom. About getting well. About going to school. I didn't know if he could hear me, but now I sense how much he does want to live."

Simeon and his wife seemed moved by her words.

"I think it would be better to take him on to Oak Glen, if you think that is possible," Oliver said to the Barts. "The child is far more fair in complexion than any of you. It would be safer to try to hide him in a colored town than with just your one family here."

"I'll get the cart hitched up," Simeon said.

The child suddenly seemed more awake. With all the strength he had, he clung to Sister Ruskin's fingers.

Oliver saw Powell's uneasiness, but the woman spoke before the merchant could say anything.

"I am going on to Oak Glen. I am going to keep my promise to take him all the way to Dr. Whitsun. You see how much Little Lamb wants and needs that."

"My sis-ter." The boy's weak whispers surprised Oliver.

"Oh yes!" Mayleda said to him. "When we are in Oak Glen, I will tell you more about that precious girl."

Powell confronted her anew. "How will you get back to Philadelphia if I do not take the wagon there?"

"By the train cars," she reasoned. "I'll do just what I planned to do before so that no one would see us driving back to the city together. I'll take the train east to the farm where both Sprague and Collin are buried. The Friends there always let me stay as long as I want. When I return to the city, Anthony will have no questions for me, for I go out to Sprague's grave often."

The child coughed. His little hand pulled away as he doubled himself against the pain. He moaned. "Sis-ter May."

"I'm right here. I'm not going to leave you."

"I did not know he could speak!" Oliver and Powell said almost the same words together.

"Yes, he was speaking in the wagon. He told me that it was his sister who died." Instantly she put his hand to her mouth. "Oh, God of mercy. I didn't want him to hear that now."

"Died . . ." The child feebly repeated the word.

For a moment she withdrew from the bed and came to Oliver. "I don't think he knows what that means. So far, I've said only that she's in a better place."

The boy called for her. "May!"

She looked at Powell. "I hope you understand why I must stay with him. I think this is the first time anyone has shown him real care, and now he does trust me." There was a deep silence exchanged between them, Oliver saw, as they faced each other.

Simeon Bart was at the door. "Brother Catos, I'd like you to consider ridin' with us for the boy's sake, 'cause the road ain't that smooth." His eyes shifted to Powell. "Sir, you welcome to stay here. Rest you'self an' you' team. Then mebbe you could come out to Oak Glen t'morrow. The way I see it, it would be best for you to take the sister to the station so that no colored brother will have to risk helpin' her in such a public kind of way."

Oliver knew how much Mr. Powell would dislike the idea of staying in a Negro's house overnight, but the man said nothing. "That load of brick an' board you got out there, sah," Simeon went on. "That promised to anybody?"

"No, it was only to make a hiding place."

Well, if we could settle on the price, sah, I could use them bricks an' timbers. I want to start curin' my own hams, but I have only a sorry kind of log smokehouse now."

Powell looked at Oliver, maybe even for advice. Some of the mental distance between them felt as though it might be narrowing.

Then Bart asked if Powell would care to go outside. "Let me have you meet my sons," he said as they were going through the doorway. "While I'm in Oak Glen, you can conduct you' business with them."

Charles went out with the African farmer. His Conestogas were standing stoically. Simeon admired them momentarily in the evening light, then he looked over the load. "I can promise you so many fowl, live or dressed, as you might want. Eggs, feathers, down too. I have pigs an' goats. You can take what you will t'morrow or spread it out over a course of weeks. My boys are old 'nough for this business of tradin'. I'll let them an' you come to agree on what's fair for all that you got in you' wagon."

"All right," Charles said, knowing that it would be to his advantage to trade, for then it would seem that he had stopped here only to make the delivery.

The Negro must have been thinking nearly the same thing. "When you go on to Oak Glen with you' wagon, you be sure to say to anybody that you gwine there for apples, cider, or honey, for those are what Pastor

Cummington Brown of Oak Glen do have for trade. His wife's quilts too. My children can tell you the way by the pike."

"Fine," Charles said, but only after hesitation. He remained against letting Mayleda go, yet by what right or power could he stop her decision? He was only the driver. He had been surprised that the Negro farmer had no qualms about him staying here with his family. He did not feel the same about sending Mrs. Ruskin off across a mountain at night with two colored men.

"I should tell you, sah, that in this township it ain't so much the constable you have to be careful of, but some of the regular men. They the ones most set against our efforts to help slaves goin' North. That's why I encourage you to act just like the merchant you are when you go on to Oak Glen." Simeon paused. "Do you know what a crazy quilt looks like, sah?"

"I think I do." Charles was puzzled by the question. "It's a random pattern of scrap pieces, all stitched together."

"Yessah, that's 'xactly what it is. Well, now, when you get into Oak Glen, the first thing you do is look up to Pastor Brown's window. If you would spy a crazy quilt there, then don't you mention us, or the boy, or Missus Ruskin at all. You just go in for the tradin', an' then you leave, quiet."

"But Mayleda Ruskin would be stranded then!"

"If there's a crazy in the window, it won't be no good for you to be seen comin' in on Underground Railroad business or gwine out with a woman what weren't in you' wagon from the start."

"You're saying there can be trouble! That you use the quilt as a code. Well, then, I'm saying that Mrs. Ruskin should not go!"

"That kind of quilt will be you' warnin', sah. Any other kind an' you be just fine. If there's no crazies, you feel free to speak with Pastor Brown about you' real reasons for comin'."

"Mrs. Ruskin should not go!"

The black man nodded. "I will take care of her, sah. Two an' more years of working as a conductor, an' I ain't never lost no passenger yet! When I first seen you two t'gether I thought you wa' husband an' wife."

"She's a widow."

The African suddenly seemed sympathetic. "I see you' worry, sah. If I done thought there was any real danger of discovery, I won't do it. But we got ourselves a good system up on the mountain. It's you out on the pike what's more likely to encounter trouble than we."

"I can be careful. There is no reason she has to go with the child. She will have to leave him today or tomorrow."

Simeon countered him softly. "I'm sure not one for caterin' to children, sah, but that sickly little boy does seem to care 'bout her in a most peculiar way."

Charles did not like the expression on Simeon's face. The black man looked down.

"I hope you don't take no offense, sah. With Missus Ruskin's eyes an' hair so dark, in the night I do believe anybody could think she wa' one of us."

"No one had better encounter you in the night! If you think it is the remotest possibility, then you have the responsibility to tell that woman to stay here!"

"Her goin' might just save the boy. Give him the will he needs to survive the mountain." He looked with searching eyes, as though to see how much this mattered to Charles. Both men then glanced to the house, for they heard the door opening. Mayleda Ruskin stepped out alone. Simeon nodded in a knowing, nearly fatherly, sort of way, though they were much the same age. "There. You can speak with the lady now, you'self. Direct."

Charles watched Mayleda come down the steps toward the wagon after Simeon stepped off into the darkening twilight. "I must see to my horses," Charles said, feeling awkward to have her come near. He started working with a harness buckle, though he had not done so while talking with Simeon Bart.

"Sister Bart has some soup for you inside." Mayleda came close enough to look at him in the dusk. "Are you opposed to eating with Negroes?"

He did not answer her directly. "When I travel, I take what I need for my team and myself. This journey is no different."

Her gaze turned sad. He changed the topic. "How is the boy?"

"He's sleeping right now. Brother Catos is with him."

Then she changed the subject too. "These are beautiful animals you have." Without hesitation, she moved ahead to Marcy's head and put the mare's soft nose between her hands. She spoke some quiet indistinguishable words to the animal in a show of real affection for the horse before she turned back to him. "I want to thank you so much for bringing us this far."

He wanted to say that she shouldn't go farther, yet he found himself talking about his mares instead. "Mrs. Ruskin, I'm surprised you're not afraid of these big creatures. You'd never guess how many are."

She smiled in the weak light that came out through the windows. "I was the only girl in my family. My three older brothers and my daddy were all excellent horsemen, so they all agreed that I must ride. I think they had me in the saddle before I could talk." She laughed. "But I enjoyed it immensely even then, I am sure."

He dared to reveal some of the past he knew about her from reports in the newspapers published during the time when the Ruskins had taken her off the streets and sequestered her in their house. "Mrs. Ruskin, I don't think of Boston families as having horses."

Her gaze turned soft and even sadder. "I'm not really from Boston, Mr. Powell. I was just living there when I met Sprague."

It seemed that she might be wanting to open the way for more intimate conversation, but Charles was afraid he might be misreading her based on his own strong desire to know her better. For that reason he spoke of nothing personal. "It's odd that you should have started out liking horses, when I started out not liking them at all."

She said she was eager to hear why. That made him painfully self-conscious. "Well, when I started working for Brother Peabody, I was only a boy and terrified of his big team. I used to stand outside their stalls and pray before daring to go in."

When she laughed this time, it made him long to protect her. It made him willing to speak his mind. "Mrs. Ruskin, I must say I think you might be increasing the danger to these people by going to Oak Glen. If the boy is content with Catos now, can't it be that way through the night and into tomorrow? Then I can take you to the train from here. Pleasant Points has a station, and there is an eastbound express train, I think, that runs before dawn."

If it had been possible, he would've taken her to the city himself, but it was true that they should not be seen together by anyone who knew either one of them. She frowned, and he sensed she might be judging him. "I am the sort of man who must speak his mind," he explained, in case she thought he was meddling. "If something happened to you on the mountain or while you were in Oak Glen, I would blame myself for not having protested your choice."

A hardness beset her face. "Do you fear for my safety because of those who might stop us from helping a slave, or do you fear for me because

Oliver Catos and Simeon Bart are Negroes?"

He knew he did fear both. Her bold confrontation made him feel instantly wrong, though he did not believe that he was. He did not want to offend her or mar her innocence, but neither did he want to dismiss a danger that was real. It was awkward and rude to speak of sexual matters, yet there was no brother or husband or father here to guard her. He tried to choose the most delicate language possible. "Mrs. Ruskin. It *is* said of Negro men that they are—"

"You stop right now! People are people, sir! They and their actions cannot be classified by the color of their skin! Do you see Brother Catos rushing out to be my defender because he mistrusts *you* being here with me in the dark? Do you want Simeon Bart to accuse you, after he is willing to have you stay here with his family and with his wife?"

"Of course not! Please!" He was appalled, for though he had tried to speak with modesty, she had gone right to the sordid point. "I know my own intentions, ma'am. They are pure."

"Then, please, have the courtesy for *your* brothers in the faith to think the same of them!"

He had never seen so much fight, so much passion inside one human being. Instead of discouraging him from any other words, her brave transparency made him willing to say more. "What about the child? Tomorrow you will have to leave him, so why not tonight? Are the risks you want to take truly worth what you can gain by being with the boy just a few more hours?"

Tears filled her eyes. "I made a promise to Little Lamb that I would not leave him until he was with Dr. Whitsun and until I had explained where his sister went in death." She took a breath and looked away. "Honestly, I don't have the courage to speak of death now, for it is so possible that this child is going to die too. If so, then no one will have to explain heaven or the Almighty Father's mercy toward him. He will see it and know it for himself. But if he lives—"

"Can't you just release him to Catos? Perhaps you have not thought enough about what could happen to you and those men if they are discovered with you, Tyrone Ruskin's daughter-in-law and Anthony Ruskin's sister-in-law."

Their answer came from outside of them both, for just then one of the Bart children started down the porch stairs and came around the corner to the wagon's edge. "Sister May?" the young girl called out with timidity. "The little boy's cryin' an' callin' you by name."

Mayleda delayed a moment. "It's not just for him that I want to stay with him." She wiped her eyes. "There's something inside me too. When Sprague died, I was not with him." She closed her fist against her mouth. "I've always regretted that, Mr. Powell. So often I dream of being there in that moment when he slips from this life. With this child now, I may have the chance to do that, to hold him as he moves from earth to heaven." She covered her face.

Charles wanted to touch her and hold her, for she seemed like someone walking near the edge of a dangerous precipice, yet he knew he had no invitation from her to be the one to offer her comfort. In truth, any touch might have been for his sake, not for hers.

She dropped her hands and again brought herself close to the velvet of his horse's face. "You think I'm wrong in wanting to be with the child. You think I'm foolish."

"I know you are not foolish. As far as being wrong, I do not know. Dr. Ellis would say that if it is God's will, you cannot judge the rightness by the consequences. Yet I greatly fear the consequences of your going."

"I think am doing this for the right reasons. If the boy does die, I can be with him. If he lives, I can show him that there is a place where black children can be free. The Ellises have told me how Dr. Whitsun and the pastor there, Reverend Brown, have established both a school and a church. My prayer is that some family in the town will take Little Lamb. Then he can be happy."

The little colored girl was still a short distance from them. "Ma'am? I was asked to call you in."

Mayleda took Charles' hand and squeezed it. "I thank you for your honesty and for your concern for me once again. I would ask that you accept the Barts' hospitality with grace, and that you know it is God's will that we be like one family in His kingdom because of the same faith we all share."

He said nothing as she went away. Within moments Simeon Bart drove his cart to the porch steps. Then the farmer went inside. Soon he brought out both Mayleda and Catos. Catos carried the boy, then handed him to Simeon. Charles continued to watch from a distance. Catos climbed into the cart's narrow bed, and Simeon gave the child back to him. Mayleda put a scarf over her bonnet and pulled her cloak about her, much in the same fashion as when he used to see her travel through the streets with her friend Harriet Mason.

It reminded Charles that Mayleda had been discovered once, much to the Ruskin family's incredible dismay and disapproval. It made him think that it could happen again. Still he said nothing. Not even good-bye. The cart, pulled by one lean horse, rolled off toward the forest and away from the pike. The same little girl soon came out to him again. "Mama wants to know if you will eat here, sah."

He had never partaken of food or drink with anyone of color. Yet now he said, "Yes, I will come in."

CHAPTER 13

THE LOFT IN JOSEPH'S HOUSE was always cold, autumn to spring, but usually he had no trouble sleeping. He had one of the two windowless rooms there. Ba had the other. Yet this night Joseph lay awake. Finally he got up, feeling it was a waste of time to be in bed, but he was so restless that he could not even pray.

Without light he went down the ladderlike stairs to the front room, full of blue shadows invited in by the moon. Only after he was in the kitchen did Joseph light one candle. He sat down at the table, conscious of the wall clock that ticked like a young healthy heart. It showed him that soon it would be dawn.

The stove still warmed the room, and Joseph was still in his clothes from yesterday, for early in the evening he had fallen asleep on his bed pondering what he should do about Cummington Brown's suggestion that he write down the story of his past.

He had wavered slightly from his original private promise to never tell any of it to anyone, though he did remain convinced that he would never share it in full. Yet he had carried down the empty journal book and the pencil that had been his bedside tormentors. He had thought much about other former slaves who now were publishing their testimonies or traveling around the North to speak about them so that more white folks might be won to the cause of abolition.

From his own observations, he concluded that white audiences had an insatiable desire to hear about the physical horrors of bondage, but that such hearing was slow to be translated into meaningful action. Right now, even a *white* woman, Harriet Beecher Stowe, was torturing the nation's heart with her fiction called *Uncle Tom's Cabin, or Life Among the Lowly*, which was being printed chapter by chapter in a national newspaper. Joseph wondered how colored men and women were able to tell their own stories so boldly, letting their private sufferings become fodder for public spectacle.

Grief coated his throat as he considered how Northern ladies might dab their eyes and Northern gentlemen might shake their heads upon hearing the specifics of his own twenty-one years as a slave. Their faces would go red if he spoke about his wife, haunted and hunted by a licentious master nearly to the hour of her death. But what good would it do? In Philadelphia he had been among gawking audiences most interested to see physical scars—as though *scars* were the only proof of slavery's horror.

At these very meetings, however, Northern white abolitionists had often not been willing to sit in the same row with him, eat with him, or speak with him as a fellow human being. Until that changed, Joseph could not believe that putting one more story out there—his own—would serve any purpose in helping to end slavery.

He put the pencil down to hold one hand inside the other, for he was trembling. There were wonderful exceptions, of course, among the white population, and he took comfort in thinking on them. Dr. and Mrs. Ellis—to those two he had bared his heart about everything except that of loving and losing Rosa. Ba, too, knew his past. The man sleeping upstairs even knew that he had been married, though he did not know how Rosa had died.

Spreading his fingers, Joseph touched the cool paper to bring himself back to the quiet present. Despite the anxiety within him, he went on to consider a more reasonable and responsible cause for recording his testimony. It concerned the need for education to undo slavery's stronghold of ignorance. Many did come out of bondage with their minds and spirits mangled.

Joseph steeled himself, almost as he had done before working on Cyrus's hand, so that he could go on thinking how he might encourage others by the printed word. With the advent of faster, cheaper presses, and with more and more black men and women learning how to read, Negro publications were creating a sense of African community nationwide. Information and inspiration could be carried on paper all through the North and even into Canada West, where many colored individuals now were residing.

There was even hope that newspapers smuggled South might give literate Negroes there the stamina to go on in the fight for manhood. Joseph remembered his own youthful years. Seeing slavery condemned in *The Liberator* had made him feel the rightness of the cause and power for the struggle. All this had inspired him to write down a few lines before falling asleep last night: *Education is essential for the elevation of my people, physically, mentally, but also spiritually. Education should be offered to every individual, regardless of gender or economic standing.*

These were not original thoughts, but rather parts of the philosophy he had learned from Daniel Alexander Payne. When he tried now to write that man's name, his hand shook again. Yet he felt determined to complete an article, even if it took him days. It would be good to honor Payne, for so many in the North knew him now. To do so rightly, some things from Joseph's past would have to be revealed. He considered that he could write over an anonymous signature but say the truth, that he had been a slave. The power of his words would have to come from his experiences, so that readers would know he was not just speculating on being bound to ignorance and then loosed by Christ-centered education. He would need to give facts and commend Payne specifically.

Almost monthly, colored solicitors passed through Oak Glen to collect fees from readers such as Pastor Brown who subscribed to Frederick Douglass's newspaper and to other periodicals. Joseph now had more than a glimmer of interest in getting something ready for the next traveling salesman, since these men carried news and submissions back to the editors. A few months ago Angelene had sold an original poem in this way through a solicitor for the *Gospel Weekly*. She now eagerly waited to see her work printed.

Joseph's mind stayed on her. He twisted the pencil. The heart of his struggle was still on what he should or should not say to her. From the first until now he continued to believe that revealing his secrets fully would destroy her lovely mind and her hopeful spirit. Yet he did not feel free to write something for the press if he would not at least do something for her first. Because she read nearly everything to which her father subscribed, it was likely that she would read whatever he wrote for print. And because she discussed so many things with him, it was likely that she would come to him with his own words in her hand. Then it would be too late for honesty, he reasoned. If he told her some things now, he could have control over what he said in order to shield her.

After this night of anguished thought, he felt he could tell her that he had been a slave and that God had freed him. He would do the telling much as he had done with Cummington and with Ba, stopping before he would say things that could wound her tenderness or defile her thoughts.

Having done this for her, then, he could in clear conscience go on to write about education and Africans to further the cause to which he had already dedicated himself. Clutching the pencil, he began. *I, Joseph, was born a slave on Whitsunday morning, 1814, in South Carolina, on a plantation called Delora.*

The moon had lighted their way over the mountain. Now it directed them onto the one narrow street coming out of a steep wooded hillside to a sleepy hamlet, stark and still, surrounded by fields and the crown of forest.

Mayleda saw lights burning in two windows as Brother Bart drove between the rows of odd-sized homes. A lamp shown from a second-story window of the tall house on their right. Its purpose even in this pre-dawn hour seemed clear, to illuminate two beautiful quilts and the sign advertising that they were for sale. She thought it odd that the house owner would spare the oil needed to let the lamp burn all night.

The other light was on her left, making gold the windowpanes in a low cabin that stood connected to a dark square building. "That's our school," Bart said to her and to Oliver, who was behind them in the cart bed with Little Lamb on his lap. "An' that sandstone buildin' we done just passed, that's our church, Mt. Hope. This all used to be a white settlement in the days when Lancaster County was the wild frontier."

"Who's house is that now?" Mayleda asked, referring to the one with the quilts in the window.

"Why, that's the pastor's house, Cummington Brown's. He's the one that bought the land to start Oak Glen. He's got a wife, Azal, an' a daughter, Angelene, that still lives at home with them. An' this house here beside the school is Joseph Whitsun's. He's got a deaf man livin' with him, a Mista Barnabas Croghan." Simeon looked at her. "He's white."

Mayleda wished the boy could see what she was seeing now. Simeon stopped the cart, then handed her the reins while he jumped down. He helped Brother Catos out first, then came back to her. With the men, Mayleda hurried up to the porch and stood outside. Simeon knocked. Surprisingly, a slender man in country dress opened the door in a moment. Quickly and efficiently as a trained practitioner, Oliver summarized their reasons for coming here from Dr. Ellis's infirmary, including the child's state as a fugitive.

"Come in at once." The slim Negro welcomed them with concern and compassion. "Instead of examining the boy here, I want to start off somewhere else. School will begin in just a few hours, and we won't want that kind of commotion being so close by." The man looked to Simeon. "Brother Bart, please go get the pastor. Tell him that I've gone down ahead to Widow Sladder's to see about using one of the rooms upstairs."

After both these men scattered, Mayleda spoke to Oliver alone and fearfully. "Is the boy still breathing?"

"Yes." Oliver moved so that Mayleda could see the child's face. "The trip was not so bad as I expected. But I still think it is pain that keeps him unconscious."

She touched the blankets as Oliver continued to hold the boy in his arms. "I hope he can soon know that we are here."

Oliver sighed gloomily. "It will get worse for him before it can get better."

Mayleda met the worry in his eyes. He was speaking of the need for surgery, she was certain. "I know."

Practitioner Whitsun soon was back, wearing no coat nor a hat to cover his short graying hair. "There is a room being readied. If you all will come this way."

Oliver and Mayleda left the house and walked into the street. They headed toward the mountain on foot, passing the school, then the church on their left. They stopped in front of an old dwelling that had it corners sinking and many of its window frames askew. Without knocking, the local practitioner led them in.

They stepped into a kitchen with a narrow banistered stairway set against a side wall. There were many children sleeping like sacks of grain on the floor in front of a huge hearth. They ascended as quietly as possible so as not to disturb the family. Mayleda soon understood why the children were by the fire, for the air upstairs was cold and stagnant. They entered a dark room, the second one to their right.

There was a low rectangular parlor stove within. A woman and a sleepy lad were putting in kindling to keep a new blaze going. The woman's eyes met Mayleda's. It seemed that perhaps long ago her face had been etched with worries that remained close to her still. A white cap completely covered her hair, helping to make it impossible for Mayleda to guess her age, whether she might be the mother or the grandmother of these many offspring.

"Hello, I am Mayleda Ruskin," she introduced herself, first name and last without any titles, as was her practice with everyone. "I want to thank you so much for helping us tonight."

"Call me Widow Sladder," the woman said with no expression in her words or countenance.

Being widowed herself, Mayleda was surprised that the other woman chose to carry the description as part of her name. The little boy beside her seemed to give insight about that at once. "The ten oldest children in this house are Aunty's. The five youngest belonged to my mama but she's gone away."

"I see," Mayleda responded awkwardly, feeling compassion for the young speaker. "Well, I thank you so much for making the fire for us. The little boy we have with us is very, very ill."

"Is he yours, ma'am?" the child asked.

"Oh no!" She answered quickly, but then grew silent, for Simeon Bart had already warned her that not everyone in Oak Glen knew about the Underground Railroad. Joseph Whitsun and another boy from the house came in carrying a table. The one bed in the room was pushed aside so that the table could be centered under the hook in the ceiling from which a light could be hung. Several glowing lamps were brought in by Pastor Brown, who introduced himself. After lights were put everywhere, the doctors made their first examination in the stark but wavering brightness.

Little Lamb was conscious, though his eyes were dull. His lips were dry and parted. Mayleda drew near. It was grievous to see him suffering and growing worse by the moment. It seemed that the boy saw her and knew her, but no sound came from his mouth. Practitioner Whitsun's words did not surprise her. "There's not much hope for survival."

Mayleda held her breath, determined not to cry and not to be so discouraged as to neglect her prayers. The men decided to remove the bone fragments and do what they could to repair the lung.

"I am a nurse," she said to the doctor she did not know. "I am ready to help in whatever way I can."

Practitioner Whitsun glanced at her, for the first time meeting her eye to eye. "We will need your help, ma'am."

"I am Mayleda Ruskin," she said to him, as she had done with Widow Sladder. His eyes stayed fixed on her for a moment, perhaps reflecting his weariness in this predawn hour.

"I am Joseph Whitsun."

Brother Catos removed his coat. She took off her cloak, scarf, bonnet, and shawl. For lack of another table, two chairs were brought in to hold the surgical supplies that Whitsun had had the same boy go back to his house to retrieve. The practitioners' talk turned to the bone fragments that were piercing through the skin.

Little Lamb turned his face to Mayleda. He drew his knees and wrists together to show how he endured the pain in silence. He looked at her as if she were his only source of comfort. "I cannot imagine how he suffers so much, yet never cries," she said, hardly able to stop her own tears.

At once Practitioner Whitsun spoke. "He's been a slave, ma'am. Look at the marks on him. He learned early that to whimper or complain would only bring more of the same to his body."

She stroked the child's hair, then bowed to kiss his forehead. "It will not be so for you anymore!" she told him. "What will happen next will hurt more than anything you may have gone through before, but then, Little Lamb, there will be rest and healing. We are in Oak Glen. This is Dr. Whitsun. When you are well, he will show you the church and the school. I've seen them!"

Whitsun looked at her again. This time she was the one who delayed in pulling her vision away.

The pastor spoke to Oak Glen's practitioner. "Brother Joseph, do you want me to awaken Angelene?"

Mayleda found herself unable to look anywhere but to Joseph Whitsun's face while he answered. "No. Let her rest. I have Brother Catos here and Nurse Ruskin. If we are successful, then Angelene will be needed often during the long convalescence." He said one more thing to the pastor. "Brother Brown, will you pray?"

Because Little Lamb stared at her, Mayleda could not bear to close her eyes. He seemed to understand completely that these men would use their tools to open his flesh.

When Pastor Brown said amen, Joseph Whitsun spoke to Widow Sladder, who stood at the hallway door. "I want all the children kept downstairs until this is over."

Simeon Bart came in as she was leaving. He reported that he had concealed his cart and horse in the pastor's barn. This met with their approval.

Joseph Whitsun began to speak to the child. His words drew Little Lamb's attention from Mayleda to himself. He spoke of the excruciating pain that would follow the surgery while at the same time taking hold of the child's limp left hand to examine the scar that formed a *V* that someone, at some time, had branded on his small palm. There was another dreadful mark to match it on the boy's right shoulder.

"With God's help," Dr. Whitsun said, "this suffering will not be like a branding or a whipping. It will bring you health, but we must be patient to wait for it afterward, for it may take some time to come. Are you willing, lad?" The doctor squeezed the little hand between his own hands, his darker, more slender fingers still extended.

The doctor's hands had been shaking, but now they were still. However, Mayleda then saw the muscles in Joseph Whitsun's face draw so tight that they twitched as he set his jaw. It made her stop breathing. Long ago her father's favored manservant on Delora Plantation would have the same thing happen whenever he was in full concentration. *And the name of that slave had been Joseph.*

"Sister Ruskin?" Joseph Whitsun's call startled her.

"Yes?" She saw then that the child had been nodding his consent. The boy's interminable gasping changed to horrendous coughing that made him draw his knees to his chest. The Oak Glen doctor waited for this to pass. "Do you think you can hold his legs? It is essential that he not move."

"Yes." She quavered inwardly.

"Pastor, you come and hold him at the shoulders. Brother Simeon, you take his hands."

Mayleda moved numbly. She leaned over the child after Mr. Whitsun had gently reextended his limbs. She pressed her hands close to the boy's knees, ready to put her full weight upon him if needed. She forced herself to watch and be ready. Another moment and Little Lamb began to scream.

"Sister May! MAY! MAY!"

CHAPTER 14

WHEN THE LONG ORDEAL WAS OVER, Joseph watched Oliver Catos wipe his hands clean. Weary, the young man sat down directly on the floor. Mayleda Ruskin, the white woman, glanced to Joseph, then hastened to leave the unconscious child while she took one of the pillows from the bed and also a cover.

These she gave to Oliver, who accepted them with a painful sigh. "Rest now, Brother," Mayleda said with great compassion, giving Joseph the impression that she and Oliver were friends. Without another thought, it seemed, the younger man stretched out and almost instantly was asleep.

"He has been up since before dawn yesterday," Mayleda said, turning back to Joseph. "First he was sent by Dr. Ellis to find a driver to take us from the city. Then he helped to build the hiding place in the wagon. And since then, he's been looking after the boy."

On the floor, Catos was already softly snoring. The woman returned back to the child. She had been strong and unflinching through the whole horrific ordeal, and she seemed alert and tireless now, though she must have gone without sleep too. Joseph thought about the doctors in New England and elsewhere who were beginning to experiment with drugs that could safely make patients unaware of their pain. It would be years, maybe decades, until countrymen like himself might have such chemicals and training.

He shuddered at the sight of the little boy's abdomen, horribly bruised, and now stitched again. He grasped his hands tightly, not trusting them to be still without some force upon them. The woman offered her help once more when Joseph finally moved to bind the child's torso firmly with a new dressing and white bandages. After that, he could do nothing more for his young patient. Still he continued to stand there, allowing himself to glance once more at the woman who had helped him. Her dark hair and eyes unnerved him, as did her name: Mayleda.

In every way but age she reminded him of his former master's daughter, who had been only fifteen when he had fled the South. Already at that age she had saved his life more than once and had vowed that she would not live her whole life where slavery reigned. Dropping his view of her sad countenance, he silently calculated that sixteen years had gone by since his leaving, so Mayleda Callcott would be older than thirty now, and so was this woman, he guessed.

To pull himself from his disquieting thoughts, he spoke to Pastor Brown, who was still in the room. "The next few hours will be a time of waiting," he said. "Perhaps you could take Brother Bart and Mrs. Ruskin down to give them some breakfast while the young practitioner sleeps. I am sure Ba would be willing to cook some ham and cakes for everyone."

Cummington stretched his shoulders stiffly while grimly looking at the boy, whose lips were blue. His mouth opened as though he were running out of strength to pull in air. Joseph was grateful when the pastor chose to pray aloud again before asking their two guests to join him for some food and rest.

"Thank you, but I need nothing!" the woman said, showing more of her great resiliency. "I would rather stay here."

"Then you at least need a chair," the pastor said, moving one that Joseph had used during the surgery. He said to Joseph, "You need one too." By then Mayleda Ruskin had moved to wrap the soiled instruments into one cloth so that the second chair would also be available.

Joseph took his advice and sat down after the woman did so. Within moments he found himself alone and face-to-face with Mayleda Ruskin, as Oliver still slept behind them.

"You did a marvelous thing," the woman said. "Dr. Ellis assured me that the child would be in the best of hands with you, and he is."

Joseph sighed, wholly exhausted, but still absolutely undone by her likeness to the girl from his past. "God's hands were in it more than mine, or the boy would not be living now!" Joseph laced his fingers, grateful that they were still steady.

"With the weakness and the pneumonia, I had little hope," she admitted.

He looked at her fully. "Truthfully, so did I. There's no doubt that God has intervened on his behalf."

Even her smile held no surprises. The beautiful pink lips that once belonged to Mayleda Callcott showed themselves now on this older stranger. Joseph dare not look at them, for fear of what the woman would think of him.

"I knew you would be a man of faith!" she said.

He spoke of the child. "You call him Little Lamb. What is his name?"

"He won't say. Or perhaps he doesn't even know. He has spoken only a few words, which makes me wonder even more about his past. The day I found him, his sister died leaping from the window with him. He did not trust me, then, but he did trust my Negro friend, Harriet Mason." She paused, perhaps uncomfortable that she had spoken about color. "I wonder about his relationship with his sister. He does know how they were related, but he's never mentioned her by name."

"Many times, ma'am, slavery is so inhumane as to be beyond all understanding."

She looked at him as though seeing into his soul. "I know."

Joseph glanced away. "Well, if he awakes, I suggest that we call him Daniel. Brave Daniel, for he's suffered much."

"Yes! He should have a strong Christian name!" It seemed that she wanted to say more. "Sir? Do you think there will be a family here to take him? As Brother Catos told you, we believe that no one will come looking for him. I saw the slave catchers who had him, but I think they chose not to follow us, either believing that his injuries would render him useless or would take his life."

"We will do our best to help him." Joseph felt his words were not enough. He found himself wanting this time of privacy with her to last, yet knowing that it could not, for soon the others would return. For that reason he dared asking directly about her. "Ma'am, how long have you been a nurse at Dr. Ellis's infirmary? I don't think I ever saw you there, but that is where I studied before I came here."

"So I've heard." Now she seemed hesitant. "I started in the fall of 1844. That was nearly two years after my husband's passing. Perhaps you knew him, for he was in the city longer than I. His name was Sprague. We met in Boston while I was living there with friends."

Joseph's nerves prickled. He almost wanted to guess aloud those friends' names, for Mayleda Callcott of South Carolina had had friends in Boston too. Instead he spoke of her husband. "Madam, I did know of Sprague Ruskin."

That seemed to comfort and please her. "I am so glad!"

"I never met him, but I know enough to say that he was a man to be thanked by all in my race. So now you are continuing to help others as he did." He felt himself smile.

Again she seemed pleased. "As much as a woman can do, sir, in this day." She brushed away a tear. "I love God and I trust Him, but sometimes I still struggle with why He let Sprague die when he had such a heart for unity among all Christian people. And such vision."

Joseph did not resist looking deep into her pain, for it matched his own exactly. "I understand, Mrs. Ruskin. My precious wife drowned sixteen years ago. Sometimes the grief and disappointment are as fresh now as they were then."

Her dark eyes grew wide. "I had a friend, long ago, whose wife drowned."

In that moment he could not stop staring at her. He felt he had to take more risk. "Ma'am, I'm interested in your name. I once knew another Mayleda. When she was a girl."

"Oh, I once knew another African named Joseph, though that is not so uncommon a name! He was the widower I just mentioned."

"Mayleda Callcott." He said it very softly.

She responded in a breath, raising her hands, then her arms. "Joseph! Are you Joseph from Delora?"

"I am, Mayleda!"

"Oh, how can it be!" She was out of the chair to throw her arms around him. "Oh, I knew you had to have passed through Philadelphia, but I thought you were dead!" She kept holding on to him. "Then this day, everything about you was just the same as the Joseph I knew and loved so many years ago. I've been watching you so intensely, all these hours!"

He gently took her hands from around his neck, then he stood, still holding to them in the decorous manner of a close friend. "Your face. Your eyes. Your hair. It was the same for me. I knew you at once, really, yet I could not believe it."

"I thought you were dead!" she said again.

He helped her to sit back down. "How could you know anything about me? I never told your brother Brant where I planned to go."

"I left Charleston the summer I turned eighteen. I ran away to keep my promise about shunning slavery. The Gilmans kept me for a year. They are good people, but they did not understand my heart. In Boston I saw the races still divided. That is not the kind of equality I had dreamed of in the South."

"I do understand."

"Mr. Gilman was good about hiring Negroes, but the family does not think it odd that they should not be friends with them. They do not expect that Africans will become equals in this land of opportunity, nor do they work to that end. Then I met Sprague. . . ."

She cried silent tears, and Joseph with her.

"Sprague understood. It was his vision, too, to have Negro friends and even a colored partner in business. He lived to make that dream come true, though his dear African friend, Collin, died with him in the accident that claimed his life."

"How did you get from Boston to Philadelphia?"

"We were married in Boston without his parents knowing it. Or my brothers either. Yet Sprague's family is from Philadelphia, so after our daughter, Judith, was born, we decided to move there so that they could know their grandchild. They never really accepted our marriage, though they immediately loved our daughter, and they never accepted Sprague's goals and his vision. It's a long story, but that is where Judith and I live now—with his family."

There was no doubting the discomfort shown by her face. "What about you, dear Joseph? If you were in Philadelphia then, where were you?"

"In the winter of '41 I found a sickly deaf man. It became my focus to learn the manual language taught by Thomas Gallaudet in Connecticut. I first learned about his work through abolitionist friends, for Gallaudet was concerned about justice and the Negro. The good man passed away just weeks ago."

"This deaf man, he lives with you now. Brother Bart told us."

"Yes."

She was fighting tears again. "So we never met in Philadelpha, though we might have. That surely would have eased my pain concerning thoughts of you."

"You said twice that you thought I was dead. Why?"

"I found my father's Bible. I knew you would not just give it up."

"I would not have! Oh, Mayleda, how was it returned to you?"

"Well, soon after Sprague and I came to the city, his family put an announcement about our marriage in the papers even though it was more than two years after the ceremony and even though they were less than pleased about our union. In that article they published my maiden name, Callcott. It wasn't long until a bookseller came to our door by night with a Bible, my father's Bible, because he had seen my name printed on the page were Daddy recorded all our family's births and deaths."

"Oh, you must know that I never would have given that Bible up by choice!"

"Joseph, I did know! That's why I had to think the worst! That something awful had happened to you in Philadelphia."

Now she waited for him to speak.

"When I sailed from Charleston I came directly to the city, but the disease in my lungs from my time in the workhouse flared on that journey," Joseph began. "When I arrived, I was so ill that I don't even remember how I got to shore. I was carried to Bethel church. Some colored Quakers called on Dr. Ellis to help me. By then I had lost every possession, except my freedom paper, which I had tied around my arm with the piece of cloth Mama Jewell had cut for me from the hem of her dress."

"So you were Doctor Ellis's patient before you were his student!"

"Yes. I was in bed nearly a year. The Ellises cared for me." His eyes welled with tears, and so did Mayleda's.

"Oh, Joseph, I know about your story. The Ellises have told me, but they always referred to you as Brother Whitsun, for you know how Dr. Ellis is about using names. Oh, to see you! I cannot believe it! I can't think of a greater joy than to know that Little Lamb—I mean, Daniel—has come to you!"

Yet when she spoke of joy, she started sobbing. "Oh, and now I know your pain, at least in losing Rosa. I was a girl when I cried at her grave.

Since then I have lost the dearest one that life could give me."

He resisted putting his hands on her shoulders while she wept. "I am so sorry for you, Mayleda. I do not believe there can be any grief sharper than that of losing a beloved spouse!"

"Joseph! I cannot believe this moment!" She rose to her feet. "That God would let me bring this child to you!"

He was standing and she instantly pressed herself against his chest, hiding her sorrowful face in his vest. He might have put his arms around her then. It seemed so natural to touch her, for he felt such deep affection, but then he saw Widow Sladder pass by the door.

It caused him to draw back so quickly that Mayleda almost lost her balance. She sensed his discomfort. "Oh, Dr. Whitsun. I-I didn't mean anything! I hope I didn't do anything to offend—"

The very next moment, the doorway was free of Widow Sladder's prowling eyes. Now again only the sleeping Oliver Catos was with them. Joseph tried to speak freely, but he felt too much caution. "No, Mrs. Ruskin."

"Before, you called me Mayleda!"

Joseph still watched the hallway. "Mayleda, there is so much I want to know, so much I want to say, but it is unwise for us to be here like this, even as it would have been unwise in the South."

He knew it was futile to seek out Widow Sladder then for the purpose of explaining. As had so many others in Oak Glen, she had served her time in slavery. Telling her that the moment of intimacy she saw was the result of a former plantation mistress meeting her past slave would do nothing but make matters worse for them both. He did not want to worry Mayleda, so he kept his silence with her too.

As Mayleda stepped back, he glanced to the child, whose condition seemed unchanged. "If you can agree to it, I would like to go find Pastor Brown. He would listen in confidence, I know, and protect us from any rumors that might spring up from how deeply we desire to speak to one another in private."

"All right," she said, shivering slightly. "I understand the wisdom in that."

"Then I'll go look for him while you watch the boy. Awaken Brother Catos if there's any need for help."

"Yes, Joseph. I will. Oh, thank God. To see you alive and following your dreams to be a doctor!"

———————

Mayleda did not speak to Brother Catos right away when he awoke from his slumber. Her mind still felt so divided between the sorrows of watching Daniel and the joys of anticipating that she was going to be able to know Joseph again after all these years, now as a free man. When Joseph returned, he had the pastor with him. One look to Joseph seemed enough to tell him that she had said nothing to Oliver about their incredible meeting. Daniel remained unconscious.

Joseph looked at the child, then at the younger man still seated on the floor. "Brother Catos, do you mind staying with the boy? I would like Mrs. Ruskin to meet with Pastor Brown and me for a time."

The young man agreed, seeming to think nothing more than it was his turn to be on duty. At Pastor Brown's suggestion that they go to Joseph's house, Mayleda donned her bonnet, scarf, and cloak before following the men downstairs. Pastor Brown kept himself between the two of them as they went out by the back door. Mayleda saw that there were children in the kitchen, but she did not see the Widow Sladder.

They proceeded to Joseph's house through the rear yards, going into Joseph's kitchen by way of the still empty classroom, the hall, and then a front room. A white-haired man sat at the kitchen table taking the sprouts off potatoes that he had spread on sheets of newsprint. Joseph touched him before he was aware of their presence. The man stood then, nodding to her and to Pastor Brown. Mayleda watched with fascination while Joseph both spoke and signed her full name, using movements of his hands.

It caused the deaf man to raise a questioning brow while he responded with hand signs of his own. Then Joseph gave his explanation to her, moving his hands and fingers again. *"Ba recognizes your name, Mrs. Ruskin. He and I have been as close as brothers for ten years. He has told his past to me, and I have told my past to him, so he knows who the Callcotts are."*

Then for Pastor Brown's benefit, Joseph said even more. *"My pastor knows that I was a slave, but he does not know about your family, as Ba does."*

Mayleda's eyes dropped painfully. She knew that he was not accusing her, but in this company it did feel that way.

Pastor Brown must have understood the reasons for her unhappy discomfort. "I am very glad to meet you, Mrs. Ruskin," he said. "And I know that Joseph is overjoyed. Just this morning he's said some of the reasons why. How you saved him and stood by him. How you have fought slavery, even since your childhood. And how your father dared to manumit him despite the dangers of doing that."

She felt her calm nearly restored. When Joseph held a chair for her, she sat down. By then Ba, as Joseph called him, had put all the potatoes back into the basket and had folded up the papers so that the table was clean. He made signs that Joseph translated as his decision to go back to work in the barn. Mayleda sensed it was the old man's politeness that had him leaving them.

When Ba went outside, Joseph started the conversation right away. "It's been sixteen years since I last saw Mrs. Ruskin, whom I knew then as Mistress Mayleda Callcott," he told the pastor.

The minister nodded encouragement for him to keep on speaking. There was a sudden intensity as Joseph turned to her. "Mayleda. What of my mother, Jewell? Is she living still? Is she well?"

Mayleda felt sorry for the answer she had. "I don't know much, Brother Whitsun. What I do know, I will tell you. The summer I turned eighteen, I ran away from the Gibbes Street house. Since then, I have not written directly to my family. You see, I fear that Brant and Eric might have the power to force me back to South Carolina, especially now that I am a widow with a daughter.

"I do communicate to my brothers at least twice a year through the Gilmans. I send my letters to them, and so do Eric and Brant. Then our friends send the letters on so that we can reply to each another, but while they still cannot know where I am."

"Then tell me all that you do know!"

She found her voice faltering. "I think your mother must be well. I believe Eric would write and tell me otherwise. He is the one who speaks most often about the servants." She glanced to the pastor, but saw no condemnation in him. "I know that Jewell and my brother's wife's slave Corinth have divided Maum Bette's work." She closed her eyes. "Maum Bette died the summer I went away. That's one reason why I decided I could leave the South then."

She opened her eyes to find Joseph's face in his hands. "She didn't suffer. I know that. One night while on the back porch of the town house, she just sat down and died. Brant and Ann arranged for her body to be taken back to Delora. Her son Parris preached her funeral. I was there. She's buried near your Rosa."

She saw the pastor's head turn slightly.

"The morning I saw Delora for the last time, I put flowers on both their graves."

Joseph stood and faced the stove. When he could speak, he said. "Poor Billy Days, or has that saintly man crossed over too?"

"I don't think so." She was speaking to his back as Joseph kept his countenance hidden. "I know that Parris is married and that a few years ago his wife gave birth to twins, a boy and a girl. Eric has written that Billy is a doting grandfather who lets the children sleep in his featherbed."

Joseph turned and came back to his chair. Again she had the terrible sense that her words were inflicting pain, but there was nothing she could do to change the facts. "Eric is mostly in charge of the slaves now. From what Brant writes, I think he's investing himself mostly in breeding horses. With the Gilmans to help him, he's brought down a small sturdy breed of horse from New England to experiment with making them popular on southern farms."

She sighed to have to speak more about this real world of slavery. "I think Brant knows the truth about the wrongness of plantation life, but he will not cut himself off from its comforts or the leisure it provides."

"What is Eric like?"

Joseph's question sounded sharp, but she could not fault him for that. "I don't know how he treats the people. He writes to me about the slaves he knows I knew. He says nothing about the others."

Pure anguish marked Joseph's face.

Mayleda spoke to Pastor Brown. "You must think me a horrible person that my people still have claim on Negroes as slaves. I am sorry! I don't know what to do!"

"You do what you can do, ma'am. And you never neglect to pray that slavery will end."

"With all my heart, I do pray."

"Whatever happened to Theodore Rensler?" Joseph's cheek was twitching now.

"Linford Rensler died the winter I was sixteen. Teddy took over Pine Woods Plantation then. Brant would not hear to any kind of agreement or merger. I feel sure that that will never change."

Joseph sat down. "Is he still so cruel to Africans?"

"I don't know. That is not something that Eric is likely to tell me, and it's not something I have asked."

"You don't think Eric would follow his example? I mean with Rensler's cousin being your brother's wife."

"I don't know." She grimaced. "I pray not! Oh, I do beg both my brothers to seek after God and be selfless and merciful, but they never write back anything of a spiritual nature to me."

There was a silent pause, then Joseph turned his attention to her. Instead of asking another question, he spoke about her to Pastor Brown. "Sister Ruskin was married to Sprague Ruskin. Do you remember him?"

"I do," the pastor said. "I met him at various meetings, and certainly I heard much about his work. It shocked and grieved so many of us to learn of his passing."

Joseph said, "Sister Ruskin's been living with his family since that time."

"I did go to Boston for a time after the funeral," she explained. "Joseph's already heard my reasons for not wanting to stay there. The whole time I was there, I was exchanging letters with a close friend, the sister of the man Collin who died with my husband."

"A colored woman," the pastor clarified. "I remember meeting this man Collin too."

"Yes, well, Harriet and I decided that if Sprague and Collin's business of loaning was to survive, then we would have to take up the work ourselves. Without telling the Ruskins, I moved back into the city. I lived with my friend for one winter. We were wholly unsuccessful in continuing on with the work, I am sad to say."

The fact still caused her great pain. "That spring, Sprague's family discovered what I was doing. They came right to my house and took me away. They obtained a court order so that I could never take Judith to any permanent residence outside their house again until she is eighteen. They gave us a separate apartment in their house. Even so, I've had no freedom to live as I truly believe God wants us to live. They do let me work at Dr. Ellis's infirmary, only because they perceive that as being the charity associated with the Quaker meetings I attend." She looked at the pastor.

"But now you dare to come here, for the sake of this little boy!" he exclaimed.

"My husband's family and my child are in Europe. I felt God was directing me. A free-products merchant from the city, Charles Powell, drove us as far as Simeon Bart's house yesterday. I believe that Mr. Powell will come here to find me later today and take me to the train so that I can get back into the city on my own without calling attention to myself or to Mr. Powell."

She looked to Joseph. "I promised the boy, Daniel, that I would stay with him until he was safe in Oak Glen. I told him that when we arrived here, I would explain heaven to him, for, as I think you heard, Pastor Brown, his sister died when they jumped from the window." In speaking about Daniel, she felt compelled to go back to see him.

"Now it's clear that he may die. Explanations of heaven may be unnecessary." She moved her chair slightly. "I think I should be getting back to him."

Without warning the front door opened, and a young brown woman dressed in dark red came in with books in her arms.

Joseph stood at once. "Angelene, good morning. This is Mrs. Ruskin."

Her father spoke too. "You heard last night that Brother Bart brought in an injured passenger. That little boy is at Sister Sladder's house now with another practitioner trained by Dr. Ellis."

Mayleda also stood, not feeling much acceptance under the young woman's gaze. "Hello. I am Mayleda Ruskin."

"Angelene has been the teacher at our school for two years. She also works as my assistant in surgery," Joseph explained, but none of this seemed to warm Miss Brown's countenance.

Mayleda tried to speak from her heart, for what she said was quite sincere. "I am very glad to meet you, Miss Brown."

"I must get to the classroom," the woman responded. "The children come in by the rear door, and they will soon be here."

"We have classes on Saturdays in the autumn." Joseph's explanation sounded uneasy. The woman went toward the hallway and the schoolroom beyond. "That starts after the harvest and continues until Christmas."

"I think I should be getting back to the patient," Mayleda said, ready to excuse herself much as the man Ba had done before her because of the awkward feelings of the moment.

The pastor stood also. "Since the children will be coming, perhaps it's better that you go out the front way. It may cause less of a stir. We don't want to have more questions raised than necessary, for not everyone in our town knows about our activity to help runaways."

Mayleda voiced a question that had been on her mind. "How will you explain this boy's arrival then? How will you find a family to take him in while he gains back his strength?"

She saw the pastor look at Joseph, whose brows knitted with concern.

"We will tell the simple truth, ma'am," the pastor said. "That he was injured and without parents, and that he was brought to us by friends."

Without being asked to do so, Mayleda concealed the color of her face and hands by her outer garments. "I can find my own way back, sir, and I will take care not to cause distraction."

But Pastor Brown came right beside her. "I will walk with you back to Sister Sladder's."

Mayleda turned to say good-bye to Joseph, yet when she saw him standing so pensively, his eyes closed, she decided it better to slip away right then without more words.

CHAPTER 15

THE WIDOW SLADDER WAS HOME when Mayleda and Pastor Brown arrived at her door, and she let them into her house without speaking. Mayleda went directly upstairs to find Brother Catos standing over Daniel.

"I am glad you are back!" he exclaimed. "Every breath may be his last. I know you wanted to be with him at the end."

"Oh yes!" she replied.

The pastor came in too, prayed once more, then left them. Oliver suggested they move Daniel from the table to the bed so that his last moments could be as comfortable as possible. When Oliver put his hands under the boy's arms, Daniel whimpered. He opened his fever-darkened eyes.

"Little Lamb!" Mayleda mourned as she held her hands under his nearly weightless legs. "We're putting you to bed."

They laid him on the thin mattress in the dreary room, as most of the lamps had been turned out.

"Now that you're here, I'll bring up more wood for the fire and put things in order," Oliver offered. "You give him what comfort you can."

When Joseph climbed Widow Sladder's stairs, it was with a heavy heart. The pastor had come back to him to report on the child's low state. This was added to the distress he already felt in having just learned of Maum Bette's death and the continuing uncertainty around his mother's life as a slave. He also carried the burden of how Widow Sladder had looked in on them and of Angelene's unusual incivility toward Mayleda. Knowing Angelene so well, Joseph did not think it should have to do with Mayleda's race, but he could think of no other explanation as to why Angelene would have shown so much coolness toward the woman.

When he reached the top of the stairs, he heard Mayleda's sweet voice. She was singing a hymn that both of them had learned at Maum Bette's knee. It drew him to the room but not inside. Instead he stood in the doorway to watch from a distance. Oliver Catos was gone, and Mayleda was bending prayerlike over the child as she sat on the bed. She was wholly unaware of his eyes upon her as she sang.

> "I'm going to leave you in the hands of the kind Savior
> Going to leave you in his hands.
> Going to leave you in his hands. . . .
> Darling Daniel, oh my dear little Daniel,
> I'm going to leave you in the hands of the Lord."

He walked in when she paused, conscious that the table had been moved to one wall and that all his medical equipment had been put away. Mostly, however, he focused on his fear that the boy was dead. As a child, he had heard singing done with sadness just as often as with joy. Yet when Mayleda saw him, she smiled.

"I think he's thirsty," she said.

Joseph thought it unbelievable that the child could even be alert. He said this aloud to her. It increased her look of cautious joy. "You called him a Daniel. I think he likes the name. I have already told him a few of the Bible stories about Daniel. How he prayed. How he survived and prospered even among his enemies."

"How long has he been awake?"

"Nearly from the moment I walked in."

"Where is Brother Catos?"

"Getting firewood. For the widow's sake, he's splitting it himself in the rear yard. I thought you would have seen him."

"I came by the street." Joseph went closer to make an examination. He looked into the child's eyes. He felt his high temperature, his shallow pulse, the texture of his skin. He didn't say anything to Mayleda, but she spoke to him.

"Dr. Whitsun, we have also talked about heaven. Daniel is not afraid to die. He knows that he should look for his sister. And of course he will look for Jesus, who will open the gates of heaven for him. I do think he understands. I even told him to look for my Sprague and for your Rosa." She did not cry.

The little boy struggled to focus his eyes. "Wa-ter?"

Mayleda looked at Joseph for advice. Surely she knew from her training that it was too soon to give the child anything to drink. Joseph remembered poignantly what it was like to suffer thirst. From his experience as a doctor and from his studies, he knew that keenness and activity like this often preceded death. "Yes, Daniel, I will bring you water," he answered.

Mayleda watched as Joseph gently supported Daniel and helped him to drink from the cup he'd brought from the kitchen. Oliver was back from getting firewood, and he, too, watched Joseph's action. The scene reminded Mayleda of the sad weeks so many years ago when Joseph had tenderly cared for her invalid father. It showed her that despite all the trials and sorrows in his life, nothing had been able to destroy Joseph's empathy for those who suffered.

To communicate her gratitude and her admiration, she quoted from the Scriptures as well as she could remember: " 'Whosoever shall give to drink unto one of these little ones a cup of cold water . . . I say unto you, he shall in no wise lose his reward.' "

Joseph nodded to her, then spoke in Oliver's hearing. "I thank you, Mrs. Ruskin, for that encouragement." His formal manner told her what she already knew, that it was best that they keep their friendship and their pasts wholly secret.

The child lay back, still licking his cooler lips. "It won't hurt him, will it." She said it as a statement so that Joseph would know that she had a realistic view. Death was coming.

"No." Joseph answered, compassion showing from his face. "And neither will your kindness and your prayers. However he wants it to be now, quiet or with conversation, it is his time."

A bittersweet stillness followed, as though heaven might already be preparing the way. Little Daniel kept up his panting, but now with eyes closed. The ethereal peace was broken when the child began to retch. His little arms flew around his body. Surely he must have felt that his sutured abdomen would split wide.

Both Joseph and Oliver rushed to take hold of him, for Mayleda was terrified in the midst of his convulsing. Just as Daniel's collapse came, Mayleda realized that the house was full of sounds. Shouting. Crying. The pounding of feet on the stairs. Then in the hall.

At the same moment that Joseph looked around, she saw a white male in the doorway. Mayleda screamed, "Anthony!"

At once Mayleda tried to put distance between herself and the boy, quickly yet cautiously removing herself from the now still child. She got to her feet, and Joseph and Oliver stood close to her. Her brother-in-law strode directly to her. She was dazed by his coming. He gave an ugly look to Oliver, then to Joseph. Physically he trapped her by taking hold of her hands. "Don't touch me!" she protested, but it was useless.

Anthony pulled her to the center of the room, then close to the door. There was another white man coming in from the hall. At first her brother-in-law didn't seem to care about this other man, for his wrath was toward her. "What are you doing back in another house full of niggers? You wretch! You slut! Will you never change?"

He would not let her go. She was glad that the boy was behind her and dying. Otherwise he would have been terrified, and he would have been in danger, for behind the man she did not know, she saw two more faces, those of the slave agents whom she had seen in Dresden Alley.

"I have her!" Anthony proclaimed to the man who was a stranger. "That is Constable Long of the township," he said to her. "I alerted him to our search, and he came with us to be a witness to all that is transpiring now." Anthony then spoke to the slave catchers. "Your quarry is on the bed!"

She screamed with all her might, "Oh, God help us! There are slave catchers here!" She hoped it would warn Joseph and Oliver, though she knew the practitioners would be as helpless as she.

Anthony yanked her once more, pulling her all the way through the doorway to the hall. Putting himself behind her, he forced her to the stairs. She glimpsed Constable Long following them, carrying her bonnet and cloak. "These are yours, I presume," he said when they paused inside the front door until Anthony had it opened.

Anthony was unkind even to him. "I can take her from here." Her brother-in-law put her own cloak on her and pressed the hat to her head. "Constable, you have other duties to attend to!"

Mayleda knew this meant the child. They had come to get him, after all these hours. She realized then how incredibly shrewd they had been. Surely they had been following, secretly and silently, all the way. That meant that the Ellises, the Barts, the Browns, Joseph, and Oliver could all be in trouble. Even Charles Powell might be within their snare. She was afraid to ask anything. Afraid to even to look back.

When Anthony pulled her into the street, she saw Widow Sladder looking through the window. Anthony had a saddled horse tied to a ring outside. He forced her up to sit upon it. He freed it, then climbed into the saddle. Without a word, he took the reins and kicked the mount fiercely. She grabbed him around the waist. They galloped off through the town to the pike.

Joseph and Oliver stood their ground in front of Daniel's bed. It did no good, of course, though at first it seemed that young Constable Long was somewhat reluctant to order the two of them to move aside. When he did speak and they would not move, Long presented them with an official paper, a warrant making it legal by even white standards for Dawes and Pudget to be there, in this house, making their claim on the boy.

The slave agents themselves carried an authorized deposition of the master's description of the child and their right to take him for remanding. Joseph felt sick as he kept his feet planted. While he faced the lawman, Constable Long called on the slave catchers by name. "Mr. Pudget. Mr. Dawes. You may take the boy."

The lanky whiskered one named Dawes squeezed around behind them so that he was between the wall and the bed. "Constable," the slave agent said, "all this may be unnecessary."

The words made Joseph turn. His first thought was that Daniel was dead, yet he saw the boy still breathing. With Dawes ahead of him, Pudget forced his way to the far side of the bed too, moving the frame with his thick, overweight body. Before Joseph knew what they would do, the men pointed to the bandages on Daniel's thin frame.

"Look at that!" Dawes said to Long, while Daniel seemed far beyond knowing how much danger was near. "They have practiced their quackery on Mr. Venor's property! Look at this, Constable! We will not let ourselves be held responsible for this slave's death! These niggers should be charged!"

Dawes waved the written deposition like a flag of surrender. Then he tore it up and threw the pieces down so that they floated to the floor and to the bed. "There! So that you know we will have no claim to him after he's been in the hands of colored butchers! Be assured! We will tell this to the commissioner the moment we are back in the city. And I hope we can also report to him that you have caused justice to prevail here by arresting these two for impersonating doctors!"

Joseph dared to face the local officer. "This child was dying when he was brought here—"

Young Constable Long cut him off by looking at him sharply. "Joe, it's quite unwise for you to speak right now."

"I see! You will let a Negro accuse us!" Dawes raged. "The boy barely had a scratch on him when he was stolen from us. That's what we'll say to the commissioner!"

Mr. Long looked as though he was at a loss as to what to say or do. Dawes spoke again. "Mr. Pudget and I have no more reason for being here! Our profit has been destroyed, and something needs to be done about that!"

The constable spoke to them as they moved toward the door. "Because you successfully trailed them, a long portion of the Underground Railroad route has been discovered. From Pleasant Points, up across Mine Ridge, and down into this town. You should take consolation in that."

"Surely you cannot think that enough!" Dawes said with oaths. "These colored boys should be arrested and put in jail to rot, just as their little victim will soon be rotting in the ground."

Joseph thought he saw worry in Constable Long's eyes.

"I'm afraid you can't have it both ways, sir," the constable said. "Either you must maintain your claim on this boy as Virginia chattel, or you must be satisfied that the invisible line for moving fugitives has been cut. Without your testimony that the child here is indeed a slave, I have no evidence that these men have been wrong in aiding one of their own. I have no evidence that they put themselves in the position of doctors."

"Sure you do! Look at the child's body."

"Around this mountain, many families and friends try to help themselves without ever consulting a physician. If you two do not stay to say that this boy is chattel, I can assume that he is one of the children from this area, perhaps even one from this house."

"We followed that man out of Philadelphia!" They pointed to Oliver.

"I know that, and you have alerted us to the possible reason for his journey from the city to here. However, you saw no fugitive with him. There is nothing substantial enough for the courts."

"You heard the nigger say it. The child was brought here."

"You know the court does not rely on Negro testimony. My first look at the boy has been here. If you want me to act under the fugitive law, then you will have to stand by your claim that he is Virginia chattel."

Dawes threw up his hands. "The next time we have cause to be in this township, you had better believe that we will bring federal agents with us to see the law enforced rightly."

Constable Long lingered for a moment after the other men were gone and the pounding of their boots still sounded on the stairs. "Personally, I am sickened that official papers can be issued to take a child back into slavery. But this has gone beyond any personal perferences now. Remanding slaves, no matter what their age, is part of the law. And I am an officer, sworn to uphold the law. Do not think for a moment that I have won protection for you, for the man who came in first is a Philadelphia attorney set on seeing every aspect of the antislavery movement stopped. The woman is his sister-in-law. No, boys, you haven't seen the end of your troubles yet."

Oliver showed the courage to move as soon as they were alone. He gathered the pieces of the torn deposition while Joseph bent and searched to find the boy's pulse. "You can read this, Brother Whitsun," he said, as he started putting the pieces together at the foot of Daniel's bed. "This child is claimed by a man named Venor. It supplies a full description of his brandmarks and his scars, and they do match the boy's exactly."

Joseph shook his head. "In a moment, or hours, it won't matter. Paper or no paper, the boy will be where no one but God can have him back. Those agents knew it too. That's why they deserted him, so they would not be fined for abusing another man's slave or neglecting him." He fought to keep his emotions from crumbling. "Can you read whether it gives the child's name or his age?"

"Sir, I see neither."

Joseph pressed his trembling hands to his face. "It does not matter. He will live and die as Daniel, and that is how we will mark his grave."

CHAPTER 16

THE MOMENT CHARLES was in Oak Glen, he lifted his eyes to the house on his left. Appalled, he saw two crazy quilts displayed in the window. There was no hiding himself, for he was on the street driving with bells on his horses' harnesses, and there was no easy way to turn his huge wagon around.

Already, dark-faced children were looking out the windows to his right. An aging Negress farther up the street left her dilapidated house to stare at him, with little children clinging to her skirts. Finally a middle-aged Negro, dressed in farming clothes but carrying himself with an air of dignity, came out of the small barn near the house that exhibited the quilts.

Charles' mind was on Mayleda's safety, but on Simeon Bart's warning too. He had no idea what to do, what to say, now that the quilts were showing. The brown man coming near him ended his dilemma. While

Charles still was in his seat, the man said to him, "You must be Mr. Powell."

"That's right!" He felt relieved that this man knew his name, but still he felt compelled to follow Bart's instruction. "I-I came to see if you might have apples or cider or honey for my free-products store in Philadelphia."

"Yes. Please step down. Come with me. I am Pastor Brown."

Charles set the brake. It didn't seem odd that the man would take him to his barn, for he had asked about his produce, yet Charles wondered with every step how he was going to find Mayleda. The moment they were inside, however, Charles' suspicions and fear rose, for this man Brown quickly closed the door behind them. At once Charles saw other Negro men gathered on the stacked hay. Then Charles saw Simeon Bart with the others.

"Hello!" Charles said, only a little less tense because of this familiar face.

Simeon stood and dusted himself off. He seemed distressed. "Hello, Mr. Powell. We don't have good news to share with you, sah."

Charles felt panic and anger. "What do you mean?"

"You all were followed, likely from the moment you left the infirmary. Us, too, comin' over the mountain. We didn't know anything 'bout it till just a few hours ago when Mr. Anthony Ruskin, the local constable, and two slave agents showed up here."

Charles could keep no secrets now. "Where is Mayleda!"

"Mr. Ruskin took her," Pastor Brown said. "Some of these men followed him at a distance. He was on horseback, but then he took her to the train station, surely to go back into the city."

"I knew we should have been more careful!" Charles fretted. "Why weren't we accosted on the pike?"

"Consider it, sir," the pastor challenged. "This way they've gotten everything they wanted. They have our whole route exposed. Mr. Ruskin was able to get Mayleda Ruskin back before any federal officers were involved. And they found the child too."

"So they have taken him! Mrs. Ruskin must be heartbroken!"

"Actually they turned down their claim on him," the pastor said. "He's still here. Still hanging on to life, but we don't know for how long."

"They followed us because of the child, then let him go?" Charles marveled.

"Yes, that makes sense, too, when you think of it from their perspectives. The agents surely saw that the child's condition would have prevented remanding. If they say they had no legal claim to him, then they dismiss themselves from every possible charge concerning his injury and his fate. From what our men saw, they have headed back to the city too."

Charles vented his worry. "Mrs. Ruskin said her presence would help to protect any rescue. She said the Ruskins would do anything to hide her involvement in such a mission, for they would not want their name associated with abolition. What do you think? Have they apprehended her to arrest her?"

"I doubt it," Pastor Brown said. "I think that's why Mr. Ruskin came without federal marshals."

All of them were startled then by the sound of the barn door opening. Charles recognized Oliver Catos at once as the young man with glasses came in. Pastor Brown, still standing closer to the door than Charles, anticipated the news. "The child is dead."

"No," Oliver said wearily. "It's nothing short of a miracle, sir. Brother Whitsun has moved him to his own house. We carried a bed down from the loft to put by the kitchen stove so that steam laced with turpentine can be made to try to ease the boy's breathing. It seems the child might survive."

Pastor Brown looked at both Charles and Brother Catos. "We should get you two on your way before anyone in Brinkerville catches news of what transpired here today."

Charles kept staring at Oliver, who looked so distressed. When the young practitioner spoke, it was to him. "Mr. Powell, we all could have been arrested. The local constable was here, and I believe he knows about you too."

"I heard that," Charles responded, then the silence grew again. He did not want to say more, but perhaps they all were thinking it together. Their arrests still could come on the road or once they were back in the city. Now that Mayleda had been removed, perhaps Anthony would testify against them and send the marshals to them.

Charles sensed that many eyes were upon him. Until that moment he had actually forgotten that he was the only white man present. Pastor Brown extended his hand. Charles shook it.

"Let's put some apples and cider in your wagon, then you and Brother Catos can be on your way," the pastor said.

"I'm afraid I have nothing to exchange."

"What!" Bart spoke up. "Did my sons fail me?"

"Oh no," Charles replied to him. "We agreed on chickens now, and hams once you have your smokehouse built. But I did not want to travel with live fowl, for I anticipated returning to the city early tomorrow, which is the Sabbath."

"No payment is needed to me, other than that which you have already given," Pastor Brown said. "Even if the boy dies, he will do so in peace. There will be a proper home-going for him. That, sir, has to do with your commitment to us and your bravery."

The other men stayed silent, but when Pastor Brown moved to get some of the baskets of apples in the barn, quite a few got up to load Charles' wagon for him. When it looked like it was sufficiently full to justify their journey home, Charles and Oliver Catos climbed in. After a few more words of gratitude from Pastor Brown and a prayer, Catos and Charles started on the long, perhaps dangerous, drive back to Philadelphia.

Watching from her classroom window, Angelene waited for the white man to drive away with the handsome stranger at his side. She could contain her own curiosity no longer, nor that of her students. Most still wanted to gawk out the windows more than work at their slates. "You wait with the others until the schoolroom clock strikes the hour," Angelene said to some of the oldest girls. "Then you let the students go, but only by way of the back door and only to head for home."

Then she herself left the classroom by the door that opened first to Joseph's house. As she went through the sitting room, she was amazed to find Joseph beside a bed that had been set up in his kitchen. The boy was in it, causing her more confusion. Joseph rose wearily to his feet when he saw her.

"Constable Long and other white men were on the street," she said, coming to him and spilling out her concerns. "I thought surely the child must be dead for they did not have him."

"He was too close to death to please them, I think," Joseph said with quiet bitterness. "They had plenty of other victory's spoils, however, for they exposed the whole secret route that Tort and others have been using. And the man Ruskin got back his sister-in-law, Mayleda Ruskin. She has been courageously helping Negroes in the city, but now that will surely come to an end."

Angelene had not planned to say anything about the woman, but this news of her relative and also of her activity only increased her own distress. "How did she help Negroes?"

Joseph studied her. "She works at Dr. Ellis's infirmary. When her husband lived, he had an incredible industry finding loans for colored men who wanted to start businesses in the city."

"So you knew her from the infirmary, then!" The thought did not make her happy.

"No. I knew of her husband, because of his tremendous work, but I was already with Ba when she came to work for Dr. Ellis."

"Do you know what her connection is with this child?"

"Yes, of course." He seemed to grow more uneasy with every one of her questions. "She was the one who found him."

"Who else knows that?"

"I don't know!" Now he seemed beyond patience with her.

There were so many things troubling Angelene's heart. She wanted to press him more, but he looked so despairing. Though Joseph could not know it, Sister Sladder had been to her house early that morning, agitated and eager to talk with her mother. Angelene had stood in the hall outside the sewing room, able to hear every word. Angelene's father had been out of the house, at the barn, caring for their horses and milking the cow.

Standing before Joseph now, she hardly felt she had the courage to carry, alone, all that she had heard. She wanted to talk to him. She wanted to believe that by talking she could help him, especially after the terrible report she had heard about the white woman's actions toward him. She hoped even now that he might say something to her.

Whatever the real nature of the woman's character, Angelene desperately wanted to be assured that Joseph had been in the right and only her victim. She wanted to be assured that no matter what the woman's forms of persuasion, Joseph would not give in to her desires. "What do you plan to do with this boy?" she said, hating their silence and thinking that her question was innocent enough.

Yet again he seemed harried. "What can be done, but to watch and to pray around that clock that he might live?"

He kept looking at her as though he were disappointed that she did not share the same depth of grief that he had.

"Look at what slavery has done!" He extended a trembling hand. "Look at him—broken in body, mind, and spirit. God have mercy, but God bring judgment too!" He crossed his arms, as one in pain.

Never had she seen him so close to rage. It frightened her. She pondered more on what she had heard Sister Sladder say. The widow from their church had vowed to her mother that she had heard the white lady singing Negro hymns. She said it made her suspect that this lady might be only "passing" for white, a term used when very fair-skinned mulattos tried to fool society and deny their own Negro blood by living as white folk.

Many a woman in the North did successfully pass for white—until her children were born. Sister Sladder reminded her mother of this too. Through a woman's offspring, her African blood could surge again, bringing forth the appearance of the Negro back to her sons and daughters. This could have happened to this woman. Sister Sladder had mentioned that early on in her telling. If so, and if this Mrs. Ruskin still was trying to be part of high society, of course she would want to look for some absolute way to abandon her unwanted issue to other Negroes.

Now that Angelene had seen a rich gentleman come to whisk the woman away, and now that a constable and two slave agents had left Oak Glen without the child, though he lived, Angelene found herself fearing that the child might be Mayleda Ruskin's and not a slave at all. If so, the woman's scheme had worked in bringing the boy, for Joseph seemed willing to sacrifice every part of his own life for this child of mystery. She stood there, not daring to speak, not daring to leave.

"What is it that has you acting like this?"

She was so deep in thought that she nearly missed Joseph's asking.

"Even this morning, I knew something was wrong by the way you came in here. What is it?"

She blurted out her feelings. "I am worried for you! Worried about how you were pulled in to be this child's doctor and now, it seems, his guardian."

"His is alive by the grace of God. I do not understand why you seem so angry."

"Joseph, I fear that he is not a slave at all, but a child unwanted and abused." She poured her grief in front of him.

He seemed amazed. "How so?"

"That woman who brought him. Truly I think she might be someone who is merely passing for white. Perhaps she conceived this child with her late husband and then tried to give him up."

"How can you link the woman with the child? You know nothing about her. Is it only because he is so fair?"

She wanted the truth out. "When you told me that she and her late husband worked among Negroes, I thought perhaps this is why, because she is Negro too, though most might not know it."

He rose and came beside her. "This boy has been branded. Would a mulatto mother brand her own mulatto child?"

She shed a few tears because of Joseph's unnerving manner, which she had not witnessed before. "I don't think so."

"There was a document that the slave agents destroyed right in my presence. When Practitioner Catos pieced it back together, it described the child's brand marks perfectly. Does that sound like the description of a mixed-race boy born in the North?"

"No, Joseph." She covered her face, but her own anger grew. "Now, just give me the answer to some of my questions, please. Why did that woman embrace you? Was it because she wanted you to take her child? Was it because she ended up hoping that you might take her too?"

He stepped away. "Sister Sladder has talked to you!"

"No!" She cried because he did not deny any of her words. "She told my mother. I was listening, I confess."

He dismayed her by his next comments and by his agitation. "I cannot speak about it now. Whatever I'd try to tell you, you would not understand."

"Say what you will! It would be better than vowing that you can say nothing at all!"

"Anything I say right now will not help you. Trust me."

"Trust you?"

"Please! Yes!" He came to her, his eyes full of desperation. "Please, do trust me! And do trust Mrs. Ruskin. There is nothing to be suspicious of. God knows! We have done nothing wrong."

"You did not repel her embrace. That I know!"

He closed his eyes. He would not speak. It made her turn away to leave him.

———————

Charles came into Easton Alley just at dawn on Sunday morning, having first taken Oliver back to Dr. Ellis's infirmary. It had been a long, cold ride but without any confrontations, even between themselves. At the end, Charles had extended his hand to Oliver Catos, and the practitioner had taken it. That simple act had left Charles with a slightly less burdened heart as he drove the last blocks alone.

The alley was darker than the streets. Charles turned his mares toward the barn. They were restless, sensing the closeness of home. But he stopped them short of his goal because he caught sight of a glimmer of orange reflected in the windows of his store's rear door. Deserting the team, he got down and walked where no lights burned in the alley. Yet still his back storeroom seemed to glow.

Then he saw another thing as he came right up to the door. One square pane of glass directly above the keyhole and knob had been removed. He held his breath and listened. There were voices inside. For a moment he drew back toward his wagon, for he was alone.

He thought of calling on Huck Baring, his neighbor, though he could hardly consider the Negro his friend. Besides the man had a wife and several daughters. He did not think he should get them all out of bed. While he stood deliberating, a face appeared at the door. "Bossman Powell's come home!" he heard one colored boy warning others.

Then, as though Charles had the right to be only a spectator, he watched the door to his own establishment swing in. A cluster of Negroes who had helped themselves to his store's interior tumbled out and headed up the alley. The last boy to leave was one he recognized. "Hey there!" he yelled. In his anger he raced after him. "You! Tom! You stop right now!"

The boy was quick on his feet, but Charles' anger propelled him. They came to a place where the way was narrowed by rain barrels set out for a cooper's attention. The boy ran around them. Charles pushed through. By doing so he was fast enough to grab hold of Tom's loose coat. The Negro fell backward, tumbling down between the barrels. Charles let go of his clothes, then trapped him by his ankles when he tried to crawl away.

The boy turned and sat upright. There was enough light to see his look of terror. Charles was determined to keep his grasp. Tom twisted. Charles threw his weight upon him. "Now you tell me who broke my window to let you boys in." He pushed hard against the Negro's shoulders and chest.

"We didn't know you'd be back," Tom panted. "You hardly ever come by night. An' never do you travel on the Lord's Day!"

Without mercy Charles kept him pressed to the cobblestones. "You've done this before, then! You've let yourselves in to pilfer my supplies!"

"No, sah! Just to keep from freezin'."

"Do you invade my property because you think you have cause?" As

Charles accused him, his mind raced from the present to imagines of his own past, when he was an envious and angry child because what others had while he suffered with nothing.

The memories tempered his emotion. "I'll let you up if you promise you won't run off. I want to speak with you, but not like this."

"Sure, sah! I won't run."

Charles lifted one hand. "Understand. I don't care what your color is. Breaking into someone else's property is wrong. But I do know the temptation. Yes, I do. For once I was an orphan alone on these very same streets. Are you listening to me?"

"Yessah!"

He pulled himself away, now not touching Tom at all. "I've had much time to think since I saw you in my stables. I could hire a boy like you. I mean, every day. And at night you could eat with me and share my house. When Mr. Peabody owned the store before me, that is how I was removed from the streets. I started to work for that Friend when I was only seven."

Charles made this invitation because of all he had witnessed in Oak Glen and with Simeon Bart's family. Indeed, his opinion about Negroes was changing. The boy seemed frozen to the cobblestones.

"If you prove yourself trustworthy, I'll teach you as much of the trade of shopkeeping as you can learn. I'll take the same chance that Friend Peabody took with me, for I might still be a thief today if he hadn't had compassion on me."

Again he said things because of what he had heard and seen. It made him willing to believe that a Negro's dishonesty might be related to his hunger, just as his own had been. He knew he was willing to test this idea for Mayleda Ruskin's sake, as though in her honor, for it might be a long time before he saw her again, if ever. He believed she would approve of what he was about to do in taking this boy in.

Tom still sat motionless.

"Boy, what do you say?"

Suddenly the colored youth was like a penned wildcat finding a gate opened. He leaped up and raced away. It made Charles tremble while he still knelt on the pavement. He was angry and confused. Had he been mistaken about a Negro's wants and needs? Had he really learned so little after being with Oliver and Simeon and the rest? In anguish he threw up his hands. Could there ever be peace in America as long as Negroes lived here?

PART TWO
The Rumors of Many

And the stars of heaven shall fall,

and the powers that are in heaven

shall be shaken.

MARK 13:25

CHAPTER 17

JOSEPH HAD NOT THOUGHT OF TIME until Ba set his squirrel gun in the corner near the front door and gave him a brief signal about going up to bed that Sunday night.

Only then did Joseph consider that the man had put himself on a voluntary outdoor watch for the second night in a row, starting at dusk and lasting hours. Numbed from intensity, Joseph rose from the chair where he had been sitting beside Daniel's bed all this time, but Ba was already through the room and to the loft stairs before Joseph could follow him. He decided to thank him in the morning.

Not more than ten minutes after his friend had gone upstairs, Joseph heard footsteps on his front porch. With the child being helpless to know if anyone was with him or not, Joseph went to the door, ready to meet trouble before it would come in on the boy. Fortunately he saw only Angelene when he looked through the window. For her, he opened the door.

"I brought you some warm apple pie." She held it out.

"Ba and I had supper," he said, then recognizing how blunt that sounded, he invited her to come in.

"How is your patient?"

Her mood seemed mild. They had not spoken since her visit on Saturday, when they had parted on ill terms. Because of the boy, Joseph had not gone to church that morning. "There has been no change." Joseph had not left the child's side once since his bed had been moved. He took the plate she had and carried it to the table. She followed him, which brought her close to Daniel's bed. Joseph watched her look at the weak, gasping body.

"Daddy and Mother are still up, praying every hour for him."

"Please tell them how grateful I am."

"Don't you think you should get some rest? I am willing to sit by his side." They looked at the clock together. It was almost eleven.

"I'm fine. You should not have come across alone in the dark so late."

Her look held him. "Would it be all right if I sat with you for a time?"

Joseph purposed to be more kind. "Of course." He brought her a chair, which he set beside his own.

She sat down. "This is your bed, isn't it?" she asked, keeping her voice low. "How do you plan to get any rest if the boy sleeps in it?"

He didn't answer. Though the question showed her concern for him, the idea of rest for him hardly mattered. His goal was to be with the child as long as there was life in him.

"I don't see how you think you're doing him any good. You're so weary now that I fear it will render you incapable when he does awake."

"*If* he does!"

"Joseph, you have had sick children in your care before. I have even been with you and watched them die. What is it that makes this boy so different?"

"He is in this condition because he was somebody's slave! When I look at him, I see injustice in the flesh." He shifted his eyes to her. "If you still think that he is Mrs. Ruskin's child, then you do see him in a different light, I know."

Her words were very soft. "I don't know what to think, but I do want to know the truth. Honestly, Joseph, that's why I came." There was silence, broken every moment by the ticking of the clock's pendulum. "Do you really have nothing to say to me?"

He answered her by getting up and going to the same shelf where Ba kept his chessboard and pieces. When he came back, he had a journal book in his hand, but he kept it closed. "I am not quite sure where to begin. It will help if you will just be willing to listen and hear me fully." He hesitated. "Mrs. Ruskin is not a stranger to me."

He saw Angelene's lips began to quiver. "You want the truth! Here it is. Sixteen years ago, when Mrs. Ruskin was just a girl of fourteen, she saved my life."

Her eyes went wide. "Where? How?"

Joseph longed to say that the details did not matter, yet he proceeded another way. "You will not like this story. Neither do I. Since moving to Oak Glen, I know I have worked hard to keep this tale hidden, even from my own memories."

Angelene showed patience with his delaying, and he thanked her for it, then opened the journal for her. "I was trying to write the short narrative for you, even before Mrs. Ruskin came." He let her read his few words before saying some of them out loud. "Sixteen years ago I was a slave on a South Carolina plantation called Delora."

"Oh, Joseph! No!"

"Mrs. Ruskin, Mayleda Callcott Ruskin, was my master's only daughter."

Instead of bringing insight, his words caused Angelene to fly into a rage. "And she touched you! After her family had held you as its brute! How vile! How despicable!"

"Angelene, she saved me on the plantation. I would be dead now if she not had intervened to help me."

"So now she brings this child to you!"

"You need to believe this. She did not know that I was Joseph Whitsun, and I did not know her either, as Mayleda Ruskin. It was only after the surgery that we recognized each other. Yes, and then she did embrace me."

"It makes no sense that you would have allowed it. She, the daughter of the man who would have you as a slave!"

"Her father freed me. That is how I had the liberty to come to Pennsylvania, by way of Philadelphia. He did it because of the conviction of his sin as a slaveholder."

Her mouth turned down. "You said I would not like this story, that you do not like it yourself, yet you do not seem the least bit unhappy about anything that you have said."

"Would you rather that I hate her? For her background? For her color? You overlook that she's an abolitionist in the North now, that she came to Oak Glen as part of a mission to save this child. Never could I have thought that I would see her again, and she felt the same of me. That is why she did embrace me in her joy, and that is why I did not resist her touch for a moment.

"But then, know this too. That is why you saw us in this kitchen together with your father. Right away, after that moment of recognition, I called on him to meet with us so that we would not have our dialogue alone. I wanted to know about my mother. My friends. They are still in bondage. But I wanted your father there as a witness to our words and to our actions."

She frowned.

"Angelene, I give you permission to ask your father. Whatever you want him to tell you about Mrs. Ruskin and me, he may do so."

"Does he know that the woman had her arms around your neck?"

"Yes! As a *sister* to her long-lost older brother. She thought I was dead. That is an amazing story too. I came to Philadelphia carrying her father's Bible. I was so ill, I could not prevent it from being stolen from me. Later it was returned to her when it was noticed that her name was listed in the family genealogy. She knew that I would never give it up willingly. She concluded then that I had died in the city."

"But you both worked for Dr. Ellis. Didn't that man ever guess the association between you?"

"No. As I told you yesterday, I was gone, committed to helping Ba by the time she started volunteering. She knew about me, but Dr. Ellis always called me only by my last name, Brother Whitsun."

"This is all very touching, Joseph," she said, but there was still fire in her eyes. "However, it doesn't address an underlying fact to this all. Her family still owns slaves."

"She cannot help that anymore than I."

Angelene got up. Unlike yesterday, Joseph went after her. "Don't go! I beg you! At least not until you try harder to understand Mrs. Ruskin and her motivations. She does not deserve mean-spirited condemnation."

"You think I am mean-spirited!"

"No. I know you are not, so that is exactly why I beg you. We must talk more. I want you to understand everything, but trust me, I don't want to reveal all my pain incurred in slavery. I don't want you to be burdened by my past. That's why the journal entry is so brief. I hardly knew what to say. Now, because of this, I know I must say enough to ease your mind. But I want to protect you too. Believe me, please!"

She turned to him fully.

"Mrs. Ruskin, Sister Ruskin, gave up her family and the wealth she was born into to fight against slavery." He saw her take a breath.

"Why does she fight it?"

"What a question! Because it is wrong, and she knows that. She is the widow of Sprague Ruskin. Ask your father about him too! More than any white man in Philadelphia, he understood equality between the races, and he worked to promote it."

She still moved closer to the door. "Did he believe in it enough to love and marry a mulatto who was white enough to pass for being white?"

"What! You still think Mayleda has Negro blood in her?"

"She's a planter's daughter. You admit it. Her mama could have easily been a slave."

"No! I was in the Callcott house when Oribel Callcott gave birth to Mayleda. I was in the very room."

She covered her ears and squinted. "I don't want to hear it. I don't want to know anything about how they used you."

He pulled her hands away from her face. "I knew you would feel this way. That is why I never, never wanted to mention my years of slavery. Yet after Renny was put on the Underground Railroad, you know that your father came to me and told me that he wanted to speak with me in private. That is because he noticed how my hands shake nearly every time I am confronted with the suffering caused by slavery."

"I know that too!"

He dared to continue holding on to her hands. "You can feel my tremors now, I know. They come because I did suffer tremendously as a slave, but Mrs. Mayleda Callcott Ruskin was never the cause of any of that suffering."

"But she knew you as a slave because her family had you!"

He started over with his reasoning. "I will keep my promise to spare you details, but you must know this. I witnessed Mayleda's birth. I was there to hold the basin, to fill the pitcher with water, to do what a boy of six can be made to do as a servant in the master's house."

"Oh, Joseph! Oh, Joseph!" She shook as she sobbed.

"I am saying this to clear Mayleda Ruskin's name and her reputation. It means much to me that you would not despise her."

She pulled one of her hands free, but only to wipe her eyes. When she spoke, the tension within her seemed to subside. "You truly think that this Mrs. Ruskin did not conceive this child."

He kept her hand and led her back to the suffering boy. "This innocent child belonged to a man in Virginia named Venor. I don't know how
or why the boy was found in Philadelphia. Or his sister either. What I do
know is that if he does not die, he will have a chance for freedom because
the deposition papers from his master had been destroyed, and those who
pursued him have relinquished their claim.

"I have my freedom because of a manumission paper signed by Mayleda Callcott Ruskin's father on the day he died. Little Daniel, as I call
the boy, may be free because now he has no papers."

She moved on her own to read his words in his journal once more.
She spoke them out loud. " 'I wanted to forget the past, but your father
spoke to me with wisdom. He guessed the truth before I had the courage
to tell him or you. He encouraged me to be honest with myself, and with
you, as an act of fairness to us both.' "

She turned and raised her eyes.

"Why Mrs. Ruskin came yesterday, I cannot explain. I submit to you,
Angelene, that it must be part of God's greater plan."

She stepped closer. Even her eyelashes trembled. "Did she save you
in the South because she loved you even then? Did you yield to her embrace today because it is your desire to love her now?"

"The friendship Mrs. Ruskin and I share is deep and innocent."

"Did you speak of love?"

He hesitated. "Yes, Angelene. We did speak of love. Love lost. How
she has become a widow. As I am a widower."

Her mouth went wide.

"On the plantation I was married. Your father knows about my years
of slavery, but I could not bring myself to say anything to him about my
dear wife, Rosa." He squeezed his eyes closed for just a moment.

"She still lives in slavery!"

"No. Ba and the Ellises know my past. They know that I had a wife,
and that she did die."

"I am so sorry."

He felt her take his hand again.

"You grieve, in part, because of how she died! Joseph, I can see that
in you."

He began to sob. She touched his face as though to share his tears,
which he could not stop.

"All this time you have been suffering not only from slavery," she said, "but from the pain of being a widower. All in silence." She started weeping too. "These are tears for your Rosa and for you, dear friend."

He sat down, suddenly having no strength to stand. There was silence again except for the clock and Daniel's gasping. "When my wife died, she was carrying our first child. We had already talked about it. If the child was born a boy, we were going to name him Daniel."

"So you are considering keeping this child for your own?"

He heard no condemnation from her now. "Yes. Yes, I am."

"I do understand! You see his suffering, but you also see your own, in him. You couldn't save your own child, but now you're doing all in your power, and more, to try to save this one."

"I am."

"Oh, I commend you. I do." She sat with him.

Joseph found himself freed from the grip of uncontrollable emotion. "The night when your father had his private interview with me, he asked how I had gained so much education while being enslaved. I told him a little of the incredible opportunity I had in Charleston, South Carolina. Even as a slave, I was able to study under a brilliant teacher, Mr. Daniel Alexander Payne."

"I know Payne, the preacher! Was he a slave too?"

"No. Mr. Payne was a free brown man in South Carolina. When he was only nineteen, he opened his first school. The persecution he received while he remained there came directly, I think, because he was not afraid to educate even slaves, men and women. And not just in reading and writing, but in all the highest of thinking skills. That's one of the reasons I call this boy Daniel, as a way to honor the man who saved me from ignorance just as Sister Ruskin and her father saved my body from death and slavery."

"It is your passion to teach Oak Glen's students as you were taught."

"Yes. Teacher Payne did shape my philosophy. I was going to write that in my journal to you too. I was going to open myself to the possibility of giving part of my testimony to honor Payne and to encourage others to work for education."

"Oh, I hope you do," Angelene said, taking his hands in her own.

Joseph did not think he could stand more of her touch or her sympathy, yet out of his respect for her, he endured both expressions of her compassion.

"Dear Joseph, my deepest thoughts and my prayers are with you. Thank you so much for sharing what you have shared with me. I am sorry, so sorry. For my words, for my actions. For my jealous heart!"

Suddenly Daniel started screaming, "May! Sister May!"

CHAPTER 18

MAYLEDA HAD NOT BELIEVED ANTHONY that Saturday on the train when he was bringing her home from Oak Glen against her will. He had threatened then to keep her locked inside the house until his parents, Tyrone and Francine, were home from Europe, and that would not be for weeks. He pledged, too, that if she went out any door or window of her own volition, he would draft a testimony concerning her insanity and commit her to a hospital ward.

Because of the demeaning court record of her time spent with Negroes in Ludlow Row, Mayleda feared he could write such a deposition against her. He had kept part of his cruel promise, for she had been locked inside the house now for a week and two days.

Instead of extending her the grace to be in her own rooms within the house, he had put her up in the drafty third floor, where the rooms were hardly better furnished than neglected attic space. It was where some of the family's Irish help slept in summer. This time of the year, the quarters were frightfully cold. There was a coal stove in one room only, so May-leda stayed in that room, which also contained a bed and a chair.

There was only one window in the space, and it looked out to the rear yard, affording her no possibility to communicate with the city. The white servants of the house brought her water for washing, good food and tea, coal, and sewing and books to pass the time, but none of them would listen to her pleas for freedom.

At the end of her ninth day in this one room, she was beginning to feel as crazed as Anthony wanted to say she was. Perhaps this was part of his inhumane aspiration, that he could drive her to insanity. Unlike his parents, who tolerated her so that Judith would be near them, Anthony cared as little about his niece as he did about Mayleda.

Four days after the start of her confinement, he had come to visit her in the night. He was as angry then as he had been in Oak Glen. By the candle he held, he showed her a report published in one of the city's most prominent proslavery newspapers, the *Pennsylvania Citizen*. The article named her and identified her has his sister-in-law. It went on to say that she had been one of the abolitionists apprehended in an attempt to steal a young slave from agents authorized to remand it to its master.

The paper still lay on the floor at her feet while she sat in the twilight that put an end to her reading and sewing for that day. The door latch rattled, and she expected that her supper would be carried in. Instead, Anthony presented himself. "Good evening, Mayleda." She had not seen him for five days.

She was amazed by his jovial mood yet instantly terrified, for he had never shown any happiness about being in her company. "Why are you here?" she asked, rising to her feet.

"To say that you will come down for supper tonight." He held forth a dark blue satin dress in the light of the candle he carried. "You will be ready within the hour, or your travel to the city hospital tomorrow will be assured."

"You would not do that to me!"

"No, because I trust that you will not offend my dinner guest, my former partner in the office, Mr. Burns. He is eager for you to join the two of us at the table."

"I won't! And not dressed in that!"

"You are crazed enough to enjoy being locked away here, in drab at-tire? I shall make note of that."

"Don't torment me with your words!"

"Do you remember, Mayleda, that our commitment to you and Judith can be terminated in the event of your marriage to a gentleman who would meet my father's approval?"

She stared at him. "You think that Mr. Burns will come and marry me, your plain sister-in-law, just like that? You are the one who is insane!"

"You will be the foolish one if you do not accept this man's offer. He is on his way to the new state of California to set up his law offices, and unfortunately, he has not found a woman brave enough to leave the East to go with him."

"You know I would never leave my Judith, and I know that your parents would never release her to move that far away."

"The girl is old enough now to write you letters."

"You are a lunatic to think I will agree to such a thing."

"It is better than being separated from your child because you are legally deemed insane, don't you agree?"

"You horrible, despicable man!"

It did not matter what she wailed, for he had already closed himself outside the door. She heard him locking it again.

———

In the years since fleeing Delora Plantation, elegance had become a stranger to her. Though Mayleda had lived in the Ruskins' well-appointed mansion for years, it was rare when she dined at the family's table. Even then, she wore only modest dresses that showed her commitment to shun vanity and every garment that carried with it the price of human bondage.

Now, though, under the glow of the dining room globes, she remembered what it felt like to be rich and living a life of ease. She loathed it, more now than even when she had been a girl growing in her awareness that injustice was always cultivated by plantation life. Anthony was at her side. Mr. Burns sat across from her. There was no denying his good looks. He was a strong, handsome man in his forties with brown eyes and black hair. He looked as though he could have been her older sibling.

As much as she could, Mayleda kept her eyes down and away from both men, who chatted about the business of law. It was a long expanded meal, served entirely by the Ruskins' butler. By the time coffee was carried in, Mayleda began to have real hope that Mr. Burns had not come to talk about matrimony, that it had only been another of Anthony's cruel gestures toward her.

The candles at the table's center sputtered as they waned. Anthony casually pushed back his chair. "Let us speak of Mrs. Ruskin," he suggested.

Mayleda found herself lifting her hands to cover her neck and chest, which the low, dark dress did not do for her. At the same time she dipped her head, warring against the ugliness of being disgraced. When she dared to glance at Mr. Burns, she felt his gaze on her as one of pity. It made her want to flee.

"Ruskin, you have humiliated her, and you've made me feel that I am only one step removed from the Southern buyer who dines with the auctioneer."

Anthony laughed profusely.

Burns reprimanded him, as much as social conduct would allow. "I was not joking, sir. If you don't mind, please, I would like to speak about this with you alone."

Mayleda was ready to rise.

"I would rather that she stay, Mr. Burns. There will be no condemnation toward you if you say you do not want to have her."

There was a heavy, disaster-laden pause.

"Ruskin. Have you read the *Pennsylvania Citizen* today?"

"No, man, I have stopped favoring some of its opinions."

The man reached inside his coat. "I feared as much. I brought my copy with me."

It was really only part of a folded sheet, which he handed to Anthony. Her brother-in-law grew paler by the moment. "This is all speculation! I say! Who wrote this?"

"Surely not anyone who supports you for senator."

"I cannot believe it. This writer says that no agents were involved with a young slave as the previous article had reported. That's not true! Agents to claim the slave were there in the Negro town. It was Pudget and Dawes. You know them."

Mayleda's hands were clammy. She saw Mr. Burns frown. "I do. Perhaps Dawes and Pudget saw a larger quarry in publicly rejecting their claim on the boy. That quarry, sir, being the reputation of abolitionists. And your reputation too, if they favor another proslavery man for the office you covet."

"But they were the ones who alerted me that my sister-in-law had been taken along on the rescue! It was my assumption that they went for the purpose of getting their slave back."

Burns looked at her. "From this article, I would say that they were looking for just such an incident. They are in the business of remanding slaves, of course, but also in the business of destroying the credibility of the abolitionists' cause."

"If they wrote this to the paper, they were in the business of destroying me and my campaign."

"Didn't I say that already? You are not the only proslavery contender for the office. Knowing those two, they could have written what they did here for a fee, paid to them by your opponents. When it comes to profit, they have no scruples, I am sure."

Anthony swore.

"They probably don't care one way or the other about you personally, Ruskin. It makes a good, hot tale for those who want to see the faults of abolitionists exposed in general. Surely being the slave agents they are, that is what they want. To see the whole antislavery cause dissolved."

"What actually has been said, Mr. Burns?" Mayleda asked, appealing to the visitor's sense of integrity.

Burns looked to Anthony. "Ma'am, I don't think you need to know the slander. The words against you are certainly meant more for Mr. Ruskin's harm."

But Anthony simply handed the newspaper over to her. "Read it! You've brought this all on yourself!" She had hardly focused on the text when Anthony demanded, "Is the Bible they describe in there something that you really have?"

"What Bible?" she asked with bewilderment. Her heart was beating so wildly that she could not read.

"The Bible with the name Mayleda Callcott in it," he answered. "The Bible that they say gives proof that you are Southern born."

Her surprise caused her to be unguarded. "How could anyone know about my Bible?"

"Then it is yours!"

She saw the words of the long article then. In part it was a testimony from a certain city bookseller—surely the same man who had visited her by night. Now he was giving information because of the report he read previously about her as one involved in an illegal slave rescue. "What do they care? Who am I, anyway, in regards to your campaign? We are not blood relations."

He had only one question. "Did Sprague know that you were born on a plantation in South Carolina, as it says here?"

"Yes, he did," she said bravely.

"Then why did you lie to us?"

"We never lied. We only said my parents were deceased, which was true. Sprague and I met in Boston. I had fled the South and left my past behind me. We agreed there was no reason to have to bring it all back just because your family wanted our marriage announced to Philadelphia society."

"Was my brother such a renegade that he would marry you despite the Negro blood in your veins?"

"What Negro blood?"

He took the paper from her. "There! Read that! They are saying that you love the Negroes, that you insist on living with them, and that my brother did too, because he knew he had married a half-bred mongrel born to a planter and his colored consort."

She fought the chair to stand, her full skirt impeding her. "For all that it's worth, I am as blue-veined as you!"

Burns looked at them both. "I'm afraid the story is going to do a great deal of damage, especially to your parents, who dote on their granddaughter. For by the law, she will be considered a Negro too!"

"But I am not a Negro, though there is no shame in being one!"

"No shame!" Anthony threw the words back at her. "That's what the men of the South have. No shame in conceiving children by Negro concubines."

She screamed at him. "You will not accuse my dear father!"

He stood and yelled back. "That is enough. Sit down."

Mayleda was forced to steady herself by holding on to the table.

Mr. Burns looked pained. "I am sorry, Ruskin. It is a risk I cannot take. I have parents and siblings, and California might not be far away enough for rumors this large." He nodded to Mayleda, not even giving her the courtesy to stand as she stood. "I do say *rumors*, ma'am, for I hope that is what they are."

"I want that Bible," Anthony said.

"No. It's the one thing I have that was my father's. He was a loving, caring, pure Christian man."

"Mayleda, you bring it to me, or I will find it myself." He pointed to the sideboard. "Take a candle. Go into your apartment and get it now."

Mayleda did flee to her own rooms with the light. Her plan for the moment was to get the Bible but then to leave, for there was a door in her apartment that opened to the garden. She prayed that Mr. Burns' presence would detain Anthony, but it was not so.

Anthony strode in by himself while she was in her bedroom. She kept the Bible in a drawer with some of her clothes. Because he was present, she would not go for it. "I'll not give it to you."

"Then I will find it." Anthony still had the evening's paper in his hand. "So, Mayleda, is the boy yours alone, or was my brother responsible for breeding two new mulattos?"

"I don't know what you're saying!"

"You did not read the paper carefully then!"

"You know I didn't. I could hardly read it at all."

"Pudget and Dawes relinquished claim to the boy you took into Lancaster County. Dawes' testimony is right here in print. He's quoted as saying that the boy did not match the description on their affidavit at all once they were in Oak Glen and could see him up close. That allows them to side with and support this newspaper writer, who chooses to say that the half-bred boy is *yours*. And perhaps a Ruskin too."

"Anthony, it is a lie, and you should know it! I don't know that child's age. You saw him! But surely he was born after Sprague's death."

He grimaced. "Then I can at least say that you conceived it unwillingly by a Negro man, if I must."

"You will not say anything of the kind! That is not true! I never saw the child before Thursday. Now, that you can say!"

He held the paper before her. "You may have ruined this family. And my career."

"I did nothing!"

"You consorted with Negroes! I found you in Oak Glen, didn't I? Dawes and Pudget knew you were there in the company of all Negro men. Dr. Dickens saw you before that in the worst part of town! Not with the boy, but wandering the streets. What more evidence than your own activity does this press need?"

"I have one child. Judith Oribel Ruskin."

"Tomorrow I will have you make that statement under oath. In sworn testimony you will deny every accusation that this Negro child, whom you helped to transport out of the city, is yours."

Mayleda considered it. "I won't, Anthony. You know it's not part of my faith to swear or make oaths. God is my judge. He knows I have done nothing wrong. Yet now you are telling me to neglect my beliefs just to prove to bigoted men that I am not the mother of that child. Well, let them think that I am. For the boy's sake, it will be better. The free status of a mother is conferred to the child, don't you know, no matter what his complexion."

"You will not rescue your own reputation?"

"I don't have to. My father used to say, 'Righteousness has no respect for rumor.' I believe that is true, even in Philadelphia."

Suddenly he took her arm. "I'm taking you to the asylum now."

"Mr. Burns!" she cried as loudly as she could.

"He is gone, Mayleda! And the servants do not care."

She tried to twist away from him. When she could not free herself, she bent and bit his hand. He let her go. While he swore at her, she raced out of the bedroom to the garden door. Without coat or cloak, she opened the door and ran outside, her only thought being to get away.

Instead of following her for the purpose of catching her, Anthony seemed to let her go. The moment she was out in the cold, the door slammed behind her. When she tried the knob, she found it locked.

Turning, she ran down the garden path to the street. She could think of only one safe place to go—Dr. Ellis's infirmary.

CHAPTER 19

CHARLES FOUND HIMSELF AT DR. ELLIS'S late Tuesday night. Because of the article in that day's *Pennsylvania Citizen*, the elderly Friend had called a meeting of men from both his own antislavery society and from the city's Vigilance Committee, composed of many of the city's colored leaders in business and in the church. Oliver Catos had been the one to invite Charles, and Charles had come, in part to show his appreciation to the young man whom he was continuing to know better. It was Oliver who now watched the doors as the rest of them were seated in a circle of chairs in the infirmary's front hall. One lamp burned, for Dr. Ellis did not want to bring attention to their gathering by having more light than usual. The draperies were drawn. It was the first time Charles had attended such a meeting since Brother Elim's passing.

A white Friend whom Charles did not know spoke as soon as the meeting started with prayer. "Sister Ruskin always trusted that her husband's family would protect her, regardless of her actions, in order to protect their own reputation."

"She never considered the reverse, that some could relish destroying the whole image of the Ruskin family by exposing her actions. That's what's happened now." This was said by another white Friend, who leaned in across the circle from Charles. "My thought is that much of this information was given to the newspaper by those same slave men mentioned in it, Pudget and Dawes. Perhaps they were even paid to say what they said."

There was a great murmur of agreement.

"Instead of claiming the sickly child, they saw the larger possibility to use the boy as their tool for destroying the credibility of our cause, first by destroying Sister Ruskin."

Charles had not come just to discuss who was responsible for the terrible report. "Where is the sister now?" he asked with urgency, and immediately every man's gaze turned to him. Though most knew him from the store, he was a newcomer to their group.

Dr. Ellis's eyes mirrored his own melancholy concern. "I assume she is with the Ruskins. I believe that Anthony Ruskin has kept himself in charge of her since he rode out of Oak Glen with her."

"Our consideration must not stop with Mrs. Ruskin." A black man spoke now. "We must think further, just as Mr. Anthony Ruskin himself must be doing at this moment. The core of the rumor is that his sister-in-law may have Negro blood in her, and that the mixed-raced boy she says she found on the street might be hers."

"A man like that is not going to leave such rumors as they are!" the brown man beside Charles said, moving in his seat with great agitation. "He'll fix it his own way now to try to help himself."

The colored man on the other side of Charles agreed. "That's my thought too! And my fear! Mr. Ruskin will try to turn this rumor around again. He'll not want anybody to be able to say that she is Negro or that she passed Negro blood onto her offspring."

"Then he'll have to fight to deny that the boy is hers!" a white Friend concluded.

Charles saw many of the colored men looking to each other.

"Yes, or he may say that the woman was a *victim* of Negroes during her time in the streets. That would work well for him, considering how Negro men are said to be."

"Aye!" Nearly all of the colored representatives agreed heartily, their faces hardened with worry. Charles felt like a tardy schoolboy trying to keep up with a lesson he did not completely understand.

"But wouldn't Mr. Ruskin rather fight the rumor that says the child is his nephew and absolve the sister's name all together?" an older white man dressed in Quaker garb asked in earnest.

"What evidence does he have to win that argument, sir?" a black man reasoned. Such a thing Charles had never seen, a Negro and a white man in equal dialogue.

"That's right!" Another man of color entered into the discussion. "But, you see, if he takes the course that the woman could have this child against her will, and to a *colored* man, then you have our race brought into it in just the way the public favors!"

"The way Ruskin favors!" the first black speaker said. "If he can make his relation into a *victim*, then he can make us all into lusting brutes."

"In that way he will end the discussion about his niece bein' mulatto!" another African agreed. "He need only call rape!"

"That could also end the rumor that his brother was married to a fair-skinned Negress!" The Negroes spilled out their conclusions all at once. It sobered everyone in the group, Charles included, to see how firmly they believed they would become the villains in Ruskin's race to clear his own name.

Dr. Ellis had had his eyes closed throughout much of this discussion. Charles assumed that he had been in prayer. The group of black men remained vocal and excited, while the Quakers were ponderously silent.

Then Dr. Ellis spoke. "If he takes that course, which will make Mrs. Ruskin a victim, then he has to name one or more black men who have preyed upon her."

"Yes, indeed!" A black man agreed. "An' *naming* him, that's the right expression, Friend Ellis, for he wouldn't have to prove it! No, not in this town. No, siree!"

The brown man to Charles' left spoke again. "A question! Will he stop at accusing only one brother? I mean, with the facts already published as they are, it sounds like Mrs. Ruskin has taken to the streets. It could give them cause to bring up the ugly opinion that more than one has preyed on her."

Many sighed with disgust while nodding their agreement.

"Then Mrs. Ruskin would indeed seem the piteous victim of the same black race that she and her husband loved and tried to help!" a white Friend said after he frowned grimly.

"It would be better for us all, if he would accuse us all," the man to Charles' right said then. "For all of us probably could not be hanged, but if he accuses one brother, then that man will go swingin'."

Charles shivered. These men were speaking in calculated measure about having one or more of them die. "Can no testimony we give stop this?" he said aloud, awkward at being in the conversation but compelled to do so.

Dr. Ellis answered him. "The only ones who could say that Sister Ruskin's story is true are the ones who saw the events in Dresden Alley too. As far as we know, that would be only the slave agents themselves, and Sister Ruskin's friend, Sister Mason."

There was a murmur of agitation. "No one would listen to a colored woman speak her mind, that's for true!"

"Or *any* colored testimony!" Others in the group revealed their rage. "Pity the brother, or brothers, who do fall prey to the falsehood that could well be brewin' now."

Charles dared to look at the Negroes facing him and at Oliver, who listened from afar, as he was still responsible for their safety. Though not completely comfortable in their presence, Charles did wholly side with their concerns. For the first time since reading the ugly report on Mayleda for himself, he saw the dangers of the matter from their perspectives. Indeed, he had only been concerned of Mayleda's safety at first, before being part of this group.

Had he heard Negroes speculating like this outside the meeting or in an alleyway, he might have focused on the lewd boldness of their words. Now he knew they had real cause for such open and grave concern. He thought of Ruskin's budding campaign to have all colored people removed from this state. A vicious, licentious story in which his dead brother's wife was the victim could serve him well.

He looked around and reflected sadly that even colored men such as these could be accused.

Suddenly Oliver turned to them all. "There's a woman running up the walk!"

Dr. Ellis got on his feet. This night he was dependent upon a modest walking cane. "Excuse me! People come day and night, for they know this to be a place of help and safety."

Oliver was again at the window. "It's Sister Ruskin!"

Charles stood. "Please, let her in!"

When Oliver opened the door, Charles scarcely recognized her. Her face was red. Her black hair hung down like a girl's, flowing over her shoulders but hardly covering her breasts, which were partially bared by the low-cut fancy dress she wore.

"Close the door!" she screamed the moment she was in the hall. "I think Anthony is following me!"

She seemed too dazed to even care about their presence. Dr. Ellis turned to Charles. "Take her! Get her out of here to someplace safe!"

"I have no horse," Charles said, reaching for his cloak on the back of his chair and racing to put it around her. "I walked."

"Oh, Charles!" Her eyes seemed to melt as he covered her.

"I have a horse!" A colored brother whom Charles did not know by name volunteered. "It's the roan mare tied up right beside the infirmary's kitchen door."

"Mr. Powell! This way!" Oliver urged.

Charles took hold of Mayleda by the shoulders. She was lost in the largeness of his thick black garment. He nearly carried her through the hall, to the kitchen, then out the back door. When he had her outside and up on the stranger's horse, he took the reins to lead her to the street. He was unsure where to go. "Not yet, no!" she cried looking down to him while they were still in the yard's shadows. "That's Anthony on his horse right out there!"

She pointed through the gate. Charles feared for the men inside. Still, the moment it was clear, he took her forth, never looking back.

Charles came to Easton Alley still uncertain what he should do. Leading the horse he passed by Huck Baring's harness shop, where lights glowed inside. It surprised him when Huck opened the door. Charles was only steps from the threshold. "Lord have mercy! Mr. Powell! From my windows I saw only a woman ridin' by. I thought she might need help bein' out so late herself."

"She is Sprague Ruskin's widow. I need a place to hide her."

"Well, you can surely come in here!"

"No, Mr. Baring. There's been a terrible report about her in the newspaper that's likely to cause trouble for all your race."

"Well, if I'm in trouble already, I don't see why I shouldn't risk a little more. Mr. Sprague Ruskin, he did everything for me to get this shop up an' going. If you need a place for his widow an' she agrees, well, consider you'selves invited in."

"I do thank you!" Mayleda said, already slipping to the ground. "Mr.

Powell could be in terrible trouble, too, if he is seen with me right now."

"Then, ma'am, you come in without delay," Baring told her.

Charles considered how shrewdly Anthony and the others had been in tracking them to Oak Glen. He feared the same thing might happen now. He stayed outside the light of the smoking tallow candles that were glowing inside. "I feel I should watch out here to make sure we weren't followed. Then I have to see that this horse is returned."

"Sure," Baring agreed kindly. "Don't you worry 'bout Missus Ruskin. She be fine with my wife an' daughters an' me."

"Thank you, sir!" Charles said it from the depths of his heart. Then he went out to the corner of the alley and the street to start his lonely vigil in the cold.

The Barings lived in two rooms above the shop, which Mayleda had never seen. The larger one was at the top of the stairs. It was where the family ate and where their three nearly grown daughters slept. It was cluttered but warm and bright, with blankets and quilts and dishes that filled every tight space with textures and colors. Mrs. Baring was a slightly stooped and graying woman with worried eyes but a friendly, courteous manner. When her husband repeated Mayleda's plight and her need for a hiding place, Mrs. Baring said, "Sure! Of course!"

Mayleda did not feel comfortable to lay aside Charles' cloak. "I'm quite embarrassed, ma'am. My brother-in-law forced me to wear the dress I have on. There is no modesty in it."

Huck Baring left the women to themselves. While the girls ogled over the incredibly fine dark satin, their mother opened her own small trunk of garments. "Here is something I was saving for my oldest. Something I used to wear when I was as small 'round as you are now." She smiled at Mayleda. "I think that perhaps it will fit you, if you don't mind my clothes."

"Ma'am, I don't mind!" Mayleda said, holding up the warm, slightly worn linen dress in shades of brown and blue.

Mrs. Baring smiled even more. "I didn't think you would mind! Welcome to our house, Missus Ruskin."

With Mrs. Baring's help, Mayleda changed clothes while the girls went down to be with their father. "I must get Mr. Powell's cloak back to him," she fretted.

"All in time."

"I have no coat. I have no shawl. I have nothing of my own!" Her mourning increased. "I am cut off from my daughter. I don't know what to do."

"We've hid other women here as sorrowin' as you, Missus Ruskin, but they wa' never white." She gazed at her. "Still, this is about the same thing, ain't it? I mean, why you' own people are treatin' you so mean that you cain't even be with them. It's about slavery, ain't it?"

"It is, Mrs. Baring."

"Then you know that God is on you' side, ma'am!"

Mayleda tried to smile, yet the truth had come too close. Colored women were often separated from their families forever. Was this to be the price that God would now require of her?

She did not cry but prayed then, for other women had gone before her in this grief, and somehow, she assumed, they were surviving.

Charles watched for an hour. When no one came, he climbed onto the horse that he had kept under saddle. Thinking that he would be less conspicious riding than leading the mare, he made good time going back to Dr. Ellis's.

Because of the lateness of the hour, he went behind the infirmary and rode to the doctor's stable. Tying the horse outside, he went to the back door, reasoning that some nurse would have to be awake. He knocked softly, not having much hope that it would be answered because it was the kitchen door. He also had great fear about what might have happened during the time when he was gone. Soon, however, Oliver Catos cautiously showed his face as he opened the way just a crack.

"Mr. Powell!"

"Mr. Catos!"

There was no need to voice the relief they had in seeing each other. "I came to return the horse I borrowed. I confess I do not even know to whom she belongs."

"I will put it in the stable. She is Brother Smithton's, and he has walked home."

"What happened? We saw Mr. Ruskin on his way to your door."

"Nothing. He searched for her, and then he was gone."

"I'm sorry about it all. It probably won't end here."

"Probably not." Oliver started out the door. "Is Sister Ruskin safe?"

"Yes! If you're watching over the patients, I can take care of Mr. Smithton's animal."

Oliver stopped and nodded. "Thank you. I am on duty while Dr. Ellis gets some rest."

There was a calm familiarity between them that felt comfortable, and it made Charles glad.

Oliver seemed in no hurry to close the door. "You were not followed?"

"No. I suppose it would be good for you and Dr. Ellis to know the secret. She is with Huck Baring, the harnessmaker, who is my neighbor in Easton Alley."

"A colored man."

"A colored family. I know, it has me worried too. But the Barings insisted, because of all that Sprague Ruskin once did for them."

"The Barings regularly hide runaways."

"I did not know that!"

Catos smiled. "I suppose that is good, sir. If even you, as a neighbor, do not know, then the secrecy has been well guarded."

"May it continue! I don't know what plans Mrs. Ruskin may have. I do know my own, and they are to do whatever is necessary to see her safely removed from that Ruskin family—forever."

"I understand. After what I saw tonight, I agree."

"Did harm come to anyone her, Mr. Catos?"

"No. But the man brashly looked upstairs and in the ward and everywhere. Some of the group were quite wise to suggest that I fill your chair. When Ruskin entered there was no indication that you had left the group already."

Charles grinned, for he felt as though they had shared a risk together and then a small victory. He wondered if Oliver felt the same. He was inclined to extend his hand. The younger black man accepted it. "Good night, Practitioner Catos," Charles said, requiring of himself that he address the man for what he was.

"Good night, sir! Godspeed to you! Divine protection."

After settling Brother Smithton's horse in the stable, Charles set out for home, feeling almost happy despite the circumstances. Though he continued looking for signs of trouble, he did not feel so wary as he traveled on foot through the dark. When he arrived at Huck Baring's, the shop and house above were both without light, making him feel more than a bit regretful, for he had hoped to see Mayleda Ruskin again that night.

Considering it best to go right to his door, he put the key into the lock while standing in the alley. Just when he did, a man approached from behind. Charles spun to see a dark face enveloped by what seemed to be a dark cape. "What do you want with me?" Charles demanded, poised for fight or flight.

"It's Tom, sah! I been waitin' to give you back you' cloak what Mista Barin', you' neighbor, done gave to me." He proved his words by handing over the garment that had just been around his own shoulders. Charles was amazed that Baring would trust him. "How did he find you for this task?"

"Why, I was outside you' door, sah. I told him I was you' regular hired help, startin' t'night."

"An' he believed you?" He was angry at both Negroes.

"Yessah. 'Cause of what else he saw me do for you t'night."

"And what was that?" Charles said, wholly suspicious.

"I was at you' barn, sah. I come 'round dark 'cause I wa' cold an' I wa' thinkin' on you' words 'bout me workin' for you."

"And?"

"There wa' two men an' they opened you' barn door. They had torches in they hands."

"Who were they?"

"I don't know, sah! It did look worrisome to me, so I braved myself an' sidled up to say real loud that I was you' hired hand an' asked if could I help them. They dropped them torches, Mista Powell, an' they did run!"

"You think they were here to burn down my barn!"

"I don't know, sah. Whether they wanted to or not, those torches caught on some of you' straw near the door. I took down you' horses' buckets an' put it all out. That's when Mista Baring done showed hisself. He got a glimpse of the men an' he thought they might be slave catchers named Pudget an' Dawes. Do you know them?"

"Thank God! You did save my horses. I transported a fugitive slave last Thursday, and those men know that. They could have been coming to punish me without taking me before the law." It could explain why they had not confronted him on the pike. They did not need the law to pressure him away from the abolitionist cause in a manner that would hurt him even more than fines.

"I can show you the circle burnt into you' stable floor, sah."

"Tomorrow," Charles said, feeling without strength. "If you hadn't been there, I could have lost my mares!"

"I won't have been here, sah, if you hadn't asked." The young man looked at him directly. "You want me to stay in you' barn t'night, I will, in case there's more trouble."

"No, Thomas. The rooms I have for sleeping look out to the alley. I say that we should go inside and watch by turn."

"That's more than fine with me, sah. I couldn't bear to see no innocent animals go up in smoke 'cause of somethin' you done to help a slave. I am a slave too, sah. I s'pose you ought to know it, in case that means that you don't want me near you. You could turn me in for profit."

"I won't. Do you trust me?"

His answer seemed meditative. "Yessah. If slave agents hate you 'nough to want to burn down you' barn, then I think you might be a white man to be trusted." He bowed his head. "But I guess you got no reason to trust me. You were right. I let all the fellers in."

"I want to trust you, but only you can be trustworthy." Charles wondered then how Brother Elim had felt the day he risked leading him up the back stairs from the alley for the first time. "We need to have an understanding with each other. I'll try to treat you fairly, and you may tell me straight out if you think I'm not. I expect you to work hard, for my occupation requires hard work. I don't think that work is shameful. Do you?"

"No, sah!"

"Then come with me and come up the stairs. I will show you where you can stay."

Charles had told Thomas he would take the first hours of watching. As much as he wanted this agreement to work, Charles knew he would have a hard time sleeping with the young Negro in his house. He actually stayed awake all night until dawn, never calling on the colored boy to take his place. When he finally went to the other room, he found Thomas watching, just as alert as he.

"I didn't want you to think me lazy an' not ready to earn my keep," Thomas explained.

"You were awake all night?"

"Yessah!"

Sighing wearily, Charles said, "Well, so was I. I guess we both learned something by losing a night's sleep together. Come out for breakfast." He had given Thomas clean clothes and a bowl of warm water for washing before he went to bed.

While Thomas sat at the table, Charles shaved and dressed. His usual morning fare was bread and cheese, but when he put it out before Thomas, the boy stood just as he sat down. Charles looked at him, puzzled. "Sit down. This is breakfast."

Still the boy stayed on his feet. "Sah, I never sat with no white man before. I never ate with none, neither."

Then Charles nodded. "Well, I never ate with anyone colored until a week ago, so we're both making progress."

He offered the chair again, and this time Thomas accepted with a hesitant smile. "Yessah, we are, ain't we!"

Charles bowed his head for prayer. He was uncertain if Thomas copied him in doing that. Afterward he said, "It occurs to me to ask you what you did in slavery." He passed the bread to him and sliced some cheese. "It could help me to know what kind of skills you already have." Charles was considering Sprague's bold mission to affirm fugitives in the work that slavery had prepared them to do on free soil.

Thomas knitted his brows. "You an interestin' gentleman, sah," he said, as though not fully trusting his motives. "I'm farm born, but I moved to the city the summer afta there wa' no rain an' the winter afta there wa' no snow. There wa' my marse an' the mistress an' twelve of us slaves on the farm, but when they moved on into Baltimore, they kept only two. Me an' my next oldest sister, Betty Marie."

There was a painful pause. "I took to doin' everythin' afta that. Fixin' whatever needed fixin'. Gwine for firewood an' coal. Takin' care of Marse's horses an' his carriage. Even bein' his butler an' his manservant. Whatever he wanted to say I was at the moment, I was."

"I see. Then you do have many skills. How long did you work for him? How old are you now?"

"I don't know, sah, for I don't count."

"Do you want to learn to count, to write, to read?"

"Do you think I can?" He gingerly took bread from the plate.

Charles reflected in that moment that he probably knew more literate Africans than did Thomas. "Yes. I learned right at this table under Friend Peabody's tutelage. Now, I suppose it's my turn to do the teaching."

Thomas looked dismayed. "My marse was not unkind to me, sah, as most folk would think of 'xplainin' unkindness. I weren't whupped or starved. Many times I was wore out to the bone, yes! He prayed like you prayed, but out loud. An' he had a Bible to read out of every morning." He pointed with some respect to the book on the table. "That's a Bible, ain't it, sah?"

"Yes, it is. So why did you run from him?"

Instantly he looked worried. "It's somethin', sah, I don't know if you can understand."

"I think I should try. I think white people should try to know how Negroes think."

Thomas's look of concern increased. "Then I think you'd have to start by being colored, sah, then bein' slave, for Negroes can think many different ways."

Charles felt rightly reproved. "Yes, of course. Let's not work on the past, then, but on the present. When Mr. Peabody trained me, he took me as a young boy, but with the idea that I would be his equal once I had matured. You are not so young. You might already be twenty years old. I don't know. But what I want to say is that I will have to treat you as someone who knows less and who needs to be learning. But that does not mean that my goal is not the same as his was. I want to see you matured, equal to any white man."

Thomas shook his head. "Whatever you say, sah."

"You don't believe me?"

Thomas gave him a furtive glance. "I'd like to believe you, just like you says you would like to trust me."

"I guess we do have an understanding, then." Charles wanted to say more, but there was suddenly much noise outside, as men were shouting, even so early in the morning.

Thomas was on his feet in an instant. "They comin' back for you' horses!"

"No, the noise is on Spruce Street." Charles rose and looked out the front window. Below was a group of twenty to thirty men. Several in the middle were carrying pieces of wood nailed together to form a model of a gallows. A stuffed sackcloth image of a Negro was hanging from a rope, bouncing wildly as the men marched along. Charles felt breathless, especially after Thomas looked out the window too. "I know that man in the lead," he confessed. "It's Mr. Anthony Ruskin. He's part of a campaign to get all colored persons removed from the state. And now I think he feels he has a cause to make everyone agree with him." He said no more.

Charles thought immediately of Mayleda, that she might be looking out the Barings' front windows. He had not stopped thinking of her all through the night and now in the day. "You stay here, Thomas, and I will be back in a moment. I must go over and see Mr. Baring next door."

CHAPTER 20

SNOW WAS FALLING when Angelene came to his door. "I'm ready," she said, not taking a step inside but staying on the porch when Joseph opened it to her. His coat and cloak were still on the pegs inside the door, so he asked her to come in. Her dark riding clothes were jeweled with large icy flakes that soon melted like those that had made her eyelashes bright with drops of water.

"I'm not sure I should go," he said, looking back to the kitchen where he would be leaving Ba to care for Daniel alone. He already had postponed his visit to Orphans' Cottage. He knew for the girl's sake he should not delay longer, yet he had not left the house since Daniel's arrival.

"Is something wrong?" Angelene asked with concern.

He could not say that there was, for the boy had been making continual and remarkable progress, which was evident even now as Ba sat beside him feeding him thin soup from a spoon.

"May I see him for a moment?"

No one from Oak Glen except Angelene's father had been in to visit the child during the first seven days when he had lingered near death. Five days ago his fever had subsided. Now his lungs were slowly clearing. Even so, Joseph chose to keep the child isolated and still.

But to Angelene he said, "Yes, of course." In part, Joseph knew that the confinement he required for Daniel reflected more his own need. He was weary from watching over him day and night. Yet there was something inside him that would not let him leave the boy for more than moments at a time, even though Angelene and her mother and others from the church had offered their help.

"This is Sister Brown," Joseph said when Angelene approached Daniel's bed. "She wants to see for herself how well you are getting along."

Daniel put his hand to the spoon and held it himself. Less than a week ago, he had still been as helpless as an infant, too weak to feed himself and with too little coordination. The boy looked between the young woman and Ba. Then he licked the spoon and laid it down upon his covers. Bringing his hands together, he clapped them with his fingers spread.

"What's he trying to do?" Angelene asked.

Joseph felt so proud that he had to smile. "He's trying to speak Ba's language."

"He is!"

"That is why Ba insists that I leave him with the child. He wants Daniel to learn."

Angelene frowned. "But what if he has some need he cannot express? My mother is ready to come and sit with him. I only need to go back and call her to come over. She could at least be Ba's ears and give him written messages, if necessary."

Perhaps Ba was able to read some of the words from her lips, for he shook his head and signed that he was capable. Even now as he spoke, Daniel tried to copy his every move, though while lying back on the pillows, for the little bit of excitement and activity had wearied him already.

"He does not know that many words, even to hear them," Joseph said, compelled to take the child's hand and not just talk about him. "But he's learning both languages. He knows what to do if he's thirsty or in pain or when he must relieve himself. I think he will be better with Ba than with anyone else, for they are already friends."

Hearing this word, the child weakly locked together his index fingers to form the symbol for "friend."

"That's remarkable!" Angelene said.

Again it caused Joseph to smile. "He's a smart little lad." He bent and kissed him on the head. Daniel puckered his lips. Joseph bowed and let him touch his cheek. "Kiss," Daniel said. Joseph could not deprive himself of the inward feeling of pride he had, just like that of a father.

"*You two should go,*" Barnabas signed to Joseph and Angelene.

"Go?" Daniel said the word, and he made the correct motion.

"The last three days he's been sleeping for a only few hours at a time, then waking up to speak until he is exhausted again."

Her look was kind. "Joseph, you are exhausted."

"Yes, I am, but I am happy too. His determination is extraordinary." He again held Daniel's warm, thin hands. "I told this to you before," Joseph said directly to him. "I must go take care of another child. I will return, I promise. I will go, and then I will come back."

The child lay back, sighed, and nodded. Still, Joseph kept a hold on his hands. "Whatever his past, it has made him as hungry for words and affection as for food." What he said then was far beyond the child's understanding, but it moved Angelene, Joseph could tell, though she kept silent.

"I love you, Daniel." Joseph dared to say the now familiar phrase in front of her.

"I love you, Dr. Joseph. I love you, Ba." The child spoke clearly, while his eyes moved furtively. He looked at Angelene but said nothing.

Joseph then felt obliged to explain. " 'I love you' is something he heard and learned from Mrs. Ruskin in the wagon on their way here. He said it to me first. I was amazed," Joseph confessed.

"You shouldn't have been." Angelene seemed pensive.

Joseph patted Daniel's fingers, then nodded to Ba. "I know we should go." He moved to the front door where he had his medical bag packed. He let Angelene go out first, then he followed her, taking his coat and cloak with him.

When he was outside, he put his outer garments on. "What? You have both horses saddled. Did you do this yourself?"

She frowned. "If two bachelors can care for a child, then one woman can saddle two horses!" Her expression thawed, and Joseph breathed easier in the fresh air. She stood for a moment more against the background of morning sky, where the clouds that had brought snow were now being swept away as high, thin wisps of whiteness.

Once they stepped down from the porch, Joseph held her big blond horse for her while she mounted. He fixed his medicine bag to laces behind his own saddle, then got up on the sturdy chestnut gelding he had had for most of his years in Oak Glen. Angelene stayed beside him as they started out, going just a short way on the street, then turning into her father's orchard. The trees there, bare and symmetrical, stood in rows as silent sentries, all at attention.

Neither of them spoke until the trail led into the forest on the southeast side of Welshman's Mountain. The sun shone on their backs with enough strength to give them warmth, and there was no wind once they had the mature growth of woodland trees all around them.

"Are you still thinking of keeping Daniel?" Angelene asked, breaking the silence as they walked their horses.

"Of course!" The idea chilled him every time Joseph reviewed it in his mind. He wondered why she would even ask. "He's made so much progress. He's been so starved for love."

She looked at him directly. "The same can be said of you."

The comment was disquieting. He tried to shrug it off.

"I mean it, Joseph. It's so clear that you need that boy's love as much as that child needs you. You're a different person for it."

"I hope I have no such selfish notion."

She sighed with exasperation. "It seems that selfishness and love must always go together by your definition."

They rode on in silence. Though it had been Angelene's nature all the years Joseph had known her to be confident and happy, it unnerved him now to see how he could plant in her the glumness he shouldered himself. "I have weighed you down by telling you my sorrows. Please, don't trouble yourself to carry burdens that are mine."

She looked across to him. "I may care about them if I want to, and I do!"

Joseph made himself look straight ahead. For months he had sensed this same kind of tension between them. He knew it was because she wanted to be closer in spirit and emotion than he would allow. He thought such anxiousness would have been resolved by his testimony about Rosa. Instead, she dared to speak of her now.

"You said that the woman who became your wife endured unspeakable trials."

"I did." Though he had kept his promise not to speak much about his past, Angelene had continued to speak of Rosa, wanting to know more about her. Usually the conversations between them lasted only a few minutes, before or after class or when she walked through his house, either going or coming from her own.

"Joseph, what if she had continued to reject your love in body and spirit just because she had been wounded?"

"She didn't!"

"I know. I'm asking because I wish you would see that being hurt and being harmed does not made one unlovable. Look at Daniel."

"I don't want to talk about it."

"You say you cannot love, but what I see between you and Daniel proves that wrong. I think what you really fear is *being* loved."

"Angelene."

"That little boy is going to love you. He already does. If I must, I will speak on his behalf only. But you must know that I want to speak on my behalf too. I have the capacity to love you, if you will let yourself be loved."

Joseph blinked painfully. "I asked you to come along today to help me through an indelicate situation. I'm not prepared to have a conversation turned on myself." He despised himself for being so harsh with her, for in the forest covered with new snow she looked as innocent and as beautiful as he had ever seen her. It made him cast his eyes down.

"I would like to help you bear your grief. The child should not do that."

"I appreciate you, Sister Brown. I hope you know that." Without being conscious of it at first, he was pulling his horse to a stop. "You are a wonderful, bright, warm young woman. I am a tired, worn-out, aging man. You may not know it yet, for your life in Oak Glen has been quite isolated, but there is a world out there for you, and you should do all in your power, with God's help, of course, to grasp it."

"What world will you raise Daniel in? Your dismal one, or the one of hope, which you can somehow still promise to me?"

"I should have the condition of the orphan girl on my mind. We should save our energy for that."

"All right but you know how I feel, Joseph Whitsun. I love you. No matter what, that is not going to change. And with time, I think I could love your Daniel too. Perhaps that will mean something to you someday. If there is a world of hope, and I think there is, then there's also room in it for *you*."

She kicked her horse, moving out ahead on the unmarred trail filled up with unblemished snow. She went so far out and so fast that he was obliged to knee his older horse into a canter so as not to lose her. Regard-less of the fact that he did not feel playful, she looked back, clearly ready to make a game of it. Since she had never ridden to the orphanage, he needed to lead the way. So he was forced to catch her. She was a confi-dent rider, but he overtook her mare at last. When he did, he saw her smiling.

"Are you angry at me?" she asked.

He told some of the truth. "No." Truly the fast ride had been exhila-rating, as had the moments when every care he had was left behind. Her face was joyful. Radiant. He looked away again, but only so she would not see him smile and grow too hopeful.

Coming out of the woods, Angelene saw a white fence against the snow. Joseph instructed her to follow the rails around to her left. Soon she saw a large stone house set on the hill away from the forest. When she looked back, she noticed that Joseph's jaw was set hard. He passed her, then led the way to one of the institution's back doors. She got down off her horse before he was able to dismount and come to help her.

She had never worked in the presence of white people before. As best she could, she hid her fears as they started up the narrow walk toward the huge white door. It opened before Joseph was even close enough to knock. A tall imposing woman stepped outside. To Angelene's dismay, Mr. Harley and Constable Long were with her, and they came out too.

Mr. Harley spoke awkwardly. "You were to be here last week at this time."

Angelene saw Joseph take in breath. He was direct with them all, not looking down or cowering. "Yes, Mr. Harley. But I could not come last week. I had another patient."

"A colored one, I hope," Constable Long said.

"Yes." As far as Joseph knew, Daniel's survival was a secret from all those in Brinkerville.

The woman had words then just as harsh as her countenance. "You shouldn't have come back at all."

Constable Long explained her anger directly. "Two weeks ago we know you looked at a thirteen-year-old white girl."

Joseph faced the woman in charge. "I did. That is one of the reasons I am coming back today and bringing Miss Brown. The girl is seriously ill. I believe she has a tumor."

"Yet you did not come last week because of taking care of your own!" the woman accused.

"That's true." Joseph remained steady. "But it's also true that I spent many hours with my medical journals. I did not want to make any kind of hasty judgment. The young patient here may have cancer in the womb. An examination after two weeks of growth might confirm it today."

Angelene saw both white men flinch noticeably.

Joseph chose to ignore their reaction. "I have a letter with me explaining the urgent need, in my opinion, to take her to the city hospital should my findings prove true. I wrote out all my observations to this point." He glanced directly at Mr. Harley. "But I did not sign my name, because I considered the dilemma of producing written evidence as a colored man. Yet I know my work is valid, and I felt it wise to say something to the other doctors who will see her."

He paused, and when they did not speak, he continued. "I know you may not think you have the funds. If that is true, then I suggest that you take her to Dr. Leon Ellis. He is a white Quaker and a skilled physician who dedicates himself wholly to helping the poor."

The woman put her hand to her face and emitted a little scream. "I cannot bear to be near you!" she said with indignation. "That you would terrorize her so, *then* send her to a real doctor!"

"I do not understand what you mean by that, madam."

"Oh, that you would have her clothes off and touch her."

"You, Madam Calley, were there. There was no immodesty."

Joseph saw Angelene from the corner of his eye. She was leaning forward slightly.

"I did not know what you were doing when you had her on the table," Headmistress Calley said. "And she's been more ill ever since that day."

"I explained that she might be. I was only looking for the cause of her illness then. I came back today knowing that I could do the surgery myself, but knowing, too, that the board would likely be wanting someone else to do it." He turned to Harley. "Thus my letter and my suggestion that you take her to Dr. Ellis. I do believe it is a matter of life and death."

"Likely because of what you did to her!" Madam Calley said.

Joseph searched the faces of Harley and Long while Angelene watched him intensely. "I did nothing but what any trained doctor would do. The headmistress knows this. She was there every moment because I requested it."

"I did not know then that you were entertaining white women in your town," she said with disgust.

Now Joseph looked only to the constable. Mr. Long explained. "The men of Brinkerville learned about Anthony Ruskin's sister-in-law being found in a bedchamber with you and another Negro male."

"Another practitioner, sir," Joseph protested, "and you saw the reason, sir! There was an ill child in that bedroom."

Mr. Harley spoke. "You were accused of quackery there. When Constable Long told me that, I knew I had better review my personal choice to have called you to this institution."

"I have cared for these children. Doesn't this letter prove it? I've asked nothing for myself. I do this so that the child might be saved. I brought Miss Brown to be a nurse with me today so that it would not be necessary for me to touch the girl again. Headmistress Calley could speak on my behalf, if she would. The girl she brought to me was sickly and losing weight. I examined the child professionally, then I told her that it might be a week or two until I could know the cause."

"Of all Negroes, I did have hope in you!" Harley said, as though he had not listened to Joseph at all.

"I came here at your bidding, sir, and did as I was asked."

His face reddened. "I will take the blame for that, but Constable Long and Mrs. Calley do know that I never expected you to be one who would take advantage. I was appalled to hear the news concerning the woman, Mrs. Ruskin."

Angelene stared at Joseph while he dared to look at her.

"Don't act as though you don't know why you're not being trusted now!" Mr. Harley said. "Truly that sickens me all the more. You think the truth needs to be told by letter, then consider this, because you are a literate Negro."

He handed a newspaper to Joseph. "You see there that Anthony Ruskin is looking for Negro males who may have compromised his dead brother's wife. And you were with her! You and that other Negro!" Joseph had no time to protest before Harley showed him another piece of paper. This was a letter signed by the slave agents, Pudget and Dawes, who had abandoned the child. Angelene was standing close enough that she could read the letter too. It gave the slave catchers' description of coming to Oak Glen to look for a fugitive. They wrote that they had found Whitsun and another Negro male alone in a bedchamber with Attorney Anthony Ruskin's sister-in-law under the pretense of being doctors.

"Mr. Long, you were there," Joseph said as he gave the letter back. "I don't believe you saw anything amiss."

"Just as I was too blind to see anything wrong here until the full picture was pulled together right before me!" Headmistress Calley said. "Now it's certain that you are just like every other colored beast, looking for any opportunity. God strike you, Joe Whitsun!"

Angelene could no longer hold her opinions silently. "That isn't true!"

The headmistress's voice stayed as icy as the air. "Get off the porch," she said to Joseph. "Take your colored woman with you. I never want to see you here again."

"We don't want you coming back, Joe," Constable Long agreed, but with far less emotion. "I'm not saying that you did do anything wrong here, it just will be better if you keep company with your own kind only, male and female."

Anglene was trembling. Joseph took hold of her arm and held it tightly. They were watched, she knew, while he helped her down the steps and out to her horse. Angelene could not even look at Joseph while he took his own. When they both were ready, he led the way back around the fence to the woods, retracing their trail, a vivid gray path in otherwise undisturbed snow.

He seemed determined to ride fast and hard. "Stop, Joseph, please!" she cried when they were far away from the house and she had used nearly all her strength to keep up with him.

He accommodated her desire. She felt her tears when he stopped. "Joseph, that was the most hideous spectacle I have ever witnessed." His eyes flashed to her, convicting her that she had been reared in a protected environment. "How ignorant they are! What stupid fools!"

He gave no verbal response. She saw the muscles in his face twitching as though violence might explode out of his mouth. She had never seen him so agitated, yet so steady, even down to his hands. He took one look to make sure she was securely seated, then kicked his horse and they rode off again at a rapid, discomforting pace.

Raised mostly on the mountainside, with three brothers as siblings, Angelene had no trouble keeping up with him as he hastened back to Oak Glen. Not a word was shared between them until they were at his door and he moved to help her down.

"Oh, Joseph!" she cried in sympathy again.

This time he let her words run off like water as he headed straight inside. "I tell you, if I risked Daniel's recovery in any way by seeing to my duties at the orphanage . . ." He did not finish the sentence but went into his house, leaving the door open for her to follow him.

It was like another world inside—warm, loving, silent. Barnabas was on the same chair where he had been when they had left him. The old man had brought down his chess board. Daniel was still lying back on his pillows but now with chess pieces spread all over his bed. He turned to them and smiled. He called out in breathy but clear words, "Dr. Joseph. See."

Angelene watched Joseph's transformation. Outside he had been riled, either hurt or angry beyond words. Now he was again the patient, tender man she knew she loved. The boy puckered his lips to kiss Joseph, then Joseph did the same. Barnabas watched them for a time, then shifted his eyes to Angelene. The old man had a keen sense for reading emotions. Without making one sign with his hands, he was able to question her with his eyes: *Was there trouble?*

She nodded glumly, knowing she was still close to tears.

"You must stay here from now foward!" the man said with silent emphasis as he signed to Joseph with the concern of a father.

Joseph shook his head as though fully resigned to it. *"There is no freedom for a black man out there!"* He frowned as he pointed to the door.

Little Daniel tried to imitate what they had said to each other, which was in sign language only. Now Angelene's tears did flow, though she turned to hide them. Behind her, she heard the little child's simple question. "Dr. Joseph. What you an' Ba say?"

When Angelene left the log house, Barnabas came out with her to take care of the horses they had ridden. The old man was grave, but he did not engage her in conversation. She respected him all the more for this. Whatever he longed to know, she knew he would ask Joseph to speak about it himself. Yet he did ask her one question with grandfatherly care. *"Are you all right?"*

She blinked away yet more tears and nodded that she was. She was conscious as seldom before that Barnabas Croghan was a white man. How could others of Ba's same race be so cruel when their neighborly friendship with this man was so natural?

He was still studying the grief on her face when her father came out from around the far side of the schoolhouse. In their absence, he had been in her classroom teaching the children Bible lessons and giving them practice in reading from the Scriptures.

Aware that Joseph should be the first to speak about what had happened, Angelene still could not resist her father's comfort. "Oh, Daddy! Mr. Harley and Mr. Long were at the orphanage! They were there to confront Joseph. They had a letter written against him by the slave agents and a copy of a Philadelphia newspaper. They nearly accused him to his face of taking advantage of a young white girl who was his patient."

His grimness was startling. Though she had sought his solace, he seemed to have none to give. "What, Daddy? Did you know this would happen even before we went out there?" She pulled herself back to stand on her own.

"No, Angel, but it does not surprise me." He did not look at her. "Where is Joseph now?"

"With Daniel, of course." She grabbed his hand. "Please tell me all that you know! I see your worry! Are you fearful that they will come and do something more to him?"

He pulled her to himself and stroked her hair. "While you two were gone, the new solicitor for Mr. Douglass's newspaper came in from Philadelphia. While I gave the children their morning recess, this young man, Mr. Dumond Holmes, had just enough time to share the news that he had heard in the city."

"What news?"

"All in time, Angel. Right now, Mr. Holmes, the man who's come to sell newspapers, is watching over your class. I want you to go inside and finish out the day with the children as usual. Little ones can see your worry or your grief, so do not show it. At the end of the day there will be time to talk and pray."

"Daddy, how can you expect me to bear this burden without knowing?"

"With God's help, we do what we must do."

"You do think Joseph is in danger. I can see the worry and grief in you!"

He was so oddly distracted that he did not answer her. "You need to be in the classroom. I need to speak with Joseph now."

He left her standing alone. Despite the snow, she waded around to the back door, believing that if she had gone in Joseph's way, she would not have had the strength to pass him by for the sake of the children.

Once she was around to the rear yard, she opened the classroom door.

The stranger standing at her desk was a young brown-skinned man flaw-lessly dressed in a fully matched suit of clothes, as wealthy men from the cities wear. She had never seen a Negro dressed so well. His voice was different too. Though he was speaking in English, it came out in deep, rounded tones.

"Children, it seems that your teacher, Miss Brown, has returned." He looked toward the door. Angelene felt herself caught in his gaze.

Angelene struggled to remember his name. She could not, for though her father had said it, her mind had been on Joseph. When she continued to stand there awkwardly, a distinct twinkle came to his eye. "I assume this is your teacher."

She was wholly embarrassed, for some of the older children were as-tute enough to observe her self-conscious actions. "Yes. I am Angelene Brown." She forced herself to walk closer to him, though she felt like peasantry dressed as she was for outside travel.

"I must apologize," he said, gesturing to those in her classroom who all seemed under his spell, as she was, and incredibly quiet. "Your father said that it was time for them to practice their arithmetic. Instead, I con-fess, I was telling them about London, England, which is my home."

"How nice!" she stammered, aware of her own feeling of plainness from being raised in the country. "I'm sure most of them have never met anyone from over the sea." She felt herself then being held by his dark eyes, which seemed quite bold and in turn made her shy. "Nor have I met anyone like that, sir." He might have been as young as she, but his de-meanor made his presence commanding.

He went for his sleek high hat that he had set upside down on her desk. "I will let you begin with your regular lesson now." He nodded to her, then to the children. "It was my pleasure to be with you, young friends."

The unnatural quiet of the classroom continued until he had walked through the hallway door, his ivory-headed cane and hat in hand. Sud-denly the calm broke like rain pummeling on a tin roof. Children giggled. Many were nearly out of their seats. No one had regard for her stern looks. Some of the boldest even cheered out loud. "We think he likes you, Miss Brown! We think you like him!"

"You all be quiet now! Get your slates so we can catch up on your ciphering."

She saw then that in the back of the room, standing in the doorway to Joseph's house, the newspaper solicitor had turned back to watch her.

CHAPTER 21

ALL THE DAYS MAYLEDA was in hiding with the Barings, Charles never ventured next door without some obvious excuse in hand. Today it was one of the harness bells that had worked loose from the leather. He went inside his neighbor's shop and did not have to say a word.

"I'll take that for you, Friend Powell," Huck said from his workbench, having taken on the practice of addressing him as though they both were Quakers. The older man's eyes sparkled then. "I could have it finished in say, three-quarters of an hour. Will that give you enough time, Brother Powell?"

Charles said an awkward yes, though he did not mind that the older married man encouraged him in every way to see his visits as courtship. It did not matter to the Negro that Mrs. Ruskin and he were from different classes. However, it was something that never left Charles' mind for a moment when he was with the lady in exile.

Even now the harnessmaker prodded him. "Go on up. My missus an' girls are all at market."

"Mayleda?" Charles called before he was at the top step.

"Yes, Charles! Hello! Come up!"

At once Mayleda was at the top of the stairs to greet him. With her to direct his way, though all was quite familiar now, Charles entered into the main room where the family had been sacrificing space and one bed to provide for Mayleda. To occupy her time, she knitted socks or mended clothes for the family. She had also taken in the seams of the dull brown dress she wore, borrowed from Huck Baring's wife.

At first, Charles knew, Mrs. Baring had been quite uncomfortable with Mayleda doing work for them. Yet after eleven days of confinement, all seemed to be going more smoothly. Still, it remained a question in his mind, and certainly in Mayleda's, how long she would have to be hiding here.

As usual during his visits, Mayleda sat on the edge of the bed she slept in while Charles took the chair. Her first question to him was nearly always the same. "What news have you heard? Do you know anything more about the little boy, Daniel?" Through visits from those involved in the Vigilance Committee, she had learned that the boy was still alive, news that had been carried by Negro travelers from the Lancaster County countryside.

"Today I don't know anything more about Daniel," he said.

Often then she would ask him about the arrival of ships, whose passenger lists were always posted in the newspapers. It was now December, and it was always on her mind that Judith and her grandparents would soon be home. "And there was no mention of Ruskins arriving in port," he said, before she needed to question him. She sighed.

"There is good news today, however," he told her with genuine gladness. "Castner Hanway of the Christiana trial has been judged not guilty by the jury. Though nothing has reached the newspapers yet, the talk in the store is that none of the other men will even be brought to trial. Everyone thinks now that it was a blessing that the charge of treason was brought against them, for Hanway and the others might not have fared so well if the accusations had been rioting, or even murder."

"God be praised!" She looked too relieved to even smile. "Then do you think that the verdict proves there are many in the Commonwealth who do not support the nation's present insanity in trying to protect slavery?"

"Yes, ma'am, that's exactly what I hear others saying."

"God of mercy!" This time her words were like a prayer. "Perhaps we will be spared from the wrath of judgment. What was the date of the decision?"

"December eleventh. Hanway and the other white men are still in prison, and the twenty-three black men associated with the uprising too. But there's talk of them being released. And more talk that no court in Pennsylvania is going to have the will or spirit to convict them of any lower crime."

"I pray that is so!" Suddenly her eyes, which had been closed, were on him. "What about you, Charles? Are you now fully convinced of the rightness of abolition and the wrongness of slavery?"

"Yes, I am, ma'am. In part, thanks to you."

She smiled momentarily. Her eyes were bright, but still her face was somber. "How is Thomas doing with you?"

"We're learning together." Charles found that he could be smiling and serious too. "Often I have to remind myself that it's probably the youth in him that does rub me and challenge me, instead of the color." He paused. "I suppose it would be interesting to hear what *he* has to say concerning me. That it is often my age, instead of my lack of color, that does puzzle him." He was able to laugh about himself, and Mayleda smiled.

"You are schooling him, I hope?"

He knew this was a tremendous longing in her heart. "Yes, ma'am!" he said with teasing obedience.

"Are you teaching him the Scriptures?"

He could not jest with her then. "I am, Mayleda, but he resists. I feel I can understand why. He said his master read the Bible to him, the same man who sold his family to have the money to keep him as a city slave."

"Read him the story of Joseph, Charles. The stories of the exodus. Read him the gospel, so that he can see how Christ was the friend of all men and women whose hearts sought after God. And read him the story of the crucifixion, how Christ suffered at the hands of evil men. Instill that hope of freedom in him, please! Instill the vision that God desires His church to come from every race and nation! Read Psalm 117. It is short and easy to remember. 'O praise the Lord, all ye nations: praise him, all ye people. For his merciful kindness is great toward us: and the truth of the Lord endureth forever. Praise ye the Lord.' Charles, teach him that!"

"Yes, all right, as I learn it myself. You have quite a passion about this all! I admire you."

"You can lose him to discouragement if he cannot soon find himself in Christ." She stopped, and her words turned gentle. "Charles Powell, you are a good man. I trust you to be doing the best you can for this young man."

"I am not a good man."

"You are."

"No, there is still suspicion in me. Your heart is so pure and so open, May. Mine still is filled with distrust. Because Thomas is with me, other Negroes are always nearby. I am not completely comfortable, I confess."

"Because they are colored, or because they are idle and restless and without meaningful employment?"

He nodded. "I see what you're saying. It is some of both, I feel." He cared about her so deeply, yet he could not bring himself to say it. "I am concerned for you too. I have been thinking what must be done for you."

She sighed. "I know I cannot hide away forever."

His words seemed to surprise her. "I'm wondering if you can. Not here, of course. But someplace where you could be at home and live free yourself."

"I have no resources, and even if I could run away and hide from the Ruskins, I would not be happy anywhere on earth without my Judith."

"I understand. But what if you were established somewhere and then started working on the problem of how to get Judith?"

"I have no resources for that! The Ruskins presented their evidence against me in court so they could be assured that Judith would remain close to them until she becomes a woman."

"I know. You've explained all that to me. But I've been thinking. I could have the resources to see that you are moved to a safe place away from the family. I could probably even have some money for legal fees on your behalf."

"Charles, I don't want you to spend your money to help me!"

"I would ask nothing in return. No obligations. It's that important to me that you be happy and not controlled by those who do not agree with your kind heart."

Her lips parted.

He would not let her speak. "Just think about it. Think about where you would want to go. Even as far as Boston. That is possible!"

"Charles, I would not let you do this for me."

"I believe it is an inspiration by the Spirit of God," he said sincerely. "Would you dare to counter that?"

"No." Tears came to her eyes. "There is no place I want to go where I will be alone."

He did not know how to interpret her words or her longings. "You would be under no obligation to me. You would be free to choose your own friends." He wanted to say her own spouse, but he feared revealing his heart.

He could bear the secret of his feelings no longer. "Mayleda Ruskin, I care very much about you. It grieves me to see you unhappy. God knows I will do everything not to let you be hurt or harmed again. And that goes for your daughter also."

She reached for his hand. "God sent you to me."

He held her fingers and felt his own on fire. "I dare to say the same of you. You have taught me much."

"The purity and strength of your heart do challenge me."

Her words made him take his hand away. "My actions are not always so right, madam." He convinced himself once more that the difference in class must keep them apart. Even though she was dressed in plain clothes and in a plain house, there was a natural elegance about her, which he completely lacked.

"You judge yourself too harshly, Charles."

"Mayleda, you don't really know me. One reason I took Thomas in is because of Friend Elim Peabody, who owned the store before me. He found me on the street, an urchin rejected by my mother's family. I am half Irish and all poor."

"Dear Charles, do you think I care?" Again she took his hand. "Much of what they wrote in the papers is true about me. I am the daughter of a rice planter, but I truly rejected that way of life. What's important to me now is God's kingdom. That we all have the opportunity to become one family in His Spirit."

He stood.

She dropped his hand but held him with her words. "I see now. You think yourself unworthy of our friendship."

"I *am* unworthy."

"Not by God's standards. No!" She stood too. "How men judge other men is of no avail in God's kingdom. I was born to wealth. I did not choose it. That is why God's commandment was applicable to me, to leave what I had to help the poor."

"I was among the poor."

"I did not mean that to be slighting. I meant to say that God has His ways of making us equal, and I think that one of them is His economy. We learn that we can hold nothing as our own within His Kingdom. That creates equality, as none of us has anything of our own and all is given over to God."

He thought again of his own untold plan to sell his store and his inventory to accomplish her rescue. "I am willing to give all that I have, no matter how little it is, to save you from further condemnation."

She went toward the window. Though it was high off the street and dusty, she followed the Barings' wishes that she not go too close in case someone might look up and see her. "Charles, I think I need to know how you would get the means to help me." She turned.

He was honest. "I will mortgage the store."

"Then you will lose the store if you use the money to get me settled elsewhere and never repay it!"

"My plan is that I would still have Marcy and Maude. They would help me to take you where you want to go, then they would give me what I need to start again as a simple traveling merchant."

"You would do that for me!"

"Yes. You have done so much for others. You and Sprague. I would do this to honor his life too."

She stepped to him, weeping. He reached and took her gently into his arms. She felt so small. He could not keep himself from being thrilled by her touch.

"Is it wrong for me to say that I do not want to live alone anymore?" she asked. "Is it wrong for me to say that I care about you, Charles, though I have nothing to give you but myself?" She paused and put her arms around his waist.

"I don't think so." He kissed her hair. "I love you, Mayleda! I cannot believe that you would love me. And I cannot believe that I am even having the courage to confess this to you."

"Hold me and tell me that you will not let me go."

In the distance Charles heard a harness bell ringing. With Mayleda still in his arms, he looked around to see that Huck had come up the stairs. Rather than feeling embarrassed or ashamed, Charles moved only one step back and took Mayleda by her hand. His neighbor was laughing good-naturedly.

"Well, now, I done been wonderin' how many days of belts an' buckles an' harnesses it was gwine take 'fore you two saw the light 'bout each other."

Charles shared his plan with Huck. "I'm going to mortgage the store, and with that money I'm going to move Mrs. Ruskin to some safe place. I've been thinking about this plan for a while." He dared to look into Mayleda's admiring, expecting eyes. "I think today my plan was confirmed. I'll take my horses and sell my inventory. But now it's on my mind not to have to turn Thomas back to the street. He's a good young man, I think, and he's proving himself to be a careful worker. I was wondering, Friend, might you consider taking him on to teach him your trade, if he's willing?"

Mayleda squeezed his hand.

"Yes, Friend Powell, I might do that if he's interested."

Charles felt a new and uncertain way had been opened to him. When he looked into Mayleda's face, he found courage to pursue it. "I'll not tell him yet," Charles said to them both. "I need to see about the mortgage. Perhaps that can be done even today."

"Be careful," Mayleda urged. "Your account is in Tyrone Ruskin's establishment."

"Better to do it now before the man is home," Charles said.

"Oh, Charles, are you sure about sacrificing your store?"

"My sweet, darling Mayleda! I am."

Angelene's classroom had been emptied of students for only a few moments that afternoon before Dumond showed himself, coming in by the back door. "I did not expect to see school conducted on a Saturday," he said, sitting down on one of the front desks while she busied herself stacking books that she had no real reason to move.

"It's because it's December," she answered, aware once more of feeling and sounding too much like a country-reared girl. "The children are needed for planting and harvesting, and then often they cannot come in the deep snow, so I have some extra days of classes in November and December until Christmastime."

"That seems like a wise idea." He had a gentle smile that she was learning to treasure the longer he was there.

"It was part of Joseph Whitsun's plan." She felt her face heat as usual whenever she said Joseph's name. "He's in charge of the school. He founded it."

"I've been getting to know Dr. Whitsun better these past few days."

She waited for him to say more, but he did not. "You've seen Daniel too, then?"

"Yes, I have. Sometimes I sit with Mr. Whitsun while he sits with the child." Some anxiety within him seemed to bring him to his feet. "Miss Brown, what do you think about the woman who brought the boy here? Is she the mother or not?"

Angelene could not hide her surprise. "What? Have you been speaking to Sister Sladder too?"

"No. I'm asking the question because of what has been published in the white city newspapers by those who wish to thwart the cause of abolition in this nation. Another issue of the *Pennsylvania Citizen* just arrived today by mail. I've written to ask men in the Vigilance Committee to keep me informed by sending the news here. I think the story is quite important to America's colored population, so much so that I have asked them to send off telegraphs to Mr. Douglass and others to let them know that I purpose to stay here a while longer to learn what I can.

"It is important for colored Americans to understand the issues here and what's at stake." He often referred to them as that, though Negroes were not citizens. "Sometimes I think the colored population of this nation can set its best course by first listening to what its adversaries say."

"So what are they saying, Mr. Holmes?"

He smiled at her interest. "The last published testimony was by Mr. Anthony Ruskin himself, replying to the many accusations put forth toward Mrs. Mayleda Ruskin."

"He is that woman's brother-in-law."

"Yes. Mr. Ruskin denies that his brother could have fathered a mulatto child. But he does not contest that the boy might have been given life by his sister-in-law. He avows that she has no Negro blood in her veins, that the bookseller's testimony about the family Bible from the South is untrue, for he says the woman's quarters in his house have been searched, and no such Bible has been found."

Angelene was surprised that Dumond knew every detail of the story. He went on. "The woman has disappeared. Did you know that?"

"No."

"In part Mr. Ruskin is writing, he says, as a plea for her to be found. In the article he speaks eloquently of his concern for her safety and her sanity."

"From what was witnessed here, the man had not much tenderness toward her."

"I know. I've been told that by others here." He did not mention names.

"Mr. Ruskin led a parade in the city to protest the licentious behavior of black males." Dumond paused and raised his eyebrows. "He concludes that his relation has been a victim. Her innocent heart and mind, he writes, led her to want to reach out to the colored poor. And yet instead of cherishing her charity, she was probably outraged, perhaps time and time again, by Negro men from the streets. Though not in so direct a way, this is the content of this day's news story."

The issue sounded too personal, especially coming from a man who was still almost a stranger, and Angelene's face flushed at the telling of it all. She began to move the books again.

"The article says that Mrs. Ruskin would be a woman too broken and ashamed to reveal her past to anyone. I think Mr. Ruskin will gain much sympathy from white readers by his writing."

"I would rather not hear about it." It was still Angelene's well-kept secret that Joseph and Mrs. Ruskin had known each other from the past. Because of Daniel always being with him, Angelene felt no freedom to ask Joseph any questions concerning the newspaper reports. Because of the child's brandmarks, she continued to believe as Joseph did, that Daniel had been a slave. Yet that fact could not naturally clear the whole character of Mayleda Callcott Ruskin. Angelene entertained the small thought now, as she had done before, that circumstances and time could have changed the scruples that Joseph once knew belonged to this woman, at least in her childhood and early years as an adult.

Dumond looked at her as if the whole issue were just one grand puzzle to be solved. "What do you say, Miss Brown? Is a black man guilty? Has Mrs. Ruskin been in the North merely passing as white? Who are the parents of the child Dr. Whitsun now holds?"

She blinked, overwhelmed. "I don't think the truth will be known from reports in the newspapers. Persuasive writers seem to have the power to say anything they like."

He showed her that warm smile again. "So you distrust the press!"

"I do unless I trust the writer, which in all these cases I do not."

"That is very good, Miss Brown! It shows you have a discriminating mind that will look for the truth and not just assume it."

"Did you think I didn't?"

He began to walk around the room, looking at the few books she had. "I've been looking in on class these past few days, you know. It seems that you teach only from a perspective of Christianity. Is that part of Dr. Whitsun's plan too?"

She had never questioned the wisdom of having their faith permeate every subject. "What else would you expect, sir?" His poise caused her to address him as her superior, then she regretted it, for by doing so she felt she had wrongly demeaned herself.

"You are teaching children of African descent. Do you not think your studies should be based on the learning and knowledge of our own people?"

She did not know what to say.

"What do you teach them about Timbuktu or Mali or Mecca?"

Her mouth opened, wordless.

"My inquiry is not meant to shame you, Miss Brown, but to confirm the reasons why I left England to come to America. And perhaps other reasons why I would like to stay in Oak Glen for a season."

Angelene had always thought of Europeans as being wholly a white race, but she kept her ignorance to herself. "Why did you come, Mr. Dumond?" She tried to sound casual.

He sat back on one of the desks again, looking satisfied that she had asked. "I wanted to see for myself how the colored race behaves within a nation that was established by revolution and that calls for personal liberty. I wanted to know for myself why black and brown men cower here instead of rising up to take what could and should be rightfully theirs."

"Revolution would bring a bloodbath. We have little, and sometimes no, protection under the nation's laws, for we are not allowed to be citizens, or colored *Americans*, as you like to say."

"Ah, there's a question too! Who does not *allow* some to be citizens, when all work and occupy the same nation?"

"The Congress makes the laws. There are no Negroes in the legislature."

"Ah, another enigma! Why does this remain acceptable? From what I have seen since coming here, there are Negro businessmen, Negro churchmen, Negro lawyers, and Negro doctors, though some like Joseph Whitsun seem content to work in secret. What keeps such talent away from the political arena?"

"Those already in power!" Angelene answered without question.

"I don't think so. And I'm ready now to say that to those of African descent in America. I think that you yourselves continue to keep your-selves shut out because you continue to acquiesce instead of rising in the power of unity to take a stand! Think of Pennsylvania. Black men had the right to vote here until the state revised its constitution in 1838. Why was there no riot and bloodshed then?"

"I'm impressed that you know our history."

"*I* would be impressed if I had heard of a revolution in 1838 because of that loss of power! I do not understand the mentality of a people who will not fight." He picked up her Bible. "But perhaps I am learning what keeps American Africans subdued."

"So many of us are slaves. We have no arms."

"Education is a weapon, Miss Brown. Surely you do know that."

"Yes, I know it is!" She was sensitive to how he might be looking down on her and on those like her, her own father and Joseph included. "But there is a political line between the states of Pennsylvania and Mar-yland that keeps education for the Negro from going South. Surely you know *that*, Mr. Holmes!"

"That is another reason I came. I think your patterns here can be changed. You appear to see things from one level only, from North to South. But I've come from outside. For us in England, the whole of America has been thought of as the West, and surely there are ways for African peoples to influence other African peoples, east to west."

Angelene looked at him with true curiosity. Perhaps he did have things to say to this nation. If so, it puzzled her that he would choose to remain in small, rural Oak Glen. "You should be in a place like Philadel-phia, where your ideas could be better heard."

It made him smile. "Whether you see it or not, your father, Cum-mington Brown, is and will be quite an influential man. The black man's podium in America is the church. I don't say that happily, for again I think it reflects on what the Black American thinks the White American will *permit* him to have. A shadow of white religion seems to be no threat to the American people at present. Well, wait until it is infused with the power and substance of African thinking. Then the sparks will ignite and burn away the impurity we see now."

Even as he spoke with so much passion, she felt him looking her over from head to toe.

"What do you think, Miss Brown?"

"I'm not sure what you mean by power and substance."

"Of course you could not. Look at the sum of what you study. There is a world of religion and experience that white Christian writers never reveal, but a world that literacy can open for the black man. So please know that while I do affirm your efforts, I would also say that your focus on Christianity will likely keep yet another generation from having liberty."

She had nothing to say in defense of what she had been teaching. "I should get home to start supper," she decided out loud, not knowing any better way to respond to her own uneasiness.

He laughed gently. "I did not think you would run away from dialogue, Miss Brown, to hide yourself in woman's work."

"I am not running. There is wisdom in saying nothing when one has nothing to say. But I will think about what you have said. I hope you would know that, even without my saying it."

"I like your spirit, Miss Brown!"

Dumond had been staying with them in the upstairs room which had been her brothers'. He had been taking his meals with them too, so he knew her schedule of responsibilities, which included much of the housework because of her mother's illness.

"Allow me to delay you just one more moment," he said, coming so close that she felt she should not breathe. "Something else came in the mail today. I asked your father's permission to be the one to show it to you."

She could not imagine what would cause him to justify himself in coming so close. "The *Gospel Weekly*." He smiled. "And a very good poem is published in it."

"Oh my!"

"Shall I read it to you?"

"I don't think so. It's not really that good. You would say that it's all from the perspective of my Christian faith."

"I'm not speaking so much of the content, but of the talent."

"Mr. Holmes, I hesitate to believe you."

"Miss Brown, I think one of my other missions in America must be to let *you* experience something about the world that is larger than this place and to help you to see what your own contribution could be in it."

She stepped back when he put his fingers at her waist. He unhanded her at once but without apologizing for what seemed to her to be improper.

"I have some book and writings of my own. Perhaps we could take time for discussion."

"All right." She still felt flustered.

"Perhaps after supper in the evenings."

"Yes, perhaps. Depending on if my mother needs me, or Mr. Whitsun, as I sometimes sit with Daniel." She was conscious of how she had called Joseph by his last name.

His gaze was captivating. "It is my hope, Miss Brown, that no one needs you this evening but I."

CHAPTER 22

EARLY SUNDAY MORNING Joseph left Daniel's bedside to heat water on the stove. Long before it boiled, he took the kettle and quietly filled the basin on the pine stand in front of the shaving mirror that stood in the kitchen's corner. Taking off his shirt, he washed himself in the warm, soothing liquid. His guardianship over Daniel all these days continued to leave him weary, yet also with an indescribable joy. The child progressed so wondrously, day after day.

Joseph could not keep his morning activity completely silent, for while he washed and then shaved, water drops tinkled lightly against the wide ceramic bowl. Conscious of the sound, he looked over and found the boy awake. He reached for his towel, and in that amount of time, Daniel was struggling to climb out of bed, something he had not done before.

Joseph rushed to him. "Daniel, no! You can't get up yet, though I'm glad you are feeling so well today!"

The child seemed dazed. Perhaps Joseph's assessment had been wrong. "What is it? Are you hurting? Are you ill?"

The boy would not speak, but tears squeezed from his eyes while he stretched out his hand. Joseph was holding him now, centering him back on the bed. Daniel's hand reached around him and stopped directly on the brandmark of the cross inside the circle that Joseph would bear to his grave.

"That!" The child articulated his thought with one tense word. "That!" he cried again, then he held out his own hand so Joseph could see the brand mark of the *V* burned into his palm.

"Ah! You saw my brand mark, and you matched it with your own." Joseph sat on the bed beside him and looked into the little boy's eyes. Daniel bit his lip, perhaps not knowing what to expect next.

"Dear child!" Joseph leaned forward and embraced him fully, careful of his still healing wounds. "Yes, I have a brand mark, and that is because like you, I was a slave. I was held in places where I did not want to live. I was made to do work that I did not want to do." He said this all because he did not know if Daniel even comprehended the meaning of slavery, even though he had endured its pain. He stopped. Perhaps it was not right to burden this child with more than he already knew.

Daniel pulled back. Slowly the boy put his hands on his own head, though the raising of his arms must have brought him much discomfort.

"What are you trying to tell me or show me, Daniel? I don't understand."

The boy ducked low. "You? In the box?"

Joseph could tell from having his own horrific memories that the child was close to having some kind of terrible waking dream about his past. "Not every slave lives in a box," he told him gently, watching the action of his eyes. "Is that where you lived?"

Daniel pressed his head until his chin bent against his chest.

"It was a small place?" Joseph guessed, moving his hands to show tight dimensions.

Daniel closed his eyes as though the daytime nightmare was coming nearer.

"Was your sister there, or were you there alone?"

The child emitted an audible cry. He had done this before when he could not understand what was being asked of him.

Daniel turned his face from Joseph. From his mouth came forth all the vile words that someone must have used like a verbal whip against him.

"Hush, Daniel! Hush! Those words are not for you, nor are they about you!"

Because the child seemed so alert and so intent on remembering, Joseph dared to ask a question that had burned within him. "Was Venor the name of the master who kept you in the box?"

Once more Daniel looked at him blankly.

"Who locked you in? Who let you out?" Joseph pantomimed his words when he spoke.

Daniel set his teeth hard as though seeing a spectre. "Big Man!" He called out the name while his jaws stayed clenched.

"Big Man is not here!" Joseph assured him at once. He tried to touch him. He understood the pain of the past being so real that it would cause the child to pull away. Joseph lifted his hands. "Big Man will not come again. Look, I am free, Daniel. And you are free! Do you understand? This is my house. I can walk, I can run, and I can ride my horse as I will. Ba is my friend. We work together. We eat. We play together." He turned around and pointed to the shelf that had the chess board. "You will be free to do all these things too, as soon as you are well."

Both of them were startled when the front door opened. Barnabas came into the kitchen from outside, for he had already been to the barn to care for the animals. At once he sensed Joseph's intensity and saw the child drop back to the pillows. *"Is Daniel worse?"* he asked, rushing close to the bed.

"No. But now he knows I have been a slave. He saw my scar."

Even though the conversation had exhausted Daniel, his inquisitiveness was not fading. "What does that mean?" the child asked. This was his usual question when he saw the two of them speaking with their hands in symbols he did not yet know.

Joseph was more careful now about saying words aloud while he signed them to Ba. *"Today is Sunday. Ba is going to church. I am staying with you."*

"Church?" While lying there, Daniel made the sign for it.

Of course he might not know. Though this was the not the first Sunday that he had been with them, it was likely the first time he had seen them speak of church. "It is where we go to worship God together," Joseph said.

Suddenly Daniel made himself sit up. "I want to see God! My sister is there!"

Joseph translated the boy's comment for Barnabas. It brought tears to his old friend's eyes. Then Joseph tried to help the child understand, signing while he spoke so Barnabas could follow along. *"Your sister lives in heaven, not in church. God is everywhere, up in heaven and on this earth. Church is like a path to heaven. Or a door. When we go there, we think of God and we worship Jesus. Jesus is the One who will someday lead us to heaven."*

"Take!" Daniel pointed to himself.

"Not this morning. Your side needs to heal. And your lungs."

"Take!" Daniel said again.

Barnabas could easily interpret the boy's desire. *"Wrap him up and carry him,"* the old man suggested. *"What harm can it do? What good might it do?"*

"What does that mean?" Daniel said once more, even moving his hands as he lay back, his eyes drooping.

"It means, Daniel, that this old brother of mine is on your side! Are you sure you want to go outside and be carried to the church?"

He did not have so much energy now, but still he had determination. "Take."

"All right. I'll get you ready for your first outing, but it will not be a long one. You need rest, and plenty of it."

———

As an elder in Mt. Hope church, Joseph most often sat up front beside Cummington Brown. This day, however, when he walked in the door with Daniel wrapped up in his arms, he sat down in the last pew with Barnabas beside him. His old friend always endured silence during the service, here in the back row, for he never wanted Joseph to use sign language with him in the church. Ba's reasoning was that being the only white man made him enough of a spectacle in this community where many once had white masters over them. It was at home when Joseph would summarize for Ba what Cummington Brown had said from the pulpit.

The moment Joseph sat down and put Daniel on his lap, he saw that the young visiting newspaper agent was sitting in the first pew with Angelene and Azal. He felt regret in that moment, but he knew it was unjustified, for he himself had been wanting Angelene to be meet educated men closer to her own age. He closed his eyes to shield himself from the distraction and tried to pray.

The service started as usual, but soon Pastor Brown called Mr. Holmes to come up behind the podium. "This morning I thought I would give Oak Glen's visitor time to say something about himself," their pastor said, both hands still on the wooden stand. "This is Mr. Dumond Russwurm Holmes, as I'm sure most of you know by now. He hopes to stay in our community for perhaps a week or so more, so I trust that many of you will get to know him. My thought is if I let him speak about himself from the pulpit, then I will save him from having to make his own introduction again and again as he meets you individually."

The congregation was amicable, nodding and smiling, showing the up-turned faces of those eager to affirm the pastor and to give attention to the stranger. There was already an animation in the people and in their hands, as they clapped and waved to give encouragement.

Cummington then stepped aside. Dumond Holmes, who was much younger but not lacking for a commanding presence, quite willingly took his place. "Good morning!"

The congregation greeted him loudly. "Good morning!"

"I am so pleased to be standing here behind one of the pulpits of the Church of Color in America! There is no doubt in my mind that by doing so, I myself have become a sentinel in the highest watchtower the African people have within this nation! Soon, I think, the whole world will be hearing us from here! A second cry for liberty in America is going to ring out. A second call to arms for another revolution! And the black man and the brown man in America will be heard!"

By now Dumond could hardly be heard, for the small country crowd leaned forward and called out for him to say more.

In the midst of this loud affirmation, Dumond bowed modestly. "I will let preaching remain for the preacher," he told them. "It is my desire to tell you something about myself, for I think that the root of what I have predicted is already planted firmly in the soil, ready to sprout and to live as we nourish it."

In his pausing, the church grew silent, as though taking its own breath while Dumond took his. "It was only a few decades ago when American foundries in Philadelphia and Baltimore started casting metal type to be used by printers everywhere: North. South. East. West." His hands pointed in each direction.

"My father was a colored man living in Georgia in those days. A literate man. He set type for a white newspaper publisher on the seacoast. Then in 1833 the state of Georgia passed a law forbidding men of color to work at any kind of printing. You know why that was!" He said it as a challenge, not as a question.

He leaned forward and the crowd kept on leaning with him. "Because the printed word is a voice that cannot easily be silenced! Because the printed word can be carried without mouths and listened to without ears. It can be carried by ship. It can be carried by letter. Now it can be carried by the magic wires of the telegraph."

There were many amens voiced, though more than half in the congregation were just now learning to read, and some, Joseph knew, felt too old or too slow-minded for literacy. Yet even they cheered him.

"My father fled from Georgia when his work was taken from him. Four years later he found himself in Alton, Illinois, on the day when the white publisher Elijah Lovejoy was murdered there and his press destroyed because of his writings against slavery. That day my daddy gave up hope for this nation. He removed himself, his wife, and his family to London, England, where we all live to this day, I being the temporary exception.

"I was born in the year 1829, prior to all these years of trouble. I was named *Dumond* after my grandfather, but *Russwurm* in honor of the first black editor to publish a newspaper in America. When my father went to England, he changed our last name to *Holmes*. In my years as a boy held away from my father's rightful home, I kept hearing news from afar about the people's struggles over here in America!

"That is why I have come back to the land of my fathers. That is why I have accepted the position of solicitor, not only for Mr. Frederick Douglass's work, but for several other publishers as well. And that is why I plan to write my own reflections, based on what I am learning and seeing now."

Pastor Brown seemed ready to claim his pulpit back, but the young man seemed ready to say much more.

"I feel I have returned after my family's sorry pilgrimage with a message to America. You who have been born here and have toiled here should not be satisfied to be driven out by forced colonization! Nor should you let yourselves be beaten into submission by unjust laws! Nor should you be ignored by a Congress populated only by white men! Nor should you be silenced, either by intimidation or violence or even death! Even from your graves, if necessary, your voices must cry out, 'liberty!'

Freedom! Liberty for *all* in this land!"

The people of Mt. Hope were on their feet by now.

"If words will not work to bring down the oppressing race over you, then let us take up arms. If arms will not get them to live by a new way, then *death* to them all!" Joseph saw and felt Cummington's tension as he attempted to wrest the congregation's attention back.

The young man remained poised and passionate when the pastor put his hands back on the pulpit. Dumond dared to speak again even with the pastor standing by. Yet now his subject was completely new and his tenor also. "Before I sit down, I would like to give my congratulations in public to Miss Angelene Brown."

Angelene looked amazed, Joseph saw, for he had been watching her, as she had her face turned slightly toward the congregation.

"I suppose most or all of you know of her writing endeavors. I just want to say that it was my pleasure to receive the first copy of her printed work in the mail yesterday. A lovely little poem titled, 'Winter's Beauty.' "

Now Pastor Brown did not seem so eager to take back his podium. The father smiled with pride, but Angelene put her hands against her face. Holmes honored her another time by asking her to stand, and Mt. Hope was more than ready to break into loud applause again. The noise caused Daniel to stretch his neck and look everywhere. Certainly all of this was new to him.

"This is called clapping," Joseph whispered as the thundering noise continued. "Men and women do it when they see or hear something that pleases them greatly."

"Ah." The boy's smile was weak but forthright. "Then you clap for Sister Brown. She pleases you!" Angelene had not been at his place so often in the past few days since Dumond's arrival. So Joseph was amazed and more than slightly embarrassed that the child so easily knew his feelings. Joseph laid his hand on the boy's neck to check his pulse. It was normal, yet the child looked pale.

Dumond was back at Angelene's side by then. Daniel shook suddenly as a slow dry cough overtook him, turning many heads around to see him.

"It's too cold for you in here." Joseph stood, even though they had not been in the pew more than half an hour. Most persons had directed their attention back to Pastor Brown, so Joseph moved without everyone's eyes upon them. Only Ba and some of the others who were closest to him acknowledged Joseph's leaving with a nod or a glance.

He was almost at the door in the rear of the church when it was thrown open. Tort and Cyrus Woodman burst in, perhaps too tense to even see how close Joseph was to them.

"Men are in Joseph Whitsun's house!" Cyrus cried to the full congregation. "They've started a fire to burn his medicines!"

Except in the nights when he was awake with Daniel, Joseph had not given much thought to the Black Guard volunteers who watched the town continuously from hiding places on the mountainside and in the icy swampy hollows. Pastor Brown came down and rushed back to Joseph in an instant, while Joseph himself stood there, stunned. Because the church door was open, he could see the smoke rising.

"Conceal the child!" the pastor called to him. "And do not come outside yourself, Brother Whitsun!"

Then the pastor turned back. "Angelene! Come, take the boy! Azal, let Joseph take you to the house. Lock the doors. If I do not knock on our front door soon, you know what to do."

Angelene was pulling Daniel from his arms. Azal, walking with a cane, was nodding, already halfway through the pews. Then Joseph noticed Ba pushing his way out through the door. Cummington followed, and also young Dumond Holmes.

"This way!" Angelene cried, wanting Joseph to meet with her mother. Other men and women in the congregation made a human screen for them, coming out of the church and milling around the street so that they could more easily get away from the church, to behind the Browns' barn, then to the house by way of the back door.

Joseph took Daniel in his arms again, for the child was nearly too heavy for Angelene.

Once they were in the hall, Azal was wholly breathless. "Into the cellar, Joseph!" She looked at Daniel. "Take the child too."

———

Cummington strode to Joseph's house, with Barnabas and Dumond Holmes on either side of him. Constable Long was standing like an inactive guard on Joseph's porch. "What is going on here?" Cummington demanded from the street.

"Men have come from Philadelphia to investigate what kind of medical practice Joe Whitsun has going on here."

"Investigate!" Cummington watched the smoke billowing behind the log house. "That is not investigation!" Then he saw that Barnabas was gone.

"They are only removing anything to do with his medicines. We should have expected it to come to this. I should have demanded it myself to save you from such scrutiny."

"Who told the people of Philadelphia that we have a doctor?"

"Actually Joseph told on himself by writing a letter to admit a child from the orphanage to the city hospital. They questioned whose letter it was when the child was taken there."

"Did they question his skill? His right observations?"

"I don't think so," Contable Long said without apology.

"Then this is not about medicine. This is an injustice against our race, Mr. Long. Will you just stand there? Then God have mercy on your soul!"

"Don't threaten me, Pastor!" the constable said, his eyes growing wide. "These men who've come are within the law."

Cummington turned away, disgusted. He then heard Dumond complaining within sight of the many other white men who were circulating there. "It this the America you want, Pastor? Call your congregation forth against them! You have them outnumbered!"

Instead, Cummington walked faster, for he wanted to be around the schoolroom to see about the fire. With the first view he had of it, he saw Barnabas Croghan nearly consumed by the smoke. His thought was that Brinkerville men had thrown the old man into the blaze as his payment for being loyal to Joseph. He started running. When he came to Barnabas's side, he saw the man kneeling in coals, his shirt scorched to the elbows as he frantically tried to pull out some of Joseph's journals from the flames. Those he was able to reach he tossed to his side. They sizzled and smoked in the wetness of the shallow covering of snow.

"Don't burn them!" Some white man Cummington did not know called out.

"Look in this one! All the nigger's lewd drawings are in it. Save these for the courtroom so that the nigger doctor will be hanged."

Cummington looked behind him. Dumond was at the fire too, and his hand was reaching into his vest. Cummington leaped up and put all his strength and weight against the young man's shoulders. "Don't!" Cummington screamed. He wrested away the solicitor's pistol, which was so small that it could nearly be hidden in the palm of his hand. "Don't you show that firearm if you want to keep us here and alive!"

Dumond challenged him with oaths. "Kill the brutes, I say."

Cummington slipped the gun into his own pocket, then he bowed down to pull Barnabas from the coals, for the man seemed to have lost

his mind about caring for himself. Barnabas fought him until Cummington dared the heat of the blaze to look right into the old man's face.
"Move back! Your flesh is burning!"

Only then did Barnabas crawl away. He stared at his own blistered
hands, then laid them in the snow, with tears washing some of the soot
from his face.

"You stay with this man," Cummington said to Dumond. "Don't let
him do more harm to himself." Rising from giving that order, Cummington found Harley, Long, and others he did not know forming a line between the fire and Joseph's house, which walled him in close to the blaze.
Barnabas and now Dumond were kneeling near Cummington's feet.

"I am Federal Marshal Nichols!" one of the young men Cummington
did not know announced with great importance as he came to stand in
front of him. "I want the Negro, Joseph Whitsun."

Cummington tasted the smoke on his lips as he spoke to this man
with thick dark brows and a curving moustache. "Why?"

"For the practice of medicine, of course. But there's more." He
opened one of Joseph's journals. Surely it was where Joseph had chosen
to hide his manumission paper, for it was there still. Nichols unfolded it
in his presence. He spoke to Cummington slowly as though he might
think him too dull as a colored man to understand the danger. "This paper
gives testimony that Joseph Whitsun was a slave in South Carolina. But
more than that, it gives the name of his former owner. *Abram Callcott.*
Do you know that name?"

"No," Cummington said, unnerved to the core.

"*Callcott* is the maiden name of the white woman whom the slave
agents Dawes and Pudget found here with the mulatto child. It is all beginning to make perfect sense now why Anthony Ruskin's sister-in-law
would *want* to come here." His eyes burned like the fire. "You bring Joseph Whitsun to me!"

Dumond stood, coming to his feet right beside him. All the people of
Oak Glen were around them. Cummington dared to say what he knew
would be true. "Joseph Whitsun doesn't live in Oak Glen anymore."

Angelene was with her mother looking out her father's study window.
"What are they doing over there? How much of Joseph's property will
they destroy?"

"I'm not waiting any longer for word from your father, Angel. If we err, it's going to be on the side of caution. I want you to run upstairs and put my crazies in the window."

"Mother, that is the least of our worries."

"No, it's a symbol that there's danger at our Underground Railroad safe house. Certainly all those in town today know it, but there may be someone or some other conductor on the way, whom we do not know and who does not know what is happening now."

Angelene had just recently been told by her father about how the quilts in their window had been used as Underground Railroad codes for years. But this was the first time that Angelene understood how much her mother knew about her father's secret operation. Many times her mother had told her to replace the quilts with this one or that. Usually the excuse had been sunlight. None of the quilts should be in the window so long that it would start to fade.

Now Angelene's eyes were opened again when her mother said more. "I'm going down to the cellar. I don't want you to follow me or to ask me any questions. If anyone comes here and you must answer about me, you tell them that I went down for a new jar of honey for my ailments. That's what I'll come back with. A jar of honey."

"Mama! What are you going to do with Joseph and Daniel?"

"Don't ask! Then you can honestly say you don't know!"

Joseph had been in total darkness. Now he saw a light and heard soft footsteps on the cellar stairs. He stayed seated on the dirt floor with Daniel in his arms, limp from all the excitement and now his struggle to breath in the musty air.

"Joseph?" It was Azal.

"Yes, ma'am!" On numb legs, he stood.

"There's a tunnel from the cellar here to Oak Glen's safe house."

In all his years here, Joseph could not have imagined it.

"I need you to help me open it. Come back to where Cummington stores his honey. That shelf there." She lifted the light nearly to the low rafters and pointed to the wall as soon as he could see her well. "Those shelves will slide to the right. That's why Cummington keeps only his empty jars upon them. Slide the whole case of shelves now, Joseph. I'm going hide you in the tunnel."

He was worried about Daniel staying underground, yet he could not let himself be parted so soon from the boy. "What is happening upstairs, Sister Brown?"

"I don't know." Her eyes filled with concern. "I want you hidden. Then they cannot take you away, if that is their desire."

Joseph put his weight to the shelving, while still holding Daniel. Well-constructed and well-hidden rollers made the work easy. The whole wooden case, nailed together, moved as a unit. "Now take the lamp. Proceed down the way until there's a turn to your right. You'll see a ladder. Take it. Then you'll find another standing on a wooden floor. With all caution and all quiet climb that one too. It will lead you to a loft, well-supplied with water and food and blankets. When we can, we'll bring you more of what you and the child will need."

"It will be too cold in a loft for him, Sister Brown."

"I don't think so. The fire in the church has been burning since dawn. When Cummington and my sons made this route, they angled the stove pipe in the church so that there would be some heat in the safe house."

"This way leads to the church?"

"Yes, to its attic. Behind the wall that they built on which to hang the cross. They left a space just a few feet wide between the windowless stone wall and their new wooden wall, so you must move quietly. As long as it is daylight outside, it is safe to have light. But orient yourself, Joseph, then turn out the lamp, for there's always danger that a light might shine out between the shingles or the boards in the church by night."

"How did this all come to be without Brinkerville's knowing? In fact, I never expected it."

There was pride in her eyes. "Many sleepless nights. Much prayer." Her smile now was placid. "Cummington will come when he can. If this is my last view of you, dear Brother, God's blessings! God's protection!"

Her mother returned with the jar of honey as promised. By then her father, Dumond, and Barnabas were in the house, having come in by the back door. All the white men were gone, but their trials were far from over, her father reported as Ba sat in front of Angelene, slumping in the kitchen chair, his head rocking as he vibrated his body against his pain.

His trousers had been burned off at the knees. The cuffs of his shirt were gone. Indeed, unimaginable concentration must have been his to sustain such injury for the purpose of saving Joseph's books.

"Dear Ba!" Angelene kissed his sweating forehead as though the man were her close relative. She wrapped his burns in soaking wet compresses. "What you did for Joseph!" She trusted him to understand her heart, for she had no free hands to speak with him while she held the cloths. For

now, his blistered hands were also useless for speaking. Then to her surprise, Barnabas used his voice. Angelene had never heard him speak before, but very clearly he revealed his anguish in loud mournful tones.

"Jo-seph! Whe-re!"

Angelene looked to her mother, who said to her, "Tell him, Angel.
He's on the Undergound Railroad."

CHAPTER 23

THERE WERE PLACES BETWEEN THE SHINGLES were Joseph could see the light of day fading. Long before that happened, he had turned out the lamp, having memorized the location of the jugs of water, the chamber pots, the tins of shelled walnuts, the hard bread, and the strings of dried apples and beans. Daniel had been so calm through the hours, mostly sleeping as Joseph sat in the attic near the stovepipe, thankful for its warmth.

Only as the horror of the morning dimmed did Joseph think on the grief to come. He was like Renny, whisked away in a moment. He meditated on losing Barnabas and Angelene. He was helpless to know what was ahead until Cummington came. This happened while there was still enough light seeping in to see by.

"Joseph."

There was comfort in hearing a friendly voice. "Yes, Brother Cummington."

Daniel stirred, then settled back to sleep in Joseph's arms.

Joseph saw the pastor's face as the man came up the ladder. They kept their voices low. Immediately Joseph felt hopeful that flight might not be necessary. "Please tell me all that happened."

"They burned your supplies and some of your journals."

Joseph's hands started shaking.

"They found your manumission paper, and they took it. There was a federal marshal present who recognized your former master's name as being Mrs. Ruskin's maiden name."

Joseph felt his eyes narrowing. "Oh, God, help us!"

"I fear it will be enough to pull you directly into the whirlwind of rumor. Mr. Anthony Ruskin is looking for some Negro or Negroes to blame for outraging his dead brother's wife."

"I never touched her."

"I believe that. And you are certain that the boy is not Mrs. Ruskin's?"

"Yes! She said she found him in the street. What she says would be truth. Practitioner Catos, then Ba, pieced together the deposition that the slave agents here destroyed. Regardless of their testimony to the newspapers, Daniel's physical description matches that of Venor's missing slave boy. And the more Daniel trusts me and learns to speak, the more I hear from him about his own terrors in slavery."

"None of this surprises me. I just felt obliged to ask."

"Do you think that I cannot go home?"

"Joseph, I know it. But I'm unsure what to do about Daniel."

The boy was now listening. He put his arms like a clamp around Joseph's chest. "I'll keep him with me," Joseph declared. "In the kitchen I had some medicine for him. Perhaps this was not taken."

"I'm not sure I can arrange passage in winter with a child who has been so ill. You know that passengers usually travel in groups. The ill and the young can put everyone else into danger. And he is both."

"Then I will take my chances fleeing by some other way. Why can't I? It is uncertain if, or when, anyone will come for my arrest, true?"

"The federal marshal demanded that I bring you to him. I said that you do not live in Oak Glen anymore, and I am right. You are a passenger on the Underground Railroad now. If any marshal or constable does see you, you will be taken. That means you cannot leave by stage or train."

Joseph sat glumly. "What of Barnabas? How is he?"

The pastor seemed reluctant to say. "He scorched his hands and legs trying to save your books."

"My dear friend!"

"He did save some of them. Angelene has been taking care of him. The burns are blistering, but she says to tell you that she is certain they will heal."

"She would say nothing else to me when I am unable to get to him myself."

"That is probably true," her father agreed mildly.

"What of Ba? Can't he come on the Underground Railroad with me? What will the man do if I leave him behind?"

"The Underground Railroad is meant to serve all in need, but he could not travel now, injured as he is. I'm concerned enough about you and the boy." There was silence. "It may be a few days until I can meet with others to find the best and safest route for you. In the meantime, think of the few most important things you'll need. We'll pack these in a sack."

It was all so final. Some things Joseph felt he needed could not be held in any bag. "Is it possible for me to go back just long enough to say good-bye?"

The pastor delayed his answer. "It is too much risk to have you possibly discovered in my house. As far as Barnabas and Angelene coming here, I must consider the consequence of revealing all of this to them. Right now, no one but Azal, our sons, and I know about the tunnel or that the safe house is above the sanctuary."

"I never imagined it."

"The tunnel you took extends into the woods. Even Simeon Bart and Tort Woodman do not know that. Do you know where we have the church picnic grove? Where there's a huge pile of stumps left from the trees we cleared out? Well, that gave my sons and me an idea about how to conceal our Underground route. There's an old hollow hemlock stump near the center so wide that we could put the entrance to our tunnel down through it."

"How did you accomplish all of this without anyone knowing?"

"We worked by night, or we disguised our work, as we did in the church when we told Harley that we wanted to narrow the meetinghouse so we could have a wooden wall behind the pulpit for the cross. That was true. Yet we left a space large enough to provide a secret way into the attic."

Daniel coughed. "I fear he will get worse as the attic chills," Joseph said.

"I'll keep the fire going in the church. How often I have had an all-night prayer vigil to keep my secret passengers warm."

"That is true! I know it now! But never did I guess that you were doing more than *praying* for them through the night."

"There is nothing greater that I can do than to pray and commit your ways to God as you travel toward safety."

"Then I will not have the chance to say farewell either to Ba or to Angelene," Joseph concluded gloomily.

"I will not say that for certain. Give me time to see what arrangements can be made."

His pastor disappeared. Joseph felt the tears coming. He wiped them away and vowed there would be no more after Daniel reached up and felt the moisture on his face.

———

Charles and Thomas sat at the table on Monday night with the Bible lying open between them. Charles pointed to every word as he read it aloud. " 'The Lord is my shepherd; I shall not want. He maketh me to lie down in green pastures: he leadeth me beside the still waters. He restoreth my soul.' "

"I don't think I'll ever be able to do that, sah."

"Be patient. You will. Now, you start at the beginning."

" 'The Lord—' " Thomas began, whether by memory or reading, Charles wasn't certain.

Their study was interrupted by pounding at the Spruce Street door. "Maybe Dr. Ellis or another abolitionist is in trouble!" Charles said, starting at once for the stairs.

"Wait, sah! I can see a carriage down below." Thomas had moved to the window. "I think it's Mista Ruskin. I can see him, sah. There's another white man holdin' a light."

Charles changed his mind. "I'm going to open the storeroom door." Anthony Ruskin had called on Charles three times before asking what he knew of Mayleda. Each time he had come by day, alone, and to the store. Now Charles feared that the man with him might be an officer with a warrant. "You stay here. If there's any cause for alarm, let yourself out the front way and get yourself over to Dr. Ellis's. Tell him what's going on."

"Yessah. You can trust me to be listenin' in the stairs."

Charles took the steps Thomas spoke of. He went down to his front storeroom door and opened it. Mr. Ruskin and the man he did not know saw him at once. Charles said a prayer as they came toward him.

"This is Marshal Nichols." Ruskin pressed Charles back so that they could both step inside.

Charles let his door stay open, and the little bell above it rang.

"I've come once more concerning my sister-in-law's welfare and safety."

"I have no new information." Charles said the truth.

Ruskin nearly smiled. "Ah, but I do."

Nichols spoke with less passion. "On Sunday I was in Oak Glen supervising the removal of Joe Whitsun's clinic."

Charles felt instantly chilled.

"We found a manumission paper that gives evidence that this Joe Whitsun was the slave of Abram Callcott, who is or was Mayleda Callcott Ruskin's father."

Charles was truly stunned. "I knew nothing about it!"

"Of that I am sure." Ruskin said, sounding suddenly both tender and sad. "It is her darkest secret, without a doubt. The slave may have first taken her when she was young. That is why she has had neither the dignity nor the will to save herself from further harm."

His vile words made Charles stare at him more.

"It is quite likely that since the slave abused her in her childhood, she simply put herself under his odious spell again once he found her here in the city."

Charles felt tortured by his speculation. *Can this be true?*

"We see then that she had no choice in conceiving a half-breed. I believe that the public will understand the situation fully once news about this manumission paper is given. It explains why she chose to go to Oak Glen." He raised his brows. "Mr. Powell? You were the driver who took her there."

"I knew nothing about this!" Charles said again, but then he grew quiet in his concern. "Why did you come to tell me?"

Ruskin nodded, as though his doubt was understandable. "I brought Mr. Nichols here to witness what I say. I think you know where Mayleda dwells. I want you to give her a message from me. Once Joe Whitsun is in custody, it is my desire that she come home. I give you my word, and you give it to her. The ordeal is nearly over. Once this Negro is punished, her name will be cleared, as well as mine. She can be united with her daughter. Everyone in the city will offer her the sympathy due a victim. If not, we will see to it that she is taken someplace where she will not be harassed, and we will give her everything she needs."

"Why do you believe she birthed the child?" Charles managed.

"What else would keep her sneaking into the streets? What else would make her ignore our best interests toward her? I pity her. She made a desperate, unintelligent effort to get the brute to take responsibility for his own issue."

Charles knew this was mere suspicion, yet Anthony spoke with much certainty.

Marshal Nichols spoke. "If you know where she is, Mr. Powell, the right thing would be to take her to her home. You heard Mr. Ruskin make his pledge to help her."

"But I'll not be home for the next few days, perhaps," Ruskin told him. "We'll be raising a *posse comitatus* tomorrow with legal jurisdiction for Brinker Township and all the countryside to the north and west. We're going to find him, and we're going to bring him in. I will use every word of the law to make an example of him that no one in Philadelphia will ever forget!"

Charles shivered when Anthony smiled.

"Perhaps you would like to join us. I believe I'm right about you, man. You have strong feelings for my deceased brother's wife, or you would not have been involved in taking her to Oak Glen or in hiding her now. So how do you feel knowing that you may have been an unwilling partner in taking her where she could be abused by Joseph Whitsun even one more time?"

Charles said nothing. When he could, he closed the door. He wanted to believe that everything he heard had been a lie. Yet he knew that a marshal would not lie about a manumission paper. It made him wonder why Mayleda had never dared to speak about knowing Joseph from the past. Perhaps the Negro *had* harmed her, if not in Philadelphia, then long ago on the plantation in the South. Surely if that were so, Mayleda might be too broken, too ashamed to ever speak the truth about Whitsun to him or to anyone.

He felt he could not ask her. As a man he would not question a woman about her most intimate times. Or her most terrible ones. But there was one other who would know the truth.

Charles purposed in that moment to find Joseph before the posse did. If Mayleda Ruskin's honor needed to be defended, he himself would bring Joseph in, bound and ready for trial.

Thomas burst into the storeroom, perhaps having waited for a time to make sure it was safe. "They want that colored brother's neck broke!" he raged as he dared to look out the window while Ruskin's carriage rolled away.

Feeling great discomfort, Charles met the black youth face-to-face.

"What! Mr. Powell, you not gwine let you'self believe it!"

He said nothing, for he had never spoken much about Mayleda to Thomas.

Then the former slave spoke again. "Sah, there's more reason in a slave's heart than stars in the heavens why he don't want nobody to know about his past. Believe me, sah! An' so, that's probably true for folks like Missus Ruskin too. She wants to be done an' through with slavery! That's why she came here!"

"Yes," Charles agreed glumly, but he was not sure. *If Joseph had harmed Mayleda in the past, certainly that could be the reason for her silence now.* It stirred other questions in him about Mayleda's suffering while living in Ludlow Row and working for the same Quaker physician who had trained Joseph Whitsun.

Perhaps this colored man *had* secretly and insidiously found ways to dominate every year of her life in the North. Perhaps she had even had to leave the security of her friends in Boston because she knew she was carrying a black man's child.

It sickened him, for her beauty and innocence could have masked any suspicion he might have had. But these men had come to his door, and now he had to face the possibilities. He tried to temper his fears with thoughts of the horrors that a colored man could face being punished for rape only because of rumors started on account of his dark hue.

Then immediately Charles considered a woman's suffering in silence, too fearful to admit that she had been used time and time again by the slave who once had been her father's. Either story, but not both, might be stark reality. Until he got himself to Oak Glen on a borrowed saddle horse, he would not know which it was.

Ignoring Thomas, he rushed upstairs to dress in his warmest clothes so that he might leave at once.

Joseph, with Daniel at his side, passed the night in the attic of the church. True to Cummington's word, the pastor had not let the fire go out. Still, by morning Daniel was restless. Joseph started to consider how they both would endure the day when he heard noise near the ladder.

Soon Cummington's solemn face appeared.

"How was the night?" he asked.

"Bearable. Thank you for the heat."

"I have found a way to get you and Daniel west on the Underground Railroad. You will do so by riding on the real one." He handed Joseph a printed paper, but in the loft it was too dark for reading. "I want you to carry this handbill with you. You do know Brother Whipper of Columbia?"

"Yes."

"You know about his successful lumber business?"

"Of course."

"Here is the way you will travel, then. When it's time, I'll lead you to the tunnel's exit. You'll find your own horse tied there. You'll ride to the real tracks, about two miles west of Brinkerville. Do you know where Brother Woodman and others got permission from the Philadelphia and Columbia Company to build a woodshed on railroad property so that they can store dry cordwood to sell to the firemen and engineers?"

"Yes, I've been there."

"Good! You'll find a white man at the woodshed. He'll say he works for Brother Whipper. In truth, he will be moving fugitives as though hiring them to be woodcutters. This is as the handbill reads. It is an advertisement for work in Columbia. Since men do sometimes move to Whipper's looking to earn wages once their farm work is done in winter, I have good hope for this plan. Some men do take their families. That's why I think no one will question you when you board the westbound train with Daniel. The abolitionist agents working on your behalf will rent a Negro car to haul all their new employees, as you will be called."

Cummington paused. "My concern now is whether or not Daniel will be strong enough for this journey."

Daniel answered on his own. "Strong!"

Joseph was not so sure, but the child's determination made him keep his silence. Somehow, with God's grace, he felt they must move on from here, for this place had its dangers too, not only for them, but for the Browns. "I think we can do this."

"I have some supplies for you." In the dim light he laid a bulging sack into the loft. "You were right about the medicines left in the house. Angelene wrapped and carefully packed these for you. I usually like to send one blanket per fugitive, but she insisted on two for each of you. There's some food and extra socks. Here's a hat and cloak for you and warm clothes for the child."

Joseph did not want to accept that he was leaving. His mind was still on Oak Glen. "How did Barnabas fare through the night?"

"His wounds are going to heal, perhaps quicker than his heart. But he understands that you must go."

"He shouldn't be alone!"

"He's not. He's with us now. When Dumond Holmes leaves, he'll have a room of his own. Right now he's in our parlor. He can still work your garden and have the animals in your barn. We'll look after him, and you know he will look after us too."

"I need you to say good-bye to him. And to Angelene. But I don't know what message to pass on to them. This is so hard."

"Give me a moment to climb down, and you can say your own fare-well to Angel."

"You brought her through the tunnel! Now she knows where the safe house is."

"Yes, she's begged to be trained as a stationmaster for so long that I've decided now should be the time."

Cummington left the loft. When Angelene came up the ladder, Joseph truly regretted not being able to clearly see her face one last time, but the light was too dim. He sat Daniel on a blanket beside him and moved closer. The instant he was within reach, Angelene put her arm around his neck and wept against his shoulder while still standing on the ladder.

"I begged him not to send you away. No one has come back to look for you, yet Daddy says that you must go."

"I trust his judgment for the safety of us all."

"Joseph, please say that I can go with you. I can be ready in a moment. I can endure whatever you must endure, and I can help you with Daniel."

"Angelene, no. You have too many responsibilities here." He felt her take a breath.

"If it were not for those, would you bid me to come with you?"

"There's no reason for you to put yourself into danger."

"I'll go by train to Ohio, and then I'll have my brothers bring me to you."

"It's impossible. I don't even know where I am going."

"Once you are near Canada, you can choose. I beg you, go to Sandwich in West Canada. Then I can know soon that you are safe."

"I don't know of this place you speak about."

"You do. Remember, you saw Dumond Holmes' copy of the *Voice of the Fugitive*. That is a paper printed by Mary and Henry Bibb in Canada. Every week they publish letters from those who have arrived safely. You can write to us. You can sign with your initials. You can tell me to come, and I will! Barnabas has spoken to me already. He wants to come too. He can't think of living without you. I cannot bear it either!"

"You will. You are needed here. And in the end you will be happier." He thought of Dumond Holmes. Perhaps it was God's timing for Dumond to be in Oak Glen just when he was forced to flee. "Angelene, I am going to miss you sorely." That was the truth.

"Then take me with you!"

"I can't. In a month, in a year, I think you will not regret it."

"Oh, I will!" But then she quieted herself. "Here is something for you that my father planned to give me on Christmas Day."

It was a slim book. In the dimness he guessed the author. "Daniel Payne's poetry."

"Yes. To bless you. More than that, to remind you that you are deeply and forever loved by me." She bowed in her grief.

Joseph kissed her forehead. "Dear, sweet Angelene. I will never forget you."

"Write for me! Tell me I can come! I will read every paper looking for a word from you!"

"Oh, you may regret that you asked for that now."

"I won't!"

"If I can get to Sandwich, I will send word of my safe arrival, and Daniel's. I promise you that."

She wiped her eyes.

"Take care of the school and speak with your father about this, please. While I've been here, I've been thinking that when the way seems safe again, perhaps your father could speak to Dr. Ellis. Oliver Catos is certainly ready for a practice of his own. Perhaps not in Oak Glen, but nearby, so our people can still be served."

She was quiet. As he thought about Oliver, he considered that the two of them might be right for each other. Perhaps they would be better matched than Dumond and she. Either way, it would be good for her that he was going. It would force her mind and heart to turn to others. Yet now his own heart throbbed painfully in thinking of her with someone else.

"You be careful, Angelene. Don't settle for a man who will not honor you and love you purely with all his heart."

"Joseph! Can't you love me that way? Won't you love me that way? For that is the way in which I love you!"

"Your father will want you to be going. Our voices might be heard through the church walls. I don't want to jeopardize your safety any longer." He took her hand and held it to his heart. "You are a wonderful young woman. There are good things ahead for you. And not the least of them will be love."

When she slipped away crying, he vowed inwardly that he would pray daily for her best all the time he lived. After she was gone, he focused on Daniel.

"We had best get some more rest. When Pastor Brown comes next, we will be on our way to Canada."

PART THREE
The Courage of a Few

In the midst of a crooked and perverse nation . . .

ye shine as lights in the world;

Holding forth the word of life. . . .

PHILIPPIANS 2:15–16

CHAPTER 24

THE WOODSHED ON RAILROAD PROPERTY stood low and snow-covered on the steep, wooded hillside within sight of the tracks. Joseph found it easily, for though Pastor Brown had led him out of the tunnel and to his horse after dark, there was moonlight to see by.

The rough log structure showed little promise for guarding flesh from the cold, yet following his pastor's instructions, Joseph approached it from the north, the side that faced the tracks. He dismounted, leaving Daniel in the saddle. Holding the reins, he moved to the wide door, partially opened. Instantly he encountered a short white man with a lighted lantern at his feet. An old handleless market basket had been turned on its side to cloak the light so that none of its glow would escape beyond the room.

Staying outside himself, Joseph cautiously gave this man the handbill. Even with the light shining Joseph could see little of what this supposed Underground Railroad conductor looked like, for the man wore a scarf and a knit cap pulled down toward his nose.

"Come in." Even the stranger's voice seemed muffled by his garb. Then the speaker saw that Joseph had a horse and a child.

Reluctantly, without asking Joseph anything about it, the stranger decided that the animal must be brought in and concealed. What would be done with it in the morning, he said, would be decided then. Everything about the setting made Joseph uneasy. He dared to ask the man's name.

"Mr. Edwardson," he replied.

That did cause Joseph to trust him more, for Cummington Brown had mentioned the names of white conductors he was most likely to meet, and an Edwardson had been among them. Joseph led his horse in, then lifted Daniel off.

By the gauze of light that stayed like mist around their feet, Joseph saw two other Negroes in the shelter: an aged, silent couple, perhaps husband and wife, seated on the dirt floor and leaning against the wall. The man was staring; the woman asleep. The woman's eyes stayed closed, but the man surveyed them dully. The couple had woodchips piled around their feet as a sorry kind of covering since they had but one thin blanket between them. Joseph shuddered, for now he and Daniel would spend the night here too.

Using his best judgment, he led his horse to the back left corner where no wood was stacked. He tied the reins to a nail and left the animal saddled and bearing the pack the Browns had made for them. Gratefully he took out all four blankets, which Angelene had foreseen they would need. While Joseph prepared a place for himself and the child, he saw the woman tremble. At once the man put his arm around her and drew her head to his chest. Their worn, expressionless faces were like a mirror to him, reflecting old countenances he had seen when he was a slave in the rice fields. He breathed a prayer that Daniel would never grow old in this way.

There was a second door in the woodshed, one that opened to the south. Because there was no latch or bolt on it, Joseph worried that the white man watched the north door only. He said nothing, though, as he finished the little platform of logs he was building to keep them from sitting directly on the ground. Once this was done, he put a blanket on the wood and put Daniel down upon it. Then Joseph sat close beside the child and cuddled him while pulling the remaining blankets around them both. The temperature was already miserable. For as long as Edwardson let the lamp burn, they could see the heatless steam of their breaths when they exhaled.

When the white man decided that no one else would attempt to join them that night, he put out the light. The icy blackness instantly took their sight and, slowly, the feeling in Joseph's toes and fingers. Every thought was toward keeping Daniel warm. Instead of holding the boy beside him, Joseph pulled him onto his lap and opened both his coat and the child's so that he could press the boy's chest to his own. He cocooned them again in all the blankets they had. He gained no sleep that night.

By first light Joseph felt Daniel's lungs rattle. At the same time he feared the renewal of the long-dead respiratory disease within himself because of the raw air. Joseph kept his fears to himself, however, as did the child, it seemed, for Daniel had not uttered one word in the dark. Now with dawn prying the cracks between the logs, the boy stared up at him with desolate eyes. Joseph bent and whispered, feeling his breath warming Daniel's hair. "We've made it to morning. It will be better now."

Joseph looked at how the others had fared. The woman no longer leaned against the wall. She was on the ground with the man bowed over her. Edwardson stood again by the slightly opened door, but this time he divided his attention between the silent blue outside and the couple within, who were surely in distress. At once Joseph used his stiff hands to settle Daniel into the covers by himself. When he tried to stand, he had no feeling below his waist, but still he straightened and took halting steps that made him feel like a scarecrow with wads of straw for feet.

He wobbled to Edwardson. "I know something about doctoring," he volunteered. There was always danger in admitting this to someone who was not colored. The Negro brother heard his words, though Joseph had intended them for their guard.

"Ain't nothing wrong with her 'cept she's cold an' sore!" the man said fiercely. "Got her leg caught when we come through the marse's fence, but she can walk."

Joseph knew the fear behind the slave's certainty. Edwardson detected it too. "You will jeopardize this rescue if your wife is ill. Soon we're going to meet another party gathered on the north side of the tracks. We can't risk bringing any attention to ourselves as we load you into the car."

"I know the plan, sah!" the distressed brother said without raising his eyes. "Liz an' me can do it."

"I'm doubting that!" Edwardson replied.

"She won't be sick by the time we need to move," the man pledged.

"The Lord done brought us this far. Our boys are out ahead somewheres, an' they families! We *all* gwine see freedom!"

"Could I have a look?" Joseph spoke only to the colored man. His own feet had thawed, giving him more stability. "I have some medicines along. Maybe something for that wound."

Seeming wary that Edwardson would see his wife's ankles, the man nevertheless drew aside the woman's skirt to reveal a long, pus-filled laceration that entangled her leg like a viper.

At Joseph's touch, the woman trembled violently. Her hands and feet twitched like handkerchiefs hung out to dry in the wind. At the same time she bore down hard on her teeth as though her jaws were glued shut by the saliva that looked like frost around her mouth.

Joseph glanced across to Daniel. The boy was standing with blankets around him. "Stay where you are!" Joseph said.

"She weren't like this yeste'day," the fugitive vowed.

"I see." Joseph looked on them with pity.

"What's wrong with her?" Edwardson demanded of Joseph.

The old man tried to answer. "She strong! She make it! Now God even sent this brother alongside to doctor her."

Edwardson looked at his pocket watch. "The train comes through Brinkerville in less than two hours."

The older man nodded. "Fine!"

But Joseph shook his head, the pain of the truth once more splitting wide the chasms of his own grief over Rosa. "I can't help her, Uncle. This is tetanus. There is no cure."

Edwardson came away from the door. "Are you sure, man?"

Joseph faced the white man's attitude. "I am."

The Underground Railroad conductor pulled at his scarf, looking amazed. "What terrible luck! How long until she dies?"

"I don't know. Hours. Even days, perhaps."

Edwardson sighed. "Your horse we can unsaddle and let go, but if someone comes in here and finds a corpse—"

"I'm not gwine leave her!" the husband cried.

The conductor finished his thought while ignoring the other man's sorrow. "Anyone who looks in here will suspect we are doing more than just *hiring* Negroes and holding them for the train."

"I'm not leavin' her!" the distraught man said again.

"Then the marshals will find you, and I'll lose two passengers instead of one. I can't let that happen. We depend on this hiding place. If you're discovered, then it will become a point of ambush for unsuspecting run-aways who are coming along behind you."

The woman writhed. She rolled her eyes as though she recognized her husband's face. The disease had stolen her voice but perhaps not her mind. Her distressed gaze seemed to shout that she wanted her spouse to go on, yet the brother in his grief did not see this.

Joseph tried to speak gently. "I think she wants you to go forth to find your sons."

"The Lord can save her!" The man declared in tears.

"He can. But the Lord can also take her home."

The husband despaired so loudly that Edwardson shut the door. "What! Do you want slave catchers to come in on us? Then I'll take that horse and leave you all on your own!"

Joseph tried to look at Daniel, but with the door closed there was much less light to see by. *Nothing must happen to him.* Yet as a trained doctor he felt an inescapable conviction that he had responsibilities toward this unknown woman too. "I think you must go on," Joseph urged the other man. "There is nothing you can do for your wife. She will go to God, and you must go to your sons. I will stay with her until God takes her. I have my horse, and I know the way to Brother Whipper's. I am from this community and am known by the men who cut wood in this place. I can stay."

Edwardson brought back the crack of light by opening the door. "The boy stays if you stay."

"Of course." Joseph would not think of sending Daniel on without him. He was already considering what to do if marshals came. The only idea he had was to be ready to hide them all between the piles of wood.

The husband kneeling in the dirt had his fists curled to his face, a sign of grief that Joseph knew completely. Then he put his hands to his wife's face and gently stroked it, whispering inaudibly his affection and sorrow. Joseph turned away, leaving the man to say his good-bye in private.

"What will you do with the body?" the conductor worried.

Joseph had already pondered this. "There are two axes there," he said, pointing to tools hanging on the wall. "If you help me, perhaps we can scrape out a grave before you go." Joseph was uncertain how his suggestion would be received by one not of his race. He saw in Edwardson one who was willing to take enormous risks for them, yet without seeming to understand that black men had emotions and thoughts just like his own.

Edwardson toed the dirt. "It's dry. It might be possible."

"I'm not puttin' Liz in the ground!" the man cried out.

"Not while she lives," Edwardson countered, even showing some sympathy now. "This local man says he'll stay to bury her."

Edwardson handed one ax to Joseph, then took the other. Walking into a clear space directly in front of Daniel they started chopping at the earth. The safety of *every* fugitive coming along this route might be sacrificed, if even one mistake were made. Even the sound of their digging might not go unnoticed, now that day was fully born.

When the weary Edwardson and the now silent, grieving brother left for the train, Joseph kept the north door open so that he could look for the smoke that would tell him when the locomotive had passed. He opened the southern door too, for the strong sun was the closest thing they had to heat, and a beam of it did come in that way. He moved Daniel into the sunlight but away from the door, then he went back to watch the woman. There was both hope and sadness in seeing the boy look like a swaddled angel in the glow of heaven's warming light. As far as being able to give help to the patient, Joseph could only wait and pray.

After hours at this awful vigil, he found his vision blurring with fatigue. All of the interior was cold and gray once more because the sun was setting. His mind and spirit felt dimmed too, as he had sat so long considering the inhumanity that would force a man to leave his dying wife. Daniel came to stand by him. The child buried his warm hands inside Joseph's collar. His fingers felt like tender shoots of life.

Quietly, without questions, the boy watched the woman struggle for breath. Joseph considered that less than three weeks ago, Daniel had struggled in just the same way. The child still wore his blankets like a robe, though Joseph had given his own to the woman. Soon it would be her shroud. Daniel noticed that Joseph had no blanket. He took off one of the three he had and put it on Joseph as though the child were the father.

"No, son, you need it!" Joseph protested while tears came to his eyes.

"I'm not sick." Daniel opened his mouth and drew in a breath, his way of proving that his lungs were clear. Thankfully, Joseph could say the same about himself. Because it was the boy's gift to him, he kept the blanket and pulled Daniel close.

The woman's body began to vibrate like an unlatched shutter in a gale. Joseph pressed the boy's face against his coat and covered Daniel's ears when the woman moaned. Daniel accepted his protection for a time, but then pulled away. The woman was completely still now. Death had come. This Joseph explained to Daniel the best he could while the boy stared at the corpse. He showed no fear, even when Joseph closed the unseeing eyes.

"My sister was like that on the street," he said.

Joseph moved to hold him once more. "Yes, Sister May told me. That's because your sister, like this sister, left her earthly body to be with the Lord Jesus Christ forever. It is a good thing for them, but a sad thing for us."

Daniel stooped and touched the body in what seemed a child's simple act of curiosity.

Joseph, however, found himself shaking so much that Daniel looked at him with worry. "I just need some rest," he said, hoping it was the truth, "and some food, as I'm sure you do too." Edwardson had left them a jug of cider and a small sack of smoked venison. When Joseph spread the blanket over the woman's body, he thought of his friend Parris as being the one to bury Rosa so long ago. Now it was his turn to bury another man's wife, a brother whom he would probably never see again. It caused bitterness within him, for here he was in the North, more than a decade older, yet nearly in the same awful setting as before.

He took off the small-brimmed hat Cummington had given him and said a silent prayer, not only for this departed one, but for all of them who lived. He felt dangerously close to despair, but he knew it would do Daniel no good if he let himself sink down. Rising to his feet, he faced the dreadful task of pulling the woman by her still-supple limbs toward the crude grave. Silent as a kitten, Daniel came beside him. Watching for a moment, the boy reached out for the shroud and for the woman's skirt beneath it. As Joseph's partner, he started pulling the body sideways. "Oh, Daniel, you don't have to do this."

The child persisted. When they had the covered body in the shallow hole, Joseph pushed in the loose soil with his hands. Daniel copied his every action, thumping dirt against the feet while Joseph worked near the head. Afterward they piled cordwood over the site to hide the grave.

When they were finished, Joseph put all the remaining blankets around Daniel. Wiping his hands on his pants, he went to get the cider and the meat. He sat down wearily and saw the boy breathing hard. "We'll rest and eat," Joseph said, trying to keep his own hope from faltering. "Then sometime after sunset, we'll take the horse and set out for Columbia."

What Joseph did not say was that the journey would take them more than thirty miles through the dark and cold.

CHAPTER 25

AFTER SUPPER Angelene's parents nearly commanded her to leave the dishes so that she could join them in the parlor. Dumond Holmes had just offered to read aloud parts of Mr. Shakespeare's drama about a black man named Othello, the Moor of Venice.

Dumond said that in Europe hundreds of people paid for chairs to see the play performed on stages and that an American-born Negro, Ira Aldridge, was favored in portraying Othello's role. Angelene found herself wholly disinterested, for Dumond had called the play a tragedy. She already had pushed herself to endure the daylight hours at school, all the while thinking on Joseph's fate. Now she was faltering through the duties of her evening in just the same way. She felt she could face no more *tragedy*.

Privately she spoke to her father in the hallway, thinking that he would excuse her to her room. Instead he clasped his hands upon her shoulders as if she was a son rather than a daughter. "They are probably at Brother Whipper's now. Once they're west of there, they'll have no trouble. It is you, dear girl, who cannot survive such worry. That's why I'm taking you into the parlor. I want you to let Mr. Holmes' story be your worthy distraction. He's traveled with this actor he speaks of, and he's recently written reports on the performances for some of our newspapers here."

She wanted to accept her father's confidence, but anxiety kept nagging like an aching tooth. Her daddy offered his hand as though he were ready to escort a lady into the theater. She took it, thinking what a wonderful time this would be if only Joseph were here, for literate guests were rare, and visitors from England unheard of.

Her mother was already seated in the rocking chair. Barnabas, who could not sleep by night because of his sorrow, now dozed in a chair by the window. Her father glanced at the white-haired man, his chin awkwardly on his chest. "You are not the only one being worn down by concern. When Barnabas awakes, I want you to make it clear what I have told you. Within a week, Joseph and Daniel can be in Canada."

She took her seat on the couch. Her father started putting a fire in the parlor stove. Dumond's eyes already seemed as bright as coals when he looked at her. Under different circumstances, his attention might have been flattering. But her all-encompassing care was for Joseph. Carefully she watched her hands instead of looking at the scholar who cradled his open book.

"Before I begin I would like to say that Mr. Aldridge and my parents are quite good friends."

Angelene felt admiration for that, but she had no spirit to say so.

Dumond began to read. He tackled the strange words with great delight. Angelene found herself helpless to withhold her interest. Dumond's portrayal of every character, not just that of the colored Moor, sounded as natural as his daily discourse. He could frown, grimace, and laugh in ways that would make her feel that he had the voices of many different persons. He spoke the language of the drama as though it were his own, so much so that it tore the veil between what seemed real and what was imaginary.

For pages at a time he relied not on the book at all but on his memory. It gave him opportunities to look into her eyes when she finally did lift hers. He recited more of Othello's words, and somehow they pricked her heart as being true. " 'She loved me for the dangers I have pass'd. And I loved her that she did pity them.' "

Before Angelene could stop herself, she was sobbing.

Dumond closed the book. He went down on one knee in front of her. She tried to make herself face him calmly.

"I am sorry," she said. "It's just that the words made me think again of all the dangers that Joseph could be going through, even now."

"I am the one to be sorry," Dumond replied with as much dignity as any character in his story. "I should have picked something better for your tender mood. Would you like to hear some of the writings of our own leaders for the recent newspapers? Their insights are no less profound than those of America's first revolutionaries, as colonists fought against Redcoats."

"No, thank you. I'm not concerned about the cause right now."

Dumond rocked back on both knees, seeming helpless to know what more to say.

Angelene's mother had been knitting and listening. She laid aside her work. "There's only one suitable activity for now," she said, not rising from her seat. "Prayer."

Unashamedly her father got down on his knees near where Dumond had been. Angelene slipped down to join him while Dumond silently walked to the stove. Barnabas was awake now. Angelene told him in his own language that they were going to pray once more for Joseph and Daniel. Because of his blistered knees and hands, he stayed as he was but bowed his head.

Dumond seemed aloof, but no one cajoled him. When Angelene closed her eyes, she heard every voice pray except Dumond's. Even Barnabas, in another rare time of vocalization, moaned out sounds, an eerie, solemn background to their own supplications. Angelene did not know how much time passed before her father said, "Amen."

While she seated herself again, her daddy stood and turned to the young man in their midst. "It is important for us to pray when the Spirit leads," he explained, walking to the stove. "The Scriptures instruct us to remember those who are in bonds as though we ourselves were bound with them. And also those who suffer, as though we ourselves suffered."

"Yes, I know," Dumond said clearly. "I believe that all comes from the book of Hebrews, directly between 'Marriage is honourable' and 'Be not forgetful to entertain strangers: for thereby some have entertained angels unawares.'"

He smiled wryly when they all looked amazed, and he teased Angelene, especially for her gasp of disbelief. "I am no angel! Just a grown-up boy who once loathed having to commit so much Scripture to memory."

"Then your parents are believers?" Angelene's father seemed pleased. "You did not mention that before."

"Not believers as you would wish them to be, sir, as in holding to the opinion that there is but one savior for this entire world. However, the tutor my father hired for my sisters and me was dogmatic in holding to that. He was a big, round-faced white man named Boskin. Much in the order of William Wilberforce, a man I know you favor."

"Indeed I do!" her father said. "He and his colleagues broke the back of slavery in the British realm."

Dumond seemed unimpressed. "Boskin believed that a thorough knowledge of the Scriptures could right every wrong and set the whole world straight."

Angelene could hardly imagine a white man being hired by a colored family. Indeed, Europe must be different from America.

"I might have liked this man Boskin," her father ventured.

"No, you would not! He was a demeaning, belittling man who felt himself on a mission to deplete the ignorance of London's colored population by three through the schooling of my two sisters and me."

"Perhaps it had more to do with your age than your race," her father suggested.

"No." Again Dumond was adamant. "In public, with his own kind, he loved to show us off as though we were his little monkeys. Of course he could not do that in the company of my parents or with our Negro friends such as Mr. Aldridge, for then it was clear that my family had much more social standing than Boskin the tutor."

"He was but one man, son," Angelene's father said. "You are wise enough to see that one individual cannot represent a race."

"I am sorry to say that he was only the first of many! That has especially been true in my short time in America." Oddly, he looked at Barnabas who was dozing again. "I know, Pastor Brown. You think Christianity can be the white man's tempering factor. My view is that it has made the race even more narrow-minded. I see so many white men demanding humility and poverty for others but never for themselves.

"My conclusion is that Christianity can do nothing positive for an African's soul. Instead, it is apt to chain it, just as Americans are apt to shackle the black man's body."

"But Christian men such as Wilberforce brought an end to slavery *because* of their reverent fear of God," her father reasoned. "They loved

God more than they loved material wealth or social status. They believed there is freedom in Christ, and they wanted all to know that freedom."

"They ended slavery by commanding a change in the laws. But who will change those things that cannot be governed by laws? Things such as attitudes and judgments of the heart? Even a Wilberforce cannot touch those deeper issues, because they are bound to the structure of power that the white population in America does not want to see changed."

Her father sighed. "Jesus said of himself, 'All power is given unto me in heaven and in earth.'"

"I do not believe it."

"Then I must challenge you to speak to Christ himself about your doubting."

"How could I know what god to address, when no god is seen?"

"Call on the name of Christ, and He will answer you."

"I have known many Christian men, sir. I do not respect the god they say they honor."

"Christians can fail regardless of their color, but Christ will not fail you. When you seek God with a sincere heart, you will find Him. It was Christ's mission to reconcile men back to God."

"A holy god should have a holy people," Dumond reasoned.

"Agreed! God makes holiness possible by His grace."

"Forgive my boldness, sir, but I do not see holiness in the church. I would think that an all-powerful god would have worshipers who do not fail him. That, to me, would be evidence of his strength and his perfection."

"But it could not be evidence of His love. Do you want to live as God's slave? The Almighty could have it that way. He could stop your breathing the moment after you say your first imperfect word or commit your first imperfect act. Sin drives us away from God's perfection. Christ's love finds us and brings us back."

"What I have seen in Christians is not love—starting with Boskin."

"Look to Jesus Christ, then. He was man, yet He is God. He never failed in His love. Others will fail. You will fail, even if you choose to be Christ's follower. Be careful, then, not to demand more of others than you can expect of yourself."

When Dumond stayed silent, her father went on. "You are being invited into the presence of the holy God now because He loves you. Even before you knew enough to look for Him or to ask the questions you are asking now, He loved you. I know that God has made a way for you to know Him, and not as judge only. That way is by His mercy. Call on Him and you will experience His greatness through His grace given to you."

"Sir, I want a holiness I can see! A holiness that will come against everything that is ungodly, including slavery!"

"Then it could come against you or me, for I cannot say that we are holy, at least apart from Christ's redeeming work. Also, we must submit ourselves to God's time."

"How often I have heard that! It's those kinds of words that keep our people with their faces to the ground."

"Be cautious, son. We all *deserve* judgment, then death. But through God's mercy, He is willing and able to save us from that."

"How can you believe this as a black man, sir? Thousands in Africa have never even heard the name of Jesus."

"God longs for those in Africa to hear! Every believer is called to share his faith. Perhaps in Mr. Boskin's Bible sessions he neglected to have you memorize the opening verses of the thirteenth chapter in the book of Acts."

"I was not a perfect student. I cannot say."

Her father reached for his Bible on the table. "Here! It speaks about the church in Antioch where believers were first called Christians. The names of some of the leaders are listed. There is a Simeon, who was called *Niger*. Also a Lucius from Cyrene. Clearly both of these were African men. Whether or not Mr. Boskin chose to tell you, Christ has been calling Africans through every century to lead His church."

"I did not know there were colored men written about in the Bible. It only makes me despise the faith professed in America and England all the more!"

"Yes, well, then let your disillusionment be with the nations and how they interpret faith, but not with God! Become Christ's follower and help us change the nations! No struggle will ever be as worthy as the great task of taking God's Word to the world."

Dumond sighed quietly. Angelene's mother had been eyeing her father. "Cummington, perhaps enough has been said. You know, there *is* a short work I would love to hear Mr. Holmes read aloud. A piece of poetry written about winter's beauty."

"Oh, Mama, no!" Angelene was embarrassed when her mother held out a clipping of her first published work.

"I will be honored to read it, ma'am," Dumond said, showing Angelene another of his wonderful smiles. "But you may keep your copy. See,

I have my own." He took a cutting just like hers from his waistcoat. He glanced at Angelene once more, but she looked away. The next moment Angelene saw Barnabas get out of his chair and peer through the window.

"What is it?" Her father said to her. Dumond waited while Angelene went to Barnabas. She touched his shoulder, and he turned. Before she could speak with signing, she saw the movement out on the dark, quiet street. A man tied his horse to the rail, then came up to their porch.

"There's a stranger here, Daddy, and I think he's white!"

"Azal. Angelene. Go upstairs," her father said as he went toward the front door. "Turn the quilts to give warning. If more needs to be done, I'll send Dumond up to tell you."

Angelene looked at their guest, then at her father. "Do you think it has to do with Joseph?"

"Angelene, do as you are told!"

"Oh, Daddy, please, be careful! We can't lose you too!"

Arriving in the small moonlit town, Charles had gone first to the log cabin to look for Joseph there, but all was dark. Lights in the pastor's house now had him standing on that porch. When the door opened, he faced not only Pastor Brown, but a gray-haired white man and a young brown man dressed in fine clothes. Both stood directly behind the owner of the house. Charles felt his voice sounding cold. "Pastor Brown, I am Charles Powell. Perhaps you remember me."

"I do." All three men facing him stayed as they were.

"I need to speak with Mr. Whitsun."

The old white man watched him severely. Charles noticed then that though the man had the centers of both hands wrapped in bandages, a hunting rifle still rested at his side. The younger Negro he did not know took several steps his way, coming out through the door.

"He is not here," the pastor said.

"Then I hope you will understand if I wait." Charles shivered, cautious because of the gun and dreading even one more minute of cold.

The minister frowned. "There is no use waiting, Mr. Powell."

"What? He's gone?" Charles' frustration flared. It caused the young Negro on the porch to set his jaw. Charles drew a breath, which made him shiver more. "I am sorry, it's just that I've ridden all the way from Philadelphia to speak with him." His clothes were damp. He felt frozen. Now he would have to ride fifty miles home and have no answers.

He turned, greatly troubled to know that Joseph had fled. Would a man do so, if he were not guilty? He felt angry and alarmed that his worst suspicions might be affirmed. Already he mourned more deeply for Mayleda. How would he comfort her, knowing what he did know now?

"What did you want with him?" Pastor Brown's question stopped Charles at the stairs. "Perhaps I can help."

Charles looked back cautiously because of the audience of three. "It has to do with what's been printed in some of the Philadelphia newspapers," he admitted, holding to the icy rail. He reflected on his first parting from this town. It had been amicable because of this man who spoke to him now. He felt sorry that it all was so different this time.

The young Negro came out at him hotly. "We know what's been printed! You didn't need to ride here to tell us that!"

"Mr. Powell, this is Mr. Dumond Holmes, recently come from Europe," Pastor Brown said, calmly taking steps to come between them. "He is a writer and a solicitor for our newspapers." Then the pastor spoke about Charles. "Mr. Holmes, this is Mr. Powell. He is an abolitionist friend from Philadelphia."

Charles did not feel he fit that description, yet the pastor's introduction was so conciliatory and without pretense that Charles felt obliged to go back and extend his hand to the younger Negro. Inside, he suffered tremendous conflict. Did he or did he not trust these people? Surely most Negroes did not trust him. At this moment, Pastor Brown seemed to be the exception, for the minister cordially extended a hand to him then.

"So you came to inform Brother Whitsun of what was being said about him?" the pastor asked.

Charles hesitated, hating the truth. "No. I came to learn if those charges were true." He dared to say the rest of it. "And to defend Mrs. Ruskin's honor, if need be." He felt Holmes' hardened gaze, yet there was no judgment coming from Pastor Brown.

"You rode all the way in this weather to hear Mr. Whitsun speak for himself?" the pastor asked.

Charles could not guess what the pastor thought of him for that. "Yes." There was something comforting about the man being so intense, so direct, but without animosity.

"For his safety, I put Joseph Whitsun on the Underground Railroad," the man who faced him said. "I was the one who made that decision, for I was quite concerned about what might happen now that a lawman has Joseph's manumission paper."

"I assure you, Mr. Ruskin did see it." Charles tried to focus only on

Cummington Brown. "He plans to raise a posse to bring Whitsun in."

"On what charge?"

Perhaps he was forcing Charles to say it in front of them all. "I think the tenor of the newspaper reports makes that clear."

"If you would speak about the charge, please."

Charles did so reluctantly. "Outraging his former master's daughter. Conceiving a child by force." He trembled, for it was not easy to say this all out loud and while standing here.

Pastor Brown's gaze narrowed. "Do you believe this is true?"

Charles felt alone, yet closed in by all the eyes that were on him. "I am not sure. That is why I came. It is too immodest a subject for me to speak with Mrs. Ruskin about."

Charles knew then that the pastor's nod was sympathetic. Had they been alone in that moment, he believed they might have spoken frankly. Instead, the company increased as a young woman came running down the interior stairs in the hallway. Charles could see her clearly because the door had been left standing wide open.

"I heard what you think!" The woman suddenly spoke and with great fervor. "Get off our porch! Get out of our town! How can you be an abolitionist if you have no respect for us?"

Holmes moved aside when she stepped outside.

"This is my daughter," Pastor Brown said.

Miss Brown stayed focused only on Charles. "Joseph is innocent! Everything written about him is a lie to discredit his character and to ruin our good people!"

Charles looked at Pastor Brown. "Then he was not formerly the slave of Mayleda Ruskin's family?"

"Yes, he was," the minister admitted. "That part is true."

"That has nothing to do with his character!" Miss Brown raged.

Charles was reluctant to speak in her presence. There was a modesty that he believed needed to be preserved between women and men, color aside. "I've heard that the child still lives," Charles dared, though unwilling now to directly question parentage.

Anger filled the woman's eyes. She made her hands move as the old white man watched her, and he returned such signs to her, though slowly because of his wounded palms. Then the old man went inside. It was obvious to Charles now that the man was deaf and that the woman could communicate with him. In a few moments the white man carried out pieces of paper that had been glued to a square of cloth.

"You think that child could be Joseph's?" the woman said without flinching. "Well, there's your proof that he's not! It's the affadavit of a Southern man named Venor identifying that boy as his slave. The slave catchers who came here ripped it to pieces, seeing that there would be more profit in going after our reputations than in remanding an abused and wounded child."

Charles was held by her passion.

"This paper describes how the boy is branded. And we all saw that with our own eyes! Do you think Joseph Whitsun, who studied under a Quaker doctor, would burn a child? Do you think your own Mrs. Ruskin would do so?"

"No, miss," Charles admitted. Nowhere in the newspapers had it said that the child bore the marks of being a slave. There was now great sorrow on the pastor's face.

Charles looked down, feeling that he had been cause for most of it. "Miss Brown, I came seeking to hear the truth from Mr. Whitsun. Now I believe I have heard the truth from you."

Despite his confession, she stayed angry. "So you think truth is useful only to make you satisfied and happy? Well, I say what good is such truth if it only serves you and your color? No matter that Joseph is kind and good and noble and righteous! He has been driven from us and from his home, while you are satisfied now that truth prevails."

He understood exactly what she was saying. "I am sorry. You are right. I can only pledge that I will do anything to help see that the truth will prevail for all."

"It is too late!" she cried. "Joseph has already gone!"

Charles kept his silence, for there was no power to right the wrong by more apology. Unable to think of anything to say or do, he turned to go. "I should not have disturbed you. I regret how I allowed the rumors to affect me."

The pastor called to him, "Mr. Powell. You are dangerously chilled. Come inside and warm yourself before you go."

"I can't, sir." He looked back. "I am not deserving of your hospitality. You heard my admission. I did come thinking the worst about Joseph Whitsun, and all my apologies cannot change that."

"But you came to speak to him. To give him the chance to clear himself. That's what makes the difference. You wanted to know the truth, and now you do because you came here."

The pastor stepped to the railing. "If you can't accept my invitation as hospitality, then accept it as mercy. Your teeth are chattering. You will be ill by morning if you don't come inside."

Charles feared it was true.

"We can give you hot cider and some of the wonderful squirrel pie that Mr. Croghan here made for our supper." He nodded toward the silent man who had gone in for the paper.

Charles trembled, tempted by the pastor's warmth but concerned what the others would think. "Thank you, sir, if I could just thaw my hands and feet for a moment."

Pastor Brown stood by while Charles came to the door again. The others went inside with unhappy countenances, surely caused by his presence. Charles stopped in the light of the doorway, seeing how completely snow-covered he was.

"Don't worry about that," the pastor said, seeming to know Charles' mind. "Flesh is more important here than water on polished floors."

Charles did step in, and Pastor Brown closed the door. The old white man's injured hands moved as they all stood in the hallway. The woman clearly understood what these actions meant, for she responded with signs of her own.

"That is a language for the deaf," the pastor explained while Holmes disappeared into the room to Charles' left. "Joseph Whitsun sacrificed years to learn the method so that he could rescue Brother Croghan from the streets of Philadelphia."

Charles looked down, ashamed once more that his appreciation of Oak Glen's people had been so lacking.

"When Joseph came here, Mr. Croghan was with him. Joseph taught my daughter the language, in order that Barnabas would not have to be solely dependent on him." The man sighed when their eyes met. "He was wise to do so."

Miss Brown spoke, a sharp edge to every word. "Mr. Croghan wants to know if you are our friend or our foe."

Charles sensed the grief that reigned in the house. "Is Joseph Whitsun safe?"

"We have no sure way of knowing," the pastor answered. "Not until we get some report from the north. He's on his way to Canada. He has the boy with him."

Charles was aware of the trust shown by the pastor in speaking so freely. He did not feel that same trust from Holmes, who was now at the edge of the hallway with an older woman standing at his side.

"Mr. Powell, this is my wife, Azal. Now, Angel, go warm some supper for our guest."

Awkwardly Charles requested that she stay. "First, could you please have Mr. Croghan understand that I do not want to bring trouble to Mr. Whitsun?"

Her demeanor stayed cool, yet she nodded. She drew the deaf man to the kitchen with her while Pastor Brown invited Charles to remove his cloak and boots. After Charles was in his stocking feet, he led him to the dining room table where Dumond soon came to seat himself too.

"Mr. Powell, again I want to commend you for coming," the pastor said as he sat down beside him. Because of the cold Charles had endured, he was shivering all over. "Not many white men would ride so far to hear what a black man has to say."

Charles was sorely aware of Dumond's gaze upon him. "I think it fair that you know what is happening to Mrs. Ruskin. She, too, suffers from these lies. At present she is hiding, cut off from her daughter. I don't think Anthony Ruskin cares if her reputation is ruined, so long as his is saved." Charles rubbed his cold arms. "That man came to my store because he believes I know Mrs. Ruskin's hiding place, and I do. He told me that a posse was being raised to find Joseph, and that's when I set out for here."

"Then you have helped us by warning us."

"Mrs. Ruskin never told me that she knew Joseph Whitsun from her past," Charles said, feeling that he was facing honesty now and not trying to justify himself. "I wondered why. That's what had me most worried— why she kept it all secret."

Dumond bristled, but still the pastor was calm. "Perhaps she was being considerate of Joseph. That you would not have to know he was a slave. If it can ease your mind, I knew about the plantation. In fact, I was with them both on that day when the child was brought here, and they recognized each other after sixteen years of separation. They had much to speak about. There was much emotion."

"Of that I am sure!" Dumond put it.

"It was not hostility." Pastor Brown looked at Charles. "Each was concerned about the other."

Charles believed him, but still he worried. "So they never met in Philadelphia even though both of them worked with Dr. Ellis?"

"That is true. If you know each of their pasts completely, you see why.

In large part it has to do with the months that Mr. Whitsun spent helping Mr. Croghan."

Charles could not stop his weary sigh. "There is no need to say more, Pastor Brown. I was wrong, wholly wrong, in my distrusting, and I am more sorry than words can say."

"So is miscegenation a slain monster now, Mr. Powell?" the man Holmes probed. "Are you convinced then that not every colored man is on the prowl against women of your race?"

Charles was taken aback at his bluntness, but he could not justify any defensiveness on his part. "I admit I did entertain fears based on such misinformation and personal judgment, and I stand corrected. What I want you to know is that this misinformation has been given against Mrs. Ruskin too. This is not just about our separate races. More and more I see it is deceit. Raising suspicions and maintaining them can be akin to holding power." The pastor looked at the younger man, who said nothing.

A little puzzled about the hard exchange of glances, Charles went on. "*That's* what's happening, I think. Individuals are deceiving others in order to maintain themselves. Before God I say, may truth prevail, in us all and for us all!" He thought of the young woman in the kitchen.

Pastor Brown nodded. "I couldn't agree more."

Holmes, however, still seemed cold. Charles could think of nothing else to say. In a short while, Miss Brown brought in a bowl of squirrel pie to him with a thick slice of bread.

"You enjoy your meal, *Brother* Powell." Pastor Brown smiled. Charles could not miss his choice of words.

"Afterwards, come into the parlor and warm up by the fire. You are welcome to stay the night."

"I am overwhelmed by your kindness." Charles bowed his head to give silent thanks. When he looked up, he was alone.

CHAPTER 26

ANGELENE WAS IN THE KITCHEN putting away dishes from Charles Powell's late meal when that white man went into the hallway to claim his boots and outer garments. She had another glimpse of him through the dining room, and of her father too. At first he stood urging Powell to stay, but soon he sent the man out with his blessing.

Dumond, who had gone up to his room, came down the moment the front door closed. "I sense a trap," he said. "I can't believe that man came all this way alone to hear Joseph defend himself."

"I can," Angelene's father said, looking at her as she came through the dining room still wearing her apron.

"He left too quickly," Dumond reasoned, holding to the banister and staying on the bottom stair.

"He had pressing business. He told me he's mortgaged his property to have the funds needed to move Mrs. Ruskin out of the city. If Joseph weren't already away, I would have pressing business too, to get him to safety in a hurry. I understand the man's concerns. God be thanked that Joseph is on his way."

"You could be in danger, Daddy, when they learn that you still used the Underground route," Angelene fretted.

"There will be no evidence of that, but we must keep your mother's crazies on display. That should help our people to be cautious, now that we know a posse will come."

"In my opinion, Charles Powell should be counted with them," Dumond said. "Perhaps he was sent here to find Joseph, not to speak with him. Perhaps the posse knew that you would be trusting of him. Yet I am not trusting of him, for he admitted his judgment against Joseph."

"Yes, that is one reason I like the man. To work for peace you must believe that people can change. I trust Mr. Powell's conscience. He is a man of faith, like me."

Dumond's mouth opened in protest, but her father spoke first. "I know that this does not sound right to you, but I believe Powell will do what he can to make the truth known. And that will help us."

Their tense conversation was interrupted when Angelene's mother, dressed in nightcap and robe, came to the top of the stairs. "Cummington! There's someone in the rear yard. I saw him from our bedchamber window."

The words were not out of her mouth before someone knocked at the back door. Angelene felt numb while her father opened it. Cyrus was there, his hand free of bandages. He was covered with snow, but his face looked hot.

"What is it?" her father pressed.

"Who was that white man?"

"Mr. Powell," her father answered. "From the city."

Cyrus rolled his eyes. "Sah, the pike is covered with men, but I daren't come till now 'cause I saw that man ride up. Papa done wanted me to hurry an' tell you, but I was scaired to come in with a white man already here."

"All right. Go back and tell your father that I know."

Cyrus said more. "Sah, we know they lookin' for Joseph."

Angelene emitted a small cry, but her father was calm.

"You needn't worry. He's already west of Columbia, I'm sure."

"We don't think he is!" Cyrus was almost in tears. "You see, we done know'd that some Underground Railroad passengers what were tooken by the train were caught this morning."

Angelene wailed. "They have Joseph!"

Cyrus looked at her, his worry way beyond his years. "We don't know. We think that 'bout half of them what were headin' toward Columbia done been arrested. The other half an' one of the white men, Edwardson, may have got away. Guns were fired."

"So this is not the posse out of Philadelphia?"

"No, sah! Most are Brinkerville men that have done been ridin' through the day."

"Well, tell the Guard, then, that soon there will be a posse from the city likely to join them!" Her father shook his head.

Dumond stepped in. "Where were the passengers apprehended?"

Cyrus stammered. "A little ways west of Orangestone Bridge."

"Where's that?" he demanded of her father.

Cyrus answered. " 'Bout five, six miles west of here." Then he glanced toward Angelene with reluctance.

She was lacing her fingers in distress. "Do you know if anyone was hurt by that gunfire?" She felt Barnabas standing near, but she had no strength to speak with him right then.

"Nobody knows what happened to those what got away. We found out 'bout it all from this colored brother what wa' workin' near the tracks. He saw white men stop the train. Then he saw them take more than a handful of Negroes off 'fore others jumped an' skadaddled with white men's guns boomin' at they backsides."

Angelene leaned to the wall, her heart pounding. "Then they could be injured out there. Left in the snow. Or dead!"

"The lawmen don't have Joseph nor the boy, far as we know. The Guard says some colored prisoners are bein' held in a Brinkerville house to await the next train gwine east."

"We can't do anything about the captured passengers here," her father said, "not with the numbers so against us, but we do need to get word to the Vigilance Committee."

Cyrus looked a little braver. "That's already done."

"Angel, explain to Ba what the whole situation is. Tell him to keep his rifle handy, if he will."

While Angelene started to sign, Dumond showed the small revolver he kept on his person. Her father chided him. "No gunfire from us!"

"You will let a white man shoot, but not we ourselves!" Dumond protested.

"They won't kill Mr. Croghan as fast as they'd kill you. Listen to me, son, and obey me, for the good of us all."

Angelene felt terrified to think of Barnabas in mortal danger. She started translating this for him, but the old man shook his head and turned to ignore her worry by pulling his eyes away. Dumond showed his fist clenched but hanging at his side.

"I must go out and see if I can find him," her father said. Again her mother was at the top of the stairs, sharing their concerns.

"Allow me to go instead of you, sir." Dumond glanced to Angelene before trailing her father to the door. "The posse can recognize you and imagine what has you out. I'm not likely to draw attention. After all, I am a traveling solicitor, with no ties to Oak Glen." His eyes shifted to Angelene again. "At least for now."

"But you don't know the way," her father said.

"I can lead him!" Cyrus volunteered.

Taking his cloak and hat down from beside her father's, Dumond quickly dressed for the cold. "Also, I will find out if Mr. Powell is, indeed, friend or foe. We will see if he truly left for home, or if he just went back to join the others." He donned his high expensive hat.

"I don't believe Mr. Powell is a traitor," her father said. "Don't waste your time on that. Find out about Joseph and Daniel."

Angelene could hardly meet her father's eyes, his voice was that full of worry.

"We will, sah!" Cyrus said. Then Dumond and Cyrus left by way of the back door.

———

Charles chose to avoid the pike because he feared Anthony Ruskin's party of men might already be coming into the region. He headed back through the woods, hoping to follow the railroad bed east as he had followed it west. Even his solitary ride in the forest was not silent. Bundled up against the cold, he could still hear the crunch of the snow under the livery horse's feet.

Knowing it was not wise to push the animal or himself because of their weariness, yet wanting to be away from Oak Glen and back to the city as soon as possible, Charles hoped to travel at a slow but steady pace all through the night. He was just deciding how he would get around Brinkerville unnoticed when he heard a horse behind him. Turning in the saddle, he saw several mounted men. One carried a lantern. "Ho! There! You!"

Charles had one split second to decide if he should flee or stay. The moment passed and he was brought into their light. The man with the lamp he knew at once. *Anthony Ruskin!* Charles backed his horse to keep his face in darkness, but to no avail.

Mr. Ruskin spoke loudly. "Well! Charles Powell, from Philadelphia! You must have raced us to get out here."

Somehow Charles found the courage to face him. "I came to defend Mrs. Ruskin's reputation. I am returning to defend Joseph Whitsun's instead."

"So you know where he is!" Another rider, casting imposing shadows, pushed his mount forward.

"I don't! Except to say that he's gone. You won't find him."

"You are obligated to say all that you do know," Ruskin warned. The man beside him was Marshal Nichols. Charles could not believe the men were already here, when he himself had made such an arduous journey.

"There's more than twenty of us that came out on the evening train," Anthony reported. "We've borrowed our horses from here. The local constable and many others are out searching already. It appears that many were coming through on what you so much like to call the Underground Railroad. Some have been apprehended. We believe Joe Whitsun is out there with those who are still trying to flee." He pointed to five or six others whom Charles did not know. "These men are riding with us because they know the territory."

"You all accuse him wrongly!" Charles dared.

"Where is my sister-in-law? Does that brute have her now?"

"She is safe. I hope the same can be said of Mr. Whitsun."

"You had better start saying all that you know about this Negro," Nichols warned.

"All right!" Charles said looking at him hotly. "I'll begin by avowing that many of you are helping to spread lies about a Christian man and a Christian woman, both of whom may well have more integrity than any of us here!" He spoke to the marshal, whom he thought might have the most authority. "Mr. Nichols, please believe me. Mr. Whitsun is innocent, and Mrs. Ruskin is safe."

"What makes your testimony worthy?" Ruskin challenged.

"For one thing I have nothing to profit by it!" Charles said, hoping Nichols would see this too. "You, sir," he said, addressing Ruskin, "desire to harm the cause of abolition, even if it destroys Mrs. Ruskin's reputation."

Ruskin swore at him. "Nichols! Long! You are witnesses to what this free-products merchant has said against me."

Charles searched their countenances. He had no allies. "Mr. Ruskin acts as though Mr. Whitsun's guilt is proven! The man is innocent. Your fears are unfounded. I know, because I came here having those same fears too!"

Nichols listened. "And?"

"I've just come from Oak Glen. I spoke with the pastor and with his daughter. Both know Joseph Whitsun well."

"Negro testimony!" Ruskin snarled.

"I believe Whitsun is innocent, otherwise I would join you to help bring him in myself."

Nichols rubbed his face. "You are neither juror nor judge. Yet you may be of help in bringing this whole matter to an end. We are set on apprehending every runaway from the train, and Joe Whitsun also. Now we will count you with us for the search."

"No, sir. I decline because of my religious convictions!"

"There is no declining. Either you join us, or I am authorized to put you under arrest. That is according to the Fugitive Slave Act."

"I won't serve!"

"You are a known abolitionist, Mr. Powell. I believe colored folks who see you will be apt to trust you, and that includes Joe Whitsun. If and when we find him, then you can draw him out to let him speak for himself."

Charles did not trust him. "I will not help to track down a man who has done no wrong!"

"You will," Nichols countered mildly. "According to section five of the law, you must. All citizens can be required to aid and assist in the capture of fugitive slaves."

"I will not!" Charles pulled at his horse's head, but Nichols, Long, and Ruskin kicked their mounts to close him in.

"I will put you under arrest if you do not cooperate," Nichols said. To make his threat clear, Nichols reached behind him and brought forth shackles from his saddlebag. "These are for the Negro. However, I'm sure they fit lawless abolitionists." The circle of men looked hard at him.

"I will not go against an innocent Christian brother," Charles said. "I came ready to accuse him, but now I know I was wrong, as you are wrong."

Many took offense. "Are you accusing us of not being Christians?"

As they spoke, Charles considered that he could be imprisoned or fined, but their discovery of the Negro could well cost Joseph his life.

"Do not think that the decision handed down in the Christiana trial means that the teeth have been pulled from the Fugitive Slave Act," Nichols warned. "On the contrary, you will face the harshest of penalties if you do not cooperate now, for we've learned much from the mistakes of that first trial."

Charles held his breath. It was not the threat that changed his mind but his desperation to help Joseph in any way possible. These men were going to keep up their search, with or without him. If he cooperated, perhaps God would give him an opportunity to warn Joseph or others if they were found. Then he'd take the consequences. He made it seem that he was reconsidering his stance out of fear for himself. "All right, Mr. Nichols, I will come with you."

Joseph waited through several hours of darkness before putting Daniel on the horse. Just when he was ready to set out, he heard a sound at the southern door. He touched the boy in the dark and felt the blankets about him. "Don't move!" he whispered. Then he fell silent. Someone pushed open the woodshed's southern door.

Joseph grappled for some weapon of defense. He touched a piece of cordwood and raised it. He worried most about Daniel. If he himself were taken, then the child's terrible fate could be sealed. The horse nickered, giving them away.

"Who's in here?"

It sounded like Cyrus's voice, but Joseph was unsure.

"Who's in here? Joseph?"

Joseph nearly cried his relief. "Cyrus, it is you!"

Hurriedly, the young man rushed in and said what he knew of the route's unfortunate passengers. Then Joseph told him how the woman had died, keeping them here.

"It was by God's grace, Brother Whitsun," Cyrus declared.

Then another voice filled the darkness. "You call this grace, to be hiding in a freezing shed?"

Joseph knew this speaker was Dumond Holmes. "Are the Browns safe? What of Brother Croghan?" he asked with burning fear.

"They all safer than you, sah!" Cyrus confirmed. "There's a huge posse out there searchin' the countryside, but Mr. Holmes an' me got this plan."

Dumond continued in his more sophisticated way. "Now that we know where you are, Cyrus can bring some of the Black Guard here. Once we know they are in place, you and I will go up higher on the mountain through their protective line. Then you can go north or west, with the Guard positioned between any white men and yourself."

"We'll make the night train our signal!" Cyrus declared. "If you don't hear nothin' more from me, you wait till that whistle blows, then you come a'runnin'."

"Dumond, you should go with him now, for there is real danger here," Joseph said.

Immediately Dumond quoted poetry that Joseph did not know. " 'How can a man die better than facing fearful odds?' " When Cyrus was gone, he said more. "I have a gun, Mr. Whitsun, and I will use it if necessary."

Joseph's thoughts immediately went to Angelene and to her father. "You must consider what would happen to those in Oak Glen if we choose violence."

"I have considered it!" Dumond said. "Let pure and holy war against our foes begin!"

Even without shackles, Charles was bound to the posse. They rode along the railroad tracks through cold scenery that the moonlight painted gray. Anytime there were animal tracks or human footprints in the snow that met the cinders from the trains, either Nichols or Long would dismount for a close examination. The men were doing that now, since the prints they had just found were abundant and human, as though a large group of persons had come out from the swampland on the north side of the tracks to meet one of the Philadelphia to Lancaster trains, which commonly stopped for passengers anywhere along the route.

"Hey, there's two more sets of prints coming down from the woods over here!" Nichols shouted. Charles looked up to the dark tree-covered slope where the marshal pointed. "There's some kind of a building up there."

Nichols got back on his horse and so did Long as the constable continued. "That's where some of the Negroes of Oak Glen split and store wood to sell to the railroad."

"Let's go up!" the marshal decided. "Negroes often aid other Negroes by hiding them."

It seemed that Constable Long would lead the way, but when he turned his horse to the right, Nichols stopped him. "Wait! Let's send Powell up to test our plan. He'll go in, and we'll stay behind him out of view. If he finds any fugitive, he'll say that he's an abolitionist come to help."

Charles knew that he would never do that, yet he moved in silence according to their wishes. Even so, Nichols seemed to think it wise to keep on threatening him.

"I've been thinking, Mr. Powell. Shackles are much too good for you. If you will not do as you are told, I can telegraph back for permission to *march* you home to Philadelphia on foot behind my horse. That way I could make an example out of you to every merchant, tavernmaster, or farmer who still thinks himself able to ignore or defy national law concerning runaway slaves."

Charles breathed a prayer, his thoughts still more with Joseph and the child than on himself. Fearfully but obediently he reined his horse upward through the brittle snow.

CHAPTER 27

JOSEPH HEARD NOISE beyond the north door. Dumond touched him, showing he had heard it too.

"Be ready to run your horse through the back door. I'll do the confronting," Dumond whispered in words hardly heavier than Joseph's own anguished breathing.

Joseph knew he would make too much noise if he tried to move the horse now. In the dark they could tell when the north door opened slightly.

"Hello in here?" It was the nervous voice of a stranger.

Joseph froze, but beside him he felt Dumond taking aim. The line of blue in the blackness, which came when the door was opened, grew to be a square as the door was pushed wide. It silhouetted one man.

"Hello! I'm here to warn anyone!" His voice was slightly softer. "There's a posse outside!"

Joseph heard the click of Dumond's pistol. The man must have heard it too.

"Hello! Don't shoot!"

Joseph touched Dumond, terrified that he would.

"Someone's in here! I know!" The voice was fear filled. "If you're colored, please take warning! Other men will be here in a moment! I don't know what else to say or do!"

The man they could barely see started turning. Close to him, Joseph could just make out the image of Dumond with his hand extended.

Outside, someone called, "Powell! What did you find?"

It caused Dumond to seethe. "You traitor!"

"Don't shoot him!" Joseph cried aloud his panic. He grabbed Dumond's hand. "I know that name!"

"Oh, so do I! The white betrayer!"

Joseph did not want to believe it, but for certain other men, their foes, were coming. He could see them when Powell pushed his body to the wall just inside the door, as though protecting himself.

"I'll kill him with the one shot I have," Dumond declared. "He deserves death."

"No! Let's try for the rear door! Perhaps he did come to give us the warning." Joseph pushed Dumond and pulled on the reins.

At once the man at the north door became aware of them. He seemed to be on their side. "If you can, escape! Hurry!"

Men outside called Powell's name again.

"Yes! Coming!" Powell shouted back to them.

Joseph and Dumond were through the rear door, then suddenly Dumond bolted far ahead of him, where he could be seen in the moonlight. Shots shattered the silence.

"Dumond!" Joseph screamed, yanking on his horse's reins while only Daniel was in the saddle.

"For freedom in the boy's time!" Dumond cried. "Flee!"

There was more gunfire. Then voices came in the dark directed toward Dumond. "Look! He's running away on foot!"

Joseph could see the shadow-cloaked crowd gaining on the young man, as he was still near the woodshed door fully engulfed by the dark. Looking inward to the shed, he saw one man coming with his own horse through the interior.

"Go! Go! Go!" It was Powell. "They're all after that other man!"

Joseph had no choice, for Powell was huge, and he used his strength and his long arms to snatch Joseph's reins. "Get up on that horse!" he barked, clearing the door and throwing himself to his own saddle. "Let's go!"

He still had control of Joseph's animal. They went downhill in pitch dark at incredible speed. Chaos reigned behind them, but Powell kept them going toward the railroad ravine.

Joseph saw the express train coming from their right. It pressed down on them as though the roaring locomotive's sole purpose was to kill them all.

With Powell still in charge, they lunged toward the tracks. It was too close for safety, yet their horses were too spooked now to stop. The lights on the train streaked toward them like flying stars. The metal was so close, Joseph could feel the heat.

Daniel screamed.

The moment they were across the tracks, Charles felt themselves in another, safer world. He stopped the reckless pace as soon as he could get the horses settled. The train clattered behind them, gating them off from that other realm of danger for all the seconds that it roared by. When he trusted the horses to be steady, he handed the reins back to the man whom he could scarcely see. "I am Charles Powell. I was coerced to ride with those others tonight. I am sorry, but this was my only plan."

The other man's voice was shaky. "I know you, sir. I am Joseph Whitsun. The boy you rescued is with me."

"God be thanked!" Even as he said it, he thought about the second man in the woodshed, but he did not speak about that now. "I don't know the land at all. I have no idea where to go."

There was silence, almost ringing after the noise of the now passed train.

Then Joseph said, "Follow me." He pushed his horse deep into the swamplands on this side.

Charles trailed him, unable to know how Whitsun felt about his company, but at this moment he didn't know what else to do. He feared for his own safety after having countered the posse.

Dead cattails and reeds snapped around their stirrups. Charles knew they must be making a path as wide as elephant tracks. Ahead, Joseph took them to where the swamp was drained by a stream. The pink of morning eventually showed on the eastern horizon, its reflection mirrored on the unfrozen patches of black, slow-moving water.

Joseph put his horse into the stream. Charles followed. The water swirled higher than the horses' bellies. Broken sheets of ice floated around them. Charles drew back his feet, pressuring the saddle with his knees. He could see that Joseph was having a harder time because the boy was with him.

Charles worried that the splash of frigid water would draw attention to them now that the morning was brightening. Everywhere around them, the landscape was quiet as a store locked up tight. Charles thought of runaways in the South who took to the streams to avoid being tracked by hounds. He never imagined that he would be hunted himself.

Joseph's choice to use the stream to hide their tracks made sense, but it left them wet and miserable when finally they came out on the other side where old pine trees grew so thickly on the bank that all snow had been blocked from the ground. Here they continued, Charles following Joseph uphill under the dark canopy of trees. When they reached a cleared rocky crest, they met each other eye to eye.

"There are men spread out everywhere searching for you," Charles warned. The little boy looked out at him from his hood of blankets, level with Joseph's chest. "Two posses have come together. One from the township and one from Philadelphia."

The black man's frown increased the weariness already showing on his face. "Mr. Powell, now they will be searching for you too."

"Yes, but do not think of me as a hero." Charles felt remorse. "Who was the man who lured them away from us? He is the hero!"

"A newspaper solicitor named Holmes."

"I fear for him."

"So do I."

"If I leave from here now, I worry that the posse may find me, and then that they might be able to find you."

Joseph's sighing sounded painful. "We must stay together." He led Charles over the rocky summit.

Soon they came to a small farm carved out of the sloping woodland on the other side. Charles dismounted with Joseph so that they could take down rails and let themselves into a pasture. A mule and two bony horses grazed around tree stumps where the snow had melted away.

Except for the movement of these animals, there was no activity in the early morning at either the log house or the log barn. They repaired the fence and mounted again. Joseph rode across the short clearing, going directly to the barn's open door. He dismounted. Charles did the same.

They led their horses inside to one of the two square stalls.

"Let's take off the saddles and bridles," Joseph said. "We'll hide the tack with us and keep the horses together."

When this was done, they both sat down with their saddles at their backs in the one empty stall. Charles' spine prickled with the intensity of the anxiety he felt. He watched Joseph frown grimly as he held tightly to the child.

"That other man, Holmes, took the risk he did for the sake of this boy," Joseph said. Charles thought the pracititioner was close to tears.

The boy looked at Charles with suspicion. Joseph seemed to counter it. "Daniel, you know Mr. Powell. He's the one who brought you out of Philadelphia in the wagon with Sister May."

"Sister May!" the boy said at once, his countenance changing.

"She's safe but in hiding too," Charles said, looking more to the man than to the child. "The moment I get home, I hope to convince her to leave the city. It can be arranged."

Joseph questioned him directly. "What brought you here?"

Charles answered with blunt honesty. "I confess I came to find you."

There was silence.

"I felt I needed to ask you some questions. I should have known better."

"What questions?"

Charles looked away, especially to avoid the child's gaze. "Concerning Mrs. Ruskin and your past."

There was sighing. "So my manumission paper has become news in the city."

"Yes. That is what brought the posse this way."

"Then Mr. Ruskin is with them, I guess."

"He is. I was not with them, Mr. Whitsun, not until they demanded service from me. I would have taken arrest over betraying you, but I acted on the slim hope that if I did ride with them unfettered, I might be able to warn you."

"And you did."

"God be thanked, not me. It was not on any noble mission that I came here." He stopped. "I came wanting to know from you if you had ever done Mrs. Ruskin any harm."

The boy said, "No!"

"My apology will ever be too feeble for my offense," Charles confessed. "I let myself be swayed by rumor."

His distress seemed to drain Joseph of every emotion. "How do you know now that I am not guilty?"

It was painful to face him. "Miss Brown spoke with much conviction in your favor. I understood her passion to defend you, for that is how I feel about Mrs. Ruskin." He added the rest sheepishly. "I also saw the slave owner's document with the boy's full description. It proves that he cannot be yours."

Joseph kissed the child. "He is mine now, until death."

"Out of respect for Mrs. Ruskin's gender and the great amount of grief she has had, I decided that I must come to you. Now I see how much I have added to your own grief and to that of your friends."

"God used it for our good. We might be under arrest by now if you had not come to the shed."

They both sat shivering in silence, their trousers soaked up past their knees. "I understand that you might want me to move on, Mr. Whitsun. If you can just tell me a way back toward the city whereby I might not encounter any of the posse."

"I don't know such a way, or I would take it myself."

"Where are we?"

"Tort Woodman's barn and property. He's one of our Underground Railroad conductors."

The small window in the horses' stall showed how dangerously bright it was outside. Charles was exhausted but alert with fear. He guessed that Joseph might feel the same.

"I suppose you are the first white man to ever see this isolated farm," Joseph told him.

"I'll not betray its location."

Joseph looked at him mildly. "I don't doubt that."

Hens came in by way of the open barn door that led out to the pasture. They clucked and scratched for their breakfast. Their activity drew Charles' attention to a large pile of unhusked corn outside the stalls.

"You are planning, then, to take Mrs. Ruskin out of the city with you?" Joseph asked, bringing them back to the subject of Mayleda's fate.

"If she will agree to it, yes. She risks losing custody of her daughter to the Ruskin family if she flees. Still, I think that the best plan is to move her somewhere safe, then work on getting the girl to come to her."

A muscle in Joseph's cheek was twitching. "So are you her suitor, Mr. Powell?"

"I am not gentry. Still, I will do anything I can to help her, and she knows that. She is a brave and good woman." He was surprised by Joseph's smile.

"Yes, she is. Does she care for you, Mr. Powell?"

Charles found himself flustered. "She says she does."

Joseph sighed and leaned back. "Then I am glad for her." He seemed desiring to say more. "When I was a slave boy, I was assigned to rock her cradle. Sometimes I carried her down to the slave street to have her suckled when her mother had to be away. She grew up being my secret best friend. As a girl she saved my life more than once. Has she told you that?"

"No."

"You did know that her family owned me?"

Charles could hardly tolerate the thought of it, seated near Joseph now, seeing him as he was. "Yes. I cannot think what it would be like to meet you enslaved."

Joseph closed his eyes. "Looking back on it now, I know it was her friendship that gave me the hope I needed to believe that I was truly human." He looked at him then. "Does that sound profane to you?"

Charles found himself drawn to the other man's agony. "I am only beginning now to understand."

"It is possible that you and Ba Croghan and Dr. Ellis might be the only white men who do understand, Mr. Powell."

"Would you call me Charles?"

Joseph smiled pensively. "Charles. I've thought and prayed much about this. If I am caught, I know the accusation will be rape, though I am innocent of ever touching any woman other than my own wife, who died in slavery."

Charles blinked, ashamed of himself again. Of course Joseph might have had a spouse, a woman he loved, but Charles had not considered that until now.

"With God's help, I will endure whatever they do to me, but they must not have this boy! Now he is my Daniel." He kissed him again. "Though Pudget and Dawes did destroy that paper, surely someone can be authorized again to do the remanding. Once they have used him to get me, I fear they will take him South."

Charles watched the boy bury his face against Joseph.

"We know from that document that he was the property of a master named Venor."

"I saw the paper." Charles' sympathy went out to them both.

"Daniel can only remember portions of his torturous life. He must not

DENISE WILLIAMSON

be made to go back! If you were not now in nearly as much trouble as I, I would beg you to take him and protect him."

"No begging would be needed, Mr. Whitsun, believe me! As it is, I still will not give up hope of seeing you *two* get away from here safely."

A small amount of light came to Joseph's dark eyes. "Let's say *three*, to include you!"

There was more silence. Soon Charles noticed that the boy was nodding, close to slumber while the imminent danger they were in kept both of them, as adults, quite wary. Perhaps it was this sense of sudden capture that caused them both to speak more about their pasts and also about their hopes for the future. The fog of mistrust dissipated as they talked through the morning. Between their times of conversation, they rested and took turns keeping watch. Both of them carried timepieces that told them when their waiting had moved to afternoon.

Having been among Friends, Charles' practice was to approach God in silence, and he was greatly moved to hear Joseph pray aloud. As more hours passed, they continued to come back to one central question. *What must they do now?*

Charles looked out upon the pile of corn again. Joseph followed the direction of his gaze and said, "All that is set aside for an annual celebration we have on the last Saturday before Christmas. Like most of the farmers who attend Mt. Hope, Brother Tort has held off husking some of his corn so that he can haul it to the all-night party Pastor Brown always has at his barn."

"The day after tomorrow is Saturday, the twentieth."

"That is the night when everyone will gather for the year's grand husking bee. It's much like the ones many of us can remember from our days of slavery." He stopped. "Of course, all is a celebration here, for men and women profit from their own crops. There's always singing, fiddle-playing, storytelling, and some courtship, just as in slave days. This lasts through the night, then all go to church in the morning for a time of thanksgiving. Later, this part of the crop is sold and the money is set aside for any who might face hardship in the new year."

Charles was touched by the plan. "I suppose Miss Brown will miss you sorely at the celebration."

Instead of agreeing, Joseph frowned. "I am not her suitor. I told you much about my wife today, much more than I ever planned to tell anyone."

As Joseph said that, Charles saw more of the torment this man had survived. "I am touched and honored to know of the courage and struggle you two shared. My life will not be the same for it, Mr. Whitsun. You have told me things today that I thought unimaginable. I will not just stand by now."

"I think we agreed that you would call me Joseph."

Charles sense the profound effect of the man's past afflictions on them both. "Do you really think that you will never love again?"

"I would say that I did believe it until I began to reflect fully on my past and my future since leaving Oak Glen."

"And?"

Joseph was hesitant. "I guess I cannot fool myself any longer now that there has been seperation."

"You mean between yourself and Miss Brown?"

"Yes, I do."

"Before you left Oak Glen, were you able to speak of what is in your heart?"

"No. There was a moment when I could have shared the truth, but I did not, for it seemed a worthless thing for her. To finally know that I do love her and had, in fact, loved her this long while, and then to be separated by circumstances forever—" He put his head down. "It is better that she never knows this longing I do have for her!"

"I don't believe that. She loves you. She would want to know that she is loved by you, regardless of the cirumstances."

"It is my hope, Charles—no, not my hope but my reasoning—that says she will soon find another man, one younger and more worthy than I am of her love."

"Friend, I think I can almost speak for this lady. She loves you, and her heart must be breaking now. Yet you do love her in return."

"I think she will find another. I even pray it will be soon."

"Couldn't she go to Canada once you and Daniel are there? Surely you think the child would benefit from having a mother."

Joseph held his head. "Angelene suggested the same thing. I said no."

The silence felt heavy. "Wouldn't you say differently if you had another chance?"

"There is no second chance."

"There could be. All it would take is having you write a letter, if we can find pen and paper. Once you are safely away and I am in a secure place, I will send it to her. Then she can know."

Joseph sighed into his open hands. "Are you going to marry Sister Mayleda Ruskin?"

Charles felt self-conscious, perhaps just as Joseph had only a few moments before. "I plan to ask if she is willing. But I tell you now, I do not know if I could live with the bliss of marriage if at the same time it were denied to you."

"I do not understand what you are saying."

"I am saying that I should not *allow* myself to marry Mayleda unless I know that you are able to marry Angelene, if that is the mutual choice between you and Miss Brown."

"I have never heard of such an agreement," Joseph said.

"I think we should call it a Covenant Day, the day when we both can be married to the women we do love."

"Charles, what you propose is impossible, but I thank you. How I thank you for showing so much unselfish commitment to me."

"So will you write the letter? That is not an unselfish question at all. You see how much I want you to be able to marry Angelene, for then I can in clear conscience enjoy the prospect of marriage to Mayleda." He smiled.

Joseph was staring at his steady hands. "Yes, all right. If it can be possible, I will write a letter to Angelene Brown."

Charles then shared a thought that had been growing in his mind for hours. "What if some of that corn out there could be put in sacks for you to sell in Philadelphia?" Charles asked. "There are many colored farmers who come into the city to trade their produce at Christmastime. Often they bring their families. Many come to my store. If you could disguise yourself as a farmer, you might be able to take the train car. And no one would think it odd that you have a child with you."

Joseph took hold of the idea. "It would be better if I did not travel alone. Once Tort and Cyrus get here, maybe they will risk taking me on to Simeon Bart's concealed in their wagon. Simeon is known for trading in the city. Perhaps he would go with me and take one or more of his children."

"Yes! His daughters! Then you could dress Daniel in some of their clothing and make him into *another* little girl. That would be safer yet. And Brother Bart already has a contract to trade with me. I could put it in writing since his older boys can read. He could bring that along as proof of your intentions to trade grain."

Joseph stroked Daniel's hair as the boy continued to sleep. "I will not be able live with myself if I lose him to agents or to the marshals."

"Honestly, neither could I. With God's help, we are going to come through this safely."

Joseph's smile was now almost wholly unencumbered. "Let's start at the beginning and discuss every detail."

CHAPTER 28

ANGELENE HAD JUST GOTTEN HER STUDENTS SETTLED for the last class of the day when some commotion outside drew their attention to the windows facing her house and the street. "Here now! Sit down! None of you has permission!" But her shouts were useless.

Through the windows, then, she saw for herself that Cyrus and his daddy, Tort Woodman, were outside and that many young men were surrounding the wagon Tort was driving in.

"Miss Brown! There's a man's body in that wagon!" screamed one of the girls.

Most of the boys headed toward the door that led into Joseph's house. "Don't you go a step farther," she warned them. They obeyed her only because Barnabas Croghan was suddenly there between his house and the class. His face was as white as his hair. "That's not Joseph, is it?" Angelene cried, numb already, while she pressed her way through the door herself.

Without signs, he understood her. "NO!" He voiced the word while he used both his hands to hold her.

Even though he had her by the shoulders, she signed to him. *"Keep the students here!"* He nodded sadly, then let her pass.

The cold air hit her hard when she ran outside and hurried down the porch stairs. Her father was already standing on the wheel to climb in to reach the victim. Her skirts prevented her from doing the same, so she raced to the wagon's gate. Within seconds she saw Dumond's face, his eyes glazed, blood coming from his mouth. "Not Dumond!" she cried.

Along with Cyrus and Tort, her father pulled the man's blood-soaked body to the wagon's edge. "He's still breathing, Angel!" She moved aside to give her father and his helpers room.

"Ba has a fire going in his own kitchen. You can take him into Joseph's house," she said, accustomed to having the clinic there.

"No! It must be away from the children's view!" Her father was adamant.

Under his direction the Woodmans carried Dumond by his knees and shoulders into her house and up the stairs to the room where the young man had been staying. Breathlessly Angelene climbed the stairs after them.

"He was shot at least three times while runnin' from our woodshed," Tort told her in his gravelly voice as they laid him on the bed.

Young Cyrus looked ill, his lips pressed together. "Joseph an' Daniel were in that shed too," he dared to tell her while Dumond groaned and muttered nonsensically.

"Where are they now?" she cried to her father, for clearly Dumond was in too much torment to know.

"No one knows, girl. You must help Dumond if you can."

"I am no doctor!"

"After Joseph, you have more experience than anyone. We can't call on a white physician, for we have no idea if he would give aid to someone wounded by a posse."

She stood dumbly, forcing her father to take charge. He used pillows to support Dumond so that he could lay him on his right side. Then he used his work knife from the orchard to cut away portions of the bloody coat and shirt.

"Angelene!"

Her father's pleading pulled her from her longing that this must all be some terrible dream.

"Do what you can!"

Cummington never left her side while his youngest child and only daughter bravely examined the grotesque holes where rifle balls had entered Dumond's back, close to his spine. They still had the young man on his side with his head against the pillows. Dumond was breathing hard, and between every breath he moaned. His eyes were wide open, and blood flowed steadily from his mouth so that the pillows were soon stained red.

Angelene looked up in stark anguish. Barnabas came in carrying what dressings and supplies had not been destroyed in the raid. Cummington prayed while Angelene tried to halt some of the bleeding. "There are injuries inside of him, Daddy. I don't know what to do."

"God knows that, Angel. No one's expecting miracles from you." He put his hands upon the young man and prayed anew.

"But I don't know what to do!" she cried again as Dumond began to choke and wheeze.

Cummington took her trembling hand, even though it was covered in blood. She started weeping. He held her while Dumond let out a fearsome roar. He cried for water, but when Cummington tried to give it to him, he was too disoriented to drink.

Cummington dipped his fingers and wet the man's lips. "Son, this may be your last moment between now and eternity! Think on Christ, and He will save you."

A spew of cursing against his attackers came forth like fire from his mouth. "My murderers' god! No!"

"Don't hold this against God! He wants to give you life—"

Angelene gripped him. "Please don't distress him more!"

"Angel, he's dying without the hope of heaven!"

Dumond's eyes fluttered wildly.

"Dumond!" Cummington pleaded. "God loves you. He wants to give you peace through Jesus Christ."

"No! No! No!" Three times he bellowed, his voice rising, then fading like waves beating against rocks before breaking into nothingness. After that he spoke no more. His mouth swung opened. His body rolled.

"Dumond!" Angelene screamed, her hands upon his lifeless yet manly shoulders.

Cummington pressed his fingers to the man's neck. There was no pulse.

Angelene looked him straight in the eye and screamed, "Oh, Daddy!"

"Yes, honey! I know!" He fought tears and felt as much rage as grief. "Don't blame yourself, Angel! Don't blame yourself."

Her beautiful face became a torrent of tears. "Oh, where is Joseph? Is he somewhere dying too?"

Cummington glanced at Cyrus, Tort, and the others who were there.

Cyrus stepped forth, trembling. "Mr. Holmes is dead?"

"Yes," Cummington managed to say while taking a sheet to cover the body. A sensation came upon him of how he had put his own sons to sleep in this same bed amid hugs and hopes and prayers. Now he was shrouding Dumond for a father he did not even know, a father who might never even learn how his son had departed this life.

"That boy done nothin' to deserve dyin'!" Tort pronounced in his rough, rumbling way.

Cummington agreed, his emotions stiff now. "Please, Brother, what *do* you know of Joseph and the child?"

"We made no attempt to look for them," Tort confessed. "We feared the posse would only be drawn to follow us. We stayed in the woods with our brother, here, a good long while. Other Guards sounded off they horns an' shot they guns in the air. But as God is my judge, sah, none of us kilt none of them in return." He cast his eyes to Dumond's shrouded form. "That brother had a gun, but he didn't use it neither. The posse didn't come into the woods to search for him. I think they knowed they hit him though. I just don't think they were ready to venture in amongst so many angry Negroes to get him out!"

"Do you think they thought he was Joseph?" Cummington speculated sadly. "Perhaps they considered it a victory, but one that no one in their group wanted to admit to. Likely the law will ignore a Negro's passing. I don't think the coroner will come."

"Or maybe the posse was smart 'nough just to turn 'round an' track Joseph, if they knew this wasn't him," Tort said sourly, not protecting Angelene from hearing any of that harsh reality.

"We don't know!" Cummington said, seeing her quiver.

Tort squinted at the corpse. "When we first got to Dumond, he wa' talkin' through his pain 'bout some white man. A Mista Powell? It wa' like he wa' tryin' to say that this white man had done already found Joseph, but that's all we could hear."

"Then Dumond was right!" Angelene sobbed. "Charles Powell may have come here to betray him!"

"We don't know that either, Angel," Cummington said. "I still believe Mr. Powell to be a fair man."

Tort scowled. "*Fair*, like Harley an' Long?"

Cummington gently tried to draw his daughter away, for again she was holding on to Dumond's lifeless form. "Girl, we're going to think the best, not the worst, till we all know differently."

"I don't think I can hope for the best anymore!" She twisted away from him and went to the window that looked out on the bare orchard. "You used to make me face the bees and tell me not to think about the stings but rather to think about their sweetness. Well, life is all stings now, Daddy!" She put her head against the tiny panes of glass that framed her portrait of misery. "God let them shoot Dumond! Oh, what will they do with Joseph and poor little Daniel?"

Cummington saw Azal in the doorway opening to the hall. He removed himself from Angelene and went to her, taking consolation in the touch of her thin, cold hands. Even with the other men present, he kissed her on the face, a sign that he felt so inadequate, so helpless, to be the shepherd of sheep being driven to the slaughterers. "Dumond is dead," he mourned. "Three gunshot wounds to his back."

He could not keep himself from saying more, though he should have guarded her from having to endure the whole truth. "He passed from this life not believing that Jesus could be his Savior. Azal, I never witnessed any consequence of prejudice more profound than that which I just saw now."

He staggered past her and sat down on the top stair like a sorry child. Azal was soon beside him, and he mourned anew, not hiding any of his grief from her. "Ah! 'What is a man profited, if he shall gain the whole world, and lose his own soul?'" he said, quoting the Scripture that most tormented him now. He did not realize that Angelene had come out of the room until he heard her behind them.

"What of those who *caused* Dumond to be unwilling to believe?" Her question was sharp with anger. "What of those who shot him? If you are going to quote the Bible, Daddy, remember Jesus said it would better for offenders if they had millstones hung around their necks before they were cast into the sea!" She showed her hands covered with blood. "I pray that his enemies will suffer eternally!"

"Angel, no." Azal looked up at their daughter with hauntingly sad eyes. "God desires that all be saved. I encourage you to trust our God of mercy and justice to care for Dumond Holmes' soul, and don't you dare try to command God when it comes to our foes. We must be faithful to Christ's call and pray for them instead."

Down at their front door someone knocked. It startled them all. "Everybody stay up here," Cummington said as the Woodmans came out into the hallway too.

He went down to find Mr. Harley alone on his porch, bright with afternoon light.

"Preacher Brown." The neighbor looked nervous in every way. "I know a Negro was wounded by the posse earlier today. I also know that Oak Glen boys were in the woods shooting and hollering up a storm so that none of the lawmen felt safe to follow up on the man that fled from the railroad woodshed that Tort and Cyrus and others use."

Cummington had no problem letting himself be cold. "Why does that bring you here, Mr. Harley?"

"Was the Negro they shot Joseph Whitsun?"

"I don't see why I have to say."

Harley scowled then. "You know I warned you about this kind of violence. I rode with those who wanted Whitsun brought to trial because, indeed, the problem did need to be brought before the law. But I never wanted it to end this way, with someone shooting him. You must believe me. I don't condone violence."

"Am I to be comforted by your words, sir?"

"Cummington! Now, don't you put the blame on the posse comitatus. Your boys were armed and they were hiding in the woods, clearly hoping for the chance to ambush officers and deputized citizens who were merely performing their civic duty. That, you must agree, is lawless behavior on the part of colored folks."

"It is?" Cummington let himself stay numb. "Is it lawless behavior for *men* who have lived in America all their lives, yet are denied every benefit of the law and citizenship?"

Harley stepped back. "What's come over you? You've never been an ugly-tempered, confrontative fellow before!"

Cummington found himself holding the door. "A man never before died in my house cursing God because he believed his murderers to be Christian."

"You folks brought this on yourselves. You've claimed for so long that you have the faculties to be *men*, yet you will not heed the laws that now are established to save the Union."

"Laws that say we can be the property of other men, Mr. Harley!

Forgive me when I say that I must stand by a greater truth, one that says we can only be the property of God Almighty, who made us in His image, just as He made you."

"Joe Whitsun should not have run. I do offer my sympathies. I believe with all my heart that his punishment should have come by civil ways, but you must see how troublesome this is, especially for men like me who have been willing to take your side. Most of us considered Whitsun to be a decent fellow and smarter than most. But then to find out that he still carried that lecherous trait within him of your primitive African ancestry! Well! I didn't come to say this, but I will. It makes me think we must suspect you all. I heartily regret that my wife's property was ever transferred to such a lot as you."

Cummington could bear no more. He closed the door, causing Harley to shout new remarks about his crudeness. He put his head against the wood once he had shut himself in, reliving the fresh, raw scene of Dumond's awful death. "Oh God!" he dared to lament in private. "Will you go on favoring our oppressors only?"

He repented nearly as quickly as he had complained, for God was sovereign, and His Word was true. If he could not hold on to that, then he was in more jeopardy than a captain lost at sea. By an act of his will he changed his prayers. "Father, I need your mercy and your grace! And wherever Joseph is now, I beg you to extend these to him too, and to little helpless Daniel."

Tort and Cyrus descended the stairs. He was not ready to face them. They seemed to understand and let themselves out by way of the back door. Angelene came down for water to wash Dumond's body. Cummington offered his help, but she told him valiantly that she and her mother would share the task.

When he was alone, Cummington went into his study and closed the door. He sat in his desk chair, feeling as though someone had come to hollow out his insides. His eyes, however, remained dry. Whatever should be done as their response to this, he sensed it was not the time to give himself over to tears.

CHAPTER 29

WHEN CHARLES POWELL was gone a third night, Thomas let himself out by the back alley door. Carrying an ember in a tin and a candle fixed in a holder, he went across to the barn and closed the door behind him before giving himself light.

The two big Conestogas seemed to welcome him as much as they did their rightful owner, now that he had been caring for them all these days alone. In a way it made him feel good. But it also was a scary reminder that something terrible might have happened to one who prided himself in them. Thomas took his time cleaning the stalls and giving the mares their supper, for there was not much he could do to pass the hours inside the store.

While the big warm animals ate fresh hay from their mangers, he curried them and spoke to them, just as he knew Mr. Powell would do. What finally drove him to think of getting back into the store was the truth that he was safer behind its locked doors. Anytime, anywhere, somebody could come investigate why he was in this barn. He had nothing to prove that he was Mr. Powell's real employee, and by law he was and always would be nothing more than chattel.

Blowing the light out and cooling the wick with spit on his fingers, he went back outside and secured the stable door. Though it was fully night, he could see by the light of Huck Baring's first-floor window. Two colored oyster sellers had their fancy dray pulled up close to Baring's door. Thomas guessed they were there because they had a harness that needed mending, but when he came across to their side he saw, for sure, that Mrs. Ruskin was climbing on board the wagon, right between those Negroes.

He did not recognize her by her face, for she had that covered up with a big scarf tied around her bonnet. But Thomas knew her still, because she was the only thin lady to stay in Huck Baring's house. His heart sank, for whether Mr. Powell would ever let himself know it or not, Thomas knew that this woman held his affections. Now that Thomas was seeing her behavior with his own eyes, everything seemed to change in a minute. He was looking upon proof that Mrs. Ruskin was the loose woman folks said she was.

This would grieve Mr. Powell so! Thomas actually found himself mourning for a white man, something he thought he'd never do. Then he noticed that Huck Baring was standing in his doorway watching this whole scene. "Unc'!" he cried, unable to hide his dismay as the wagon pulled away. "What's gwine on? That sure enough wa' the widow Ruskin leavin' with those drivers!"

"I hope to goodness you the only one 'sides me to know that, son!" Baring anxiously ran his hand through the white cloud of hair growing above his ears.

"What are they all doin'?"

"You step inside an' I'll say."

They went through Baring's door into his shop that smelled of oil and leather. The balding man drew him to stand back from the window. "Those fellows know Mrs. Ruskin. Her late husband helped set up they business, just the same as he done mine."

"Well, that sure ain't no cause—"

Baring cut him off with a disappointed look. "Cocheron an' Jamison are those men's names. They wa' deliverin' shellfish to the Ruskin family kitchen t'night, an' they got to talkin' with the cook, who is the only colored help that family has. An' Cook told them that Mrs. Ruskin's daughter was home from her travels, an' that Mr. Tyrone Ruskin an' his missus wa' both gwine out to a Christmastime party, while Mr. Anthony Ruskin is off on some kind of business.

"Cook says they wa' plannin' to leave the child behind an' that the girl has done nothin' but cry for her mama all the time since she wa' home. So them brothers came here, thinkin' they would dare take Sister Ruskin for a secret visit. They knowed she wa' here 'cause I got word to her colored friend, Harriet Mason, so that that woman wouldn't worry none."

"Haven't they thought what will happen if they caught?"

"Sure, but Mrs. Ruskin decided she's gwine try to bring her daughter here. It might be her very last chance to have the child with her."

"This could be puttin' you an' you' family at death's door!"

" 'Course, I know that."

"It's not safe, no-how!"

"I agree. Not for the lady neither, but if she's gwine get her Judith, now's the time to do so. Then Mr. Powell can help them both to move away onc't he's home." The man studied him hard. "What's got every tooth in you' jaw looking down?"

"What's Powell plannin'? He never told me nothin'!"

"To help Mrs. Ruskin. To take her away. Now you tell me what's wrong with you."

"I got a job with him. What am I gwine do?"

Baring smiled. "I knowed that was it! I'm just glad to see you start speakin' the truth, son."

"Well, I'm not glad! Somehow I wa' thinkin' that Mista Powell done cared 'bout me more than just for my bone an' muscle."

"I'm standin' proof that he does. Mr. Powell's already asked if you could have a place with me. Only difference is that I cain't teach you to read like he can. For that, Mr. Powell told me he would set aside 'nough money from the sale of the store for two whole years of Quaker colored school for you to go to by night."

"Then he's gwine leave! Sell his place?"

"I think he will. But don't you start thinkin' that he wa' plannin' to go without makin' sound agreements with you or sayin' a proper good-bye. No, sah! He wouldn't do that."

"Where's he at now? Did he tell you that? He won't tell me."

"No, he didn't say. But I tell you one thing, I think you should be worried about him—I know I am. It's not like Mr. Powell to be gone from his horses an' his business so long."

Thomas knew he was feeling that way already.

Baring toed the leather shavings on the floor. "I got an ugly kind of feeling that Mr. Powell's in trouble."

Thomas kept on looking down. He didn't want Baring to know how much he cared, and it wasn't just because Powell had showed him kindness. Deep inside, where he could not deny it, he liked the man, something he hardly wanted to admit even to himself. He walked closer to the window, thinking he had heard some noise outside. From his angle it was hard to see over to the store right next door. Still he could see some movement out there. "Maybe he's home now. Look! Somebody's there!"

The store was so dark that Joseph was uncertain about knocking. He had expected Charles to be watching for them, since the storekeeper had set out almost a whole day earlier than they had to cover the fifty miles by horse. Joseph looked to where Brother Bart was standing beside him with three tired children, two of them his own, and then Daniel, also dressed as a girl.

"Are you sure this is his place?" Simeon asked.

"It is," Joseph replied, for Simeon could not read the signs as he could. Daniel tottered across to him and leaned on him. Their spirits were low and still on edge, for from Cyrus and Tort they all had learned of Dumond Holmes' terrible fate. Now Charles Powell appeared to be missing. It sent a shiver down Joseph's spine.

"Maybe we should go directly on to look for somebody from the Vigilance Committee," Simeon suggested.

Joseph agreed, though it would mean that he would have to leave Philadelphia without knowing whether or not Charles was safe. And he would leave without his letter written to Angelene, for the pen and paper he needed to do that were inside this establishment. "Let's put the sacks of grain inside his barn," Joseph said. "Then when he *does* come, he'll know that we've already passed through."

Though it meant a loss to the members of Mt. Hope to leave corn without being paid for it, Simeon nodded. They were just about to move across the alley when a young colored man without a cap came out from the next shop.

"Hallo!" he called. At the same time, an older Negro walked out behind him. He had a ring of white hair that stood out in the dark.

"Hello," Joseph said back, with caution. Then he consciously adopted the slave language of his youth so they would not question him. "We lookin' to trade, though it's afta hours."

The old man did the speaking. "The man what owns this store ain't here. You all will have to come again."

"It's too long a way, sah," Joseph risked. "We hail from Pleasant Points an' a town called Oak Glen."

This animated the younger listener. "Oak Glen! That's where Joseph Whitsun lives."

Joseph spoke in his natural tone. "I am Joseph Whitsun!"

The older man grabbed him. "Has Powell been with you?"

Joseph felt he could trust these two. "Yes. We took the evening train to come here, but he left the township by horse this morning, well before the dawn."

"Lord have mercy!" the old man fretted. "This whole day I thought somethin' wa' amiss!" He nodded to the young man. "Tom, you got the key. Let these brothers in."

The younger man did put the key in the lock. "I'm Mr. Powell's neighbor, Huck Baring," the white-haired man declared. "An' this here's Thomas, Mr. Powell's apprentice."

The door opened and they went in, blessed in a moment by the warmth of coal glowing in the brazier. The children went over at once to extend their hands to the black grate and orange glow, the room's only light.

"We'll get you all something to eat an' make you all comfortable," Huck Baring pledged. "So Mr. Powell knew you all wa' comin' here?"

"That's right," Joseph said. "We brought along corn to trade so that no one would question our travels. But the truth is, sir, I need to be onto the Underground Railroad at once. There's a posse looking for me in Lancaster County, and Mr. Powell nearly got trapped by it too."

He saw young Thomas's eyes flash with concern.

While Simeon went back outside to bring in their heavy corn sacks, Thomas came straight up to Joseph. "You think Mista Powell's in danger now? They might have tooken him?"

"Son, all I know is that we expected him to be here."

"So you all need to be led to the Underground?" Huck Baring clarified.

"No, just help me and this child, please. Simeon Bart and his two daughters are free. But he came along to help make my way safer, for the posse's looking for one African with a fair-skinned *boy*."

Baring favored Daniel with his chuckle. "Well, you sure don't look like no young man to me, child! It wa' very clever an' very wise of you all how you did come."

"If only Charles was here, safe." Joseph noticed how they all looked at him, surely because he had used a white man's Christian name.

Thomas studied him anxiously. "The lawyer Ruskin an' a marshal wa' here three nights back talkin' 'bout you an' the widow Ruskin. An' Mista Powell went out right afta that."

Joseph chose to keep secret most of what had happened. "Mr. Powell's coming to Oak Glen did save my life and Daniel's."

"Now may God have the same mercy on him!" Baring said before inviting them all to sit on the floor by the fire. Soon the two men from the city carried down bread and cheese and even hot, chocolate-flavored milk. Being so weary from the cold and having sat in the rear bench of a train car for hours, away from the heat of its stove, Joseph now had trouble staying awake even to drink and eat, though the food was delicious.

Daniel, for sure, had never tasted chocolate. He cleaned every drop of it from his cup and Joseph's too, using his fingers. "You all rest a little while longer. We'll keep the lights low," Baring said. "Then I'll take you out to a safe house. I know plenty."

They removed their cloaks and put their feet to the fire. Joseph hardly had words for these luxuriant moments, yet his mind was continuously on Charles' absence and on Anthony Ruskin's location now. Beside him, Daniel pulled off his girlish blue bonnet. Because of the seclusion of this place, Joseph allowed it.

The child's face glowed red because of the heat, but clearly he was unhappy. "What will they do to Mr. Charles if they catch him?" His eyes were wide and sad.

"I'm not sure, Daniel. They could charge him money or put him into jail, I think. If they could do more, I do not know."

The child looked around. "Where is Sister May? Brother Charles said she was here."

Huck Baring stooped like a friendly grandfather. "Don't you worry, she's safe."

All this time Thomas had been watching by the back door. Suddenly he turned and smiled. "No bad's gwine come to our Mista Powell—'cause he's here in the alley, big as life and safe."

Then Joseph himself saw Charles' face as the door was opened.

Huck hurried to him. "We all sure done been worried 'bout you, sah!" Huck did not hesitate to express his care, but now Thomas seemed quiet. "You' company's all here, safe an' sound."

Joseph left Daniel. Having stood, he went and shook Charles' freezing cold hand. "The horse I had lost a shoe," his harried friend explained. "While I was searching for a smithy, some of the posse from Philadelphia came through. It was hours until I felt it safe to be out on the roads again, and I never took the pike. It was quite an ordeal."

"Welcome to your home!" Joseph felt himself able to breath and smile.

"I've already returned the horse to the livery, and I am glad I'm here!" Charles sighed. "I hope you had a better trip than I."

"I think we did," Joseph told him. Now with Charles here, he could think on the blessings of having come this far without discovery. "Mr. Baring and Thomas have been most kind."

"Tom an' me fed 'em, an' now I'm willin' to lead Brother Joseph an' the boy on from here," Huck said.

Charles looked right at Joseph. "Brother Whitsun, did you go up to my counter and take advantage of pen and paper?"

Joseph had been thinking on doing it every moment since he'd come in. "No, I didn't. I didn't want to leave a letter behind that might put you into even more danger."

"Well, now I'm here to conceal it. And once I know you are safely out of this state, I will put it in the mail for you." Charles smiled. "I'm determined to hold to my promise, Joseph. I'll not speak about marriage to any woman until you do so."

Joseph watched the reaction of others.

Huck dared to celebrate. "Well, now, you two both contemplatin' matrimony? Good for you! Look at me! I'm a walkin' testimony that a good wife can keep you lookin' young, fit, an' handsome."

He winked at Charles, and Joseph felt warmed by sudden joy.

"Mrs. Ruskin sure gwine be glad to see you, I know."

"I must make plans to leave right away." Charles turned to find Thomas. "It's not safe for me here, nor for Mrs. Ruskin. Thomas, I hope you understand. I expected that I would leave, but not so soon. Anthony Ruskin found me in Oak Glen. I know that soon he will come here. Mr. Baring and I have spoken—"

At that Huck held up his hand. "Sah, Thomas an' me already done talked 'bout all that when you wa' so long in comin' home."

"Did you? So will you agree to it, Thomas?"

Though looking bleak, the young man nodded. "Yessah."

There was no doubting the need for haste. "I need to make plans for leaving, and Mrs. Ruskin must be ready too," Charles said with much distress. "But first to your letter, Joseph. I'll keep it with me and mail it to Angelene after we are out of this city."

While Daniel sat with the little girls and Simeon, Joseph followed Charles up the inner set of stairs. His friend brought out pen and paper, then lighted a candle.

Huck came up to join them. "Sah, you need to know that Mrs. Ruskin's away at this very moment, tryin' to bring her daughter here."

"What? She's not safe in your home?"

The older man grimaced. "Two oyster sellers what knowed her husband saw her child in the house kitchen t'night, an' they went back to try to get her with Mrs. Ruskin aboard they wagon."

"What a foolhardy plan!"

The harnasssmaker nodded but defended it too. "The Ruskins are out at a party, sah. Sister thought it was the best time to bring her child here. Maybe you should come and spend the time with us till she do come home."

"No, I think I must get my wagon readied. The moment she comes, I think we must leave."

"You want me to put Marcy an' Maude in harness, then, sah?" Thomas said, for he had been standing by too, his own sadness showing.

"Yes, indeed!" Charles tensely agreed.

Through all this, Joseph still gripped the pen and grappled with what he should say. Then Charles put his trembling hand upon Joseph's, which held the paper. "Please don't neglect to tell her about our idea for Covenant Day."

Yet Joseph did neglect it, because he did not want to add pressure to Angelene's decision. In truth, he did not feel confident of his own fate when even his white friends were in so much danger. As he finished the last line, not signing his name, Joseph's heart beat hard, almost as if he had proposed marriage. But he had told Angelene only that he did love her now, and that he had loved her for some time. His only promise, though, was that he would print a notice in the *Voice of the Fugitive* if he could. Yet such foreboding filled this room that flight to Canada seemed impossible.

Thomas left for the stable. Joseph blotted his letter dry, amazed that his hands were steady. In a moment, the young man was back.

"Mista Barin'! Mista Powell! The oyster men just done drove off, leavin' Missus Ruskin at the harness shop with her child!"

Charles felt elation and apprehension. He ran toward the alley door with Huck beside him.

"Sah! You get ready what you need! I'll go an' make sure the lady an' Judith are safe inside my place, then I'll be back an' lead Brother Joseph an' his child on to a safe house too."

"Yes! All right!" Charles felt light-headed as he stopped short of the door. "I'll get food and blankets. You tell Mrs. Ruskin that she and Judith need to be ready to travel by wagon, by night, and in the cold."

Huck went out and Thomas with him. Charles felt Joseph's eyes upon him. "So it's an exodus for us both, I guess," Charles said, walking back toward the counter while trying to sound steady, even as he was able to see the worry in Joseph's eyes that matched his own.

"Is there anything I can do to help you?" Joseph asked.

Charles went to take the letter. He folded it and put it in his waistcoat pocket. "I need to go up to my rooms," he said. "You need to be ready to go on with Mr. Baring." He blew out the candle, then extended his hand, realizing that he would never see Joseph again. "I will not forget you, ever. I myself will be reading the *Voice of the Fugitive* looking for good news from you."

Their hands clasped just when Thomas came back inside once more. He slammed the door. "The alley's full of white men!"

————

To Mayleda's distress, Judith had been crying since the moment they had entered the Barings' house. Though the child clung to her, joyous about their reunion, she was also weeping for having been taken away so quickly and so strangely, to be hidden among oyster barrels, and now to be here in this dark shop.

"Hush!" Mayleda scolded her, not losing patience but gaining fear. "There are men outside." Cautiously Huck Baring was surveying the scene they could not see as he stood near the window. Mayleda still had on the hat and cloak Charles had given her from his store, and Judith still wore her warm coat. The child did listen too.

"It's Uncle Anthony! I hear his voice. He's come to find us!"

"Oh, God help us!" Mayleda stifled her cry.

"You'd best get upstairs, ma'am!" Huck said. "Have my family hide you."

Mayleda hardly reached the top of the stairs, pulling Judith with her, before she heard the shop door open. A breath more, and Anthony was at the top of the stairs too, part of a great commotion as some of the white servants from his house and also some of his influential friends were with him, filling the steps and the shop below. "How did you find us?" Mayleda sobbed, standing where she was in full resignation and keeping Judith close to her.

"Did you think my father would go off and leave the house unguarded?" Anthony answered in a rage. "He and my mother are waiting for me to bring Judith home. Those who watched our house followed you on that nigger wagon." He pointed to the servant closest to him on the stairway. "He went and called for Father just when I was coming home from my long ride to Oak Glen."

Joseph! Only inwardly did she cry his name, for she would not reveal any feeling concerning him. Her daughter let go of her hand and took her uncle's, though the child did not like the stern, selfish man. "Uncle Anthony? Are Grandmama and Granddaddy here?"

"No, darling!" he said with a tenderness that was wholly foreign to him. "I know you must be terribly frightened, but don't worry. All will be well now." His eyes flashed to Mayleda.

Mayleda begged, "Allow us to go away, Anthony, please. I want my daughter to know her father's goodness, and that can't happen as things are now."

"Indeed!" he roared. "Not in a Negro's house!"

"Let's go home, Mama. I want to be at our house—with you." Judith separated herself from Anthony, as though working on her own plan now to bring them together with the innocence of childhood on her side.

"Before long you will be home, dear," Anthony said, taking Judith's hand. "My coach has probably been brought around by now." When he turned, Mayleda's eleven-year-old child became wary and uncooperative, as though Anthony's odd brand of kindness was suddenly frightening to her. He kept Judith's hand, while speaking to Mayleda. "Will you come of your own will, or must some of these men drag you away from yet another Negro house?"

"This family meant no harm to me, and I demand that no harm come to them. Please, Anthony!"

He faced her fiercely. "You will never jeopardize this child's safety again. If you come now, these Negroes may stay as they are, as far as I'm concerned."

"Mama!" Judith cried, sensing his malevolence. Mayleda had no recourse but to follow him down the stairs and through the dark, silent shop that still was filled with men going out ahead of her. The moment she was in the alley, she looked to her right and saw Charles by his own door, restrained by several burly lawmen.

He saw her too. "I'll come for you!" he pledged boldly before Anthony pushed her through the open door to the family's coach. She had difficulty getting into the seat, for someone she could not see lay on the coach's floor. Anthony followed her in, with Judith still in his grasp.

Mayleda could not believe her eyes when they adjusted to the light of streetlamps that shone in once the coach was driven out of the dark alley. Joseph was in the narrow space between the coach seats, right at her feet. His wrists were bound. He appeared unconscious, or worse, while the little boy they had tried to save was huddled on the same bench seat where she sat now.

Despite Anthony's presence, Mayleda tried to speak to the child, but he turned his face to the coach's wall in perfect fear. "What have you done?" she raged at Anthony while the vehicle rolled.

Anthony would not answer her. "This is the one, isn't it? This is the one who took you first. The one whose filthy violence seered your sense of rightness and your sense of shame! How old were you when this nigger first preyed on you?"

"Anthony, you are sick with hate! This man has done nothing. He served my father to his dying day with kindness and compassion."

"How did he find you in the North? Or did you come to him? I only hope your meetings happened after my brother died."

"Joseph Whitsun is a good and godly man!" She shed angry, indignant tears, not knowing if her friend was alive or dead as he lay there.

"Those two descriptions don't fit a nigger."

"What have you done to him? Is he living? Is he dead?"

He swore at her. "I don't want to know if Sprague knew or not that you loved a nigger."

Mayleda let herself grope in the dark, hoping to feel if Joseph still was breathing. "Get your hands away from him. Woman, I can't believe you will touch him even as I am with you!"

"I am a nurse! You have injured him! Have you no compassion?"

"You tell me, is the little mongrel here yours and my brother's, or yours and this *brute*'s? I surely do hope you do say the latter."

"Anthony, you shut your mouth in front of these children!"

"Why? I am not the one corrupting Judith's innocence! It is the slut who is her mother who will ruin her if we do not protect her, starting this night."

Mayleda heard Joseph groan.

"Stay by me, dear Judith," Anthony said. "That nigger might just wake up, and I don't want him harming you, child."

"Mama, what's happening? Who is that Negro on the floor?"

Anthony would not let Mayleda answer. "Soon none of this will ever have to trouble you anymore," he pledged while the coach rolled to a stop. "I am so sorry, dear Judith, for what you had to see tonight, but you must understand how it is with your mother. She is very ill. So ill that she will not be able to come home with us."

"Uncle Anthony!"

"I know it is terrible news. Your little heart will break, just as when your father died. But soon it will heal, and you will not remember your mother's shame anymore."

Mayleda screamed. "Anthony! You cannot take my child!"

Judith tried to reach her, but Anthony held her back. "This one I know does belong to my brother," he said of Judith, "so I will fight for her well-being. But after tonight, our family will have nothing more to do with you, Mayleda Callcott Ruskin! Nothing more! Now be quiet, or I'll take you to the asylum directly." He nodded toward Joseph, who was moving his legs to straighten his knees as much as possible in the space he had. "We now know the reason for your sad moral impairment."

Mayleda's blood ran cold.

"Where are we, Uncle?"

"Trust me, child, I have only one matter to attend to. Then we will go home."

When the coach door opened and Anthony moved out, Judith reached toward her, but fearing Joseph so much, she would not come across to her. "Mother!"

"Get out, Mayleda!" Anthony stood in the street and ordered her. "Get out and bring the half-breed boy with you."

CHAPTER 30

JOSEPH KNEW HE HAD BEEN STRUCK unconscious soon after Charles had let him and Daniel out to Spruce Street and after Anthony Ruskin and others had rushed into the store from the alley. Now he understood quite well that he was on the floor of Anthony Ruskin's carriage, crushed between seats, his hands bound.

He saw Ruskin and Mayleda outside, as the coach door stayed open. Light and cold air flowed in, sharpening his senses. He looked for Daniel but could not find the child. He was numbed, not only from the pain in his head, but from fear. Then he saw a blinding torch pressed close to the doorway.

"Get out, boy!"

Though movement nearly made him vomit, he turned his throbbing head.

"Get up! Get out!"

It was Anthony Ruskin's voice. He tried to move but not fast enough for the vile, angry men he saw glowering. They pulled his feet, extracting him like a cork from the neck of a bottle. When his hips hit the coach's step, he was painfully able to stand on his own. He did see Daniel then in the torch's light. And Mayleda. And they were flanked by the slave catchers, Pudget and Dawes. Joseph wobbled to find his balance.

"There, you have them all now," Anthony said to the agents. Joseph moved his eyes. Knowing the city fairly well, he guessed they were standing in Dresden Alley, perhaps directly where this part of Daniel's nightmare had begun. The boy broke from the slave agents and ran to cling to Joseph's legs. All the other men except Anthony, Pudget, and Dawes seemed to melt into the darkness.

"Take them and make what profit you can for yourselves. I want none of it," Anthony said.

Joseph heard the words, but he could not believe them, for then Anthony put himself back inside the coach, leaving Mayleda with them in the street. There was the sound of flicking reins. The coach began to roll. Then Mayleda screamed. "Judith! My Judith! He's taking my child!"

"Come on! We don't have all night!" Dawes said, his whiskers bright in the light of the torch Pudget now carried. Dawes pointed the way to a canvas-covered wagon already hitched to a horse. "Get in, and not a word, or Venor's slave child will be the one to suffer first." To prove this, Pudget reached out and pulled Daniel from Joseph while he had the burning stick in his other hand. He spoke again. "We gave up our plan to profit from this boy once. Now, if we have to, we'll sacrifice him again to make our profits from you two." He held the torch close to Daniel's innocent face.

"God judge you!" Mayleda dared as Pudget pulled the child even farther from them.

"God help you, woman!" Pudget said back. "Do you understand what's happening here? You're bound for the auction block with your daddy's nigger as escort."

Joseph could not keep silent. "Mrs. Ruskin is not a Negro!"

Dawes came and looked at him with evil eyes. "She consorts with Negroes! That is enough. Now she will be what she wants to be." Dawes spoke to Mayleda. "Into the wagon!"

When she struggled because of her dark cloak and skirt, they helped her with the rudeness of men loading livestock, and then laughed at how they had gotten their hands on her legs for one moment. They turned back to Joseph. "If *you* touch her on this journey, we will beat the boy, then make a sorry mess of you."

Joseph knew better than to reveal any concern for Mayleda now. Secretly he admired her courage, for she was not crying despite the atrocities brought upon her.

"Get in, Black Joe!"

Because his hands were tied, they picked him up and shoved him in. The putrid straw was spread too thinly. His chin, nose, and already painfully bruised forehead hit the floorboards hard.

"Oh, Joseph!" Mayleda dared to help him turn his body over to get his face to fresher air.

The agents watched them, delighting to outdo each another in rude remarks. "There's a picture of lovers painted in hell!"

"Now you stay in there, and you behave yourselves!" Dawes warned them. "That is, unless you want to see the half-breed whipped and paddled for your own lewd crimes."

"Don't you hurt him!" Mayleda cried, on her hands and knees.

"Then don't you cause us any trouble, you high yellow Negro!"

———

Like a drunk man, Charles could scarcely concentrate on what was happening. Ruskin's men and law officers from the city had detained him right on Easton Alley until they were convinced that it would be futile for him to leave and try to follow the dark coach that had taken Mayleda and Judith away.

The moment after Charles had been freed, Huck Baring had come out to take him into his house, which is where he sat now on the second floor. Water in the wash bowl near his chair sounded like little tiny metal bells as Mrs. Baring squeezed out the cloth she had been using to wash the wounds on her husband's face. The harnessmaker had fared worse than Charles, for men had struck him down right in his shop when he had tried to stop their search.

His neighbor insisted now as he sat there that he had been unconscious for only a few moments. The rest of the time, Huck said, he had just lain in the shadows, praying, listening, and wondering what he would be capable of doing if white men harmed his family.

Charles could only hang his head while Mrs. Baring again put the cloth to Huck's face. Their daughters, youngest to oldest, stood around their father, eyeing him warily. Charles knew he should go out to contact other abolitionists in the city for help, but he feared the mob's last threats to him. They had told him if he tried to leave either by Spruce Street or the alley, he would be charged for aiding fugitives and that Huck would be jailed for having had Mrs. Ruskin in his house.

Their inactivity felt like death. Charles worried about Joseph and Daniel and Thomas too, for though he felt that they all had been out in the street in time to avoid Anthony Ruskin, Thomas had not come back. Charles considered his pledge given in Tort Woodman's barn that he would help Joseph, no matter what the cost. Now he felt like Christ's cowardly disciple, Peter, having heard the rooster crow. Yet even Baring, speaking through his lips that had been split by violence, told him not to go, not to move, for their arrests would not help anybody—Joseph, Thomas, and the boy included.

Simeon Bart and his daughters had been able to hide themselves among crates in the storeroom during the raid, and now they all were safely away, Charles hoped and prayed. He kept thinking about Mayleda. Surely she was back in the house she abhorred.

It was morning. They heard activity down in Baring's shop. Huck pushed aside the cloth from his face. He touched his wife, then stood. "I'll go down to see who it is. For sure my customers are ignorant of the trouble we've seen."

"It might be law men or marshals." His wife clung to him. While she held him back, Thomas suddenly presented himself at the top of the stairs, holding onto a bridle.

Charles took a life-giving breath. "God be praised! I thought the mob had you, son!" He stood to greet the young man and ended up embracing him fully.

The youth threw his hat off and dropped the bridle as though it were of no use to him now. "I got this from a colored wagoner, an' my cap too. I hoped it would help me look like I was just comin' in as you' first customer of the day."

"You a smart fellow." Huck nodded his bruised head.

"Are the streets still being guarded, then?" Charles asked with impatience.

Thomas's brows came down. "Yessah. There's white men in clumps on the corners, an' no colored folk at all."

"What's happened to Joseph? To Daniel?" Charles could not wait one second more. He thought then that Thomas might be ill by the way the young man closed his eyes and swallowed hard.

"I followed them, sah, as far as I could. You know they were put into Mista Ruskin's coach."

"I didn't know! I saw Mayleda and Judith taken!"

"Yessah. I saw that too. But 'fore Mista Ruskin had his coach in the alley, he had it out on the front street. An' some of his men struck Joseph down."

"Where did the coach go? Did you see that?"

"Yessah. I done followed them all the way."

"All the way to where?"

Thomas seemed to turn painfully timid. "It's gwine break you' heart, sah. That coach stopped right in Dresden Alley, an' then they put Missus Ruskin an' Brother Whitsun an' the boy all into a wagon. Then they took the wagon to the train. I ran afta them that time too. Then they put them all on the train."

"You mean Anthony Ruskin did this? Where would they go?"

"No, sah. Not Ruskin, sah. Slave catchers, sah."

"Slave catchers have Joseph and Daniel!"

"Yessah! An' they got Missus Ruskin too!"

"But she's no Negro!" He felt the shame of his complaint, yet he was now beside himself with grief.

Huck said, "Lord have mercy, to think they might sell her for bein' dark 'nough of hair an' eyes."

"We must save them all!" Charles cried.

"If you go out there right now, sah, it will mean all our lives," Huck warned. "You know they won't let you chase afta her now."

"We can't just do nothing!"

"Sah, I made certain you weren't the only ones to know," Thomas said. " 'Fore I came here, I ran straightway to the colored infirmary an' I told Dr. Ellis an' Practitioner Catos too."

Charles's head was whirling. "Oh, that was so wise, Thomas! Oh, that was so wise!"

Huck moaned. "What evil men will do for money."

The truth struck Charles like an arrow through his heart. If they could not find them, if they did not rescue them, then Daniel, Joseph, *and* Mayleda might be sold into slavery.

Charles found Thomas's eyes fixed on him. "Do you know what it means, sah, to sell a 'fancy woman?' "

Charles looked away, fearing that he did know.

"She won't be sold for no fieldwork, Mista Powell," Thomas went on as though Charles must face the full truth now, just as Thomas must have faced it when he had his family taken from him. "She'll be somebody's mistress, sah."

"You don't know that for sure, son," the harnessmaker cautioned.

Charles started reeling. Thomas took hold of him as Charles' knees buckled and he fell toward the floor. With Huck's help, they got him up, then sat him down on the chair near to where he had been standing.

But Charles was up again in one moment. "I pledged to Joseph I would get him to freedom! I pledged that no harm would come to Daniel! And now Mayleda!" He could say no more without risking tears. "Oh, Thomas! Oh, Huck! There must be some way to save them!"

"Lord, Lord, Lord. Mista Powell! Out of you' own mouth are comin' words what have been said by countless brothers. But all of them colored!"

———

Late that night Thomas dared to go with Mr. Powell back to the store. Working by lamplight upstairs, they packed the things Mr. Powell would need to go South to look for the three who were about to be betrayed for handfuls of silver and gold, just like Mr. Powell's Savior.

Thomas felt sure the searching would be useless, but he didn't have the heart to say that, for Mr. Powell was nearly like a madman already because of his grieving. He remembered his own first days, knowing that he would see his family no more.

While they worked in the storekeeper's bedroom, there was a knock at the Spruce Street door. Cautiously Thomas went down, for Mr. Powell was too weak with heartache to move or think quickly. Thomas called out, "Who's there?" much as he had done in his days as a servant. Dr. Ellis identified himself while the door was still closed and locked. Thomas let him in, knowing the name well.

He helped the old Friend climb the stairs, then set out the Windsor chair, not caring if he was doing the duties of a slave for these white men. Now they were his friends.

Charles came out just as the wall clock struck two times, telling them that it was really early morning. The soft-speaking old man began to give his counsel while Charles just stood in front of him, white as the walls. Thomas put himself slightly behind the huge man, in case he started fainting again.

"We know that Pudget and Dawes often go to small auction houses just across the border," the old man said. "Places like Hagerstown or Frederick Town in Maryland. But since they have the boy, they may go back to Virginia, since we know from the men of Oak Glen that the child is claimed by a slavemaster named Venor."

"Can't you tell where they might be because of the train they were put on?" Mr. Powell asked, sounding pained.

"The train Thomas saw was heading toward Baltimore, we think. So far, I have twenty white, literate volunteers ready to go South to start searching through the newspapers to look for advertisements on slaves to be sold. They will gather the auction houses' handbills and read them also. They will spread out through Maryland and Virginia and use the telegraph to send us word."

"Only twenty! The search sounds impossible!" Mr. Powell mourned.

Thomas bit his lip, suffering the pain rather than giving any more of it to the storekeeper. He could have said it was impossible.

"This is bound to fail! We have to do better!" Mr. Powell cried, his fists at his hip and then at his face.

"I don't think there is a better way. Every hour there will be congregations, small gatherings, and individuals committed to prayer. Brother Powell, *God* knows where they are."

The other white man's words did not seem to comfort Powell at all.

"Sister Ellis and I are ready to go down to Baltimore too. We'll rent a room there in the Harrison House and stay through the holidays. Even longer if we must. I will visit some physicians and think of medical topics that might be worthy of their time, but really I will be going to be of assistance to others and to thee."

Mr. Powell looked at him.

"Thee did mortgage the property already? True?"

"I did!"

"Then when thee comes to Baltimore City, thee should establish a bank account and rent a respectable, gentlemen's room in a good boardinghouse. Not the Harrison, but close by. Thee must act and think as though thee were planning to have some business as a merchant setting up his trade there."

Thomas cautiously looked at Dr. Ellis. "He should have a slave to attend him. I will go with him, sah."

"You won't, Thomas! No!" Mr. Powell had tears.

For the first time that day Thomas did counter him. "Sah, is this the nation where you says Negroes should be free to act like men? Well, then, sah, I hope you will not dare tell me what I can an' cannot do, as other white men have."

Mr. Powell stared at him. "I care about your safety! I would say the same to you if you were my son!"

An incredible feeling welled up inside Thomas. "I can drive a coach, sah. I can wait on you, head to toe, dawn to dark, January to December. I've done it all before."

"I don't want you to!"

"I know, sah. That's why I'm so willin'. They might not think you' like the South if you don't have no waitin' boy like everybody else down there. Besides, I know the city, sah. That's where my marse lives."

Charles turned to Dr. Ellis. "You hear him! He wants to go to the place where his master might be able to apprehend him."

"Harrison House is a long way from where my marse is. See! I do know the city! You told me to believe in God. Well, mebbe this is one of those reasons He let me suffer, so that now I can lead you all, the best way I can, to help these others."

"Thee mustn't argue, and thee mustn't delay," the old Friend said to Powell. "Thee must come down before Christmas. Sister Ellis and I will travel as Friends, but thee must come as a gentleman full of himself and full of the world." He pulled money from a purse. "This is from our society. Thee must buy clothes befitting a gentleman. God will have mercy. And rent a lavish coach once thee is in the city."

"But what then?"

"Thee comes to visit us at Harrison House without delay. We will speak more then. With God's help the handbills and advertisements will be the Spirit's tools. When we find descriptions of those going up for sale that match our friends' descriptions, then thee will go and try to buy them back. Bring the money thee has from Friend Peabody's property, and I will give what funds we have when we meet next in the South."

Thomas saw Mr. Powell's wooden stare.

"I don't know anything about buying slaves!"

Thomas spoke, though he had not planned to do so. "I do, sah! I've seen it in my time, more than I want to remember or say."

"There is too much risk in this. Dr. Ellis, you understand! I could not take Thomas, a fugitive, into a slave market."

"Then you' friends will be better off dead," Thomas said, not mincing words, regardless that he had the only colored face there.

Dr. Ellis was nodding glumly.

"This is my fight too!" Thomas added. "I am willin' to suffer if you think you can truly save one child, one woman, an' one man from slavery."

Mr. Powell looked at him. "You know that once we start, I cannot come back to this city again. Not with the Ruskins here and not with news that my store has been mortgaged. I cannot even have Maude and Marcy this way, for I must go by stage or train." The man paused, hiding his face in his hands for a moment. "You must excuse me. I must go and tell Huck Baring this news right away. I must ask him if he will quietly find a buyer for my Conestogas as well as for my store supplies."

"The Viligance Committee and our society can help him so that he doesn't draw attention to himself," Dr. Ellis said.

"Yes," Mr. Powell agreed breathily. "I'll ask him to divide whatever profit between himself and the abolitionist cause."

Then Thomas watched Mr. Powell leave by the inner stairs, the store owner's pain so much like his own.

———————

Before morning had fully come, Charles went in to be with his horses one last time. "So, Marcy. So, Maude. Tell me what future you would like to have. To be put out of this city perhaps? To be in pastures as far as the eye can see? And in perfect peace."

He sighed, knowing that the images in his mind had been dreams for himself. How he had longed to put Mayleda on his wagon and drive off to start a future somewhere, just like that.

His eyes started to sting. "There's trouble. Real trouble, my girls." He went into Maude's stall and put his hand against the sleek warmth of her neck. A moment more, and he was like a little fearful child, crying and kissing his animal. "I will never see you again. I may never see Mrs. Ruskin. Or Joseph. Or Daniel. But I must try. You understand, I must try."

The door opened on his privacy. With much anxiety and shame, Charles wiped his tears. To his relief and to his surprise, it was Dr. Ellis, who had been to his house only hours before. "I am sorry to intrude. I knocked at thy house door. Thomas couldn't find thee. He said thee might be out here."

"Yes. Well, I didn't expect to see you again, sir."

"I have news that must be told."

"Yes?" Charles was petrified, but Dr. Ellis smiled.

"Little Judith Ruskin is with us. Sister Ellis has her now, getting her ready for the trip to Baltimore."

"How can that be!"

"About four o'clock this morning, Harriet Mason brought her to us. The night after seeing her mother deserted in the street with Joseph and Daniel, Judith spoke to the Ruskin's cook in secret, and with many tears, I'm sure. From what Sister Mason and the child have told us, the cook must have rightly guessed that the plan was for Sister Ruskin to be taken away forever. When she told the child that her mother must be among Negroes now, Judith ran away out through the kitchen door."

"But how did the child find Harriet?"

"She didn't. Apparently she wandered the streets all that night and the next day too. Toward dusk last night she saw an oyster wagon and climbed up among the barrels to hide, as she had done before, coming here. It was not until brothers Cocheron or Jamison were home that they found her. Sister Mason hid the child in her outdoor kitchen until the first hours of this morning. Then she dared to bring the child across town to us."

"How dangerous!" Charles exclaimed, his thoughts drawn wholly to the doctor's story at first. Then he thought of the future. "What will happen if we cannot free Mayleda?"

"I am not sure." The doctor paused. "That is one reason I came to thee."

Charles thought of Joseph and Daniel. He had calculated the cost of trying to save them. Now he had to consider the risk of being accused of kidnapping Mayleda's child and the possibility of caring for her as an unmarried man and a stranger if her mother was enslaved. "The girl does not know me," he said with gravity. "Yet I think we must take her in the hope that in God's mercy Mrs. Ruskin will be found."

Dr. Ellis nodded. "That is what Sister Ellis and I believe too. But once we leave Philadelphia with her, there is no possibility of coming back here as her guardians, for the Ruskins will search the infirmary to look for the child, I am sure."

"I understand. If we cannot find her mother, then I will take the responsibility and the risk to rear the child on my own somewhere away from Philadelphia, for I cannot return here either." Even as he said it, Charles had no idea how he would fulfill such a promise if the worst should happen.

"Then you will see her at Harrison House. For the moment, at least, she seems pleased to be with us because she knows that soon we will be traveling to search for her mother." The aging doctor came near to shake Charles' hand, reaching into the stall to do so.

"You caught me crying over the loss of my horses. You must think me an ignorant, selfish, immature man."

Dr. Ellis shook his head. "On the contrary, Brother Powell."

CHAPTER 31

EVERYTHING MAYLEDA KNEW ABOUT SLAVERY from grow-
ing up in the South could not have prepared her for what she was living
through now. After two full nights and almost two days of weeping for
her Judith, she was still huddled in the corner of a moving train car, her
fingers and toes so cold they felt on fire all the time.

Often on this terrifying trip they had been made to change cars. More
than once they had been put into the back of a wagon to be hauled between sections of railroad track. Mayleda never knew where they were.
And since Joseph had warned her to make no conversation with him, she
suffered in silence all the way. Until the last few hours they had seldom
seen Daniel, as the slave catchers had kept the boy with them.

Since leaving Philadelphia, eight other poor souls had been added to
their lot. Though she remained the only woman, dazed, grim-faced male
captives had been made to join them, all of them being together in this
one train car now. And Daniel was with them too. Looking across the

way, she could see the child on Joseph's lap in the drafty, rattling car.

When the train stopped perhaps an hour later, they seemed to be at their destination, for Pudget and Dawes were there to see the door being opened. Several brawny white men held iron prods. The first thing the two slave catchers did after climbing aboard was to surround Joseph where he sat. They commanded him in harsh terms to be still. Then they stole his boots and shackled his feet. Mayleda cried into her hands. Joseph might have heard, but he never dared to look her way.

Daniel did, however, while holding onto Joseph's shoulders until the men pulled the boy to stand apart. After that, they called Joseph to his feet. Stiffly, he stood in his stockings. Guards went before him and behind him as though they had some riotous criminal in their midst. They let Daniel follow like an ignored little shadow while Joseph was forced out of the car to the dirty street that Mayleda could see beyond the door in the broad daylight that burned her eyes.

Not long after they had rudely pulled Joseph from the car, men she did not know came back for the rest of them. When it was Mayleda's turn to be taken toward the opened door, she saw Dawes and Pudget standing down on the street looking up at her while she was still in the car. She got up and walked as two men stayed beside her. The slave catchers watched while two more guards on the street reached up and put their fingers around Mayleda's ankles.

Their actions made her draw back because of the immodest hold they had on her. But instead of freeing herself, she aided them as they pulled at her feet. She tumbled backward, and the men beside her caught her at her elbows. She was lifted into the air and she felt the wind blow her skirts. They brought her down by force to stand in the dirt.

She was breathless, but still she cried out, "I am not a slave. I have brothers in the South. Help me. Please help me." Her words were witnessed by Pudget and Dawes. She gained a ray of hope when they came forward to talk with the men who had handled her with no degree of respect. "Soon a *gentleman* will pay for the privilege of touching her!" Dawes said. "We're not remanding her to any owner. She's to go from the block to the highest bidder."

The guards shook their heads, as though wholly disinterested. Pudget then found Mayleda's arm under the bulk of her cloak. He led her while she walked unwillingly, hardly able to see, hardly able to think after even this much abuse. She tried to make herself think on God, and to think on Charles, for in the slave agents' wagon, Joseph had counseled her to picture herself the wife of this kind man, no matter what happened to her in the flesh.

She shuddered, not able to hope that either her imagination or her faith would be strong enough to save her from the shame she knew must come. Her whole body crawled with terror, inside and out, as she was taken closer to a set of low, unpainted buildings that rambled into one. Words upon the walls read *Pearson's Auction House: Livestock & Slaves. Sales Tuesday & Saturday. Holidays excepted.*

Pudget still had her by the arm, but now Dawes walked in front of them. Right inside the doorway of the awful place that reeked of urine and unwashed bodies, there was a dusty hallway lighted by a few dirty lamps. As she was taken in, Mayleda saw to the right a large pen made of wide board fencing and lined with straw, as though it might be used as the indoor paddock for horses or cattle. But when her sight adjusted to the light, she viewed colored men and heard them as they milled wordlessly by the closed, slatted gate. Those in front peered out with sullen but curious eyes to see who was being brought in next.

Her breath caught within her throat when she glimpsed Daniel and Joseph already locked in. Yet her attention stayed there only for a moment. Someone at a small booth to her left reached over the low counter to turn her toward himself. "Mr. Pearson, her name is Muncy," Dawes lied, looking alert while speaking with the false air of a gentleman. "We acquired her in Baltimore. The man who had her liked her well enough, but his wife did not." He paused, but the man Pearson, with a head of wavy gray hair, only kept writing on the sheet in front of him.

"Her age?"

"Twenty-seven," the slave catcher lied again.

Pearson looked up, weary at first, but then a light came to his eyes that looked dark compared to his silver hair. "Man, I know she's not that young, but if you get a good price for her here, I will be satisfied with my commission and fees for selling her. If the auction goes badly, I will bid on her myself and save her for resale at one of the larger markets closer to the seacoast where men with greater wealth have more room to hide their treasures away." He smiled.

"Thank you, sir. That's a very fine plan," Dawes said without flinching. "In winter I like to make my transactions quickly, for there's always risk of sickness in cold weather."

"You have her papers. I needn't ask that, I hope, after all the times you've been here."

Mayleda quivered while documents were handed over. "He can't have papers for me!" she dared to protest. "I am not a Negro!"

Mr. Pearson raised an eyebrow. "I work for profit here, not for trouble, Mr. Dawes."

"The only trouble, sir, is this wench's mouth and her lewd behavior while she was being brought here. One of the ebonies did have his hands on her because she sought him out."

"I did not!" Mayleda cried.

"Any black buck should be punished for touching such high yellow flesh!" the auction house owner said with true concern.

"Let's say I agree, Mr. Pearson. And let's say I will tell you which buck that should be if she opens her mouth again. Otherwise, there's no use degrading the price you will obtain from any of the males I brought just because of *her* bad behavior. The buck was only yielding to his own dim-witted, earthy instinct."

"That yellow boy you just put on the list is hers, I guess," Pearson said, looking back on his records. "Yes, the paper you have for him is from Baltimore too. The same owner."

"Didn't I say the master's wife was displeased with her?"

Pearson sighed. "It all gets wearisome after a while. So you've registered nine bucks, this woman, and her issue. Is that your full shipment for this day?"

"Yes." Dawes leaned to him. "I think we stand to profit more if you keep the boy in the pen but treat her somewhat better."

Pearson rose. "Man, you don't need to advise me on the stratagems of my own business. Of course I see the advantage of selling her as a 'fancy' without the complication of offspring. Yet I fear she is too light. Gentlemen in this part of Maryland may be unwilling to take her home, yet we will try. If not here, then elsewhere. I am not displeased that you chose to come here, Mr. Dawes. I thank you for the opportunity to sell what you have." The men shook hands.

"I am not a slave!" Mayleda cried once more, thinking on her brothers, Brant and Eric, and how they might come if someone would just telegraph them now.

"Would you like to see which of those bucks did touch her?" Dawes threatened in a breath, looking back toward the pen.

"No!" Mayleda screamed. "Don't hurt any of them!"

"No," Pearson echoed. "I believe you have made her obedient. I'll keep her in one of the separate rooms I have, and you needn't worry a moment more about her. I'll take my commissions from the sales, as by our regular agreement. Except, of course, for that one you want held and remanded to his master in South Carolina."

Mayleda stared at Dawes, but he said nothing to her, for her voice, she knew, had already been silenced.

"For your sake, Dawes, I hope the planter comes as you say he will. Otherwise you'll be charged a fee for every day Black Joe is penned up after the sale of these others."

"Oh, he will come. When we stopped in Baltimore, I sent another telegraph to him, giving your establishment as our destination. In his original telegraph, sent after he read our advertisement in the Charleston papers, he said he would pay any price to have the buck back."

Questions pressed on her throat, but Mayleda kept silent. She could not imagine her brothers coming for Joseph when he was legally free. Who else might come for him, she did not know, and she felt she could not ask, for then Mr. Pearson might explore the connection between them.

The auction-house owner left his booth. "I'll take Muncy myself and make her comfortable so that you need not worry about any guard or Negro trusty I have."

Mayleda was numb when the man told her to walk in front of him. "Girl, this way."

Though Joseph could not see Mayleda after she was taken, there was no doubting that Pudget and Dawes had put her on the roster of slaves to be sold. Trapped as he was, Joseph could only pray for her. He found himself mourning for Charles, for Joseph knew what it was like to love a woman while having no power in this world to protect her from other men.

He held to the fence that blocked him in like an animal, remembering Mayleda's innocence, but also her passion for fighting the demons of slavery from the time she had been only a girl. He thought of her father, Abram Callcott. One of the man's deathbed miseries had been his fear that the sins of his own slave holding and that of his father would be visited upon Mayleda and her two surviving brothers. Already back in the holds of slavery himself, Joseph still begged God that it would not be so. Then he turned his attention once more to Daniel, still in a dress but with no bonnet now to cover his unruly, boyish head of curls. Joseph had never been subjected to a holding pen before in all his years of slavery. Every smell, every sound, made his flesh quiver.

Over the next hours, blankets were pushed in to those who did not have them. Also wooden bowls, which would be filled with grits or mush twice a day. There was a trough by the gate where blackish, scum-covered water could be dipped. He took Daniel to the outer wall, solidly constructed of horizontal boards. Though it was colder there, the straw was fresher and the air seemed cleaner. With two soiled blankets he made a place for them to rest.

Before sitting down, Joseph took a more careful look at their surroundings. With so many victims already gone before him, he was certain there was no easy, overlooked way for escape. His search gave him a glimpse of their more awful future, for when he looked right and stood on his toes, he could see a room beyond the pen. The enclosure they were in came right up against it, and beyond the last fence there was a plastered section of the building with long bright windows and neat rows of chairs. This would be the place where he, Daniel, Mayleda, and all the others would be sold.

He guarded the child from knowing about that distant room. Sitting down on the blankets, they spoke quietly of many things unrelated to their captivity until evening came. Then Joseph noticed how a cluster of white men along the fence were spying on him. He recognized the faces of Pudget and Dawes among them. Mr. Pearson was there too. The auction-house owner soon sent two young Negro trusties inside the pen, possibly two of his own chattel. They came directly to Joseph and called him out by the name under which he had been registered: Joe.

Unnerved and cautious, Joseph stood, still having on the leg irons that collected clumps of straw when he was told to follow them. Daniel came with him. White guards were by the gate. Pearson told his Negroes to bring the "boy" forth, his term for Joseph.

The gate was open enough to let him out. Daniel squeezed through too. With the guards alert, Pearson himself pulled opened Joseph's coat, his waistcoat, and his shirt so that his chest was exposed to them all. Inwardly, Joseph began to steel himself for whatever physical abuse would come. Daniel was holding his hips, yet he dared not look at the child.

The same two Negro trusties came again, this time with a wad of rags tied to a stick and a bucket of white paint. Joseph kept his vision as high as he dared. He glimpsed Pudget and Dawes nodding to Pearson.

"You don't want to sell him away by mistake," Dawes said with confidence. "His master will come and pay more for him than you could get by putting him on the block."

With that, Pearson told his boys to mark him.

From his mouth, down his chin, over his neck and chest to the waist, Joseph was slopped with the cold, thin, white staining liquid. It ran in rivulets and soaked the front of his trousers.

"There, friends," Pearson said to the slave catchers, "this is the best means I've found for marking those to be remanded. Collars and brands can leave scars, but paint is simple and painless." He then told the trusties, "Now you can put Black—and White—Joe back into his place again."

Going back inside at least allowed Joseph to turn his back on their raucous laughter. What he could not shake was the content of their conversation. What master could be coming for him when Abram Callcott was dead and he had been legally freed sixteen years before?

CHAPTER 32

OAK GLEN'S CORN HUSKING had been held Saturday, December twentieth, despite the sorrows of Dumond Holmes' passing and the fact that the Black Guard had no good news from abolitionists who were searching through the South looking for Joseph and Daniel, both having been captured in Philadelphia.

Since there was no school from that day until after New Year's Day, Angelene spent much of her time right before Christmas upstairs, quilting with her mother. It was as unhappy a task as the husking had been. Less than a week ago her mother had been joyfully anticipating having this quilt finished in time for Dumond to carry it west of Pittsburgh and on to Angelene's oldest brother, Earl, in Cincinnati. Instead of delivering a lovely family present for them, Dumond lay buried in her father's orchard.

For that reason alone, no work would have seemed worthy of Angelene's time, but every moment she now had to worry about Joseph's fate, which drained her energies even more. So different from Angelene, her mother could make perfectly neat lines of stitches regardless of her health or mood—ill or well, happy or sad. Angelene, on the other hand, could only sit and brood, the needle never moving as it was pressed between her thumb and finger.

"Perhaps we need to talk some more," her mother suggested, trying to dispel her gloom. Even while she said this, she still sewed, rocking her needle to deftly prick the fabric in several consecutive places before she pulled the thread through.

"Mama, I'm thinking I don't want to wait for Joseph's arrival to be printed in the Bibbs' *Voice of the Fugitive*. I want to leave Oak Glen now and get on to Canada, so I can be there, maybe even before he arrives."

Her mother now stopped moving her hands. "Angelene, you must wait. They are looking for Joseph everywhere in Maryland and in parts of Virginia." Her mother's mouth closed, her lips pressed tight as her eyelids fell.

"You're trying to make me see that it's nearly impossible for him to be rescued, but you don't want to say that."

"Angel, I'm just trying to say that your going North is not going to help him to get there any quicker."

"I don't want to stay here. It just makes me think that I am doing nothing."

"This town needs you. It has lost its doctor. It doesn't need to lose its teacher too."

"I've been thinking on that. Some of Widow Sladder's girls could run the schoolhouse now. They are bored as students. They have all the skills they need to do it."

"You want to live in Canada, even by yourself?"

Angelene hesitated, praying that her mother would understand. "Barnabas wants to go to Canada too. I would not be traveling or staying alone."

"Angel, you cannot be serious. You? Traveling with a white man! What people would say!"

"I don't care what people say, Mama! That has been the whole of all we've suffered. What people say! What people think! Joseph once told me a saying that he learned as a boy: 'Righteousness has no respect for rumor.' Well, my relationship with Ba would be only righteous. He's like the granddaddy I never had."

"I know, girl, but everybody on every train or barge or stage would think you are Mr. Croghan's colored mistress."

"Let them think what they want to think! You see, I could ride in the cars that way. I could be close to Ba always. He would protect me, and I would translate for him so people would know that he is dependent on me."

"No, Angel." She started sewing again.

"Mama, I can't go on living here without Joseph. Please let me go to Canada. If he's trapped in slavery, well, then, let me do something to honor him. I'll help those who do get free. I'll teach them or nurse them. Please let me do something besides just sit here like a child."

Her mother pointed across to her needle as though overwhelmed. "Just sew!"

"I don't mean to hurt you, but I do need to know what God is asking of me. And I think I am supposed to go to Canada with Ba!"

They heard the front door open down in the first-floor hallway. "Who can that be?" her mother said, seeming eager to have a reason to change the subject. Angelene rose at once, since both her father and Barnabas usually used the back door throughout the week when they attended to their work in the orchard and barns. She got as far as the hall and saw her father at the top of the stairs.

"Angelene. We have company. Practitioner Oliver Catos from Dr. Ellis's colored infirmary."

"Does he know something about Joseph? Anything?" Angelene cried, standing alone for a moment, but then throwing herself into her father's arms as he came to her. She searched her father's face.

"He doesn't know a thing more than we know, but he brought you something." Her mother came out from the sewing room while her father said more. "Brother Catos brought you a letter that Joseph wrote to you from Philadelphia. It had been Mr. Powell's intent to send it here once Joseph was safely on his way." He stepped back. "Before Mr. Powell set off for the South, he gave it to Dr. Ellis, who gave it to Brother Catos to bring here." He handed the letter to her.

She glanced at the precious handwriting. It had only been folded, never sealed. She put a hand on her heart as she read each word, the vision of his penmanship a familiar comfort. "He says he loves me! He says he regrets leaving Oak Glen without saying that to me! Oh my!"

She covered her face and her flood of tears. "Now I know I must go to Canada, no matter what. I must honor him in some way to keep this love of ours alive!"

Her parents exchanged woeful glances. "Brother Catos is downstairs," her father said. "He'll stay for supper."

———————

Mayleda and two other women were kept in a bare room at Pearson's Auction House. Now that another evening was coming on, Mayleda shivered while she sat on the low bench along the wall that had a window. Outside the dirty glass she could see the blurred shadows of the normal activities of a small town—men and women on the street walking or in wagons, and lights coming on in stores and houses as twilight grew stronger.

She thought of those in freedom who probably cared not at all that humans were in bondage here, fearfully counting the days until they would be sold. She also reflected on the pen where Joseph and Daniel were held. She prayed, for it had become her only occupation. When at last she opened her eyes, she lifted her vision to her two female companions once more.

By now she knew much of Kate's story but little of Evelyn's. Kate was talkative, while Evelyn, with the complexion of a red rose viewed by night, was always silent, usually keeping her head tucked into the twist that she made by having her arms entwined. Kate stood when she saw Mayleda look at her. "You hear those bells?" she said, putting aside her awful blanket, very much like the one Mayleda had for her own covering. "That means it's Christmas now."

"No. Christmas Eve," Mayleda corrected sorrowfully, looking gently at the brown woman who was about her age. "I've been counting the days. It's the twenty-fourth of December now."

"Shoo! Muncy! You best stop talkin' 'bout countin' an' readin' an' all them other things you say you can do." Kate always called her by the name Pudget and Dawes had written on her papers. "You get you'self sold South, not to some rich body here, if you talk that way in front of them." She nodded toward the door.

"I must think on the life I've known. If I ever forget, I fear it will be the first step to going mad!"

Kate drew near and looked at her sharply, while Evelyn sat in a world by herself. "You so white, Muncy, I don't see how no gentleman's gwine be brave 'nough to buy you. What man's gwine dare take you home in the back of his wagon if his own wife be at the door to see him do it?"

"Please, don't talk to me about it!"

"A bachelor, maybe! Or maybe a man that's got someplace to hide you. That could be good."

"Please!" Mayleda—she nearly thought of herself as Muncy—covered her ears.

Kate went away. Mayleda looked at her with remorse. Despite her own suffering, she must remember that these other women were suffering too. "I didn't mean to be rude, Kate. It's only that that kind of talk could bring me to the brink of despair. I've told you already that I'm a widow. I have a daughter. And I was close to being married to a fine man whom I dearly love. Then to think that tomorrow, or the next day I will be *sold* to someone—oh!" She put her head to the wall. "Kate, don't you feel like you want to die before that happens?"

The other woman laughed. "Won't that be sum'thing! If every colored gal died just 'fore the white man pulled her into his bed, well, that would soon end slavery, sure 'nough. Muncy, you' talkin' about 'xtinguinatin' our race. At least the brown part of it!"

Mayleda could not bear her joking. She turned back to the window.

Kate spoke again. "Why you always lookin' out there?"

"Because it's the world I knew," Mayleda said bitterly. "I thought it being Christmas Eve, I should have courage to gather us all for a night of prayer."

"Prayer! You believe in that? Well, girl, then you pray for me! Pray that I gets me a man with a sweet mouth that likes my embraces better than his paddle or braided-up leather."

"Katie, don't! I know your last master beat you, but it's not for joking. There is a God in heaven who made you to be a woman, not to be somebody's mistress or slave."

"Then, shoo, why don't God come down here an' take back what he made."

"I don't know the answer to this suffering except that it is caused by greed and by sin, so God himself must hate it. God must have some way for us to walk through this, never departing from the fact that we are His children. You and me. And Evelyn too."

Katie twisted her head. "Give you'self a month after somebody's puts down his money for you. By then you'll know it's enough to have one marse to please. You won't need a god too. You won't have time for him an' all his heavenbound rules. 'Cause you'll be breakin' at least one of them anyway to keep the whip off you' back."

Mayleda sighed. Kate's eyes looked very dark because of her serious gaze.

"I hear'd 'bout Jesus when I was a girl. I know how He don't want the niggers He made to steal or lie or drink! But I'll tell you somethin', Muncy, that ain't my gospel now. You steal a little somethin', and it will give you comfort. You learn to lie, and it gets you a little piece of rest. You drink when you can, and you'll have a little bit of freedom."

Mayleda did not know how to counter her, for she had not lived the life of an enslaved woman—yet. Still she prayed God would hold her to His truths. "I won't forget you, Katie. I will continue to pray for you and Evelyn." She bowed her head.

"You best pray for a sweet-mouthed man for you'self, Muncy, 'cause somebody's gwine be holdin' you soon."

Outside, church bells chimed again.

———

Sleeping in the cold pen lined with foul straw was too similar to the life that Daniel had known as a slave in Virginia. From their first night there to this night, the boy had had horrid dreams. Joseph slept lightly because of it, and now the child was screaming out again. "No! Big Man! No!"

A guard passed by the pen's slats. "I've told you ten times just tonight to keep that boy quiet. One more time, and I'll flog the screaming out of him." Joseph saw the horsewhip he carried as he pulled Daniel out of the straw to himself.

"Hush! It's only another dream!" He kissed Daniel's face, waking him. Mucus ran freely from his nose because of his crying and Joseph wiped him clean with the hem of his own shirt. Inwardly he fought tears, knowing that soon Daniel again would be a slave, alone, without him.

The boy hugged him and started to scratch at the dried paint covering Joseph's chin and neck. Daniel had his own childish hope that if the paint could be removed, then they might be sold together. Usually Joseph told him not to pick at the flaking whiteness, but tonight he had no heart to do so. It was Christmas Eve. By the watch he still had hidden in his pocket, he'd been keeping track of time. "Do you know what Christmas Eve is, Daniel?"

The boy looked at him blankly. Joseph adjusted his view to make certain there was no guard watching them now. He took out his silver watch and put it into Daniel's hand. He opened the clock face. "What time is it?" he asked the child in cautious whispers. Because lamps were always burning around the pen's exterior, there was light to see by.

"Eleven." Daniel pointed to the numbers.

"Good for you! Never admit that you know such things. But never forget them either! And never stop learning as much as you can."

"Yes, I know, Dr. Joseph." The boy smiled up at him. "Make these your three best secrets. Talking to God. Knowing. Learning."

"That's right!" Joseph closed his eyes, but he could not stop the grief of soon being parted from this special child. "Are you fully awake now?"

"Sure. Do you want me to practice the things I know?" The boy was eager.

"If you will make your words so that even the rats in the straw cannot hear," Joseph whispered, with true fatherly love.

He felt the boy giggle against his chest. "Not even the mice," Daniel whispered back, his voice truly hardly more than a breath against Joseph's down-turned face.

Joseph closed his watch and hid it once more, deciding that he would tell Daniel about Christmas later. "What does Isaiah chapter sixty-one and verse ten say, child?"

" 'I will greatly rejoice in the Lord.' "

"Yes! Say that whenever you can look at the sky or feel the coolness of water on a hot day or hear birds sing. These are the marks of God's world, as He intended it to be. Slavery is not of God. Remember that! Rather it comes from the sin of man."

"I know the next verse too."

"Do you?" Joseph's pride swelled, as did his sorrow. A family and school should be this child's lot, not fear and drudgery.

" 'God will cause righteousness an' praise to spring forth before all nations.' "

"Yes, Daniel. I asked you to remember that too, so you will not lose hope, even if this promise does not come true in your lifetime. The Bible says that the stars will fall down some day and then judgment will come! Until that day, you must ask the Spirit of Jesus to help you to be *strong*—"

" 'And fear not.' " Daniel immediately quoted another verse of scripture that Joseph had been diligent to teach him, reciting it to him many times each day. " 'God will come with . . . ah—' " Daniel stopped, unable to say the next word.

" 'With vengeance,' and 'with a recompense.' "

He felt Daniel tremble. "I'm sorry, I didn't remember!"

"Daniel, hush! Don't be afraid. I'm only telling you these things so that you will know them. I'm not going to punish you for what you can't remember. And neither will God. He is pleased that you desire to hide His words in your heart. This is not like studying mathematics or reading. God is actually *with* those who speak to Him, for He will never leave you nor forsake you."

At once the child continued on, reciting the next verse from that same passage in the book of Hebrews. " 'The Lord is my helper, an' I will not fear what man shall do unto me.' " After that the boy sagged against him. "Oh, there is too much to remember."

"When you can do nothing else, call on Jesus' name." Joseph looked up at the other men huddled in the pen, and silently he did that now.

"What is Christmas Eve?" Daniel asked.

"Tonight is Christmas Eve. It's the night before the day we celebrate Jesus' coming to earth, leaving heaven to be our Savior. Jesus Christ was born as a baby to a woman who had to spend her night in a barn because they were travelers and they had nowhere else to sleep."

"Was Jesus' mama a slave?"

"No, she was a woman chosen of God to give birth to His special son. She was a servant of God, just as we are called to be." He paused and reached for some of the straw around them. "In many ways Jesus was as poor as a slave. He owned no house on earth. He gathered no wealth. He glorified God by being friends with others. He healed them. He taught them. He gave them the hope of heaven."

Joseph was cut off from saying more when the guards came by, their faces peering in through the slats and even the gate.

"Hey! It's Christmas Eve. Which of you darkies will sing for a dram of whiskey? Don't be scared! Mr. Pearson's home drinking his own!"

The jangle of the key in the lock rattled Joseph's nerves. It was dangerous to have drinking white men come in on black men who had been penned up for days. Yet one guard did step inside, then another, whips curled in their hands. By their gait, even by their imprudence in coming in, they proved their intoxication.

Slowly Joseph pushed Daniel behind him. Tonight might not be the first time a Negro was killed by an inebriated keeper. One young colored trusty loomed outside the enclosure, not coming in.

"Mr. Paul! Mr. Carson! You fellers shouldn't be in there!" he called.

One of the men turned on him. "Ain't you the perfect nigger." His companion was showing a clay jug to those in the pen. "Come on! Come on! Don't any of you sad boys want a drink?"

The white men laughed and teased because the black men cowered. The Negro youth ran in, taking the keys from the man who did not have the jug. "Please, sahs, come out now! Leave them poor tortured souls."

Then Joseph saw that some of the male slaves were slowly inching their way along the edge of the pen, their eyes fixed wholly on that still open gate. The young sober Negro guard saw this too. "Get out, you all! You gwine let them all loose!"

Joseph shared a moment of hope in freedom as he, too, got up on his feet, poised to run even in his chains, his hand gripping Daniel's hand. But before he could move, the two men in the pen turned savage, like dogs suddenly gone mad. Their whips unfurled. The leather sliced the air. Every colored man close enough to their reach felt the lashes' bites. Despite their drunkenness, their aims were sharp and sure. Their talent in using the whip was well practiced. Within moments the jug was spilled, and the slaves were driven back.

Backing their way out of the pen, their weapons of torture still poised, the guards went beyond the gate, and the trusty slammed it shut. Joseph could see him locking it with trembling hands.

Then the white guards turned on him. "You black fool! To let our good whiskey jar stay in there among those colored pigs!"

"Me, sah?" the youth screeched like a child now.

They answered him by throwing him down and applying the lash to his legs. The whole ordeal for the boy lasted only moments. Joseph wondered if it had all been planned that way from the start by the two white guards, for then they came back to the gate while the Negro youth crawled away.

"Merry Christmas, you all!" they called out, laughing all the while.

When the white guards left, Joseph kept his eye on the Negro youth still on the ground nursing his wounds. Joseph had had this idea before, but not until now had he seen one colored auction house worker to be on his own. While others in the pen watched him, Joseph dared to go up to the fence. "I can pay you well, lad, if you will only help me in letting my child escape."

The young man, hardly more than a boy, looked around, then came near.

"I have a silver watch," Joseph said. "It can be yours if you will let my boy out through the fencing and take him to free Negroes who can house him and keep him safe."

The worker glanced behind him. "I don't have the keys no more."

Joseph looked upward. "There's enough space between that last board up there and the ceiling to let the child crawl through."

The trusty looked up too.

"You let my Daniel crawl out, then you take him outside to safety. When you come back, the watch will be yours." Because the boy did not have the keys, Joseph risked showing him the timepiece from a distance.

Without a doubt the lad was interested, but he said, "I got me Mista Pearson as my marse, so's I know that property cain't own property."

"I was a free man in Pennsylvania. I had a house, a horse, and wages. This watch is all I have left of that."

The boy seemed fascinated. "Sah, he can start climbin' now."

Joseph's heart missed a beat. Once over the barrier, Daniel would never see him again. "My precious boy!" he called, his voice shaking mightily. "Come, this man's going let you go. He'll take you to free colored folks who are outside this pen. Now, you behave yourself. And you pray. And you don't forget me, please!"

Bewildered, Daniel hugged him and kissed him, then climbed the slats as Joseph told him to do. He struggled because of the dress he wore. Joseph watched, praying every second until the child was up to the roof and then starting down the other side. When Daniel's feet touched the ground, other men in the pen who had not come to him all week gathered around Joseph now, patting his shoulders, shaking his hand. "Hey, ho!" They celebrated in tones no louder than light breezes. "At least you' boy gets free!"

"God be praised!" Joseph cried a mixture of tears, both for joy and sorrow. They all grew quiet, worried about any danger that might have been stirred by the escape. Yet all remained as it was until the colored trusty came back a long time later to reach his hand through the fence.

"All right, Uncle, I take the watch now."

Joseph handed the silver timepiece to him. The way the boy smiled worried him. "Where is Daniel? Where did you take him?"

The young Negro hid the watch in his shirt and would not answer. "Where is my boy?" Joseph clutched the boards and pressed his face against them.

"Property don't own property," the colored trusty said again. Then he held up a coin. "But now I also got myself this for goin' to tell my Marse Pearson that you' child done tried to run off."

"You thief! You scoundrel!" Joseph shook the fence. "Where is my boy? What have you done with my child?"

"Hush your mouth, Black Joe Whitsun!" Three men strode in while he was crying against the barrier. "Here's your boy, back again!"

Joseph opened his eyes to Dawes, Pudget, and Pearson. The auction-house owner used his own key to undo the gate. With the two slave catchers as guards, Pearson opened the way just enough to push little Daniel through. Then he locked it again.

Daniel tottered toward him like a child walking in his sleep. Joseph rushed to him. Others in the pen gathered slowly, but only after the white men were gone. The child had his hands extended in front of him. His fingers and knuckles had been struck until they were swollen and bleeding. "Oh, Daniel!" Joseph gasped, careful not to touch his wounds. "I wanted you free. I didn't want you to suffer."

The trusty called in, "That child will not climb again."

Joseph left Daniel to go to the fence, to the one of their own color who dared to linger. "How could you betray a child? You stole my watch, knowing exactly what you would do."

The boy hardly looked ashamed. "Marse Pearson's good to me, so I's good to him." He took out his coin again and then the watch. "Property don't own property. But see what I got now."

"You!" Joseph sighed when the boy just walked away. He turned to find Daniel standing behind him, his hands still in the air. Joseph tore strips from the bottom of Daniel's dress. With these he bandaged the ugly sores. "I'm so sorry!" he said to Daniel over and over.

Daniel smiled. "I like bein' back with you."

All of the sorrows of the world seemed to open up to him once more as Joseph sat down and took Daniel upon his knees. To know it was Christmas Day only made the pain more real, but it also reminded him of the mystery of God's mercy, that He would send His own son into such a wicked world.

Some brothers across the way carried over what was almost an empty jug. "Let the boy drink. It will help his pain."

"No!" Joseph said in horror.

The other men looked at him as though he were a beast for not letting them soothe his child. For long moments after that the pen stayed quiet. Then someone with a rich strong voice began to sing, not for bribery's sake, but for the comfort of them all. The music carried Joseph back to his plantation friendship with Parris, who always sang more than the rest.

The song this imprisoned man sang was one that Joseph knew from those days.

> *If religion wa' a thing that money could buy.*
> *The rich would live an' the poor would die.*
> *Some gwine come in crippled, an' some in lame*
> *But all what come will come in Jesus' name.*
> *Oh, there'll be a fire in the east an' fire in the west*
> *An' it gwine burn up everybody, but God's own best.*

"Quiet in there!" The guards were back suddenly. The man who sang merely laid back on his elbows and took a rest, until the white men were gone another time.

Then he lifted his voice, going back to the start,

> *If religion wa' a thing that money could buy . . .*

No one came this time to shout down his song. And soon Daniel was asleep in Joseph's arms.

CHAPTER 33

DURING THEIR DAYS IN BALTIMORE, Charles Powell had paced like a cat in a crate, waiting for news in the rented boardinghouse room. White messengers, secretly come down from Pennsylvania, and Dr. Ellis himself had been their frequent visitors, bringing them all kinds of information on printed handbills and scraps of newsprint cut out of the newspapers.

Now with only one auction notice in hand, Mr. Powell was pacing again, but this time Thomas was with him watching the sun rise over Pearson's Auction House in Hamberstown, Maryland. It was right across from the hotel where they had been since yesterday night, after coming in from Baltimore on the train. Thomas had done his best in their time of waiting to teach Mr. Powell what it meant to be a master.

Mr. Powell, in return, had continued taking time to teach him the skills of reading and writing, even though they were now south of the dreaded Mason and Dixon Line.

This morning the slave handbill had been Thomas's sorry kind of primer. Sitting on the bed beside the white man, he had gone over the letters and words so many times that he knew them all by heart. Mr. Powell had some of them underlined with pencil. First there was a notice about a boy to be sold later that day. His name was given as Dan. His age listed as eight. The auction-house printer described him as being in "good condition, his ribs mending from a teaming accident."

This more than anything else had caused Mr. Powell and the other white abolitionists to choose Pearson's over every other auction house, all of which put out advertisements in advance of their days of sale. Thomas was not as hopeful as Powell that they were in the right place at the right time, since he knew auctioneers were quick to change a slave's name, make his age more desirable, or lie about his health.

The delay of Christmas and then of New Year's Day had given them extra time to decide what to do, since slaves were not usually auctioned off over the holidays. Dr. Ellis and others who had been with them in Baltimore had spent hours studying the stacks of notices. They all felt that Joseph, Mrs. Ruskin, and the boy might well be locked inside that building right across the street from them. But only Mr. Powell and Thomas had come to find out. To bring everybody would have stirred too much suspicion.

Though Thomas kept his worries to himself, he could easily think of men like Dawes and Pudget arranging private sales so that the transfer of Sister Ruskin or Brother Joseph, or even little Daniel, might have already happened in some planter's house or alley. In the Pearson Auction House notice, Mr. Powell had also underlined the description of a woman, one of three in a short column labeled, "Vigorous Young Housemaids to be Sold."

In the notice this woman was called Muncy. Her age was written as twenty-seven, which was younger than Sister Ruskin. The description given for her read "light mulatto, charming, quiet." The first time Mr. Powell read that all aloud, he had put his hand over the words and wept. It was the first time Thomas had ever seen any emotion other than lust or greed in a white man looking down over a list of slaves to be sold.

Now with the morning getting brighter, Thomas took up the advertisement once more. He considered how members of his own family had probably had their names in print just like he was seeing now, though they did not have the skills needed to read about themselves. He imagined his own name printed, for now he knew its spelling and what the letters looked like.

Powell turned to him and let out one of his many sighs of anguish. "We're getting closer to the time."

They had been careful in what they said to each other, for the walls were thin, and everyone around must see them as master and slave. "Yes, Marse," Thomas practiced. The man grimaced that he would call him that now. Thomas, however, knew well the price of failure. He was nervous, for if Powell made even one mistake, it could put him back in bondage. The shopkeeper reached for his new high hat set upside down on the table. Thomas hastened to get it for him. "Remember! Do nothin' for you'self! Pretend you' hands is wood if you must."

"Oh yes. Right. I won't be careless when we are out in public."

Mr. Powell allowed Thomas to put his cloak around him, before opening the door. Thomas had his hand upon the knob when Powell spoke again.

"One more moment. I want us to pray again."

Thomas was getting used to this man's piety. It surprised him less than seeing him grieve over Negroes he did not know. They prayed, though the white man said no words. Then they stepped out into the hallway of the boardinghouse. From that moment until they would come back again, danger would be all around them, like the air they breathed.

———

The three women had been told the night before that they would be put up on the block this day. Mayleda had been startled from her uneasy slumber of the night by the sound of a key in the lock. Pearson himself stood before them in a moment. He had a white guard on each side of him and a young colored worker behind him.

"Auction day!" he said most brightly.

The Negro lad laid garments down near their feet. Two other Negroes came in carrying buckets filled with water.

"Wash yourselves and dress yourselves up right," Pearson said, "or I will come back and do it for you." He grinned when Mayleda lifted her face in horror.

She looked away, knowing how the guards and Pearson himself chose to eye her. She believed it was only by the mercies of God that no man had come into the room to take advantage of any one of them. But how would God's mercy protect them now, when today was the day they all would be sold?

The door closed. The key rattled. She was grateful for the privacy, for as a child raised in the South, she had heard of Negro women being stripped and sold naked. Indeed, she herself had seen bare-breasted Negresses paraded in Charleston's market. Kate chose the best dress for herself. Evelyn waited long minutes before she moved from the corner. Mayleda shuddered when she picked up the dress that was left.

As were the others, this one she had was sewn of flimsy calico, being no more than a collarless shift with a wide neck that could be tied up with laces. Turning from the window, Mayleda took off the simple dress she had been wearing since the days of living in the Barings' house. She left on her undergarments. The other women had none to wear. With them, she washed her hands, her face, her feet with cold water and no soap. When she pulled the strange dress over her head, she was surprised to find it scented with lavender.

For the first time in days Evelyn spoke. "You a fool, Kate, to delight in they sin."

"You the fool!" Kate shot back. "You gwine be *some* man's pillow t'night, whether you like it or not, so it would be wise for you to charm the best man in this house instead of mopin' an' gettin' you'self the worst." Her eyes shifted to Mayleda. "That goes for you too, Muncy."

Mayleda struggled with the drawstring lacing at her neck.

"No use fussin'," Kate said. "Those strings gwine be undone faster than you can breathe a breath."

Mayleda tried to go on about her own business, numbly wrapping her old dress under her cloak, hoping she would be allowed to take both garments with her. Mr. Pearson soon let himself in alone. Like a gentleman inspecting horses that had been groomed, he walked to each of them in turn. They were told to stand straight. Told to keep their eyes low but their chins high. Told not to whimper or give voice, no matter where they were touched. When he came to Mayleda, he stole the pins from her hair, then adjusted her freed tresses to his liking. "If it weren't for your hair and eyes, I'd wager you didn't have a drop of nigger in you. But it's not my business to know."

Mayleda would have pleaded again except for her fear that Joseph might be singled out and harmed because of it. Still, she thought on her brothers and on something she hadn't thought of for a long time—how to get home to be safe with them.

To torment her or to test her, Pearson started at her chin and drew his thumb slowly down until it touched her waist. "You're flinching, Muncy!" He laughed with evil intent.

Then Mayleda did more than flinch—she fainted straightway.

When she came to her senses, Kate was standing over her, reaching down to extend her hand. "It's our turn on the block."

It was only a few minutes past nine when the three women were brought out into the bright sales hall in front of all the chairs filled with men. Charles knew the time by reading the bill of sales, but more so by having studied his watch with such nervous diligence. Most of the slave-buying colleagues here smoked and talked congenially with friends and strangers. Charles spoke to no one.

He sat in the last row, with Thomas behind him holding his hat and cloak. Pearson rose from a seat in the front.

"Gentlemen, the terms of sale are as usual. A minimum of one-half in cash paid today and the remainder in notes, with prior approval from this establishment, to be paid within ninety days of this day, January third. Special mortgages are on slaves until your final payment. Any questions? No? Good! Auctioneer! The gavel."

Charles rocked at the sound of wood hitting wood up at the podium where one of Pearson's white workers grinned. The twenty or so men who formed the audience turned their attention to the front. Many started making negative comments about the women on display. "Too old!" "Too wicked in the eyes!" "Too white for any wise planter's tastes!" Charles could only shiver, for the woman who was made to stand up on the low table ahead and to his right was Mayleda.

The man next to Charles nodded at him in a carefree manner. "Pearson always does it this way. The sweet gals go up first so a feller knows how much he's got left to spend on help for his fields!" He chuckled and drew on his cigar.

Charles was overwhelmed and speechless, which made his auction neighbor take a harsh look at him. Charles dared to glance at Mayleda. She had her eyes down. It was possible she did not know he was there. Behind them was a fence that divided the building into two different sections. What little Charles could see beyond that fencing reminded him of an indoor livestock holding yard with a rough wooden pen.

The auctioneer started the bidding by taking offers for any one of the three females. He set the low price—eight hundred dollars. At that the men roared and joked with Pearson, who seemed to delight in circulating among his customers. While many laughed and declared the price outrageous for any one of those on display, Charles nearly raised his hand to bid. He might have done so except that Thomas suddenly draped his cloak around his shoulders. "I did hear you say you wa' chilly, sah?" the young man asked, making it his opportunity to look at Charles directly.

Charles understood the warning Thomas was giving him. He must not seem too eager nor too intent on just the one. Someone in the crowd challenged Pearson that they should be allowed a closer look before being asked to buy. This suggestion Pearson entertained with magnanimity, actually leading the way as several prospective buyers went up. Following Pearson's own activity, these other men parted the women's lips with their fingers to look into their mouths. They pressed on their stomachs and on their backs. They even felt their breasts.

Charles felt he could not look, for he was so protective of Mayleda, yet so helpless.

Thomas put his finger lightly to his shoulder. "I'll have you' cloak back while you look, sah."

Charles did not think he could stand. He needed to lean on the walking cane he had purchased as part of his gentlemanly costume. Weak-kneed, he moved forward to meet each woman, shyly touching only a hand or an elbow until he came to Mayleda.

Perspiration beaded her face as she kept her eyes closed. She was pale. He touched her wrist, and it was cold as ice. She flinched mightily. He could not resist a word to her. Touching her soft lips as he had seen others do it, he whispered, "Mayleda."

Her eyes flashed open, though her lashes were heavy with tears. He knew she saw him. He also knew that he must walk away. A man came behind him. He dared not turn to see what further rudeness she was made to endure. When he got to his chair, he had to hold to the arms before sitting down.

Bids were being made in earnest. "Nine hundred! One thousand!" Thomas set his cloak back around him.

The man beside him tried his friendliness again. "It's too close to holidays. Nobody has much money to spend."

Charles made himself nod. He was in terror. Someone could buy Mayleda while he sat there! The numbers whirled aloud in the air. He honed his concentration. When Thomas touched his back again under the pretense of holding to his chair, Charles managed to say, "Twelve hundred for Muncy!"

"Thirteen." A man in the front bid against him so casually.

"Fourteen!" Charles screamed, his hand going high. His anxious bid seemed to draw many eyes to him. There was no hiding the fact that he was a stranger in this town.

"Sixteen!" A man to his left made an offer.

"Seventeen," Charles said when the auctioneer again looked at him. Pearson moved to the front. It was then that Charles saw how the two other women had already been sold and brought down. Only Mayleda was left to face the crowd, now animated like bees warmed in the sun. There was more interest directed toward him, as Mr. Pearson himself took the auctioneer's gavel. "Let's see if we can increase the pace a bit for the lovely porcelain lady."

Pearson knew every buyer's name, because of the requirement that they be registered beforehand to prove their credit. "Mr. Powell, isn't it? Will you consider a bid of two thousand dollars?"

Charles knew it should be ludicrous, for he had been told that a prime field slave could be bought for sixteen hundred dollars. Yet he answered in the room where no one else now seemed inclined to speak, "Yes!"

Charles' neighbor looked at him, as did others. Pearson pointed to the man up front. "Your competitor says twenty-three!"

A whistle went through the crowd. It was a huge jump in price, and one that the men probably considered unnecessary. But now Pearson was facing him with a smile. "Mr. Powell, would you care to offer twenty-four?"

Charles wanted to look cautious, and indeed he was, for he realized he would still need funds to bid on Joseph and Daniel. But if he said no or offered a lower price, the man up front could bid higher and perhaps win the day. He was unfamiliar with the house's exact etiquette on men buying women, but he could not fail now. "Yes!" he said, not knowing what else could be safe.

Oddly, the man in the front row turned and took off his hat to him. "You enjoy her."

The gavel struck. Thomas, without Charles' direction, went forward to take the roll of clothes Mayleda couldn't seem to carry by herself, as she staggered when the auctioneer took her hand to bring her down. When she was finally standing safely behind his chair, Charles felt her sink to her knees. Thomas had counseled him not to make any commotion over her if she came to them. As much as it hurt, Charles took the young man's advice.

Thomas was careful to guard his actions too, for much criticism could be laid upon them both if a servant showed attention to his owner's new acquisition.

Mr. Pearson came to Charles with a temporary bill of sales. "Congratulations, Mr. Powell. No one has ever paid more for a wench in this house than you did this day."

Then Pearson addressed the crowd on a completely different matter. "We'll get the male field hands out of the pen and up here for you all in short order."

Charles dared to glance at Thomas. Surely Daniel and Joseph would soon be within view.

No Negro males had been allowed near the front fence while the three fancy ladies were being sold. Yet Daniel, his hands healing from the punishment, was able to sneak up to see what he could of Mayleda's fate. Joseph had not wanted him to do that, but the child would not be held back from knowing what Sister May's master would look like. Joseph had imagined that the child would come back trembling and in tears, for those were his own emotions. Instead, the boy came back smiling, hardly able to hold his tongue until he could whisper into Joseph's ear. "Brother Powell came! Brother Powell got her! Oh, Brother Powell will buy you an' me!"

There was only a moment to share this wonderful news and only an instant when Joseph could decide if it might be true or only the boy's wishful imagination. Right then, Pearson opened the gate.

"All of you step out, but not Black Joe." Guards came in to make them stand up in the straw.

Daniel clung to Joseph as he held fast to the child.

Pearson had a whip. "You can make this parting simple or hard. Your choice, Joe."

Daniel looked upward into Joseph's eyes. The child was not devastated, surely because of the hope he had in Charles Powell's coming. But Joseph felt his own heart crushed. Within moments a buyer who was not their friend could take Daniel. Yet speaking any warning to the child was useless, for the dangers of auction could not be avoided. "God bless you!" Joseph struggled. "God be with you! You remember all we have said, my dear, precious son!"

Pearson took the child by the hand, a wolf in disguise taking away Joseph's little lamb forever. As soon as the pen was emptied of all men except Joseph, two white guards whom he had not seen before came in to him. They waited until Pearson came back without Daniel.

"I just earned more from the sale of a wench than ever before," Pearson boasted to Joseph. "And now I'm anticipating my biggest profit from remanding a slave. You."

With only three of them there, Joseph dared to speak. "I have no master! I was manumitted in 1835!" While he spoke the guards came forth and put cuffs upon his wrists. Already he had been enduring blisters and swollen ankles as the only man in the pen to have leg irons on through his full confinement.

"Come on!" a guard told him roughly. "Mr. Pearson doesn't want to hear a black tongue wag."

But Joseph continued to stand still. "The master who freed me is dead. I have no other master!" For this he was struck hard across the mouth. The blow caused him to reel. He remembered what it was like to live with no more say than an animal.

Strangely, Pearson spoke on his behalf. "Don't give him more blows. I want him conscious."

Squinting as his head continued to spin, Joseph looked at the auction-house owner.

"Buck, I know your story. Mr. Dawes left a good summary for me based on his investigation of why he should find you living in Pennsylvania and having manumission signed by a South Carolina master."

"Because I was freed!" Joseph was desperate. He spoke under his breath, and they did not strike him.

"Using the telegraph, Mr. Dawes contacted the newspapers in Charleston and Columbia. He placed an advertisement with your description and the name of the planter whose name was on that manumission paper, as you call it. And the gentleman who *rightly* owns you has responded. A lawyer from Charleston too. It is all quite fine with me. Quite legal and quite profitable, though I cannot know why anyone would pay so much to have you back."

"What is the man's name?" Joseph asked with dread, thinking that it must be one of Mayleda's brothers, Brant or Eric.

Pearson laughed. "Do you really not know? Why, Mr. Theodore Rensler is the gentleman coming for you. So how does that make you feel?"

"I am not Rensler's slave!" Joseph cried. "I was never his property!"

Pearson shrugged, then spoke to the guards. "All right. I've said what I wanted to say. You can quiet him now."

Joseph was struck on the head from the rear, and all the world turned dark in an instant.

He awoke with a throbbing headache. The cuffs on his wrists had been adjusted during his unconsciousness. Looking around, still much in a daze, he found himself anchored to one of six vertical iron bars in the gatelike door of a small dirty cell. It was night, he thought, by the darkness and silence present.

The auction-house lamps still burned around the empty pen that he could see through the bars of his cell. He was trapped by three brick walls and this gate in front of him. It was much like the prison he had known in Charleston's workhouse, except that the auction house was deathly quiet, as though he were all alone in the building. Because the chain between his hands could slide freely up and down, Joseph found that he could stand. His feet were no longer held by shackles.

He did stand to examine his situation. He could not touch the back of his head or move his body more than two feet away from the gate to which he was held. It puzzled him why they decided to chain him in such a small, inescapable place, unless their business was only to humiliate him more or to keep him from harming himself. He knew of those who had killed themselves rather than being taken alive back to slavery.

He thought of Daniel. Because of his own trials, he had not even been conscious while the boy was being sold. Now he stood on tiptoe, straining to see across the pen to the sales room. But all was dark out there, and his looking was in vain. The boy's fate had been sealed, and he had not been even alert enough to pray. Now he did pray, the pain in his head nearly darkening his vision. He sank to his knees, not having the strength or even the will to stand as he wept and grieved.

———

After dark Thomas risked bringing pails of water into the hotel room to fill the brass washtub he had borrowed on "Marse" Powell's behalf. Though the water was cold, Sister Ruskin was eager to wash Daniel in it. Then she dried the naked little boy with a sheet she took from the bed. Over and over she kissed the child and thanked Thomas and Mr. Powell for their rescue. Then she and the boy shed more tears for Joseph's unknown fate.

Indeed, to Thomas, it all seemed unbelievable. Yet here they were, sharing the room the evening after the auction. Both Thomas and Mr. Powell then stepped out into the hall while Sister Ruskin washed herself and changed back into her own set of borrowed clothes from Philadelphia. When Sister May called them back in, she still had not found any way to pin up her hair. Thomas saw how Mr. Powell looked at her when they came in and closed the door.

It caused Thomas to decide that now was the time to go searching for why Joseph had not been brought to the auction block. At first both Powell and Sister Ruskin tried to stop him, but then they listened to his reasons. "I can travel the streets better than you 'cause many servants are at work t'night. Even when I was drawin' water at the boardin'house well, I met gals what said they could show me to certain of Mr. Pearson's trusties that might be able to help me get inside that man's place."

"No!" Sister Ruskin told him at once. "It is too dangerous!"

"Ma'am, we got to know somehow!" Thomas pleaded with her. "We don't have no more chances if we don't know where he is."

The woman looked to Mr. Powell. Then all of them looked to the bed where Daniel sat bravely but silently weeping.

"They put paint on him," the child said between his tears. "They said they would hold him for his marse an' not sell him."

"He can't have a legal owner." Sister Ruskin looked at them. "I know because my daddy willed him to me before we knew that the state would grant him freedom. When it did, my brother Brant took him to an ocean steamer, so he could go free."

It was an ugly thing to hear of Sister Ruskin in her time of owning slaves. It made Daniel sob harder. She seemed to know that the boy felt betrayed. Then Thomas felt himself making things worse by daring to ask his question. "Is it you' brother, ma'am, who might be comin'?"

"I can't think that Brant would do that. Or Eric, my younger brother, either. I don't think anyone can take Joseph legally."

"Well, that sure ain't the same as nobody bein' able to take him at all," Thomas mourned out loud, feeling close to these others and determined that they must not just let the moments fly by. "I'm gwine to look for him!" This time they didn't try to stop him. He glanced toward Mr. Powell. "If you will, sah, you could pray for me."

CHAPTER 34

ALL THAT DAY AND NIGHT JOSEPH had had no water or food. The whole place was still as quiet as a cave, and the lamps were burning low. Some were even out, and no one came to replace the oil now that he was the only prisoner there.

When he moved, the chain between his wrists would sing and squeal against the rod as he forced his numbed hands to go higher or lower. There was no good position that gave him comfort or rest. When the last of the lamps burned out, he was in total darkness. Then he heard rats squeaking louder than his chain.

It made him think of Daniel's sweet laugh, expressed even here when they had been penned together. He closed his eyes to the horrible wondering about where the boy was now. There was only one thing that made him grateful to have the boy gone from his side. If miscegenation was pronounced to be his crime in front of Rensler, then Joseph was sure that his end would be hellish and slow, for black men accused of outraging white women were often burned, then hanged. Preceding that, there could be emasculation and flaying. He held his breath, making himself happy that Daniel would not be present to see any of it. He shivered as his mind flashed to images of Jesus in His agony. He had seen such mental pictures before when he had suffered at Delora. He was not a holy man as was his Savior, but in his youth, thoughts on the suffering of Christ had helped him to endure. Now he wondered if his faith would help him this time. Bowing his head against the bar, he thought on the physical and mental pain to come.

Asking God without words if this cup of suffering could pass him by, he thought his imagination of freedom had opened some unreal door, for he distinctly heard the creak of hinges. Instinctively he crouched lower, though protecting himself was impossible. There were footsteps in the dark. He made himself still. Only prayer and God's mercy could be his defense now.

"Joseph? You here?"

He did not know the voice. It sounded black, maybe even southern, but he did not trust it. Daniel had been betrayed for a watch. "Joseph? The brother what let me in said he wa' sure you wa' in one of these cells. Now, come on! Speak up if you here."

The one who said this was directly in front of him. Joseph could have stretched his fingers and touched the stranger's trousers.

"It's Thomas. You remember me? Mista Powell's apprentice."

At that news Joseph stood, the bar singing. Thomas shrieked in fright.

"I am right here!"

"Sure you are!" Thomas cried, regaining his courage in a moment. "Ghost an' all!"

"You must be careful!" Joseph whispered to him as he felt the heat of the man's face near his own. "The Negroes that work for Pearson may have the will to betray you."

"We just had to find out where you were an' why."

"Do you know what's happen to Daniel? To Sister Ruskin?"

"Yes! Hush! They safe! Mr. Powell got them both. Now we plan to get you."

"Thomas, they are saying I'm being held here because my master is coming for me, but I have no rightful owner! Even so, Pearson gave a name I do know from my past. Theodore Rensler. He was my master's neighbor. There were several times when he tried to kill me in the South."

"Lord of mercy!"

"I know it won't matter what I say in my defense."

"Sister Ruskin says that she once owned you. Can such a thing be true?"

"Yes, but don't you ever hold it against her. It was the best she and her father could do, given the times in which we lived."

"Do you think her brothers would help you now if Mista Powell would telegraph them?"

"No, I've pondered that. I don't think any southern white man would help me, because of the rumors all around me that I did harm her. I would appreciate it if you would tell her to stay away and out of sight now that Rensler is coming."

"What do you think we should do, other than that?"

"I don't know." Anguish gripped him.

Thomas found his hands and squeezed them hard. "Somehow we gwine get you out of here."

Joseph held to him, though the movement of his fingers caused him pain. "Will you remind Daniel that I love him? Will you give Charles Powell my thanks? He pledged he would do anything to save us. I believe him, but tell him I can endure as long as I know for certain that Daniel and Mayleda are safe."

"Don't you give up, Unc'!" Thomas pulled away. "I be back! I must hurry so's I don't miss my chance to tell them where you are!"

───────

The next dawn brought Sunday, Joseph knew. He expected isolation and even prayed for it, though always wondering at what moment he would see Rensler again. Dim, unnatural-looking light filtered through cracks in the high ceiling, so he again had sight, even with the still-dark lamps.

Joseph stood when he thought he heard the front door of the auction house being opened. Muffling the sound of his chain against his chest, he stretched on tiptoe to view a lone man in a high hat coming in. The slave pen obstructed his vision greatly, and the front door was far removed from him, yet he could see movement against the brightly lighted windows.

The man came through the sale room to the holding area. He walked with purpose, coming directly to Joseph. It was Mr. Pearson.

"So, buck, here you are, all alone." He stopped a few feet from the cell.

Joseph looked no higher than Pearson's waist. He gave him no response. The auction-house owner breathed deeply. "You stinking animal, standing in your own pool of urine."

Joseph watched the lower tip of the man's walking cane move side to side on the bare dusty floor. It was true, for he had not been able to move or reach to open his trousers.

"Boy, the Bible says an ox or an ass may be pulled from a pit, even on the Sabbath. Surely it would be better for me and for you if your confinement would end today. On my way home from morning services, your master was introduced to me on the street. I told him I would make no transactions on Sunday, but seeing you now, it must be a mercy that I would let you go today." He sniffed. "For your well-being and the cleanliness of my cell."

Joseph calculated he had nothing to lose. He raised his eyes. "The Lord of the Sabbath knows I am a free man, Mr. Pearson. You try to humiliate me by keeping me in this way, and you have not fed me or given me anything to drink."

Pearson disappeared for a moment. He came back with a water gourd. "Do you want to drink? Take it."

Joseph was so thirsty he endured the shame of awkwardly spilling what water he could into his mouth and onto his lips. "No matter what you do, I am still a man," he said, letting the gourd fall from his hands. "You would look the same and feel the same if you were the one chained here instead of me."

"You pig! You cannot hold your tongue for an instant, can you? I should have let it shrivel. All you say and do convinces me that this wealthy gentleman Rensler does know you, and well! He told me that a decade ago you were as brash as you are now. A conceited mimic of sophisticated speech, he said. Well, I do believe him. I'm not selling you today, understand, but today he did lay the fees for your keep into my hand. If he wants you now, he will have you!"

"I had a manumission paper! He is not my master!"

"You talk to him about that, if you dare!"

"The man tried to kill me before, when I was another man's property."

"He carries proof that you are his own. Perhaps he will succeed in ridding the South of you. What he does with you is no business of mine."

Pearson stepped away, putting his walking cane between his polished boots.

"I am free! I am free!"

But no one heard his shouts as they echoed from the rafters.

The rented room was like a prison for Charles, even on Sunday, for he could not leave it without fear of being accosted by men who had witnessed the auction. In the auction house after Charles had paid the tremendous price for both Mayleda and Daniel, Pearson had to come to him with several of his white guards.

The auction-house owner took his payment in full and in cash, then accused him to his face of buying the woman and child to sell back to Yankee abolitionists across the border. Pearson boasted that he was not ignorant nor uninformed, that he knew the mulattos Charles had paid so dearly for were too overpriced to be economical as slaves. The woman Charles might have lusted for, Pearson said, with rudeness like hot coals in his mouth. But the boy must be a rescue, pure and simple, for no one would have paid so much for a recently injured child.

Fortunately for Charles, Dawes and Pudget never showed themselves during the confrontation, or he might have been identified as one from Philadelphia. Pearson made a final point before allowing Charles to remove Mayleda, Daniel, and even Thomas from his establishment. He ordered Charles to never again be present at any of his sales. He threatened to investigate Charles' business in Baltimore if he ever saw him trying to buy slaves in Hamberstown again. He promised to spread the word that Charles was probably a Unionist traitor willing to work with the North's antislavery faction at a profit, selling slaves to men who would pay to set them free.

Charles had stayed quiet through every accusation, yet now in the room he felt as vulnerable as he had been then. His thoughts were on them all, but especially on Joseph, for Thomas had come back with his first bleak report of how he had found him chained inside a cell.

Now Thomas was gone again, this time with the hopes of recruiting local Negroes, free and slave, to secretly watch all sides of Pearson's property so that Joseph could not be moved without their knowing it. With Thomas absent, Mayleda sat on the bed with Daniel still in his tattered dress. The child had been obliged to hear the ugly full report of Joseph's abuse. As they waited for further news, Charles stayed at the window. He had seen Pearson let himself in and later come out, but still alone. There was a coded knock at the door, the one that he and Thomas had agreed on. Quickly Charles went and let Thomas in.

"I seen Joseph once more."

Mayleda leaned forward.

"He says Pearson told him his marse will come to him today. The one I named to you before. This Marse Rensler."

His words made Mayleda leap to her feet. Thomas looked grim. "Brother Whitsun says the same thing again, ma'am, that this man Rensler must not know you here, or it will only go that much harder for him." Thomas looked at Charles. "Joseph says he can endure, knowing that the child an' Sister May are well. He encourages us to go up across the border to find safety now."

"We won't leave without him!" Charles went back to one of his first ideas. "I'll confront Rensler and buy Joseph from him."

"It won't work," Mayleda mourned. "I know Teddy Rensler. He'll want to make Joseph suffer. I can't imagine how he thinks he has the right to come here, but I can imagine that he did come, for he hates Joseph with every nerve of his being."

"There's enough brothers and sisters now to watch every door," Thomas told them. "They'll see if and when he comes."

"Knowing Theodore, he could murder him right inside Pearson's!" Mayleda fretted, hugging Daniel against the power of her words.

Thomas grew as silent as Charles, for that possibility could not be denied. Then Thomas said, "I'm gwine let myself in by that broken auction house door one more time, an' this time I'm gwine stay hidden on the inside to watch. If anything happens, I bring you word myself."

―――――――

Joseph felt that time had been imprisoned with him, that is until he saw Pearson and Rensler come to stand before his cell in bright new lantern light late Sunday night.

When Rensler gazed in through the bars at him, the planter's vile look momentarily erased all memory Joseph had of ever living free for sixteen years. The man had not changed, either inside or out. He was still the small, narrow-faced being in spectacles Joseph had known from the southern parish where he had suffered so much. Joseph decided after that first minute of meeting that he would not avert his eyes.

"Well, here he is for you, sir," Pearson said. "I guess as ornery as ever."

"I guess!" Rensler shook his head, his mouth sealed with a thin, tight-lipped smile. "Well, look at you, Joseph. Now I hear they call you Black Joe."

"He has the branding on his back and the scar on his tongue."

"I'm sure he does. There's no doubting him, even after all these years."

"You are not my master," Joseph said under his breath.

"You will pay for saying that," Rensler fumed.

Pearson chuckled. "He's not afraid to use that tongue."

Joseph's flesh crawled. He could not move away. "I should take it out," Rensler said, "but I'll let the next man who has him make that decision. I apologize for having you come in here so late to show him to me. The dregs traders you directed me to, Mr. Pearson, are not leaving for Richmond until tomorrow on the last train coming through. They don't want to hold him more than an hour. So I'm trying your patience again, I know, to ask you to keep him one more night and day, now that I know you do have him."

Joseph had never heard the term "dregs trader," but it seemed clear enough that he would be sold south to others by Rensler's agreement. The deeper south a man was sold, the less his chances for survival, Joseph knew, and many a slave suffered a slow death doing outside work there.

Rensler struck the bars with his fingers and made the iron ring. "Finally, Joe, you will have your lessons learned. You stinkin' fool, I will make you wish I had taken you out and slaughtered you tonight."

"I am not your slave," Joseph spoke louder than before.

"Oh, but you are, buck, for the one who owns the mother, does own her offspring."

"You don't own my mother!"

Teddy smiled instead of reprimanding him. "But I do, and we always have at Pine Woods. She never was Delora property."

"She was! Mr. Callcott took her in trade for two ewes."

"A Negro story," Rensler huffed, shaking his head toward Pearson as though Joseph were piteous. "There is no record of any such transaction. Therefore, the courts affirmed that you are mine. I have come with proper deposition papers that prove your manumission invalid. It was kind for slave agents in Pennsylvania to go to the trouble of checking on the status of your freedom. I was only too happy to pay them for their services in order to savor these moments now."

Rensler clucked his tongue. "You have no right to know these things,

of course. I just thought you might sleep better not dreaming of freedom."

He then turned the conversation casually toward Pearson. "I have no
more to say. I will claim him tomorrow."

"I close the office at six."

"Then I'll come before six."

They took the lantern with them, so soon there was no light. After a
long while Joseph heard sounds in the dark. For the third time since his
confinement, Thomas came to him. His brave friend touched his hand. "I
was over by the pen. I hear'd all they had to say. We ain't givin' up, so
don't you!"

Despite his courageous words, Joseph felt Thomas shaking when he
took his hand. He himself had no strength to even lift his head. And his
own hands were quaking as they had done so many times in Oak Glen.
"Thomas, do me two favors. Tell Charles Powell to take you all far away—
now! Then ask him to have Daniel named after me. Ask him to let everyone know that he is *Daniel Whitsun*, my adopted son, when he gets him
North. At least I will have a namesake. Again I say, rescue is hopeless.
Save yourselves!"

CHAPTER 35

BY THE TIME IT WAS DAWN on Monday, Mayleda was ready to leave the boardinghouse room at a moment's notice. Without scissors or needle, she had managed to make a scarf for Daniel from Pearson's calico dress to cover his hair. With another square of material torn from the slave auction dress, she had fashioned a better skirt for him, tying it over the one he had.

Thomas had been gone all night to be close to Joseph. Though she and Charles now knew the whole story about Rensler, why he was here, and what he planned to do, she felt more helpless than before because of Joseph's worry that Rensler might discover her too. All through the long day she and Charles and Daniel waited, praying every hour as Charles continued looking at his watch.

As it neared six o'clock they were about to go to prayer again, though Thomas had reported that Rensler was to come for Joseph before that twilight hour. Mayleda was not yet on her knees, nor was Charles, when the coded knocking sounded at their door. Charles rushed to let Thomas in. The young man entered completely out of breath. "Marse Rensler an' two others, they got Joseph now. They've tooken him out that broken door to the tracks to await the Richmond train, they says. He's in chains with a sack over his face."

Mayleda pulled Daniel to herself, knowing the strength they all would need now.

"Get to the train station!" Charles told her, giving commands she knew would come, since he had already given his money to her. "Buy passage for all of us and for Joseph. Thomas and Joseph will pass as our slaves. Lord willing, we can get him now. If not, we will put ourselves on the same train to Richmond that these dregs traders will take with him."

In the time it took Mayleda to put her cloak around herself and Daniel, Charles and Thomas were already gone.

Thomas and Mr. Powell headed to the tracks at a run, Thomas in the lead. As they raced west after sundown, a slow-moving locomotive steamed east, exhaling fire and smoke like a dragon coming to eat up the town.

Mr. Powell passed Thomas by when he slowed, uncertain what to do. Cinders crunched under their feet until Powell stopped suddenly, spying a lantern set down in the dirt no more than twenty paces in front of them. "That's them!" Thomas whispered, nearly as out of breath as Powell was. There were at least four men casting giant shadows as they milled around the light. One man was in chains, his face covered. Joseph.

Another man held him, a blunt stick showing in his free hand. The last two seemed content to linger close to the cargo car on the now stopped train. The car door was open. It was all just as Thomas had feared. Rensler planned to beat Joseph soundly, then hand him off to those who still could profit from his broken body. Charles had only a gentleman's walking stick for a weapon. This the man raised when he heard the oaths being poured forth at Joseph. Thomas held him back. "Not yet, sah! If you go in too soon, they will overcome you."

"Go for the light, Thomas. Kick it out, then run to find Sister May. Get on board this train no matter what happens. Go to Richmond!"

"Mista Powell, not without you!"

"Go. Don't look back. I will find you!"

A terrible cracking sound told Charles they had waited too long. Thomas disappeared in the dark. Charles saw Joseph fall. The man above him struck him again. Then again. Suddenly the lamp was put out, surely by Thomas, who did it with the stealth of a moving shadow. The men yelled and cursed. Charles feared for Thomas, for he could not see the young man either going in or getting away free. Then Charles rushed in, striking by remembrance, trying to make contact with Joseph's torturer.

Charles hit flesh and bone, his brute force stirred by his rage. He felt his unseen victim fall. There seemed to be no others. Charles went to his knees, scrambling in the dark, feeling for Joseph who must be lying somewhere.

The ground seemed empty. The train whistle pierced the night. Metal wheels squealed as they were pulled into motion. Charles looked up. He could see the train roll.

The car with the door open moved away from him and closer and closer to the station. Charles struggled to his feet, his cane lost in the dark. He was undecided. Must he go or must he stay? Where was Joseph if not unconscious on the ground?

While he worked his mind, his feet were moving to keep up with the dregs traders' car. Suddenly Thomas's hand was on his shoulder, though he had sent the youth away. "Didn't you see, sah? The traders have him! They picked him up an' threw him in, then them two jumped in too!"

Charles gasped. "Thomas, run! We must get on this train."

———

It was still night when the car slowed and shimmered to a halt at the junction station. Mayleda had ridden through the hours with Charles by her side and Daniel on her lap. Charles was still visibly shaken by all that had taken place, and he had not been free to tell her anything in the crowded car. She tried not to fear the worst, that Joseph was either lost or dead, but this was hard to do, because she saw Charles's hands and cuffs flecked with blood.

At the first stop east of Hamberstown, the conductor had come in to say that their Negro help could not ride with them because the car was filling. The train worker relegated their "boy," Thomas, to another car, one filled with slaves. Mayleda worried about him without end. For one thing, he had no travel papers. For another, the night had turned cold, and the Negro car surely had no heat.

Now they were at the junction where different trains had to be boarded to go either north to Baltimore or south toward the capital, Washington. Mayleda feared there could be trouble if anyone questioned who they were. Even their discrepancy in dress could work against them, for Charles was in fine clothes, while she and Daniel were clothed like servants. Beside her, Charles wore his cloak in order to hide the stains on his clothes. She kept hers around herself and the child to cover their drab garments.

At the start of the journey, Mayleda had given Charles' remaining money back to him. Now he reached for his purse in the tails of his coat. "Here, I want you and the child to go on to Baltimore. The Ellises are staying at the Harrison House, and your daughter will be wanting to see you."

These facts Mayleda already did know, except that it would be Charles' plan to send her there alone, and now.

"When you get to the city, hire a driver." He pressed his purse into her hands.

"But, Charles!"

He warned her with his eyes so that she would make no outward protest. "I will write to you or use the telegraph. Now, please go. It's the Harrison House."

She could not bear the suspense. "What of Joseph?"

He lowered his face and his voice. "I don't know. I will do the last thing in my power to get him, but while I am doing that, I must know that you and Daniel are safe. I will keep Thomas with me or send him with you, whatever he desires. Now, you go to the Ellises and to your little girl."

The train was idle, but there was much commotion outside. "Come. I'll take you to the Baltimore tracks."

He looked so anguished that she decided she would not worry him more. "I can find my own way." Their eyes met, full of fear and sadness but of fierce affection too. "Charles, the most important thing is to get to Joseph." He took her hand and kissed it suddenly. She brushed the straight hair from his forehead. "You be careful."

"Dear May, you must be careful too!"

She smiled, though she was wholly uncertain. "Of course."

Frozen to the bone, Thomas climbed out of the car for colored passengers. Wrapping his arms around himself, he hurried toward the crowd disembarking from the other cars. Because of Charles Powell's size it was easy to see him, even in the station's dim light. The first thing Thomas noticed was that the man was alone. Powell was looking for him too. They met in the shadows.

Thomas had news to share. "I was in the same car as Joseph, sah! He's unconscious. An' it's freezin' in there. I took my coat an' laid it on him. I tried to take off the sack from his face the best I could."

Powell shed his cloak at once, and Thomas was quick to give assistance in case others were watching. "Here now, you wear this!"

"No, sah! Not now! I can't!"

"Then take it with you, in case they say that you must ride in a Negro car again."

"I will stay with Joseph, sah, if I can. They gwine move him now to the Richmond-bound train. I hear'd the traders say it."

"Maybe I should try to bargain for him now!"

"How would you 'xplain you' interest? Or even that you know he's there?"

"You're right! Stay with him. Take care of him, and take care of yourself."

Thomas raced off, fearful to leave Joseph on his own even a moment more.

———

Angelene and her father were still working at midnight, for every time they thought they had everything packed into their two traveling trunks, Angelene or her mother would think of something more.

"You must get some rest, Azal!" her father said while they all stood in the kitchen. "I'm sure we can do this well enough ourselves. You don't have to stay up any longer to help us."

"Who was the one to remember you had no iron for your clothes and no sack of salt?" Her mother gave Angelene a sorrowful kind of smile. "Besides, tomorrow is now today. You are about to leave me, Angel. I'm not going up to my bed now."

Angelene feared that she had lost her mother's blessing. "I'm sure I must go, Mama. Barnabas senses the same thing. *If* Mr. Powell can find Joseph—" She stopped herself. "*When* he finds him, it's going to help him if Ba and I are already in Canada starting to make a way." She touched the letter in her pocket that she always had near her.

Her mother wiped away tears. "I'm just so concerned that you'll be in this strange place, all alone if and when you do have to face the worst, child."

Angelene did not blink an eye. "I've thought about that so many times. Daddy will be staying with us till Ba and I are settled. Maybe Earl or Wesley or Jack will come too, once we get out by way of Ohio and can telegraph word to them."

"But will you stay on in Canada even if Joseph does not come, ever?" her mother asked with hesitation.

"I've decided that I'll try to stay. To honor him by helping others, just as I said before." Her voice broke then. "Mama, I do fear being alone! Almost like an unmarried widow."

Her mother hugged her hard.

"Oh, I said I wouldn't be able to bear news of his passing. Now, sometimes I pray that God would take him instead of letting him suffer slavery again."

Her mother said, "Just pray for the strength to face the troubles of each new day that comes, when it comes."

"Well, I'd like to say that we have everything now." Her father sighed, changing the subject as he put into the trunk a brown paper sack filled with nails. "And I'd like to say that we are going to leave at least *some* things behind. Ba and I will put all this in the wagon as soon as it is light. I was inside his house tonight, and that man has a trunk too, and a box with all of Joseph's medical journals that survived in it."

Her mother turned to reach for a soft package wrapped in old calico that she had laid upon the table. "This is for you and for Joseph, dear. If you want to, you can open it now. It is my gift to show you that I will pray and believe that Joseph will come to you, and soon, to be your husband."

There was a lump in Angelene's throat as she unwrapped the parcel. "One of your signal quilts! Oh, Mama!"

"It's the first one your papa and I ever used for Oak Glen's Underground Railroad station. The bright flying geese pointed the way to freedom, giving folks hope of new homes in Canada. I never thought when I was sewing this that I'd be sending my own little girl that way."

"Our girl!" Her father gathered both women into his arms.

"Mama, Joseph and I can wait to marry. Daddy can come back for you and bring you to Canada for our wedding day."

"No, Angel. I saw what your father packed with his things. His pastor's leather book. He'll officiate your wedding, and then he'll come back to tell me all about it. And I will cry my eyes out then, just as I would if I was there."

"Are you now ready for tomorrow, Angel?" her father asked.

Angelene lifted her trunk's lid one more time to hide away the treasured quilt. "No! And yes!" She was trying to be brave.

"Then go up one more time to that bedroom of yours. Say your prayers and get some sleep." He smiled and held her mother's hand while both of them cried.

In the throbbing darkness of the moving train, Joseph felt someone touch his face. He knew that blood soaked the burlap sack still so close to his mouth and nose, though some attempt had been made to tear the fabric to let him breathe.

He tried to move, but in vain. He had an awful sense that the skin on his lips would peel away if he lifted his head or spoke through his dry mouth, which was pressed to the floor. The tender presence he felt seemed never far from him. When he took to shivering uncontrollably while lying helpless on his belly, the presence came and laid a cloak upon him. He could smell the wool and feel the warmth soak his neck and shoulders like a balm.

Even when the car floor no longer rumbled, Joseph still lay sprawled, too exhausted to move. Yet he was fully awake and listening, though a terrible ringing filled his ears. He knew he had survived powerful, repeated blows to his head. He knew he was a doctor, but he could not heal himself. He remembered faith in God. Because of the caring presence with him, he felt close to God, despite his misery.

Joseph could picture what had happened to him before he was put to the trains, though his memory seemed like sand, readily sifting away. When he was still chained in the cell, Rensler had taken only fifty dollars from the dregs traders who agreed to move Joseph down to Richmond and re-sell him there. This terrified Joseph, for he knew that Rensler had paid much to Pearson for his remanding. He feared what would make the greedy and merciless man willing to sell him for so very little.

Now he knew. Dazed and beaten as he was, he might not be worth even fifty dollars in the southern slave market. Rensler knew well that to let him live as a slave would be worse for Joseph than killing him straight out.

After the exchange of money, the cell door had been opened and Joseph had been helpless to move because he was chained to the door. They put a sack on his head before they loosed the cuffs. He was driven outside then, stumbling and blind. They led him a long way on foot. Then they struck him with some hard object until pain meant nothing to him. It all made him despair, for he knew he was a prisoner of the South unless he died soon.

Suddenly the presence with him had the face of Thomas, looking straight at him while the young man was bent close to the floor. Joseph blinked his one working eye. It could not be so, but as hard as he strained to reach reality, he stayed trapped in this place of illusion, for the face of Thomas would not go away.

While staring at it like a beacon in the night, Joseph felt himself being touched again. This time his ears and brain seemed absolutely broken, for he heard words but could not understand them. The face of Thomas moved. The precious cloak was taken off. Joseph knew then that he had been loaded into the train without his coat or vest or shirt. Strange voices came over him anew. The scar on his back was being traced as he felt the cold fingers.

He thought for a moment that he might be dreaming in his mother's language, Gullah. But this coldness and those touching him were real, as was the one word that he heard repeated time and time again. "*Bakongo. Bakongo.*"

Then he watched the face of Thomas speak. "I don't know what the brand mark means, and he's too sick to tell us. Mebbe his people were Bakongo. I don't know."

Thomas's lips stopped moving then, but English now came from other mouths Joseph did not see. As words were spoken, one or many persons traced the scar of the cross and circle burned into his back. "Day," they said. "Night. Death. Life. Evil. Good. The ways of our fathers are written on him."

After this interlude of English, all became as dialect once more. But now Joseph realized what was happening, for he could still dimly see movement from his weary right eye. Two or three bony-fingered old men were crouched over him. They had seen the mark while he lay almost naked, and they believed it was a sign that he was one who honored their own ancient African beliefs. Joseph longed to speak. He longed to call out to see if Thomas was really there.

Suddenly the world changed. The dimness of the car became light. The Africans speaking among themselves grew silent, then scattered. White men climbed aboard. The face of Thomas went away.

Rough hands tore Joseph from the floor. His whole body throbbed.

As they moved him forward, he vomited out two loose teeth and blood. He was sworn at for the mess he made. Slapped. Then carried more. He felt his head as one huge, frail bubble ready to explode. When it did, he fainted.

———

Charles was out of the passenger car the moment the train stopped in Richmond. Pushing his way with no refinement, he freed himself to get down the steps and back to other cars in the mild morning weather. Immediately he beheld the Negroes being unloaded. Thomas was there to meet him cautiously. The young man was dazed, and his mouth was gaping. "It's a wonder that he still breathes!" Thomas said after Charles pulled him aside. He shivered violently.

"It's a wonder you're still breathing. Where's the cloak I gave you?"

His terrible answer came as Charles looked toward the tracks just in time to see two white traders dragging Joseph by the arms to the railcar's edge. They unloaded him like a large, unwieldy sack of rice, wrapped in Charles' garment. It did not bother them to lay him on the bare ground, the cloak draped over him. Had Charles not known this was Joseph, he would not have recognized his friend. His face was distorted like a warty, rotting gourd stained black, brown, and red.

Charles could see only one of Joseph's eyes moving rapidly in fear as he was put on his back and left helpless. Joseph's other eye was lost in the pussy swelling that covered more than half of his face. "What shall I do?" Charles cried, looking askance at Thomas, only partially prepared to be on a southern street again, playing out the role of master and slave once more.

Thomas adjusted Charles' coat. He straightened his high hat. "You must offer to buy him," Thomas said glumly as he came close. "But you best be prepared to say why you want a dyin' Negro."

Charles shuddered at the youth's directness. He backed closer to the stores that lined the railroad street. "And just what am I going to say?" he mourned.

Suddenly Thomas was not paying attention to him at all. "Please, Marse! Buy an apple for you' Thomas!" It was as though the young man had instantly lost his mind. Yet out of caution, Charles followed him along the curb to where a thin colored woman about Thomas's age had apples for sale in many different baskets. The Negress had been watching them. "An apple, please, sah! I been good this whole journey!"

Charles paid the woman with a coin he had in his pocket. She curt-seyed, never looking at Charles' face. Thomas continued on with his strange behavior, going back behind the young woman's high stand of shelves. He crouched against the wall while taking his first bite.

"What are you doing?" Charles asked.

"You gwine need to take off that hat, sah, an' take off that city coat, I reckon, if you gwine buy Joseph without stirrin' up a fuss. That's why I come back here. I think the gal can be trusted. Take off you' things, sah, while nobody's lookin' this way."

The apple seller, small and as brown as Thomas, watched them while keeping her eye on the street as well. Charles did as he was told, for he had no ideas that were better than Thomas's.

"Take off you' cravat too! Undo you' cuffs an' roll you' sleeves so's to hide those blood marks! Now I think you ready to go out there lookin' like a farmer eager to buy hisself a bargain brute for to do his haulin'. Tell the traders you want one half-blind an' dim-witted so's that the nigger don't run off like you' last one did."

Charles felt frozen. Nevertheless, he started walking. It was his only opportunity to save Joseph, if his friend could live. Thomas and the copper brown maiden both watched him go.

When Thomas stopped looking at Mr. Powell crossing the street, he saw the young lady eye him.

"What are you doing?" she asked, looking him over from head to toe as he leaned against a store's brick wall. He had Mr. Powell's hat and coat in his arms.

"Tryin' to help that wounded brother 'cross the way," he admitted, though there might be danger in doing so.

"You're not helping him, not if you stand there with the label from that white man's coat flapping in the breeze for all to see."

Thomas looked down to see the small piece of white fabric with words sewn against the lining. "What's it matter?" he braved.

"It matters 'cause it says to all who can read that that coat was made in Philadelphia." She showed a wiry smile. "And that includes me."

Not wanting to seem too much like he was thankful for her counsel, he slowly folded the coat another way. His eyes went back to what was happening across the street, and the girl watched too.

"Your white friend's planning to buy from Duncan and Cain?" Her lips pursed to show her worry. "Is that a blood brother of yours? Or does that white man have some other reason?"

"How can you dare have so many questions?" Thomas said, never moving his vision from the spot where traders had gathered their small sorry band of Negroes unloaded from the train. "An' why do you call that white man my friend?"

"How do you dare use my stand to hide behind while that man's putting himself in danger? He sure ain't your master, so he must be your friend, for men from Philadelphia don't own slaves."

"You think a coat's enough to say he's from Philadelphia?"

"No," she said, haughty as a springtime bird. "That coat, plus how he was following *your* commands, just like a fish on a stick. And also how you both got off of cars that have just come down from Washington and points north."

"You think you're smart, don't you, girl?"

"So is your friend a good abolitionist?"

Thomas closed his mouth, wise enough to know that loyalty did not always stick with color.

She squinted toward Powell as though thinking hard. "Is he a Quaker Friend or just a God-fearing man?"

"Why do you ask so many questions?" he said again, inwardly marveling at her refined use of English.

"Because I've been to Philadelphia. That's where I learned to read and write, in the Friends' school. But I don't remember him."

Thomas stared at her. "You slave or free?"

"Slave," she said mildly. "I live on the property of a spinster lady, Madam Esther Lerew. About ten years ago she inherited her daddy's colored people, but not his love of slavery. Since that time, she's been doing her own kind of crusade to have us work for wages. And to get our education. Even a few of us she let go north. I could have stayed in the North, but I came home because I didn't like being in that city alone, able to be no more than somebody's laundress or maid."

He found himself reaching for his cap. "You right 'bout Philadelphia bein' no colored man's heaven. Or woman's, neither."

She smiled, but then grew worried again. "Whatever that man's reason for trying to buy the injured Negro, he needs you to do more than just stand here and spy."

Thomas felt careless and cowardly, for he saw that this was so. Across the way Powell was bending over Joseph, who was slouched against a stake driven into the ground to hold a sign about the sale of slaves going on there. Immediately Thomas ran to Powell's side.

"Thomas, you've got to help me!"

It was worrisome to see Powell trembling so in public.

"I bought him! Now I have no idea how to get him to his feet."

Thomas thought he would be sick, looking at the raw flesh on Joseph's face. "Looks like he got hisself a purty strong back, Marse," he forced himself to say it loudly, knowing that there were traders near. Joseph did not even know they were there. Thomas willed himself to go near the injured brother. He put his arms under Joseph's arms to try to raise him up, though he was smaller than the older man. When he saw that Joseph did have some alertness, he tugged at him again. "Uncle!" he called sharply. "My name's Tom. I been told to help you 'long."

Joseph's one eye opened. "Tho-mas?" he panted, his lips split in several places. Thomas quaked to be holding all of Joseph's weight, but somehow the sight of Joseph this way welled the strength within him. "Marse Powell done bought you, so you comin' along with him."

Thomas then determined to move Joseph in the direction of the apple-seller's stall. Amazingly, while some white persons watched and some Negroes too, he managed to get Joseph all the way across the street. But then Joseph's knees buckled, and Thomas, exhausted, let him fall into a heap at the curb near the baskets filled with apples. Seemingly unaware of what any passersby would think, Charles ran and dropped down to cradle Joseph's head to keep it away from the bricks and out of the stinking mud of the gutter.

"Do you need help for him, sir?" said the girl from the apple stand.

Charles covered more of Joseph's piteous, convulsing body with his cloak.

"I can get a wagon for you, sir. You could doctor him at my mistress's plantation, just out of town."

Thomas stared at him as the girl did speak. "You can trust her, sah," he whispered. "She's been to Philadelphia."

Charles looked dubious, yet responded, "I don't want him to die in the street."

When the Richmond gal picked up her skirts and ran off, Thomas thought he heard and saw the flutter of angel wings. There was no time or energy to speak of the miracle then, for it took only minutes for the woman to return in a wagon brought around by a Negro driver as young as she was but as dark as Joseph.

"This is David," she said as the man hopped down to help Mr. Powell and Thomas load Joseph in among the many small sacks of cornmeal.

They moved with haste through the town, Thomas in the wagon bed beside Joseph's lifeless form and the girl across from him on the other side of Joseph's body.

"Are you Quaker?" the young woman pressed as they flew along a road outside the edge of the city.

"I'm Thomas!" he answered dumbly, nervous for Joseph but for himself too, being so close to such a pretty, smart woman.

She looked at Joseph sadly. "Are you two free or slave?"

He didn't know if he should answer.

She twisted her long fingers into the apron that covered her lap. "You don't have to be afraid, Thomas. Madam Lerew will help you. I know she will. Though she owns slaves, she thinks the wrath of God will soon come on the South because of the sin of slavery."

Thomas turned his head to account for his surroundings. David was driving them through an open pair of iron gates and then on the tree-lined lane within. Thomas caught sight of the river off to his left, down beyond fields, then across dry winter lawns as they came closer to the big house. "So what's your name?" He finally got courage to ask because their ride was ending.

"Lydia." Her eyes were lovely enough to be scary, especially now as they were shining with tears on Joseph's behalf.

"He's been a doctor for our people in the North and a teacher!" Thomas said, letting some of his own grief show. "He wa' beaten by a marse who claimed him as him own. Mista Powell an' I done been on the road for days tryin' to buy him back to safety." He was ashamed of how his speech sounded, but she didn't seem to care. There was no time to say more, for they were stopped by then, and David and Mr. Powell were already out of the driver's bench.

They carried Joseph up the long walk to the mansion's rear door, with Lydia leading the way. They laid him on the back porch while the girl went inside to find the woman who owned her. Thomas fought the notion to run, his fear of masters and recapture being so strong. Yet he stayed, in part because of Lydia's quiet kind of confidence.

Within minutes Charles was let in to have an audience with the thin, somber woman of means who was dressed in black. Though fearful of her reaction, Charles found himself explaining that he needed a doctor for a black man, and that right away. The woman, who introduced herself to him as Madam Lerew, replied sorrily that this was impossible, yet she herself pledged to do everything she could for the wounded man. Charles took note that she did not call Joseph a "boy" or even a "Negro." However, instead of letting them stay in her house, she sent Lydia ahead to open a sturdy cottage at the top of her slave street, which had once been used by the white overseer her father paid.

Because of Joseph's condition, Charles dared to go a secont time to the mansion to ask if he could have transportation back into Richmond to use the telegraph in order to summons a Quaker doctor, Leon Ellis, who was waiting in Baltimore for word from them.

Immediately the solemn woman became as animated as a child. She knew Dr. Ellis, she said. She had met him at a meeting of Friends in Philadelphia the summer before her decision to send her personal maidservant, Lydia, north to attend school. At once she sent David back to town with the message Charles hastily scrawled on paper to be sent by way of the magic wire. Charles asked only that Dr. Ellis come at once to Lerew Plantation outside Richmond to meet with a Quaker lady. He did not say why.

That being done, Charles went back to stay by Joseph's side. He knew little about nursing and less about prayer, it seemed, with his friend so close to death. Yet he cared for him and prayed for him the best he could for the next two days and nights, without sleeping himself.

In all this time, Joseph did not open his eyes or say a word. In the nights, however, when the man's fever raged, he would writhe and cry out against his pain, leaving Charles helpless to comfort him.

When Charles despaired at having no strength left to go on, the Ellises and Mayleda arrived, along with Judith and Daniel. They found their way to Madam Lerew's plantation under the guise of being Friends from Maryland coming down to visit the Quakers of Richmond. Even the children wore the plain garb of young Friends. From the first hour of their arrival, Dr. Ellis took over, doing what Charles could not do. Charles watched for a time, but then he staggered from the room that smelled of death. Only reluctantly did he take comfort in Mayleda's arms and in her kisses on his face. Joseph loved Angelene Brown, just as Charles loved Mayleda. Could he allow himself the happiness of love if his friend died? The haunting question made him pull away from his own beloved. "Not now, May. Perhaps not ever, if Joseph does not get well."

"You must not blame yourself! You did everything you could."

"No! I cowered in the shadows, considering my own safety too much."

"He is still alive because of you and Thomas. I urge you! Now that we all can take turns watching over him, you must have rest. Come out here to the front room. Bedsteads have been set up for you and Thomas near the windows. Lie down and sleep, or soon you will be ill."

All her coaxing only convinced him to head again for Joseph's room. "I will not desert him. If he can awake from this, then I will be there to meet him."

CHAPTER 36

JOSEPH HAD MANY KINDS OF DREAMS. Grotesque. Bewildering. But now he had one that was more real than all the rest. He dreamed that Daniel came to lay his head upon his chest. Strangely he could not see the boy, but he could feel the outline of his warmth, and he could stroke the child's hair.

Time and time again he moved his hand to touch that softness, dreading the moment when the precious apparition would fade. Then, as though a heavy curtain was pulled back from his eyes, he saw the blurred faces of many friends—Mayleda, Charles, the Ellises, Thomas. All around him they hovered, like welcoming saints.

He heard Dr. Ellis's voice. "Joseph, can thee hear?"

He knew his name, but he could not answer. Then he saw Daniel raising before him, closer than the others. He knew he was not dreaming now, for he felt the weight of the child leave his chest. This name he could speak. "Dan-iel!"

The boy put a kiss upon his cheek. It burned like fire. Tears drowned Joseph's limited view. Someone called the child away. Joseph grasped cold space where Daniel had been. A chill crept over him like a winter vine. He felt bound and unable to keep himself seeing. Then all was dark and lonely again.

When Joseph's vision opened next, he saw only two white faces. He was terrified, for he instantly remembered the stinking, suffocating sack Rensler had pulled over his head. He groaned as he felt the blows again. He tried to roll from the danger. Then he realized that the hands that caught him belonged to Charles.

As in his other time of wakefulness, Dr. Ellis had words for him. "I will be as gentle as I can. I must see thy wounds."

Each word falling on his ears was like a seed instantly growing and multiplying his understanding of things both past and present.

"Be at peace, brother." This was Dr. Ellis again. "God is doing wonders on thy behalf."

Joseph endured the pain of being touched around his jaw, his ears, his nose, his eyes. Then he slept again.

Joseph knew that time had passed when he opened his eyes, yet his two friends were still there. He could not know if unconsciousness had walled him off from them for a moment or an hour or even a day, but now he could consider such questions clearly. Unlike his healing mind, however, his vision stayed fogged.

"Thee is doing better." Dr. Ellis's kind, nurturing voice came once more. "Thy periods of consciousness are longer. There is hope for full recovery."

Pondering that message, Joseph willed his hands to rise. He found himself able to touch his aching skull. It was wrapped in bandages. He touched his face and found his left eye covered. Along with Dr. Ellis's evaluation, Joseph's own exploration gave him hope. Perhaps he could not see well because one of his eyes was hidden. He started to uncover it but felt Charles take his hand.

"No, friend, not now."

He was aware of the moment when Dr. Ellis left him and when Charles stayed, seating himself in a chair pulled close to the bed. Joseph saw dark circles under Charles' hollow eyes. He closed his own eye to rest for only a moment, he thought. When he looked at Charles again, the other man's smile was like liquid warmth flowing to all parts of Joseph's still throbbing face.

Charles touched his hand, nearly like a handshake. He held his fingers, squeezing them intensely. "You were dreaming just now. Do you remember?"

Joseph did remember then, so clearly that Charles seemed a natural part of it. There had been a church, unfinished. And then marvelous visions of Angelene standing in it. He tried to speak this all out to Charles so that the wonder of it would not be lost. But in the end he was uncertain whether or not he was making any sense. Even whether he was speaking aloud or only in his mind. Then another message pressured him, nearly like his desire to share his dream. "I am thirsty."

Charles must have understood, for he brought him water. "Here. See if you can take a sip."

Charles was like a huge but tender nursemaid, cautiously putting his arm behind Joseph's head. The movement was dizzying, but Joseph chose to welcome it as progress. He did drink, but at the terrible expense of swallowing the horrid tastes in his mouth. He put a finger between his lips and found two molars on his right side gone. He looked at Charles with desperation.

"Yes, you lost a few teeth. Dr. Ellis says it is divine providence that your jaw was not shattered."

The news discouraged him, though Charles had meant it for good.

"Do you remember that you took a drink this morning?"

Joseph surprised himself almost to terror by hearing himself say, "No." It frightened him more that he could not know what had happened even hours ago.

"Don't worry! Dr. Ellis says that little by little your memory and your strength will come back to you."

Joseph furrowed his wrapped brows, sending intense pain shooting through his head. His tongue went to the right side of his mouth again. Charles still hovering over him, seeming to be in as much distress as he.

"I was there from the first moment Rensler started clubbing you! I waited too long! You would not be suffering so if I had come in sooner!"

Joseph remembered his betrayers. Yet until this moment he had not considered that Charles could have been there too. He had not known how he had escaped his enemies, but now he knew. Charles and Thomas had worked together to rescue him. "Thank . . . you." He reached for his mourning friend.

"Don't thank me! I am part of the reason you suffer!"

"No."

Joseph saw Charles sit down once more. He extended his hand far enough to put his fingers against Charles' sleeve and wondered at the man's weary and pensive expression. After a long time, Joseph tried to speak. "Where are we?"

Charles looked up, but he did not answer, making Joseph fear that he had not formed actual words.

But then Charles said, "Somewhere safe. As you get better I will tell you more. I think that is enough for now."

The door to the dark room opened. Dr. Ellis came in. Joseph watched Charles smile. "He's speaking quite a bit, sir. He told me about a wonderful dream he had of seeing an unfinished church and Miss Angelene Brown standing in it."

Dr. Ellis leaned over Joseph, examining him closely with a physician's knowing eyes, which, in that moment, Joseph longed to have again. The Friend then turned to Charles. "Doctor's orders for you, Friend Powell: Get some rest! Thee has kept this vigil for so many days. Thy brother in the faith *is* out of danger now." Dr. Ellis looked back to Joseph as Charles was leaving. "That man saved thy life."

Joseph reached for Charles, but he was gone. Joseph now could see the door, and he thought he saw Daniel peeking in. "Is that Daniel?" Joseph asked, thinking of their parting at the auction house and hardly having hope to believe it was the boy.

"It is! We all are here—Daniel, Sister Ruskin, even her daughter, Judith, Brother Thomas, Mr. Powell, and Sister Ellis."

"How?" Joseph whispered.

"We were all in Baltimore, praying and searching the papers to find the auction house to which thee had being taken. After much searching, Brother Powell finally gained custody of thee in Richmond. He sent a telegraph to us, and we came by train to be here."

"We are in Richmond? In Virginia? There is danger!"

"Yes, that is true, but lie still, Brother Whitsun. We are at the home of an antislavery sympathizer. A southern Quaker lady, Sister Lerew. She still holds her slaves legally, but has made changes so they can obtain education and work for wages. A few years back she sent one of her house girls named Lydia to Philadelphia for learning. I knew that girl from our school."

Joseph felt his whole body stiffen with fear. "Rensler? Where is Theodore Rensler?"

Dr. Ellis touched him as though to keep him still. "No one has come searching here."

Joseph sighed, but tension still had his body wrapped in pain. Friend Ellis, however, did not seem anxious. Joseph tried to feel the same. "I would like to see Daniel."

"Of course. Each day as thee grows better, thee will see him more. But first, there are things we must talk about."

"What?" Joseph worked hard to keep thinking despite his aching head. The doctor sat down where Charles had been sitting. "I'm not sure this is yet the time."

"Try." Painstakingly Joseph added, "Worry is harder than truth."

Dr. Ellis raised up out of his chair to honor God. "The Lord hath removed thee from death's door *and* hath restored what thy enemies tried their best to take from thee—thy intellect!"

Joseph covered his face with his hands, for he understood the truth spoke so eloquently in this unrehearsed benediction. The intensity of their conversation made him weary, but he tried to hide it because he wanted to know what the man had to say.

Dr. Ellis faced him somberly. "There is infection in thy left eye that has not diminished, even with treatment and prayer. It may mean the end of hope that thee will ever see from it again."

Joseph blinked, concentrating on the fact that he had only one eye to see by now, and even this was blurred. "I can remove the tissue of the injured eye, or we can wait longer. My concern is that raging infection might claim thy life."

Joseph thought about the need to get to Canada and to support himself there as a teacher or a doctor. His eyesight would be needed for either occupation. "Don't do surgery, not yet," he pleaded weakly. "God saved my life. Perhaps He will save my vision also." He changed the subject. "How is Daniel?"

Dr. Ellis patted his shoulder. "Fine! Most days he's off with Thomas, who spends much of his time working with a man named David, the smithy. Thomas came down to feign the role of Friend Powell's manservant so that Powell would have a more convincing presence among real slaveowners."

Joseph's injured mouth was bothering him greatly, but still he spoke. "I thought so. Thank Thomas for me! I know the dangers!"

"Yes, thee does! I will thank him on thy behalf."

Joseph thought on Angelene. His longing for her was like a physical pain. Dr. Ellis even interpreted the agony of his thinking in that way.

"Son. Where are you hurting now?"

Joseph held his breath, for he knew then that he had moaned aloud. He pressed a hand over his heart. There was too much sorrow for words. Then a sweet, strong voice called in to him. "Dr. Joseph, please don't sleep again. It's me, Daniel!"

Joseph drew a breath and smiled. "Come in, my son!"

Angelene had expected Canada to be snow covered, wild, and beautiful, wholly different from what she saw now in the mud-filled town of Sandwich, directly across the river from the American city called Detroit.

While the weather proved unpleasant, she still had the joy of having her oldest brother, Earl, in Canada with them. Having arranged a leave from his work with the railroads in Toledo, Earl had helped Angelene, her father, and Barnabas secure passage on a steamer to cross the huge sealike lake called Erie. All of Angelene's learning from books could not have prepared her for the sights she encountered on her travels. With regret and sadness she thought often of Dumond. What he had told her was true. The world indeed was much bigger than Oak Glen.

While colored individuals were fleeing from the United States of America into many lakeside towns in Canada West, and though many of these villages were closer to Toledo than Sandwich, Angelene and Barnabas had held to their resolve to settle in this town where Joseph could most easily find them. Here the *Voice of The Fugitive* was prepared and printed weekly by two renowned American leaders of color, Henry Bibb, who had escaped slavery in Kentucky, and his second wife, Mary, a freeborn Quaker native of Rhode Island.

Having been in this cold, bleak place for almost a week, Angelene had already published one report about their safe arrival in the *Voice*, which hopefully her mother and the folks of the church would be reading soon. Now setting out on Monday morning, leaving her father, Earl, and Ba behind in one of the two small rooms they rented, Angelene went back to the newspaper office a second time and with a different purpose.

As before, the place smelled warmly of ink and paper when she entered. Sister Bibb herself was at the desk. When the woman looked up, Angelene tentatively handed her a folded letter.

"I remember you came last week," the newspaperwoman said.

"Yes, with a letter to publish for our family back home. But now here is another." She felt her face grow hot as the older woman read her written words aloud.

" 'J. W.: You have friends waiting for you in Sandwich. God speed your way. A. Brown.' " The woman nodded, seemingly more interested in the writing than in the message. "Did you prepare this yourself, Miss Brown?"

"Yes, ma'am."

"Your skills are excellent."

"I was not a slave, ma'am, but a teacher in Pennsylvania."

Sister Bibb's smile turned motherly. "But your J. W. is a slave?"

"Oh no, ma'am! He is a doctor! Well, a practitioner in America, for prejudice will not allow him to be more." Angelene felt flustered, for surely this other woman was reading between the lines about her private love.

"I am glad to meet you, Miss Brown. You are here alone waiting for Mr. J. W.?"

"No, ma'am. My father made the trip with me, and my brother and an old friend, Mr. Croghan. Mr. Croghan and I plan to stay."

"Would you be interested in teaching school in Sandwich?"

"Why, yes, ma'am! I would be!"

"Fine, for I am the one in charge of efforts to establish classes here."

Angelene could scarcely believe her words.

"Come back tomorrow morning, Miss Brown, and I will have time to show you the schoolroom, such as it is. We have no desks or books at present, but someday soon I hope for better."

"Yes, Mrs. Bibb! I will come back!" She curtsied, then nearly felt like a schoolgirl as she raced out of the door to go home with such wonderful news. When she got to the rooms, she found Brother Croghan grinning for reasons all his own. While she had been to the newspaper office, Barnabas and her father had taken a walk through the town. Their dialogue carried on by way of chalk and slate had gotten the attention of a well-dressed man leading a sick milk cow.

The man had stopped to look at them writing in the street, but then Barnabas had taken notice of the animal. Immediately from his experience, he knew what was wrong with her, so he wrote it on the slate. Her father then read the note to the other man, because though prosperous by Sandwich's standards, the colored Canadian was still illiterate. Now her daddy was explaining everything from his point of view while Barnabas was speaking in signs. All this time Earl was standing by the wall watching Barnabas's hands.

"The man took us to the farm," her father said.

"But, Daddy, Ba keeps saying *our* farm!" Angelene questioned.

"That's right, sister!" Earl put in. "It is your farm now. The man wants Mr. Croghan to manage the property and the crops and livestock he has on it. He says he would rather live in town."

"In exchange for Brother Croghan's work, there's a small house on the property for you to live in," her father said, now hardly containing his joy, "And there's something like a summer kitchen with living quarters in there too." Barnabas was telling her then that she would have the house.

She went up and lightly kissed Ba at once, with her father and brother watching on. The old man's pale white cheek turned as red as cherries.

"*Is there any doubt that God does want us here?*" She said and signed, for everyone.

Her father looked at her brother. "How can I be glad that you are settled so quickly? For soon I will be leaving my only daughter."

That afternoon they moved their things to the farm. In her travel trunk, Angelene had old curtains from her mother and she hung them over the farmhouse windows. She put an ordinary quilt on the bedframe that stood in the chilly, first-floor chamber. A thin but satisfactory straw-filled tick lay upon it. Angelene saved her mother's signal quilt, leaving it wrapped in calico, even after everything else had been unpacked.

Her father and brother came in to find her filling up the small set of shelves in the kitchen. "Ah, the last visage of my little girl gone. Already it seems that Earl and I have no more excuses for staying on in Sandwich. You have a house and work and good company to look after you." Her father sounded mournful, but he was smiling. She saw mistiness in his eyes.

Earl looked out through the sitting room windows, which could be seen from the kitchen. Cold rain poured down in sheets. "I think we must stay for at least a few more days to see how sister cooks and how she manages this house," Earl teased. "I, being a married man myself now, can rightly judge these things."

Angelene laughed, for it had been a long time since she'd had the odd pleasure of being tormented by any of her brothers. "I shall burn the biscuits and serve the beans hard and raw if it will make you two stay on. Perhaps I *could* gain some skill by spring with you both here to encourage me."

"I would like to see about the church here," her father said, putting all joking aside. "I want to know what kind of spiritual nurturing you and Barnabas will have." Then her father tried out the kitchen's rocking chair, painted green, that the owner of the property had left along with the many other simple furnishings. "This chair I like!"

"My! This being only Monday, you will have to stay at least a week until church comes around again!" Angelene said with joy. Just then Barnabas came through the back door without knocking. It all seemed so familiar and pleasant already. Angelene had a hard time thinking she'd only been here hours, not months or years. *"We will have company in this house for at least one week!"* she signed with enthusiasm to Ba, who had started taking off his boots inside. *"Father and brother will stay!"*

Ba stopped, grinned at her, then straightened. *"The landlord has hens too old for laying. I will make one Canada chicken sorry that the pastor decided to stay for supper."*

She had to laugh alone until she had translated his thoughts for her family. That moment she missed Joseph all the more, for now she and Ba were alone in this world of silent language. She held her composure until Earl followed Barnabas outside, an ax in his hand.

Her father rose from his chair to meet her as she ran to him in tears. "Oh, do you think Joseph is safe? Do you think he's on his way here?" She touched Joseph's letter from Philadelphia, which she had in her pocket.

"God knows, Angel."

Of course he had no more answers than she. Still, Angelene felt the strength of his faith as he held her and let her sob.

CHAPTER 37

JOSEPH HAD ENOUGH STRENGTH to put a clean dressing over his own left eye, but Charles was there to tie the bandage that held it in place. "Am I making the wrong decision to wait for this to heal?" Joseph asked mournfully, bearing his soul only to Charles, who still insisted on being his nurse day and night.

"I don't know, brother. Dr. Ellis and you are the men of medicine."

Charles' voice could be so quiet for the large man he was, and there was something intangibly precious about his frankness, like the gleaming of gold.

"We prayed that you would have your sight restored for Canada. Perhaps we have no right to question why it is not as we had hoped." There was a catch in his voice. "I thought I'd lose you to the traders, then to death. You cannot know how this galls me that you could lose your occupation by losing your sight! Do you remember what I said to you in Pennsylvania?"

"Yes, of course. That you would fight to the death to keep slavery from taking me again." The promise made Joseph shiver.

"Yet this woundedness, I cannot help you fight."

"No. But you have helped. Look how much strength I've gained. And there's no fever now. That is in answer to your prayers." There was silence before Joseph spoke again. "Now I pray I will soon be strong enough to travel."

Charles bowed his head. "I've thought much about how to get you away from Virginia. I can think of only one solution—that we travel as master and slave, for I do legally own you and Daniel." Charles' eyes filled with painful shame. "That might prove to be your best protection until you reach Canada."

"Perhaps Daniel and I need to get west on our own."

"You know how unlikely that would be for the two of you to get away free from the heart of Virginia!"

"But what of the others? They all need you too."

"The Ellises will soon go back to Baltimore, but I think that Sister Ruskin and Thomas need to stay here. No one has come searching for any of us, so I trust this is a refuge. I've been thinking that I could travel as a merchant, for that is what I am. I have been to New York before to establish accounts. I can go again, but this time from Richmond, and with you."

Joseph felt pain. "But not Daniel?"

"I'm unsure. We might be questioned about bringing a child."

"You have thought about this much!"

"I have! For I have a promise to keep, not only to you but to Angelene Brown and to her family as well."

Joseph touched his swollen face. "Perhaps it's better that she never had the opportunity to know of my feelings toward her. Perhaps the solace of writing that letter was for me. As things are now, I take comfort that it was never sent."

"But it was! I'm certain that she does have your letter."

"You mailed it? From Philadelphia, in all that chaos?"

"No. I gave it to Dr. Ellis, and he said he would give it to Oliver Catos to deliver in person when he felt it safe."

"But I was captured, not freed to get to the North!"

"Forgive me! I did not think that that would have anything to do with your love, or Angelene's." Charles was surely distressed. "Brother? You regret that I forwarded your words? Oh, I am sorry!"

Joseph's head was splitting. "Does Angelene know I'm in the South? Does she know what's happened to me?"

"She knows that you and Daniel and Mayleda were taken by Pudget and Dawes. The Vigilance Committee was giving information to all the colored churches and collecting funds to aid us."

"May God have mercy!" Joseph held his head. "All this time I was being comforted by the thought that she *did not* know!"

"I encourage you, be at peace concerning Miss Brown's feelings for you. Let them be a comfort, not a trial."

Charles' compassion was like a sword cutting a path so that Joseph could proceed. It hurt to speak, yet he felt he must not delay. "If you had not rescued me, I would have died somewhere between the trains and the rice fields of Louisiana. Think of Angelene knowing of my love and the anguish that would have caused her to wait and never hear from me again. That may still prove true!"

"No! Your life has been preserved. She will hear from you!"

Joseph then became extremely concerned about his weary friend, for Charles sat down and put his hands against his brow. Joseph extended his hand to him. "Please know I am grateful, Charles. You have sacrificed everything for me, for Daniel, and for Mayleda. Dr. Ellis told me how you mortgaged your property and how you dared to pose as a buyer to free us. Now you need to take care of yourself, to keep up your own strength. I did not mean to discourage you."

Charles gave a tired but gentle laugh. "Are these doctor's orders from you? Well, then, I will heed them, but only if you promise not to be discouraged either. You are going to get to Canada, and we will see our Covenant Day come. Yes? Brother Whitsun, will you agree?"

Joseph closed his eyes with a sweet yet sad feeling. "Friend Powell, I will try not to give up hope."

Charles stepped out of Joseph's room to find the house oddly silent. Under each of the two front windows a bed had been put up, one for Thomas and one for himself. Both were neatly made and empty. Mayleda had her nighttime quarters with the children in the loft, but there seemed to be no one up there either, though it was after supper, and Daniel and Judith should have been in bed.

With concern Charles opened the front door and went out to the porch. It was deserted too, but across the way the small shop where David and Thomas often worked was brightly lit. Drawn there, Charles found everyone but Judith inside. At once he saw Mayleda's tears. "What is going on?" he demanded out of concern for her.

"Something you will disapprove of, I am sure," she said.

"What?" He was protective of her and went to her side.

Even though Thomas was able to sound out simple words in his reading, as Lydia had become his daily teacher, the young man handed a newspaper to him. "This was just brought up for Mistress Lerew, sah, from off a riverboat comin' in from the coast."

"A paper from Baltimore?" Charles twisted it in his hand so that he could read the largest print. But Thomas reached and turned it another way. "Lydia done found this report when she wa' takin' the paper up to the big house."

Charles looked to Mayleda. "What's this about?"

"See for yourself. There's a report of a Virginia coal baron named Venor who confronted Pearson at his auction house after receiving reports for the exorbitant price you paid for Daniel. The man's convinced from everyone's description of the child that you have his slave, and he's looking for you. There's also a description of you as an abolitionist sympathizer."

"That news reached the Baltimore presses?"

"Yes, because you claimed your residence in Baltimore. Venor and others who want to see you captured paid agents to find you in that city. This article says that they found your room deserted."

"I had to tell Pearson my residence in order to be registered by him as a buyer," Charles mourned.

"We know. That is how they got information on your bank account in that city too. Attorneys have seized it, Charles, until it can be proved in court whether or not you purchased us with the intent to free us."

"May, I would be found guilty on those charges."

She laid her head to his arm. "All you had left from Mr. Peabody's store is gone!"

By now Charles was reading some of the terrible words himself. "It says that Venor has printed up one thousand handbills and one thousand placards with descriptions of both the child and myself. That he is offering a grand reward for anyone who will turn us in to either local or federal officers. Why would he do that for one little boy?"

"He ain't all that interestin' in Daniel, for true!" Thomas said bleakly. "What he wants is you, sah. What he wants is slaveholders in all of Virginny an' Mary-land to rise up 'gainst all abolitionists so they can keep to they own ways down here."

Mayleda eyed Charles. "There is another article immediately following this one." She took the paper and started reading. " 'Along the track in Hamberstown, a cowardly nighttime attack was made upon a visiting slaveowner as he acted within his rights to discipline his own servant.' "

"It was not discipline!" Charles cried.

She wiped her eyes. " 'The vicious assault drove the slavemaster from South Carolina to the edge of death, where he lingers still. Investigations are being made that could connect this act of lawlessness with the great abolition conspiracy being carried out by Charles Powell, who falsely introduced himself to this town as a slave-holding merchant.' "

"Read no more!"

Thomas faced him. "They lookin' for you from Ohio to the coastlines, an' for Daniel too. That's why we done what we done."

"What did you do?"

Slowly Thomas extended his left hand while unwrapping the wet cloth he had around it. There was a fresh ugly burn, a brand mark more than half the size of his palm. Three straight lines came together in raw pink flesh to form a rigid looking "P."

"What is that! God help us!"

Thomas then exposed Daniel's left hand too, which had been bandaged in like matter. "The *V* on his hand was for Venor, sah. We changed it into a sideways lookin' *P* for Powell an' then made mine to match his, so we bear the same proof of bein' yours."

"I am not your master!" Charles made a fist in fury. "Why in heaven's name did you do this!"

" 'Cause the boy needed his brandin' changed in case somebody comes here lookin' for him. An' 'cause mine might prove that we did not change it. Since you hold the bill of sale, even sister here agreed to my idea. I had David do it on my shoulder too, an' to Daniel's. If Joseph weren't so low, we would've put the iron to him too."

Charles grabbed Mayleda's hand in a panic and opened it.

"She would have done it, sah, but we didn't think nobody would look upon her as Negro if she stays with you. It would be best, I think, if you destroyed the bill of sale on her, sah."

"Thomas! This is devil's work! To brand a child!"

"You are stormin' the gates of hell, sah, to keep us all out of the devil's hold. I'd *cut* off my hand—Daniel's too—if that would guarantee our freedom. Most colored folks, I think, would say the same."

Lydia nodded, her eyes wide and sad. Then she spoke to Charles for the first time that night. "Mr. Powell? Thomas says you let Negroes have their own say."

Her words were troubling. "Miss, say what you want. We all are equals here. Has that not been made clear?"

She blinked as though hardly ready to believe him. "Thomas did what he did to guard the child. And he did what he did without your permission because he trusted that you would think he had the freedom to act for himself and for the boy, to protect him."

Mayleda agreed. "They know the risks so much better than we do. They know what price they'll pay if they are found out."

"But I am thought to be a criminal, and you have nearly burned my name upon your flesh!" he said to Thomas. "What good is that?"

"It's still better than Daniel havin' his old brand marks, sah. The problem now is that it's gwine take time for them to heal 'fore they look like we done had them for a long, long time."

Charles shuddered. How could he hope to move anyone out of the South with more than two thousand published reports against him? He thought of the confidence he had just tried to instill in Joseph. Now his whole plan might soon amount to failure, and failure could mean slavery or even death for these innocent people.

Thomas seemed keen to his despair. "We all agree, sah, the capital city of Virginny's prob'bly the last place any lawman's gwine look for two abolitionists an' some runaways."

"I think Madam Lerew must see this news," Charles said. "She must decide whether or not she wants to risk hiding us now." He felt overwhelmed and looked to Mayleda. "Joseph is alone. Someone needs to go up to stay with him."

"Judith is there too, asleep in the loft," Mayleda said, her voice and her eyes heavy with care. "I'll go to the house. You speak with Sister Lerew."

"Do you want company, Mista Powell?" Thomas asked him.

Charles did not refuse it. Mayleda took Daniel, while David stayed in the shop to melt down the crude branding tool.

"I been thinkin', sah," Thomas ventured once they were out in the dark. "A Negro can get his name changed in a minute, dependin' on his marse's will. But can a marse do that? I mean, change his name? If so, then I can see that mebbe you shouldn't have to be Mista Powell *of Virginny*. That could help us some."

"It's odd you should say that." They stopped under large bare trees. "Powell is not my real name, but because of a prejudice in this nation even older than that of white against black, I was not allowed to keep my father's name after he died."

"Shoo, sah, that's too much for me to understand."

"My father, Patrick Parnell, was an Irish sailor. Somewhere in a church along the coast I'm sure my name is recorded Charles *Parnell* because of my infant baptism there. I remember being called by that name, for after my mother died I lived with my father, most times at sea. Then when I was six, my father died. Sailors brought me ashore to some of my mother's relatives in Philadelphia. Even after his death, they abhorred his nationality, for they were all of British descent. They took away his name from me and called me by their own, which is Powell. But soon after that, they locked me out to live in the streets, not wanting me at all."

"Sah, I never took you for bein' a man of such great sorrows. You said you wa' without a family, but this is a heap more than that."

Charles had to smile. "That was all long ago. When I lived with Brother Peabody, I thought about asking him if I could change my name back to Parnell. Then he passed away suddenly, and I found he had named me, Charles *Powell*, his sole beneficiary, so I kept my peace."

"Parnell." Thomas pondered it and looked at his injured hand, though it still was wrapped. "That sounds like it starts with the same letter."

"It does." Charles closed his eyes, to think that he knew what Thomas was thinking. "I hate what you did tonight, but I have to say I admire your courage and your love for liberty."

"Sah, what I did, I did for Daniel, 'cause no little boy should be a slave!"

Charles felt his blood chill. "I respect that. What you have endured gives you wisdom that I cannot fathom, though God knows I try. Surely Joseph would be dead and Mayleda and Daniel lost if you had not dared to come with me."

The young man extended his burned hand. "I sure never thought I'd come South as my first decision as to what to do as a free man. You different, Mista Powell. A Negro can trust you! Or should I say, Mista *Parnell?*"

"Brother Parnell. That's what I'd like it to be." He sighed. "I am going to consider the idea. I am. When I speak with Madam Lerew, I will seek her counsel."

The handshake Charles extended was soon transformed into a fatherly embrace. "God bless you, Thomas! God protect you."

———————

Mayleda was still at the table long after midnight, sewing a shirt for Charles when he came in. The children and Thomas and Joseph were asleep. He seemed grateful that she had chosen to wait up for him. "What did Sister Lerew have to say?"

Wearily he pulled out a chair across from hers. "More than you could ever believe."

She put the needle into the fabric and stopped sewing.

"Madam Lerew is willing to let us stay. She feels strongly that no one should stand by idle when any slave is in danger of being physically abused or inhumanely treated. She knows that will be Daniel's lot if he's discovered. And she knows what dangers Thomas, Joseph, and even we face if we leave this place too soon."

"God be praised."

"What would you think of living here for at least a year?"

"A year! Why?"

"Madam Lerew told me that when her father lived he had a hardware business in Richmond to supplement the income they received from this farm. In poor crop years, it did more for them financially than did their farming with slaves. Yet when he died, she had no resources to keep his business going. She felt it was impossible as a woman to enter into any agreements or contracts with local businessmen."

"How well I understand!"

"She says it was by the counsel of the Spirit of God that she received revelation to establish this community of workers rather than to keep her father's people as slaves."

"She has said the same to me."

"Yet now she can hardly maintain herself against the creditors."

"So she thinks if you start up the business again, it might provide for us and help to protect us all?"

"Yes, exactly."

Mayleda put the shirt aside. "She is extremely pious, Charles, almost to the point of seeming odd."

He laughed. She looked up with no humor until she considered her own words. "Oh, I see! Others have said the same of me! But Madam sees visions. I've heard from her workers that many in the city believe she's gone mad. To me she has said she is certain of God's judgment on this nation for the sins of chattel labor if we do not repent. She's told me of dreams where she's seen the blood of Negroes and whites mingled and rising to the level of war horses' bridles."

She shivered, as did Charles. "I can only admire her, for I know she is depleting her inheritance in trying to maintain her holy cause."

"She is," he agreed, "and that does worry her, for she wonders what will happen to the people should she lose the property to debtors, or if she would die. She even spoke of writing me into her will so that her people might be safe. May, that does terrify me."

"I understand her fears. And yours! I also understand her thinking. My father struggled in just this way to protect his slaves when the laws prohibit mass manumission."

"Would you think of staying here with me, Mayleda, if we can find no better plan?"

She focused only on his face. "Yes, Charles."

"I have discussed another matter with Madam Lerew. My true name is Charles *Parnell*. This could help us now, I think. It could help to free me from the information spread about me."

For a moment her heart beat fast because of the danger they could not easily flee. Across from her, Charles seemed to bear the weight of the world. "We must pray about this plan, but one thing is certain—if I start a business for Madam Lerew, my only goal will be to make a way for us to travel north. I will gain the trust of the people here, only so that they will not question me when I leave with any of you. The children, Thomas, and Joseph included. Already I'm thinking that I might be able to get Joseph to Canada. There he could establish himself and wait until it is safe for me to bring the child. As a southern merchant, I would be able to travel easily with a valet. Thomas's presence has proven that to me already."

"Joseph will never agree to leaving Daniel in the South."

"I think he will if he sees that we can eventually bring Daniel to him. At that point I see us all leaving the South as soon as we can without raising suspicions. Perhaps we can all move west, as a family with 'slaves.' Do you see?"

She looked at him quietly. "Does this mean I should be considering the name Parnell as my own?"

His face turned bright red. "Oh, Mayleda. Yes. I meant that all along. That we would be together. Does this displease you?"

She reached across the table and took his hand, for he seemed in need of so much comfort. "No, it does not displease me at all."

"Forgive me. Right now, I think so much on them."

"Them?"

"I mean on Joseph and Angelene. I want to know that they will have the freedom to anticipate marriage even as we have."

"You know that Joseph and Angelene are considering marriage?"

"Joseph and I have spoken of it, yes."

"And Miss Brown?"

Charles looked uncomfortable, but in a pleased sort of way. "Not about marriage, I guess, though she must think that it is coming. He did write her a letter to tell of his love."

Instantly, Mayleda was out of the chair. "Oh, that is wonderful. For them!"

He stood and enveloped her in a mighty embrace. "And for us?"

"Oh, that is wonderful too!"

He kissed her hair. Despite their joy, she sensed the tension that filled him.

Soon he stepped back. "I need to see that Joseph gets to Canada. Then he can write to Angelene and ask her to come—I know she will—and they can create a home for Daniel. If I establish myself as a merchant here, I think we can be safe. But I tell you, as soon as we can safely leave Virginia, we will."

"You have considered this all so thoroughly!"

"Yes, but mostly tonight. After my conversations with Madam Lerew and with Thomas."

The weight of everyone's safety hung heavily upon his shoulders, she knew, and it kept him frowning. "Before I can think of marriage, May, I need to take Joseph to Canada. I hope you understand." He reached for her hand. "I have already spoken much to him about this, even to the point of making a covenant with him that I will not marry until I know that he can marry also. I am sorry, so sorry, if this hurts or disappoints you."

Once more she threw her arms around him. Standing on tiptoe, she whispered while he bent down to put his face toward hers. "I am proud of you, and I do love you, Charles Parnell."

The door to Joseph's room creaked on its hinges. They turned, amazed to see Joseph come out, walking tentatively. He took a seat at the table. It was the first time he had been out of bed since being carried to this house. "You could have called us," Mayleda said with concern. "We would have come to you."

"I wanted to see if I could be on my feet. Besides," he paused, "I could hear much of what was being said."

Mayleda felt her face getting warm.

"I apologize for the intrusion, but I thought it necessary." Joseph's good eye shifted to Charles. "I know you spoke just now of Covenant Day, as we imagined it while hiding in Tort Woodman's barn. But, Brother Charles, so much has happened since then. I needed to tell you both that I don't expect you to keep that promise, not with all the complexities that have arisen."

As Charles faced Joseph, Mayleda watched the two men she so much admired.

"Brother Whitsun, as of yet, you don't even know how great the complications are, but I will tell you. Even so, nothing in the present or in the future will shift me from my course. I stay committed to our promise."

CHAPTER 38

MORE THAN A MONTH WENT BY, giving Joseph time to recover and Charles time to start his work as the merchant Mr. C. M. Parnell. Every weekday, Thomas went with him as his driver while they explored the countryside, which was beginning to thaw under the stronger mid-February sun. By night Charles stayed at the table after supper, making lists of inventory to show Madam Lerew based on his conversations with local planters and farmers as to what they thought was needed in the way of dry goods and tools.

Feeling some apprehension, Charles set Thursday, the twenty-sixth of February, as the day when he and Joseph would leave together to go north under the guise of setting up accounts for this new business. With Joseph, Charles planned that they would go to New York City, where he already had accounts with merchants. It was their hope that some of these northern abolitionists might help them make arrangements to get into Canada.

The terrible scars on Joseph's face were healing. Instead of bandages, he now wore a neat leather patch over his still battered eye. He suffered severe headaches and dizziness if it was exposed to too much light. Sooner than Charles wanted it, the start of their dangerous, perhaps impossible, journey was upon them.

On the eve of their trip, they packed as gentleman and slave.

———

Before dawn Joseph dressed for the day in the same room as Charles. His friend put on fine imported clothes purchased in Richmond, while Joseph wore a livery borrowed from Madam Lerew, once used by her father's waiting man.

Joseph said no good-byes to Daniel after he was dressed as a servant. He had put the boy to bed in the smithy David's cabin the night before, so that his adopted son would not see him go off clothed as a rich man's slave. It was painful enough to do what they were doing without having to worry about frightening or confusing the little boy. They also kept the scene from Judith, so that the girl would have no misconceptions of the man who soon hoped to become a second father to her.

On the porch after they had headed outside, Charles dared to kiss Mayleda on the mouth. There was a feeling of dread, as with men going off to war. Though everyone tried to keep the leave-taking bright, all of them knew that one mistake in the next few days could send Charles to jail and Joseph back into chains.

Sadly Joseph stood thinking of Angelene while his dear friends cried in each other's arms and embraced. Then Mayleda came and kissed Joseph lightly on the cheek below the patch he wore.

Charles stood, approving. Likely they were seeing each other for the last time on earth.

"I cried over you at Delora," she said, managing to smile. "But I dared not to embrace you then." Then she hugged him with all her strength, unashamed. "Now I can show my affection and my tears. Joseph, I do love you as my precious brother."

Joseph took her hand and kissed it, saying what he had longed to say so often. "Dear, sweet Mayleda!" Then he added. "God be with you. I will send Charles back to you soon, and then you take good care of him!"

"In time for Covenant Day! Yes!" she agreed. "You decide on the date and write to Angelene. Whatever you decide will be fine with me." Then she and Charles embraced again.

As Joseph turned to give them privacy, he considered his doubts about ever writing to Angelene. He knew that at some time on this journey he would need to speak with Charles about it, for after more than a month of recovery, he still could not see well even out of his good eye. It limited him to reading for no more than a few minutes at a time. And deep concentration sometimes still brought on terrible headaches. All this he had hidden from Mayleda, though Charles knew his plight.

"Give a kiss and a hug from Daniel to Miss Brown when she joins you!" Mayleda called as they eventually started for the wagon that Thomas would drive. Joseph did not answer as he climbed up into the wagon bed. It was so much like his life of long ago, filled with humiliation and physical distress.

———

The small riverboat Charles and Joseph boarded in Richmond moved them to Norfolk. From there Charles arranged passage on a large seagoing steamer called the *Eugenia*. Wholly reliant on Madam Lerew's financing, Charles rented one of the many private state-rooms flanking the "gentlemen's cabin," so he and Joseph would have a private place in which to dismantle the awful disguises of master and slave that galled them both.

All went as planned. Because of Thomas's selfless, patient instruction while he had been with Charles in Maryland, Mr. C. M. Parnell played the part of gentleman merchant well as Joseph carried the trunk and kept his face down everywhere they went. As soon as they were alone behind the closed state-room door, however, Charles was quick to say again. "I abhor all that takes place outside this sanctuary."

"Yes, Marse!"

Charles felt wounded and amazed.

Then Joseph bowed close to him, even with no one there to see them. "Please be cautious, even here, Charles," he whispered. "You cannot know which walls have ears."

Just as he said that, there was a knock at the door. Charles was startled. Joseph looked at him, then took the one step needed to get to the door. "Who is it, sah?" He made his voice thick and slow, causing Charles to watch him with much worry.

"Is Mr. Parnell within?"

Joseph looked at Charles, who could not answer because he was so mortified. "Sah, my marse wants to know who it is."

"Captain Lang, boy!"

Charles struggled to straighten. Joseph opened the door.

"Good evening." The blond captain seemed congenial. Joseph was quick to look away. "I understand you've come from Richmond, that you're heading to New York, and that you plan to take your Negro with you."

Charles answered the best he could. "I am a merchant. I plan to come home with a full trunk of new inventory. I would not think of traveling without help."

"Aren't you afraid of losing him among northerners? In truth, your speech sounds much like theirs."

Joseph kept his eyes on the floor.

Charles shivered. "No."

"I am a native Virginian, sir. You are not."

There was hesitation. "You are right, Captain. I just recently started my business in Richmond. That is why I am on my way to New York to establish accounts."

The captain looked at Joseph then. "Is he a good worker?"

Charles remembered Thomas's counsel and chose to demean his closest friend. "Only fair."

"Trustworthy, I hope!"

"As much as they ever are."

"What of his face? His eye? That seems to be a recent wound."

"An unfortunate event."

"I would like to have a steady boy. I like them dark. And I don't mind a scar that can make him easy to identify from the rest should he consider sneaking off."

Charles probably spoke too soon. "He is not for sale."

The officer laughed. "I just wanted to come and warn you, which has become my policy. I do not recommend that servants be taken to the North. Some have just walked away from owners. Others, I think, have been lured by the cursed abolitionists."

If this were his test for Charles, it was one of verbal fire. Charles tried hard to keep himself from shaking. "He will not disappoint me on this journey, Captain. That I know."

"Then I am glad for you." The man stepped back. The door had been opened this full time. "Supper will be served at six in the second-deck saloon. Please bring him with you for all meals, even after we have passed north of the line. I would not want you to feel inconvenienced in any way. This is a southern vessel."

"I thank you for your concern," Charles managed.

"Of course, sir."

Waiting no more than a few seconds after the door was closed, Charles fell down onto the narrow bed, then to his knees, as though he might be sick. Joseph went to his side. "I was not so convincing, Joseph! Oh, and how am I to dine as a master? I cannot do it! I will say I am ill before I agree to come out in public with you as my slave in that way!"

"We have several hours. I can tell you what you need to know so that we will draw no attention at the table."

Still in agony, Charles looked up. His friend's face was twitching.

"I can do almost anything for the hope of liberty. Can you, brother?"

Charles hung his head. "This is all so evil."

"I think it best that you follow the captain's wishes. Otherwise, he may begin to think he has reason to suspect us. Here. Let's pretend the plate is right there in front of you."

The heavy rain falling in Sandwich on the second Saturday of March nearly convinced Barnabas to stay home and not leave the warm second cup of chicory coffee he held between his chilly hands. He was done with the work in the barn, having risen as usual before the light of day. The chores had left him feeling damp and achy and eager for the breakfast Angelene had set before him. Her father was at the table too, sitting across him.

The other man's fingers also embraced a steaming cup. They were the only ones in the farmhouse, for Angelene had gone out by then to the newspaper office where she worked every Saturday morning, the one day besides Sunday when she did not teach school.

Hearty chicory-root coffee was one of the luxuries they had here because of Sister Azal Brown's thoughtful packing. To sit and enjoy it in the northern cold made Barnabas long once more for Joseph's company, for his wisdom, and most of all for the easy conversation they had had for so many years. Sadly he reflected on their time in Oak Glen, so viciously stolen away by hatred and rumor. He was as proud of Joseph as any father could have been of a son, and he mourned his absence as a father mourns.

Pastor Brown was first that morning to take up the slate that Barnabas constantly kept at his side. *I will go down to the river dock with you,* he wrote, *to see if your shipment of pigs comes in, even in this weather.*

Barnabas nodded, then erased the board with the soft piece of cloth they had for that purpose. He showed a skill in conserving words, which Pastor Brown had yet to learn. *Too wet. Need not go. Think on your sermons. Your Bible studies.*

The pastor took the chalk from him and squeezed another line across the bottom. *Are* you *still going out?*

Barnabas nodded once more, though not happy about the work. These shoats, however, were the first livestock he had ordered through the mail to be shipped with Mr. Henry Bibb's approval. Finding ways for black settlers to support themselves in Canada was one of the pressing issues on this farsighted Negro leader's mind. Because of Barnabas's literacy and his skill as a farmer, everyone thus far seemed quite willing to overlook both his deafness and his lack of color in order to have his help.

Since Pastor Brown had decided to spend a few more weeks with his daughter, he often worked with Barnabas. He could read Barnabas's chalkboard notes, then act as his interpreter. The pastor and he were making slow progress in communicating by manual signs, for the reverend remained more comfortable using the written word. Sometimes words were not needed at all, as now, when the other man got up and went to the door to claim his hat, coat, and cloak. Barnabas knew he planned to go to meet the vessel coming across from Detroit. That made Barnabas get up also, and to take his own hat and coat.

They went out into mud that was as common to them here as the smell of fish and the sight of moody gray skies. Whenever they met other persons on the street, they were greeted heartily, for Pastor Brown had been preaching at least two or three times each week at the small unfinished church that was being built as time and supplies allowed. In addition to preaching, the minister conducted a weekly prayer service for fugitives who bore the grief of having left loved ones behind. And when the man wasn't at the church, he was often at the makeshift school, helping Angelene, who had an overwhelming number of students in her classes and still no books.

Going in search of his shipment of pigs in the rain held no pleasure for Barnabas, but Pastor Brown's company made it bearable. The other man set his mind on practicing signed language as they walked. Rightly, the man of God made the symbol for *"rain"* as they were being soaked by it. Then he pressed the manual symbol for the letter *"r"* hard upon his shoulder, the sign for *"responsibility." "Rain and responsibility both on our shoulders."* Pastor Brown signed the words slowly as he spoke. Then he smiled.

"*Good!*" Barnabas affirmed him, but deep inside, their awkward dialogue only made him long for Joseph more. Certainly the pastor was looking to encourage him, but the effort made it harder for Barnabas to face the truth that likely Joseph was lost to them, either dead or suffering indescribably as a slave. Only God could know.

He tried not to let it be known that his heart was gloomy. He did not want Pastor Brown or anyone else to think he was ungrateful to be in Sandwich. He knew that the reverend bore great sorrow too, not only for himself but for his precious daughter.

"*I hear boat whistles.*" Pastor Brown said this with a rough mixture of gestures and words from his lips.

Barnabas nodded, and both men walked faster as the rain pelted down on them.

———

His vision fixed on Canada's shore, Joseph walked out from under the steamboat's roofed deck that was drumming with rain. Until he was away from it, he could hear nothing but the rattle of boards overhead. These were the final moments of a long, fatiguing trip that had taken them seventeen days. It was the first time Joseph had been alone in all those many miles that so often had been mired by bad weather, primitive conveyances, and prejudicial treatment that forced them to continue the ignoble roles of slave and master, even as they were crossing the state of New York.

Only since boarding this last vessel, which was to take them upriver to Sandwich itself, had he and Charles finally laid aside every part of their demeaning pantomime. Even so, Charles still was not eager to let him out of his view, for his practice these past days had been that of a watchdog guarding one sheep.

Yet now Joseph's walk in the rain felt like a rude precursor to the real freedom that would come the moment this boat reached shore. From the railing he stared at the dull land drifting closer. He felt the rain on his good eye while not being able to feel anything against the leather patch he wore in public.

Leaning out over the choppy gray river, he knew he still had not dealt with the unsettling belief that he was arriving here as a man less desirable than his former self because of his half blindness and the headaches that plagued him. Regardless of Charles' full forgetfulness of his deformity, Joseph began to look again at the reality that might meet him here. In

Sandwich he would be alone, with no one who knew him either as a doctor or an educator. Indeed he felt that he could no longer think of himself in those ways, for he did not know if mental keenness and visual accuracy would ever be gifts to him again.

Though he had been working hard to read when Charles and he could open the Bible in private, the terrible truth was that his sight, both far and near, still was not completely clear. If he could not do the things he was trained to do, then what would he do? With all this uncertainty came the most raging question of all: Should he send word to Angelene of his arrival?

Charles came to his side. "Are you all right?"

"Yes."

"I thought you would be elated at this moment."

"I think the word is *numbed*."

"I'll get the trunk and meet you." Charles smiled encouragement as the rain ran in rivulets off the brim of his high hat. The boat slowed, then sidled to the land. A gangplank was extended from shore to deck. Since they now had no fear that anyone could judge them or accuse them simply by how they divided their duties, Charles came shouldering the trunk, which Joseph had been obliged to carry until now, though it often gave him tremendous headaches to do so.

"Perhaps I should take it one more time," Joseph said, "just in case there are any federal marshals on board. They could take us yet, I think."

"The *maimed* land of liberty is behind us!" Charles declared with excitement in his voice. "The mainland of freedom starts just ahead. I hope!" Joseph knew Charles was accustomed to physical work and not ashamed to do it. "I regret I could not carry this before," Charles said as they headed to the shore. "I know that you are still not well, and yet you had to endure it."

Joseph let himself be hopeful now, with the soil of Canada only feet away. He drew breath in the wet, fresh air and looked around as his feet met the miry land. No one seemed to notice their odd partnership. All around them there were passengers, most of them colored, who carried their own belongings.

"Where do you think we should inquire about a room?" Charles asked as they turned right to enter the closest street.

Joseph could not answer as he took in more of the truth that they were on foreign soil—therefore, safe and therefore, free. Charles seemed to understand his moments of silence. He affirmed the reverence due them by putting the trunk down on a stray piece of planking so that he could hand over to Joseph the odious bill of sale with the name Joe written on it.

Solemnly, with constriction in his throat, Joseph went back to the water. Shredding the small document, he dropped piece after piece into the black river. "God be praised! God be praised!" First he whispered it, then he nearly shouted.

When he came back, Charles was still uneasy. "Do you think they will accept a *white* man and a *black* man wanting to room as equals here?"

"I do hope so, or Sandwich will be no better than the towns we just left." While Joseph spoke, he surveyed the riverside crowd. In the distance he caught a blurred glimpse of one face as white as Charles'. "Let's go this way. I think I see a black man walking with a white man. We'll approach them."

Their clothes were quickly drenched. The mud came up around their boots with the consistency of mash fed to horses. "Excuse me, sir!" Joseph nearly had to shout to the older colored man to be heard above the din of men unloading and loading the vessel nearby. "I was wondering if you could tell me—" Joseph stopped when the man turned. The sight made him speechless, but not so with the other man staring back at him.

"Can it be? Joseph! Mr. Powell?"

"Brother Cummington! Dear Ba!" Joseph cried. "What are you doing here?" He could not see for the tears and for the rain, yet self-consciously he turned away, about to cover his eye. He could not do it, though, for old Barnabas had already grabbed him.

"*Miracle! Miracle!*" Ba's fingers flew to spell and respell the word they had never had to use until now.

Pastor Brown waited, then eagerly explained. "Angelene and Barnabas felt so strongly that they should come here, Azal and I could not say no."

"Angelene is here?" Joseph felt himself grow weak.

Pastor Brown took him by the shoulder as though he were able to see his grief. Joseph bowed. "I am blind in one eye," he mourned, not having to say what was utterly clear. "I am not sure about the sight in my other eye—"

The pastor would not let him go on. "You are walking! You are talking! You are free! You are the answer to our prayers! Don't you mourn now! Dear Joseph, we were starting to fear the worst."

Joseph remembered Charles. He turned back to take hold of the huge, unassuming man. "*This* brother has been the answer to your prayers! I would be trapped in a living hell now, or dead, if it had not been for Charles and for another brother, Thomas. Daniel and Sister Ruskin were saved too, because of the courage of those two."

Charles would only tip his dripping hat.

The pastor's eyes were wet. "The Vigilance Committee kept us well informed until we ourselves left Pennsylvania." He grimaced and blinked away his tears. "We need to get you two inside out of this weather!" Beside Cummington, Ba was happily signing nearly the same.

"How is it that you just walked off the steamer and straight up to us?" the pastor asked. "We were waiting on a boat from Detroit that has yet to appear."

"I saw this rare friendship of mixed color, so like our own." Joseph smiled, sensing the marvel of a deep relief that was starting to fill him up. "But I could not see well enough to recognize either of you. Not until you turned."

Pastor Brown laughed. "We came down here looking for pigs. I'm not the least bit disappointed to find you two instead!"

"Pigs, sir?" Joseph asked.

"Yes, your Mr. Croghan is rapidly making a name for himself here as an agricultural advisor. And Angelene is already teaching."

Joseph felt overwhelmingly pleased, yet also hollow, as he struggled with a new sense of uselessness.

"Come, we'll take you up to the house they have rented." Cummington grinned.

Joseph found himself pausing. "Angelene is there?"

"Yes, she should be. She does spend time working at the *Voice*, but she should be home for the noonday meal by now." The pastor gazed at him. "You're not concerned about how my daughter does feel toward you now, are you, son?"

Charles drew close while Joseph stammered, "I am."

"Oh! My only concern is that Angel will not suffocate you with her hugs and kisses, and that after we have made you stand out in this weather. Come!"

————

When Angelene came home at midday, she found the house empty. Two cups were still on the table, a sign that Barnabas had left in a hurry, for usually he was meticulous about keeping rooms in order. She guessed that the men were out looking for the shoats Barnabas had ordered from a farmer in Michigan.

Taking the cups from the table, she replaced them with a jar of her father's honey and a plate with thick slices of bread that she had baked yesterday after school. Since she anticipated that the men might soon be home, she put the kettle on to boil water for tea. It was then that she heard footsteps on the porch. Her father opened the door. "We have visitors, Angel. I thought you might want to come to greet them."

She looked at him with some puzzlement, for though he was getting to know many people through the church, folks did not often come to the house. "Who is here?" she asked, pressing slightly at her braids under the linen cap she wore.

He didn't answer her. When she went to the door, the latch on it suddenly became her anchor, for she saw Joseph on the porch, his wet hat in his hands. She could not test the realness of her vision because of her tears. She could not move. And she could not speak. But she did hear his voice.

"Dear Angelene."

It made her wholly incautious. Even though she saw Charles Powell, Barnabas, and her father, she did not hold back. Flying into Joseph's arms, she flooded him with kisses. He started crying too, but soon it all turned to laughing.

"Is this a Canadian lady's welcome?" he teased.

She put her hands to her heated face and looked at her father. His eyes were merry.

"So, Dr. Whitsun, is her love sickness fatal?"

"Come in!" she cried, finally gathering some of her wits. She saw the weariness so plain on Charles Powell's face and the worry on Joseph's. It compelled her to embrace Joseph again, for indeed she had been fighting secret demons every day that made her want to despair about ever seeing him again. This time she stood on her tiptoes, leaning as close as she could to his cold wet clothes. She refrained from kissing him more, but swept her hands over his rough damp hair.

Her fingers met the band that held his eye patch in place. "Oh, what did they do to you?" She pulled his face down. "Oh, what did you have to endure?" She lightly kissed both his eyes.

She felt his weary sighing. "Later. All later." Suddenly he was struggling to look away. "I cannot see well, Angelene. I can't read for long periods, or concentrate—"

Once more she kissed him, but this time on his lips to stop his words. "Later. All later!" she said back to him. "Oh, Joseph, I don't care about anything except that you are here."

Late in the afternoon the rain stopped. Angelene and her father prepared to show Joseph and Charles the town, while Barnabas insisted on staying home to make an evening meal. As Joseph donned his still damp coat, Ba signed to him as he grinned mischievously. *"A second Canada hen is about to be sorry that Ba has company!"* Joseph was not sure about the joke, but Ba and Angelene laughed with merry abandonment.

Angelene was dressed in the red gown her mother had made for her in Oak Glen. There was an awkward moment when Joseph as well as her father moved to help her take her shawl and then her cloak. Barnabas kept grinning, Cummington laughed, and Charles looked away. It made Joseph feel boyish, but also like someone high on a mountaintop. In a better show of manners he then asked the father's permission to escort his daughter. It was granted.

With Angelene's small frame pressed close beside him, they walked through the miry streets, looking into the windows of the closed newspaper office and examining the interior of the poorly furnished school. Finally they went into the little church where Angelene's father had been preaching. It was still under construction, with no plaster on the walls or trim around the windows. The moment they were inside, Joseph felt so faint he was forced to close his eyes.

"You are exhausted!" Angelene showed worry. "We walked too far."

"No." He looked for Charles. He could hardly bear that they all were staring at him. "Brother, this is the church I saw in my dream! You may think it impossible. I would, but I know what I saw!"

Angelene held him tighter. "Joseph, what dream?"

His grimacing pulled at his facial bruises. Though he had told them much in the past few hours, he had not said anything about how close to death he had been because of the beating. He found Charles answering for him, when he could not.

"It was a few days after we had brought him to the Lerew property, miss. We didn't know if we could hope for recovery."

Angelene hid her face against Joseph's coat.

"Every day, every hour we were praying, not knowing anything about your decision to come to Sandwich. Joseph had this dream—"

Joseph's own emotions moved like waves as now he tried to tell his own story. "While I lay unable to see or hear much of anything in the natural, I saw an unfinished church under a great expanse of sky. It was this church! The windows there. The door. Even the altar table and the benches, just as they are here."

"Oh, Joseph." Angelene raised her face. It sparkled with wonder.

Charles said what he remembered of it. "I was sitting next to him, Miss Brown, and all at once he started speaking like one coming back from the dead with some urgent message. It causes me to shiver now to know that it was a vision from God. Back then, I admit, I took it to mean that he might soon be bound for heaven."

"There is something that I think I never told you, brother," Joseph confessed to Charles. "I saw myself standing by the altar table." He looked to Angelene. "I was standing there with you."

"At our wedding?" she said boldly, her eyes so bright.

"That I couldn't tell." Joseph smiled slowly. "I only saw your face." He felt embarrassed, but he held her tightly.

"I am sure it was a vision of your wedding," Charles said as he raised a trembling hand toward heaven. "You started getting stronger after that. I think it was God's way of telling you to keep fighting for life and wholeness."

"This brother never left my side, day or night." Joseph could not boast of Charles enough. "He risked all. He sold everything, and his own loved ones are trapped in Virginia yet, with Daniel."

The huge man trembled from head to toe. "I am so grateful to have seen this church!"

Pastor Brown listened with intensity. "Brother Charles, perhaps God allows you to share in this vision to give you hope that He has had His hand on you all."

"Perhaps to confirm our plan of a Covenant Day?" Charles said this breathlessly to Joseph only.

With awkwardness, then, Joseph found himself explaining his friend's words to Angelene and to her father. The woman he loved kept squeezing his hands.

"Let it be so!"

Even after everyone showed so much joy, Charles' face continued to look heavy with concern. "Joseph, if something happens to me, you must marry. Surely this has been confirmed."

Angelene reached for Charles. "We are going to pray for you day and night until you do get back to Sister Ruskin. As Father said, I believe the truth of your safe travel has been confirmed by Joseph's vision since you each promised the other that you would not marry until you both could. We will stand at this table on the same day you stand with Sister Ruskin. We will set a day and trust God for it. It will be too dangerous for you to receive letters in Virginia. We will trust the Spirit of God to make a way for the promises we exchange."

Suddenly Charles' knees bowed, and the huge man crumpled his hands before his face. "Oh, I confess! I am so full of anxiety! I fear not getting back, and I fear how we will live in slave territory after that! And I don't fear for myself only, but for Thomas and Daniel and Mayleda too."

Gently Pastor Brown took Charles by the elbows. With Joseph's help also, they moved his friend to the nearest bench. "There are many ways in which injustice makes men suffer," Cummington said. "You are suffering now, Brother Charles, much as our Lord suffered. Grieving for the sin of this world. Could we have your permission to lay hands on you to pray for you?"

Charles wiped his eyes. "Oh yes, sir, please do! Nothing could comfort me or help me more."

Joseph put his hands on Charles' shoulders. "I have learned to know God better as my Heavenly Father," he said, "by knowing you as my brother."

Pastor Brown touched him. "Joseph, please. You start our time of prayer now."

CHAPTER 39

HAVING STAYED A WEEK in Sandwich, Charles experienced a parting like no other, full of hope, but full of sadness too. As much as Joseph and Angelene longed for Daniel to be with them, Joseph urged Charles not to risk coming again until the fervor had died over Venor's stolen slave and over Charles' identity as an abolitionist thief.

From Canada Charles crossed Lake Erie once more, arriving in Buffalo, then going by rail and stage to New York City. There he spent two days setting up accounts, as had been his plan. He made arrangements to order rubber products, glass, pottery, fabrics, and other wares that he and Madam Lerew had already agreed on as wise investments to please Richmond customers.

The morning he was to leave New York, he packed samples of these products into the same trunk he and Joseph had shared. He had already arranged passage south with the same company that had brought them north, but he was careful to choose a different vessel, not wanting to see the *Eugenia*'s captain again.

When he came to the harbor, he found it fogged in with mist as thick as wool. The steamboat office where his ticket had been purchased was crowded with passengers, as vessels had been postponed, delayed, and even run off course by the March storms all up and down the coast. From a harried man behind the counter, however, Charles received the good news that passengers for Norfolk were still embarking, as weather was better in the South. Shouldering his trunk, Charles followed others who, like himself, were dressed in cloaks and hats to ward off the dampness that clung to them.

Having handed his ticket over, Charles arrived on deck only to learn then that a second captain had been assigned to accompany the first because of the rigors of navigation that the fog imposed. This second captain's name was mentioned by other passengers only moments before Charles caught sight of him. It was Captain Lang.

Charles turned frantically to see what might be done, but returning to shore was impossible because seamen at the railing were already casting off lines. Staying close to other gentlemen dressed as he was, Charles moved from the crowd outside to the men's humid social hall. Others stopped at the large elaborate stove to dry their clothes, but Charles hurried on to the state room he had secured. For the next three days he fasted and prayed instead of taking any meals in public. He read from his Bible, as he had done with Joseph. Only by night did he leave his quarters to use the toilet in the dim portside gangway and to drink water from the rain barrel set out on the open deck.

To finally hear the departure bell ringing in Norfolk, Virginia, felt like his release from prison. Hungry and weak, he emerged, wisely leaving his trunk to be carried by someone else. Finding a Negro youth, he offered a coin to have him take his luggage for him. The young porter scurried to come behind him with the load. Unencumbered then by everything except his winter clothes, which were much too heavy for Virginia's clear sky and burgeoning spring, Charles headed rapidly toward the gangplank, his thoughts on Mayleda.

Out ahead, Captain Lang was socializing with passengers, tipping his cap, and giving pleasant farewells. Charles looked for a way to pass unnoticed, but then the captain saw him. "Mr. Parnell?" Charles stopped in his tracks. "I saw your name on the roster, sir, but not you in person, not even once. And where is your one-eyed waiting man? The passenger list,

I noted, did not list a servant being with you on this journey."

Charles stammered. "Captain, I don't think I am obligated to say. I thank you for the safe passage. Good day."

"Good day, indeed!" The words came sharp behind him. "You did not heed my warning, did you? You lost him to the Yankees!"

Charles considered that in a few more strides he would be off the vessel, but before he could span the distance, three men from the steamboat's crew came around him as the captain shouted for their help. Then Lang joined these others who surrounded him.

"What is the problem?" Charles breathed with rapid breaths.

"For one thing, *Mr. Parnell*, if that is your name, I want a direct word from you. Gentlemen do not just turn on their heel and go off. Now, I ask you again, what happened to the slave you took with you to New York?"

Charles was hardly better prepared to give answer this time. "As I said, I believe I should not have to say. It concerns my *privacy*, my *property*, and my *privilege*, three words that all Southerners should cherish well. If I lost him, then that is my own fault and my own business."

The captain squinted against the sun. "I would not accost a gentleman unless I had reason to believe he was engaged in illegal activity aboard a company vessel." From inside his coat Lang then took a folded piece of newsprint. "The port authorities are looking for a man named Charles Powell. Perhaps you know that. Your physical characteristics match those of the man described in this paper. He is known to be a slave stealer, and you have come back without a Negro. I think I have a valid reason to detain you."

"You know almost nothing about me, yet you accuse me?" Charles spoke with courage he did not really have. "That is an insult to my integrity."

"If you are really the southern gentleman you say you are, you will forgive me my passion for not allowing abolitionists to employ our boats for their purposes. Thousands of bondsmen are being lost every year, and many, I am convinced, are being stolen. However, it will not be so aboard our steamers."

"I am Charles Parnell," Charles said truthfully. "I went to New York to establish trade accounts. I have samples of products in my trunk. If you want proof of what I say, I will show you hot-water bottles and linings for ladies' bonnets."

"Don't joke with me, sir! I don't care for your obvious lack of concern.

This man Powell has not been captured. The uproar started with a slave boy sold away from his rightful owner, and then with the beating of a planter in the same town who had come to retrieve his slave. But it hasn't stopped there. The indignation concerning this affront now has supporters everywhere. If you are the man you say you are, I think we should see displeasure from you, as well, concerning these events."

Charles quaked. Joseph had told him the tale of one abolitionist who had been tarred and feathered. Now Charles was surrounded by men who knew the facts about him.

"Can you prove the one-eyed slave was *your* slave?" Lang asked.

"Of course. I have a paper for him at home."

The captain frowned. "I could have agents follow you so that they can see this evidence for themselves, or I could have you detained until someone brings that paper to the authorities."

"I tell you, I am Mr. Parnell, a merchant."

"Then say what happened to the Negro you told me you did not want to sell. If that is so, where is he now?"

Charles was praying silently, longing to know how he should answer in the presence of his enemies. "I won't lie." His hands were sweating. "I released him far from the Line and for the good of us all. I could have sold him to you, yes, but then I would have made you a victim of deceit!"

"Sir, there is no good reason to free a slave!"

Charles' stomach soured. "There is, Captain Lang. He could read and write. The scars you saw on him give testimony to the many unsuccessful attempts that were made to break him."

"It sounds as though *you* were at *his* mercy! God forbid!"

"I could have sold him to you without saying what I've told you now, but I hold myself to be a man of integrity."

"You could have put out his other eye and sold him south!"

Charles shuddered. "I acted on my privilege to do as *I* see fit with my own property." He dared to touch his hat, while hardly having any feeling in his hand at all. "Now that you have made me bare my soul, I once more bid you good day."

The skin on Charles' back felt alive as he walked from his adversaries. They did not follow him, yet he stayed wary every moment of the next hours until he took his seat on a James River steamer bound for Richmond, ninety miles upriver.

Though now Richmond was to be his home, the way to Madam Lerew's was unfamiliar to Charles. After a grueling journey that took him all through the night and well into the next day, the steamboat finally quaked and quivered as its engine growled and it was brought to a standstill along the river's edge. As on bigger vessels, a brass bell was rung, though everyone on this simple boat could see that it was time for passengers to disembark.

Colored roustabouts came aboard, their caps in their hands, looking to carry the travelers' possessions. Two boys approached Charles. He nodded to them, and they each took a side to tote his trunk between them. It was pressing on his mind that he had no idea how he should get from the wharf to Madam Lerew's. He should not carry the trunk himself, nor did he think it wise to pay for these youngsters to come with him.

The thin black children put his trunk on the landing, then he waved them away. He hardly had a moment more to consider his dilemma, for someone called to him. "Welcome home, Marse Parnell!" The Negro who came toward him was Thomas.

Charles could have hugged him, but he understood that he must not do that now, for there were many dangers unless they played their parts well. "How could you have known that I was coming today?" Charles dared to ask.

"I didn't, sah. But in faith I knew that you would be comin' one of these days, so Mistress Lerew's been allowin' me to bring her coach down every morning to wait out the time." Thomas lifted the trunk easily. "Sah, this way."

As soon as the coach stopped, Charles reached for the door but then hesitated, knowing that he must keep to his role. When Thomas came to him, Charles could read no expression on his face at all. Stepping out, he was surprised at how close to dusk it was. They were in the middle of an unfamiliar stable yard. One lantern burned from an iron bracket mounted on a post.

Looking around with much apprehension, Charles thought they were alone. Yet he whispered, "Where are we? I don't remember Madam Lerew's house being so far away from the city."

Thomas seemed nearly drained of strength. "I took a long way in case anybody would decide to come after you."

"So there has been trouble here?" Charles panicked.

"No, sah!" Thomas vowed with much sadness in his eyes. "But the news they keep on printin' in the papers 'bout you sure ain't good. Honestly, sah, there wa' days when I had to talk myself out of thinkin' I was waitin' for you in vain. Every marse, it seems, north to south, east to west, wants to see you brought 'fore the law for slave-nabbin' an' cudgelin' that man Rensler."

He pursed his lips as though fearing to go on. "What of Joseph, sah?"

Charles could not resist taking the young man by the shoulders. "He is safe! And Miss Brown and her father and his friend Ba Croghan were already there, set up in a house and having employment. It could not have gone better." Having said that though, Charles thought of the confrontation yesterday in Norfolk. "I was stopped once on my way home. I was questioned concerning my likeness to a certain Charles Powell."

"Oh no, sah!"

"I'm telling you, Thomas, because it's right and fair and safest if we hold no secrets from each other. But I don't think I was followed here. Do you?"

Thomas looked out in the gathering night. "I don't think so neither, but now I feel the need to be on guard more than ever."

"We both will be," Charles promised him.

"I drove you to the back side of Mistress Lerew's stable, 'cause they's only one way up an' down the lane to her house, but they's two roads leadin' out from here, one to the mansion an' one to her fields."

"I thank you for your caution! And for being there! Truly I might have drawn too much attention just walking home." To call this place home felt odd. Perhaps Thomas noticed.

The youth turned his face upward. "What is Canada like, sah?"

Charles heard the longing in his voice. "I wouldn't choose it for its weather, but there is freedom there to study, to worship, to own property, to have your own business."

"Umhm! I think I could do with a little ill weather."

"Thomas, I want you to get there. Believe me. However we can get Daniel there, I want you to go too."

"I don't know 'bout that, sah."

Charles could not believe his reluctance. "Did I say something wrong? I thought you'd want to leave instantly."

"Maybe not. Not 'less Mistress Lerew would be willin' to let her gal Lydia go too."

"I see," Charles said. They exchanged sad smiles.

"We want to commit ourselves to marriage just like you an' Sister Ruskin. An' Joseph an' Miss Brown. You think there's any chance of Mistress Lerew lettin' that happen?"

"Are you sure Lydia is the one for you? You're so young, and you haven't known her very long."

Thomas smiled a second time. "As sure as you an' Sister May. Don't worry, sah. I done a lot of talkin' an' prayin' with both the Lord an' them ladies. An' I think God is ready to give His blessin' to us. So will you ask her for me?"

"You mean Lydia?"

"Oh no, sah! I mean Mistress Lerew, 'cause I don't think she gwine want no Negro what ain't hers traipsing up to her door."

Charles was still by the carriage. He leaned against it. "The more I hear you talk, the more I think it's very wrong for any of us to be here. I was pleased with my plan at the start, but now I'm unsure of it. It's not fair for you to have to live here beholden to white people, as though someone owns you."

Thomas sighed then, as though there was a great weight on his heart. "Knowin' how things are, sah, I cain't think of any place we all can go what's safer than here."

"Have you been treated fairly?"

The young man eyed him. "I guess it depends on what you mean by fair."

"I want to know what you mean by it. I want to know how you really find it here."

"Well, Mistress Lerew ain't done gone so far as you an' Sister May in believin' that colored folks is equal. That I'll say. She likes to be the Negro's protector, I think. An' mebbe *sometimes* she even likes to be his releaser, but she always needs to have somethin' *over* us. Do you see what I mean?"

"I do see. There was time when I would not have seen it, but now I see it everywhere, even in the North among well-meaning antislavery people."

Thomas's eyes softened. He nodded. "A Negro's always got to be careful he don't step over *white* lines what are laid down by *white* people, or soon he finds himself in the place called Trouble." He stopped.

"Say the truth! Say it all! I want to know. I am listening."

"That's how you learn to carry you'self on the safe side."

Charles was discouraged. "Yes, you still do that even with me. I know, and in a way I still do it with you."

Thomas nodded as though the truth were sad. Charles extended his hand. "Look! The *safe* side for us is going to be the place where our races can be equal, even if we can only find such a place in spots as deserted as this one is now."

Thomas reached out his hand to take Charles' while falling silent. They shook hands.

"It does worry me, Thomas, that all must be so temporary here. I mean, men are looking for me. And then there's all the concern about Madam Lerew as well. In the event of either one of us getting sick or into debt or even dying, all of you could be put out to other masters."

"Yessah."

"What are we to do?"

"I cain't think of anythin' better, leastwise for now."

"That's the problem! Neither can I." Charles stared off for a while. Then he saw Thomas frowning sternly at him. "What is it?"

"Ain't you got no interest in gwine up to see the Widow Ruskin? I tell you, she gwine be happy to see you! I weren't alone in my worry for you, sah, nor in my prayin'!"

Charles sighed, the longing for Mayleda's face and touch deep within him. "Yes, I do want to see her! But first I think that I should tell Madam Lerew that I am here." He remembered Thomas's request, and he wanted to start showing his gratitude to the young man by more than simple words, so he said, "I'll help you cool down the horses and put the carriage away. Then we'll *both* go up to see Madam Lerew together concerning *our* business."

A genuine smile came to Thomas. "Thank you. Yes!"

CHAPTER 40

"TELL ANOTHER STORY," Daniel said as Mayleda and Lydia had both children sitting at the table while they were knitting socks. "Another story 'bout Daniel in the Bible."

"You know every story by heart," Mayleda told the boy, hoping to affirm his confidence and his young mind, which was getting sharper by the day. "Besides, it's time for bed."

"Why wasn't I named for someone in the Bible?" Judith asked, perhaps jealous, as she was still getting used to sharing Mayleda's attention and affection.

"Your name is in the Bible, dear, but your daddy really chose it because he thought it was as beautiful as you." Mayleda stopped her work, having a sweet remembrance of Sprague, but not one that brought her tears as the memories once did.

"*My* daddy named me," Daniel said with a boldness that no one could have expected from him even weeks ago. The child seemed almost like a butterfly birthed from a cocoon.

"Joseph Whitsun isn't your daddy, if that's what you mean!" Judith argued harshly.

"Judith, he is!" Mayleda looked to Lydia. "A daddy can be someone who *chooses* to love you as his child. Think of God. He does that for us. The Bible teaches us that we all are adopted into His family." Mayleda paused, hoping Judith's heart would be touched. Yet her child seemed unsettled, even angry inside.

Daniel smiled at Judith, something he would not do when they were first brought together. "I think you gwine get a new daddy. Brother Charles."

"First he has to marry my mama!" Judith said, as though she needed to have the last word.

"Well? So? My daddy's gwine marry Miss Brown, the teacher."

"We pray so." Mayleda again looked at Lydia. "We all pray that Brother Joseph is safe in Canada and that Brother Charles will be here soon."

Then she heard bitter doubting from Judith. "I don't pray for that, even when you see me close my eyes!"

"We cain't see you' close you eyes," Daniel said with innocence. " 'Cause then our eyes are closed."

Mayleda put down her knitting. "Judith, how can you dare to say you do not pray?"

"God didn't watch over my first daddy. He died!"

Mayleda did not know how to respond. Beside her Lydia looked down, appearing uncomfortable to see Mayleda's pain. But Daniel spoke clearly. "Dying ain't bad like slavery. Dying's good 'cause you get to see heaven an' live there forever." He came and laid his head on Mayleda's arm. "My sister's there, ain't she?"

Judith shifted. "You still talk like a slave boy!"

"Hush!" Appalled once more, Mayleda took Judith's wrist. "Why are you so mean-spirited? I didn't raise you to be like this."

"Maybe my sister's already met you' daddy," Daniel continued, not giving up on his goodwill. "Wouldn't that be fine? For them to start a nice family up there? Then my sister could have a daddy—"

"You're so dumb, you don't even know what sadness is!" Judith shouted before Mayleda could stop her. "Or love!"

"I do!" Daniel jerked up his head, having no caution about defending himself. "I know Dr. Joseph wants to be my daddy, but he's in Canada. So there—that's *love* an' *sadness* all at once!"

"Judith, apologize. You don't call anyone dumb."

"Grandpa says all colored people are dumb!"

Her child had never said such a thing.

"That they aren't really people at all."

"Judith, you know that's wrong. Your grandfather knows a great many things, but he is wrong in his judgment of the Negro."

Judith started to cry. "I don't want just colored friends. I don't want to keep on sleeping in some attic. And I don't want to just have one dress to wear. I want to go home! Home to Philadelphia. I don't like being poor and living like a Negro."

"We aren't living like Negroes. We are living as God wills, according to what He has for us to do."

"I want my granddaddy and grandmother!"

"You can't. Not now." Mayleda stood. Judith was reluctant to take her hand. "You need to go up to bed. Things will look brighter in the morning. But first, you must apologize to Sister Lydia and to Daniel. You said hurtful things about them that are not true."

Judith would only stand wordless, while Mayleda's heart was breaking. Then the front door flew open.

"Hey ho! Guess who I found down by the river!" Thomas rushed in with hands held high. Mayleda fearfully let out her breath. Then she saw Charles. He came over and swept her up into his arms, and Judith too, like they were feathers lofted on a breeze.

"What about Joseph!" She could hardly speak, she was so happy for herself.

"He's fine and more than fine! I will tell you everything!"

Then Charles bent and kissed her with exuberant joy.

The next night they had a celebration. Sister Lydia, who never looked prettier than she did by candlelight, and Sister Ruskin both worked happily long past dark to put a feast upon the table. There was suckling pig that Mistress Lerew gladly donated for the occasion, sweet baked apples, corn pudding, and dark greens, withered and smothered in bacon according to Lydia's own recipe, which Thomas had already learned to love quite well.

Everybody except Charles had gotten used to sharing meals under this roof. Now with much gratefulness Thomas set a chair for him at the head of the table where nobody had ever sat while he was gone. But the big humble man would not hear of claiming the seat of honor.

"Go on! Just once!" Thomas urged, feeling nothing but happy to celebrate him being home. But Charles protested, even though they all had the treatment of equals here.

His glance shifted to Judith, seated beside her mother. "With the permission of all in this room, I'd like to call Miss Judith to sit in the seat of honor, if, in fact, that is what this is." The child looked surprised, but more so the mother.

Charles smiled at the girl. "Miss Judith and I had a little talk today and she made two important decisions. The first: to love God most of all. The second: to love others as she loves herself."

"That sure deserves a seat of honor!" Thomas cheered because he knew how hard Charles was trying to win the child by kindness. Mayleda's daughter had been quiet at first while living here. But the longer they stayed, the more she wanted to be the child of wealth and ease once more, the way her grandparents had treated her back in the city.

Thomas had heard her discontent most when Judith was without her mother. The girl's tongue could wag with a very sharp edge then, whenever she was with colored folks alone. Thomas had had more than enough experience already with young white children saying things in public that they had heard in private from their elders. No one could fault Sister Ruskin, he thought, for it was the grandparents, not her mother, who Judith mimicked most in her unhappiness. To Thomas it was like the Bible story he had only recently heard read where somebody came by night to sow in tares among the good young wheat.

That's why he kept his attention on what Charles was saying to the little girl now. "It is not natural for even a grown man or woman to choose what is *right* over what seems *best* for them, Judith. But that's what you have promised you will do in thinking of others before thinking of yourself. Such words, when followed by good deeds, please God."

Judith smiled out at them all from under her long dark lashes while she claimed the chair. Thomas thought then that Charles would call for a time of silent prayer, but this time he asked Thomas to pray out loud. When Thomas closed his eyes, he knew he was speaking to the real God who loved them all. He prayed from his heart, giving thanks for the food and for their shelter, but most of all, for bringing Brother Parnell home to this house.

Charles was the last to start eating despite his days of fasting. He felt so overwhelmed by this true family of faith, and he kept looking at Mayleda, who this day had agreed for certain to be his wife. Gladly she had embraced his hope that their wedding could be on the same day as Joseph's and Angelene's, the last Sunday of May, their shared Covenant Day.

After the meal Charles opened the trunk he had previously set near the table. It was much lighter now, for everything he had brought for the business had already been unpacked for Madam Lerew. Even though he had been raised by Friend Peabody, who did not celebrate Christmas, Charles felt a little bit like St. Nicholas with everyone's eyes upon him.

Without comment he took out yards and yards of folded fabric, bringing Lydia and Mayleda immediately to their feet. He had chosen quiet colors suitable for ladies of conservative dress, yet with a weave and texture that were the best he could secure.

"Are these slave-free products?" Mayleda marveled.

"Yes. I met some new abolitionists in New York, and they were glad to tell me where to go for the best inventory. I didn't mention, of course, that I was buying for ladies in Richmond!"

They laughed. "This all is so beautiful!"

Charles looked deeply into Mayleda's happy eyes. "Well, I do take satisfaction in knowing my customers. Now, I hear that there's to be more than one event this spring where new dresses and shirts will be needed."

Lydia's glance skipped across to Thomas. He beamed a smile. "You told him what we were thinking?" she scolded merrily.

"I sure did! An' last night I spoke to Mistress Lerew too! Brother Parnell's of the same mind as me. It will be mighty fine to have *three* weddings on Covenant Day!"

Charles leaned back in his chair while Lydia came around and kissed Thomas on his cheek. It would have been more than enough satisfaction for all the adults present, yet Charles turned his attention to Daniel and Judith. "All right. Let's see. I think I may have few things from New York in here just for the two of you."

Both the girl and the boy were at his side in an instant. "Show us, please!"

––––––––––

The dishes were done, the children put to bed, and Mayleda suddenly found herself alone with Charles as he sat at the table writing. A timidness crept over her while he was hard at work. She found pleasure just in stealing glances at him, savoring the truth that he was here, unharmed, having been the whole way to Canada and back to help his brother in the faith.

Charles had told her about the men who had confronted him on the coast. The worry from that stayed with them. Often Charles looked toward the door. And he listened. She glanced at him again when he set aside a paper. His eyes met hers, then he reached across to take her hand.

His questions poured forth like water. "Are we foolish to think of staying here? Am I my brothers' traitor, or their keeper, in designing this business for a woman who owns slaves? What of Daniel if I am arrested? What of Thomas and Lydia when the law will not allow them to truly be husband and wife?"

"It seems the safest place for now."

He let go of her hand. "But am I compromising, May? We know from what has happened in the North that compromise can kill the power of truth."

"The truth is that you cannot travel with Daniel now. In fact, I even worry about you on the roads for this business. Someone might recognize you. Someone might guess your real intentions."

"I know how sad Joseph is not to have Daniel with him."

"But think how sad it will be if we lost him back to slavery by moving too soon. Indeed, that could happen to Thomas too."

"It's so confusing to my spirit to think of staying here. Can it truly be God's will?"

"We must walk by faith, not by sight! Think of the providence that led you to this place. When it is time to move on, I trust we will gain divine assistance again."

He closed his eyes. "Oh, how I need you, May! Sometimes I falter on my own."

"I want to thank you for spending time with Judith today. She listens to what you say. Sister Lydia thinks that she might be blaming Negroes for her daddy's passing."

"I can see that. She's had many hurts and disappointments. I was a child like that, and I told her so. I told her that both my parents died when I was younger then she. Then I tried to assure her that death is not the limit of God's love."

Mayleda smiled. "Upstairs, tonight, little Daniel wanted to *kiss* her. In his innocence, he wants to follow that first expression of love I showed him while we were trapped inside the hiding place of your wagon."

"That seems so long ago."

"The amazing thing is that Judith nearly let him do it!"

"Maybe even at her young age she senses no guile in him. When I look at him, I think of Christ's saying, 'Blessed are the merciful: for they shall obtain mercy.' For all he's suffered, I see God's mercy in him. He is so kind to all."

She could not resist taking his hand. "When I look at you I think on another beatitude, 'Blessed are the pure in heart: for they shall see God.' There is so much love and mercy inside you."

"I think I know now that there can be no love without mercy. Not even God's love. We all need mercy, and God gives mercy. It's something I want to share with others so that mercy might be the beginning of love for them too, as it was for me through Brother Peabody. Now I see it between Thomas and myself."

"You should be a preacher, Charles Parnell!"

He seemed embarrassed. "I don't think so. Here. I have something to show you. Two things really. Both are from Sister Angelene."

He appeared more at ease once he had opened the trunk. He took out a soft parcel wrapped in brown paper. "Angelene had me bring this to Daniel. I want to give it to him when we have time with him alone. It's a sampler that she will eventually make into a quilt when he brings it back to her. She designed it just for him, and she calls the pattern Daniel's Stars."

Mayleda undid the paper. A large, beautifully sewn square of fabrics appeared, made of small triangle-shaped pieces of material fitted together to form four stars set against a background of browns and blues.

"She says it is to remind him of God's care, which will remain until the stars begin to fall." He pointed to a piece of the blue fabric near the center, unique from the rest. "This is cloth that Joseph's mother cut from her dress the day he left the South. It is the only thing of hers that our brother possesses."

Mayleda could hardly see for tears. "I know that fabric. Dear Maum Bette wore such dresses too!"

"I didn't mean to upset you!"

"You didn't. It's just that it came as a reminder of continuing injustice. I'm sure slave women are dressed in that kind of cloth still. What will be sufficient to change it?"

"I think only God can answer that. I see myself now only like a small piece in a quilt. Whatever God asks of me, I pray I will do. But likely that will not be sufficient in itself. The answer may come when there is suitable obedience from *all* who say they have a Father in heaven."

Suddenly Mayleda found herself weeping. Charles came around and held her close. "Oh, for so long I've been so alone! Yet you do understand my heart so very well."

He kissed her head. "We are not alone now. There's still something else I want to show you." He spoke gently while she struggled to gather her emotions.

"This is for us, from Angelene and Joseph."

Again it was a soft package, but this time wrapped in calico. Inside Mayleda found a quilt made of many different but equally sized triangles, their high points all oriented to the top. It was a familiar pattern she recognized.

"The central pattern is called 'flying geese,'" he told her.

Mayleda nearly laughed at his expertise, sounding so strange coming from a man. "Yes, I know, but how do you know?"

"This is a special quilt from Angelene's family. It's the first quilt her mother made as a signal quilt to hang in the window for the Underground Railroad."

"I saw her quilts when I was in Oak Glen."

"So did I, but I didn't know their importance then. The quilts are signs that can be read by those who know the local routes. Men like Tort Woodman and Simeon Bart. The 'flying geese' are used to show that the way north is open. She gave the quilt to Angelene, a symbol of faith that Joseph would get to Canada. This was to be their wedding gift."

"It's too precious. I wish you had refused it!"

"It was Angelene's choice. And soon another very much like it will be pinned into her quilting frame up in Sandwich." He grinned so strangely. "Joseph and I spent several days working to finish the one she's doing now so that she could start this new one."

"You are teasing me!"

"I'm not! I didn't go to Canada to learn to sew, of course, but the truth soon became clear. The fine work of quilting is wonderful therapy for Joseph's sight. He gained so much confidence, just in the time I was there. When I left, Barnabas and Pastor Brown were going out to purchase lumber so that they could build a clinic for him."

She felt herself smiling and crying all at once. "God has answered our prayers!"

"Joseph and Angelene have decided that he will train her as a practitioner too. Then they can work together."

She hugged the quilt. "Oh, to know that Joseph is happy! Oh, to think that he will have such a wonderful wife!"

"Just as I will have."

"I wish we were able to give them something in return."

"We will," Charles said with soberness. "We will keep Daniel safe and raise him in the love and nurture of the Lord until that day when we can take him home."

Just as Charles was speaking about Daniel, Mayleda saw the boy climbing down the ladder. "You should be asleep!" she said with concern.

He did look weary as he came to her. "I heard you crying."

"Sweet lamb!" She cuddled him as he came into her arms. "Actually, you heard tears of happiness and joy."

He blinked up with uncertainty.

She saw his quilt upon the table. "Look what Sister Brown sent to you. A gift that she designed herself. A piece of the new quilt you shall have in full when you go to Canada. She's named this pattern after you— Daniel's Stars. And this is a precious bit of cloth that once belonged to Dr. Joseph's mother, your grandmother, Jewell."

Daniel did not seem to understand that the gift was for him. With care she draped it around his shoulders. "Sister Brown wants this to remind you of God's faithfulness, just as the stars do."

He stared at Charles. "You know that promise?"

"Yes, we do." Charles said, and Daniel moved to be near him. "The man who wants to be your father is my brother in the Lord. Can you understand that? We share many things in common because of it."

The child smiled as though it were no mystery at all. Standing on his tiptoes, he kissed Charles on the face, as he often had Joseph. They allowed the little boy to stay with them until he was drowsy with sleep. Then Charles lifted him up into his strong arms and carried him back up the ladder, while Mayleda stayed in the little Virginia kitchen, overjoyed.

———

Charles sat up after Mayleda had gone to bed. He blew out the candle he had worked by, leaving him with only the light of the moon coming through the back window. Before retiring to the same bedroom where he had kept watch over Joseph, Charles stood and walked to the front of the house. He looked out the window down toward the quarters where most of the colored workers were surely fast asleep. Again his conscience pricked him. He considered Dr. Ellis's counsel to him so many weeks ago. It made him decide that if he must live here, then he would find ways to socialize with Madam Lerew's *other* workers, for in truth he was only her employee, as were they.

It startled him when a man rose up right before his eyes out on the porch. It scared him. At once he thought about the law, but a moment later the moon showed him that it was Thomas. Apparently the young man was standing after having been seated on the steps. At once Charles opened the door. "Brother! It's chilly outside. Why didn't you come in?"

Thomas looked sheepish as he walked to the threshold. "I just had a mind to look afta the place, you know, in case somebody decided to come seekin' afta you."

"Well, you could have come in and watched by a window. Please, come in now. You must be cold."

Thomas smiled. "I thought you an' Sister May would like some time alone."

How different this encounter from that first day when he had judged Thomas to be only a rowdy colored boy content to loiter.

"Besides," he continued, "I don't want to distress you with my worry."

"You don't distress me, for I share it. That's one reason I've been cautious about going to bed. Last night I found myself listening and watching almost till dawn."

"I was doin' the same from you' porch."

Charles shook his head. "When are we going to learn that it's wiser to keep watch one at a time, so that we each might get some rest?"

Thomas laughed. "You do remember the first night, then, when neither of us closed our eyes that time?"

"Yes! We should be smarter by now, I hope."

Thomas followed him into the room with two windows, one looking out toward the river and one toward Richmond. The room was cold. The bed, dresser, and chair all were clearly visible in shades of gray and blue.

"If you like, you can sleep first," Thomas said, looking out first one window and then the next.

Charles took off his boots and sat down on the bed. "You don't mind?"

"No, sah. I'll wake you in a little while."

"Fine."

Yet despite his promise, Thomas seemed eager to talk. "You know,

I've been thinking on somethin' Lydia told me that Miss Judith said today. How she doesn't like having to be as poor as a Negro."

"I'm sorry she said that. You know there's no truth in *poor* and *Negro* having to be put together in that way."

"Sure, I know, but part of what she said do ring true. I mean 'bout bein' poor. Look at you, Brother, all you done give up."

"I was never a rich man."

"I don't think that 'rich' is a word one man can use on hisself. I think it's more like a judgment, what one man makes toward another."

"You have a point there." When Thomas was reluctant to speak on, Charles encouraged him. "I am listening."

"Well, sah, I been thinkin' that rich men do have hard times lovin' God, just like little Judith do. You take a po' man. He's got nothin' to lose an' everything to gain by cryin' out to God. A starvin', freezin' man can be full of faith, for sure, 'cause it ain't gwine cost him nothin'. He might even get a blanket or some bread for his prayers. But not so a rich man. Likely when he calls out, God's gwine come straight down an' say, 'Why, I done helped you already. Now it's my will that you go out an' help somebody else.' See? It's gwine cost the man what's got something already. Just the way it done cost you."

"I can think about what I've gained, not what I've lost. This is part of faith too."

Thomas closed his lips with a quiet smacking sound. "I never thought I'd be some place like this, I mean, just talkin' an sayin' what's inside of my heart to you, a white man. Truth be, sah, I saw you as a rich man when I was out on Easton Alley. An' I had hate inside my heart for you."

"I understand, for when I was out on the street, Friend Peabody was like the rich man to me, and I felt jealous of him. Thank God he was willing to share the mercies of heaven with me."

Thomas stayed silent for a time. "I'm not just pretendin' when I says I love God now. I do. An' that's 'cause of the mercies you done showed to me."

Charles looked out against the night as he stayed on the bed. "Thomas, I did not always feel kindly toward you, I confess. I thought terrible things about you at times in my ignorance."

"But you did what was right, an' then so did I. An' now I gwine keep on tryin' to do that, though the whole world still does feel like it's gwine wrong."

"I know what you mean."

"I don't want to keep you from sleep, sah, but there's one more thing I would like to ask of you."

"Yes?"

"I've been thinkin' that on my weddin' day I'm gwine need some last name."

"You can pick any name you want, you know that," Charles said.

"But I want a good name."

"You sound like you might already have one in mind," Charles said, covering a yawn, then leaning on his elbow.

"I do. I was wonderin' how you'd think you' old friend Mista Peabody would feel if I done considered takin' his name as mine. Then, of course, I'd soon give it away to Lydia too, an' someday, I hope, to our children."

Charles sat up in honor of Thomas and his idea. "I think Brother Elim would be pleased. The store used to bear testimony to his right way of living. Now you will bear it in the flesh."

"So you think that's all right, sah?"

"I do, indeed. Good night, young Mr. Thomas Peabody."

"Good night to you, too, sah, Brother Parnell."

CHAPTER 41

THE HOLY UNION of Joseph Whitsun and Angelene Brown took place during morning worship the last Sunday in May 1852. Praise rang through the whole wooden church, now called North Shore Chapel, making nobody feel sorry that there was no bell as yet to sound from the spire.

When Joseph and Angelene were called up to stand before the altar table that Joseph had seen in his dream, everybody clapped, and even the air Angelene breathed seemed blessed, for every brother and sister in the house knew what wonders God had performed to bring this day to pass. Her father smiled, while his eyes had that same misty gaze she had often seen in their months of trials.

With dignity he opened his small church book, brought from Pennsylvania in anticipation of this event. She thought of her mother and brothers, who would learn of this moment only in the days to come through her letters. Though everyone was watching, Angelene still slipped her hand around Joseph's, happy for its strength. She held on as though she would never let go. Joseph's gaze on her seemed as comforting as sunshine.

They said their vows. Vows to love, vows to honor, vows to keep one another in sickness and in health, vows to forsake all others as long as life should last for each of them.

When her father was ready to give the closing prayer, he asked the congregation to rise. They were told not only to bless Mr. and Mrs. Joseph Whitsun standing here, but also Mr. and Mrs. Charles Parnell, to be married outside Richmond, Virginia, that same day. It was wonderful to hear the thunderous applause.

The service ended then, but not the celebration. That went on far into the night, filling up the whole town with excitement as Angelene's classroom had been cleared for the banquet and for the dancing with violins and trumpets to follow.

A vacant chair was placed at the table where Joseph and Angelene sat together for the wedding meal. The chair was to be a symbol of hope, Angelene's father announced to all, that the young fugitive Daniel would soon be brought to Sandwich. With pride, her father said that the child already bore their last name, Whitsun, and that his daughter and son-in-law eagerly anticipated raising the boy as their own.

At that point in the classroom-turned-banquet-hall, Barnabas Croghan asked Joseph if he might say something on his behalf. The only white man present, Barnabas had been seated across from Joseph and Angelene so that they could take turns translating what was being said. Now Barnabas relied on Joseph to speak his thoughts aloud. When Joseph translated the language, which so captivated and mystified the others, he shed tears as he spoke out loud for his old friend. *"Wherever we live, whoever we are, the love of God makes us one family. Today, I bless my brother and my sister in Jesus' name."*

Silently, Angelene's father rose to his feet out of respect for the older man. Others followed his example. Then her father showed the people how to say *"Amen!"* and *"Yes!"* with their hands only. All around the tables, hand signs were displayed, accompanied with loud cheering. Barnabas seemed so overcome with happiness that he bowed and sat down, grinning with more joy than Angelene had ever seen in him.

Then the singing and clapping started in earnest as the small orchestra began to play. Hardly able to believe that she was now Mrs. Whitsun, Angelene reached out and took her husband's hand.

Charles and Mayleda's solemn moment of matrimony came when Madam Lerew opened her spacious parlor late in the afternoon to all those living on her plantation. Though Charles' business was growing, no one from outside was invited to attend, for their wariness remained high about lawmen and inspectors.

Madam Lerew oversaw the event, patterned after Quaker weddings each of them had attended elsewhere. Young Judith and Daniel had seats on either side of the solemn, dignified lady of the house, as though she were their grandmother for that day. Thirty or so colored friends from the plantation filled the chairs that formed a square in the center of the room.

The ceremony began with silent prayer. When Madam Lerew nodded toward Charles, he had a fantastic sense that a gate in heaven was being opened to them. He stood and took Mayleda's hand. Her smile was as radiant as the candles flickering overhead in the chandelier. Charles' voice was tremulous and so was hers as they said their pledge aloud. "In the presence of God and these Friends, we promise, with divine assistance, to be loving and faithful as long as we both should live."

Madam Lerew rose and read a letter of blessing to them that would be signed by all the witnesses who could write their name or would make their mark upon the paper. Then Thomas and Lydia stood to speak special words of encouragement to them. It brought the pride of a father to Charles to be honored by this young couple, who, just one hour before in front of this same group, had received their letter of nuptial blessing too.

Afterward, while Charles and Mayleda still were standing, they spoke about their desire to have the small fellowship pray for two friends not present: Joseph Whitsun and Angelene Brown, who were to be married that day in Canada. Charles saw Daniel beam as he said their names out loud. It caused him to put his hands upon the little boy when the ceremony was ended. "As soon as I can, Daniel Whitsun, you know I will take you to them."

The child turned his happy gaze upward. "I know!"

Asking Daniel to walk in front of them, Charles took Mayleda and Judith by their hands. Together they entered into other rooms where tables had been set so that everyone present could share in the meal. In this mansion that had once known only masters and slaves, all sat down together. Winding through the magnificent scene, Charles escorted Mayleda, Daniel, and Judith to seats reserved for them next to Thomas and Lydia. "I believe a little bit of heaven has come to earth," Charles said to all who were close enough to hear him.

Yet when he sat down he became aware of the window close to his left shoulder. It gave him a view of the distant James River, and instantly it was his poignant reminder that this speck of freedom ended where the outside world began. Still he chose to rejoice in what they had. For now, he would choose to look at Mayleda, at the precious children in his care, and at their friends who had left their labors to celebrate. Rising, unable to contain his smile, Charles said, "Let us bow our heads for prayer as we continue on in the blessings of this day."

———

On their walk home in the dark hours of early morning, Joseph and Angelene Whitsun stopped at the edge of town. Enduring the raw air, they embraced each other while looking up at the stars splashed overhead. There and then they said their first private prayers as husband and wife, never taking their gazes from heaven.

———

In Virginia under a sky flecked with celestial light, Charles and Mayleda Parnell did the same.

HISTORICAL NOTES

THOUGHTS FOR THIS NOVEL started in Lancaster County, Pennsylvania, while I washed dishes at a camp for churches from Washington, D.C. My original purpose was to develop a story to inspire urban youth, but soon I became inspired myself by history that seemed so neglected and forgotten.

Those who know the area see that I have taken liberty to change locations and names, yet the story starts with a real event: the bloody confrontation of masters and fugitive slaves in Christiana, September 1851.

For the sake of simplicity, only Friends are mentioned as ardent abolitionists. In truth, Christians of various denominations and both races participated in the Underground Railroad. I want to honor Grace Kurtz, a Mennonite friend, who went to be with the Lord the week I finished this book. She and her brother took me on an unmarked historical trail, drawn from remembrances of their childhood, that linked former small black settlements and Quaker and Mennonite meetinghouses in and around Christiana.

I also want to honor Dr. Dorothy Martin, a resident of Virginia, who joined the saints in Glory while the book was in production. She supported ROOTS OF FAITH in many ways. Those who live in Virginia will know that I have changed the names and settings there, as well, since my interest is not to replicate history but to distill its truths.

Every step of the way I thank Billie Montgomery Cook, as story consultant, and Sharon Asmus, as editor, for continuing on this difficult road of researching the truth and telling it together.

For those who want to know the facts behind the fiction, I recommend the available records concerning Christiana, the Vigilance Committee of Philadelphia, Black newspapers, and Black conventions. Information can be found on the Bibbs of Sandwich, on the Reverend Daniel Alexander Payne's life and work during abolition, and on others such as Frederick Douglass, Angelina Grimké, and Theodore Weld. The autobiography of Solomon Northup, who was kidnapped from the North and endured twelve years of slavery, stands out to me because it reads like a novel.

While all the main characters in my novel are fictitious, you will find similar persons and events as you study the facts. My favorite overview of this period is *In Hope of Liberty: Culture, Community, and Protest Among Northern Free Blacks, 1700–1860* by James Oliver Horton and Lois E. Horton.